The Redshirt

# THE REDSHIRT

*A Novel*

## Corey Sobel

UNIVERSITY PRESS OF KENTUCKY

Scholarly publisher for the Commonwealth,
serving Bellarmine University, Berea College, Centre
College of Kentucky, Eastern Kentucky University,
The Filson Historical Society, Georgetown College,
Kentucky Historical Society, Kentucky State University,
Morehead State University, Murray State University,
Northern Kentucky University, Transylvania University,
University of Kentucky, University of Louisville,
and Western Kentucky University.
All rights reserved.

*Editorial and Sales Offices:* The University Press of Kentucky
663 South Limestone Street, Lexington, Kentucky 40508-4008
www.kentuckypress.com

This is a work of fiction. The characters, places, and events are either drawn from the author's imagination or used fictitiously. Any resemblance of fictional characters to actual living persons is entirely coincidental.

Library of Congress Cataloging-in-Publication Data

Names: Sobel, Corey, 1985- author.
Title: The redshirt : a novel / Corey Sobel.
Description: Lexington, Kentucky : University Press of Kentucky, [2020] |
   Series: University Press of Kentucky new poetry & prose series
Identifiers: LCCN 2020017977 | ISBN 9780813180212 (hardcover ; acid-free
   paper) | ISBN 9780813180229 (pdf) | ISBN 9780813180236 (epub)
Subjects: LCSH: Football stories.
Classification: LCC PS3619.O37377 S63 2020 | DDC 813/.6—dc23
LC record available at https://lccn.loc.gov/2020017977

This book is printed on acid-free paper meeting
the requirements of the American National Standard
for Permanence in Paper for Printed Library Materials.

Manufactured in the United States of America.

Member of the Association
of University Presses

*To Seyward*

"Bartleby!"

"I know you," he said, without looking round,—"and I want nothing to say to you."

"It was not I that brought you here, Bartleby," said I, keenly pained at his implied suspicion. "And to you, this should not be so vile a place. Nothing reproachful attaches to you by being here. And see, it is not so sad a place as one might think. Look, there is the sky, and here is the grass."

"I know where I am."

—Herman Melville, "Bartleby, the Scrivener"

# PROLOGUE

Athletes die twice. That's the hoary, comforting, horrifying mantra that circulates among us ex-jocks, and its meaning should be obvious enough: The muscle and speed, the stamina and quickness you spend your best years building up, the discipline and the single-minded drive, all are bound together by the sport, *are* you, and as soon as the sport leaves your life, that which united you is gone, and so you are gone, too, unraveled like a scarecrow stripped of its stitching. The second you is left to take over, eke out whatever it can before the ultimate death comes. But what nobody has ever told me is what happens to that first self after it breathes its last, where the first you goes. Does your living body become a kind of mausoleum for the corpse and you have no choice but to feel it rot away inside? That would explain the terrible stink I've been carrying around the last ten years.

—Friend of Steven? a man asks.

It takes me a moment to realize I'm the one being addressed, and another moment to understand that I've been staring. The man is sitting a few stools down the bar. He's twenty-five maybe, with round-rimmed glasses, close-cropped curly brown hair, and a red Arizona Cardinals jersey whose baggy short sleeves come down to his elbows. He smiles, hands placed expectantly on the bar in anticipation of moving closer; but I have no clue who Steven is, and zero desire to explain to this man that I hadn't been staring

1

at him so much as at his jersey. I shake my head apologetically and look past him toward the entrance.

I usually avoid blind dates, but a colleague in NYU's English Department has been nagging me to go out with Horace for months, and this week I finally relented. We agreed to meet here at the Raven, a watering hole indistinguishable from all the others in this stratum of western Brooklyn: a bar top made of recovered timber, a ceiling of antique hammered tin, light fixtures that are clusters of pendant bulbs with custard-colored filaments, the kind of place where the bearded bartender moodily explains the difference between single barrel and blended while the television above him plays vintage music videos on loop—big hair, parachute pants, bold letters that leave a neon residue as they streak onto the screen.

Horace arrives. He's about my age, petite and handsome, with a trim black mustache that stands starkly against his pale skin. We shake hands as he takes the stool next to mine, and there is something efficient about him that appeals to me immediately. We run through preliminaries—he's a lawyer, corporate malfeasance, I'm an assistant professor, secularization in nineteenth-century American texts. We have an easy rapport, he's drily funny and much more confident than I am, and within an hour we're already reaching back into our pasts. He tells me about the disaster of his parents divorcing when he was eleven, the depression and alcoholism that forced him to raise his little brother on his own. As he talks, I sort through my own traumas, trying to decide which one to trade. I'm not precious about sharing this kind of stuff, except for one thing: I don't tell anyone I used to play football or about the events that forced me out of the game. In fact, I've been so disciplined for so long that I've managed to cultivate a whole community here in the city that has no idea what I used to be.

The date continues to go well. Our stools have scooted closer, Horace insists I try his pilsner. I feel happy, buzzed, and am in the middle of explaining the tenure process when a group of men pushes into the bar—khaki shorts, flip-flops, many of them dressed in Cardinals jerseys, one of them inevitably named Steven. They gruffly hug the man who tried talking to me, and after some cajoling they prevail on the bartender to pick up the remote and turn the TV to the Sunday night showdown, Arizona versus Green Bay.

—Want to go somewhere else? Horace asks, which tells me I'm not hiding my panic very well.

—No no. This is fine.

The fans are harmless, as football folks go. They aren't pounding tequila shots or climbing onto the bar, and when one bumps into our stools, he sincerely apologizes rather than calling us faggots with his eyes. But I'm still having trouble concentrating on what Horace is saying, struggling to watch him rather than the game that's flashing in my peripheral vision. Horace himself is growing agitated, and I worry this is my fault until Green Bay scores and the group erupts into boos. With that, Horace sets down his beer, raises his eyes toward the ceiling, and sings out:

—Enjoy it while it laaaaaaaasts.

He lifts the long *a* up an octave, his voice tight and tart. The fans don't hear it over the broadcast. Horace sighs and says to me:

—That game is dying. Peewee enrollment, plummeting. Ratings, too. The bodies are going to run out, then the money. Nobody is going to even know how to *play* football in a hundred years. And good fucking riddance.

Defensiveness rises in me for the game I despise, but speaking out now would only force me to confess everything, so I fake a laugh and clink my glass with Horace's. After taking a sip of his beer, Horace lays his hand on my thigh. He asks again if I want to go somewhere else—except the way he's looking at me signals that "somewhere else" is no longer a different bar, it's one of our apartments. I say yes and he smiles and hops off his seat, excusing himself. I watch him walk to the back and join a long bathroom line of full-bladdered Arizona fans.

I am fine, I am better than fine—until I look up and see that Reshawn, *my* Reshawn, is on TV, or at least a photograph of him is. He's wearing dreadlocks these days, designer dreads, short and tight and henna-tinted, forming a kind of starburst around his head. He's gotten so muscular that he looks slightly unconvincing, like a sculpture by an also-ran Renaissance artist who mastered individual muscles but lacked the skill to make the muscles cohere into a living, breathing whole. But the eyes work, they're just as I remember them, dark brown, smolderingly intelligent, and I can't believe I'm seeing him, Reshawn.

The photograph occupies the top right corner of the screen while a halftime news announcer says:

—The legal saga continues between the Seattle Seahawks and Reshawn McCoy. McCoy, a six-year veteran tailback, was a lock for the starting spot this season when he unexpectedly announced his retirement from football during training camp. The Seahawks have initiated proceedings for breach of contract. McCoy was in the middle of a three-year, four-million-dollar deal.

The announcer moves on to the next item without giving more information. For years—for my health—I've abstained from reading anything about Reshawn, but I can't help myself now and take my phone out to search for mentions. He must have been euphoric when he made the announcement. He must have waited until the worst possible moment to retire, just so he could throw his team into chaos. It's over. He's free.

The first articles I read focus on the legal battle, but then I land on a more in-depth write-up of what happened. And there, in the second paragraph, is a sentence that makes me feel as if someone has plunged his dirty hands into my gut and roughly flipped my stomach inside out:

*McCoy's mother died of a treatment-related infection two days before the announcement.*

Heat gathers fast in my eyes, the phone screen starts to blur. An insistent phrase—it was all for nothing—repeats over and over in my head, pairing with the image I have of Reshawn's mother, an image that's years out of date, an image I know doesn't reflect all the ravages visited on her body since I last saw her. I try to keep the tears at bay by keeping myself perfectly still, like holding a cup filled right to the brim. That's when a hand lands hard on my back.

—Have faith, brother!

It's the man whose jersey I'd been staring at; he must have been keeping a curious eye on me all this time. Beads of sweat tremble on the top rims of his glasses, and he's so soused that his other hand, the one not resting on my back, is holding on to the bar to steady his wobbly self.

—We've got a whole, a whooooooole other half to play! Those guys—

He lifts his chin scornfully at the television, which has returned to the game and is showing the Green Bay sideline.

—They're a bunch of jokers. *Jokers.* We'll pull through!

Something between a sob and a laugh escapes from me. How could I have expected this moment to go any differently?

Horace returns from the bathroom. He sees my eyes are red.

—What—? he begins to ask.

—He's glass-half-empty! the drunk exclaims, clapping my back again. I told him just wait, *wait* till we get going!

—I'm okay, I tell Horace, attempting a smile.

The drunk ambles back to his friends, leaving us to try and recover our momentum. But it's no use. Horace gently hints that he knows I'm upset, and I play dumb. I can feel myself going cold, resenting Horace for his solicitude, hating myself for resenting him.

Soon we're splitting the tab and stepping out into the warm, clear September night. The air is scented with the rich smoke of a nearby halal cart, and down the slope you can see a tiny Statue of Liberty glowing green in the harbor.

—Should we get you a cab? I ask.

—*Cab?* he says, mock-offended. That's not what we agreed to.

I'm about to say I'm too tired, but before I can, Horace hooks his arm around mine and asks the way to my apartment. I give in and lead him up 9th Street, passing between brownstones and a line of sycamores where invisible insects make insistent clicking noises that put me in mind of a stove burner failing to catch.

Horace tries to lighten the mood by telling me why autumn is his favorite season, but I'm only half listening. Maybe my athletic self has not only been rotting away inside me, maybe it's also become a ghost that's going to haunt me for however much time I have remaining. The ghost is the voice that taunts me whenever I lose my wind during a morning jog around Prospect Park. The fingers that mockingly pinch the love handles that sit stubbornly on my hips. The saboteur who finds a way to ruin every single one of my dates.

We reach my stoop and climb two flights of stairs to my studio. I live in an old brick building that gets stuffy with the day's leftover heat, and I crack the windows before retrieving two beers from the fridge. I hand Horace a bottle and join him on my little blue IKEA couch. We sit there in awkward silence, listening to traffic sounds filter into the room from 7th Avenue.

Finally, Horace finishes the question he'd started asking back at the bar:

—What happened?

# ONE

I was raised in Sillitoe, Colorado, a suburb in the foothills of the Rocky Mountains, ten interchangeable square miles of sagebrush, strip malls, cacti, and ticky-tacky subdivisions. My parents both worked administrative positions for the same multinational mining company that employed most of my town, and like virtually all our neighbors we were as pale as the snowy peaks visible from my bedroom window and Christian in a perfunctory, most-Sundays sense—Roman Catholic, to be exact.

Such relentless uniformity magnified the smaller differences between people, which is how a white-bread kid like me got singled out as a weirdo. It started with my voice, a faint, airy, tentative thing that my classmates mockingly transformed into a lispy soprano and that the adults who called our house would mistake for a little girl's (failing to stifle their laughter when I corrected them). Raising my hand in class, yelling out on the playground, even saying good morning to the school bus driver could lead to humiliation, and by second grade I had developed a quiet, watchful manner to limit my exposure. In the way these things go, it was my quietness, and not the bullying, that prompted my teacher Ms. Munson to call Mom and Dad in for a conference one autumn afternoon. Ms. Munson informed my parents that "Miles displays antisocial tendencies"—which, in a town that prides itself on sunny friendliness, was like saying your son's got a horn growing in the middle of his forehead.

My parents scrambled to find a cure. They conscripted class-mates into play dates, but since those kids were often the same ones who bullied me at school, the sessions just led to more alienation. A halogen lamp was set up in the corner of my bedroom on the theory that I needed more light, but all the lamp got me was scalded fingers when I tried removing the bulb. I was taken to something called a "friendship specialist," a charlatan who conned my parents out of a sizeable chunk of their modest salaries via hourlong sessions in which I practiced things like shaking hands or making eye contact.

The next, worst remedy came after I sat for a state-mandated aptitude test that spring. Ms. Munson called my parents in again, but this time she was all smiles as she showed off my unusually high test scores and pronounced that the *real* root of the problem was that I wasn't being challenged enough by my classwork. It was Ms. Munson's recommendation that I skip a grade, and my parents, blinded by the pride of having a gifted son, didn't consider the questionable logic that led my teacher to her conclusion, nor the disastrous implications of me going from being the meek, weak-voiced kid in class to being the meek, weak-voiced kid who was also a head shorter and a year younger than his peers. Which is precisely what I became when I was advanced to the third grade.

At this point, a lot of kids in my position would have thrown up their hands and cultivated rich interior worlds to compensate for the exterior one that insisted on misunderstanding them. But I was an only child, and the last thing I wanted was more alone time to crawl even further inside my wormy brain. No, beneath my shyness was a burning desire to be accepted, a sharp hunger to homogenize. And in Sillitoe, Colorado, the easiest way for a boy to do that was to love football.

Organized ball started in fourth grade, and I spent the preceding summer reading *Sports Illustrated* articles and counting down the days until my first practice. When the holy morning finally arrived, Mom took off the first half of work to drive me to my state-mandated physical. I doubt a pediatrician has ever had a patient more eager to drop his drawers and cough as her cold hand cupped his testicles. Then we visited a sporting goods store downtown, where I obtained a jockstrap as big as my face and the first cleats of my young life, low-cut Nike Sharks the color of tar. My parents switched duties at noon, so that Mom headed to work while Dad drove me to a municipal park with the Rockies' Front Range lording over it. When we pulled into the parking lot, I begged Dad to stay in the car—I wanted to show off my independence to my new teammates—and as I stepped alone into the hot, dry August afternoon and crossed the parking lot in my cleats, I felt like an astronaut taking his first steps on Mars. My confidence lasted until I spotted my teammates on the practice fields, the same kids who bullied me at school, including Gus Mintaur, an ice-eyed Aryan who was in the habit of "accidentally" pouring milk down my back in the cafeteria. I began wishing, desperately, that Dad was close by.

A whistle was blown and we took a knee around our head coach, Frank Johannsen. Coach Johannsen was redwood tall and just as mightily built, with a broad hairy chest that imposed swirls through his T-shirt's fabric and gray cloth Champion shorts that showed off calves so big I was put in mind of a *National Geographic* photo of a boa constrictor that had swallowed a deer whole.

—Afternoon, gents.

I didn't catch much of his opening speech, distracted by Gus and the other kids who were looking at me and whispering. Johannsen ordered us to form a line for warm-up sprints, and as we did, Gus made a crack about the supposed tightness of my shorts. I looked over at the parking lot, where Dad had gotten out of the car to watch us. I could run over and tell him to speed us away from this horrible place. I could beg him and Mom to homeschool me and never say the word "football" again. But then the whistle sounded and I was sprinting in my gangly boyish way, my anxiety receding a little bit more with each step forward. I wasn't at the head of the pack, but I wasn't bringing up the rear, either. I was right in the middle, happily absorbed into the thudding, gasping masses.

I was euphoric by the time we returned home, and while Mom finished cooking dinner I locked myself in my parents' bedroom to rehearse the aspect of football that excited me most. I donned the gouged helmet I'd been given by Coach Johannsen at the end of practice, buttoned the sweat-crinkled chinstrap, and knelt on my parents' mattress to stack two pillows widthwise. I took a third pillow and leaned it vertically against the stack so that it was standing—and I watched the thing mutate into Gus Mintaur, the villain I and only I was heroic enough to tackle. I stared him down as I tiptoed backward. The moment my butt touched the door, I was off running, steaming, and at the lip of the mattress I launched myself through the air, sailing, *obliterating* Gus with a ferocious tackle. I landed on the mother-father-fragrant duvet cover and paused there a moment, gripping the pillow to my breast, luxuriating in the softness. Then I was up again, righting my helmet and restacking the pillows for the next round.

My thirst for contact made me a natural outside linebacker. I took to the position fanatically, and within a few weeks Coach Johannsen was bringing me magazine profiles of greats like Lawrence Taylor and Junior Seau, loaning me hand-labeled VHSs of all-time college and NFL games, staying after practice to work with me on stance and footwork. Dad was delighted I'd been singled out, but Mom grew suspicious of a man with no wedding band showing her son so much individual attention. One Sunday, she invited him over for dinner to get a closer look, and her fears were quickly allayed. Coach Johannsen was simply exhilarated to have found a player so precociously obsessed with the game, and by the end of that dinner Mom had gone from worrying my coach was a pedophile to insisting he come over again the next Sunday.

It became a weekly tradition, these dinners, and over the course of that season we learned Coach Johannsen's improbable story. He grew up in a Montana town too tiny for a traffic light, the youngest son of a ranch manager. His two older brothers dropped out of high school to work with their father, and Coach Johannsen would have followed suit had he not been encouraged by his high school's football coach to put his unusual size and strength to use in another way. He started playing eight-man ball and became a legend in the area, feared by opponents and cheered by a town that didn't have much else to cheer for. Toward the end of his senior season, a University of Wyoming recruiter drove up from Laramie to watch him play. The fantastical stories the recruiter had heard were true, and the man was so impressed by Johannsen's performance that he offered him a scholarship in the school parking lot after the game.

Rapt, I listened to Coach Johannsen tell how he went on to be the first person in his family to earn a college degree and, more important, a four-year starter named All-American in his final two seasons. He was selected in the fourth round of the NFL draft by the New York Jets and signed a contract for more money than he'd thought a man could earn in his entire lifetime.

But then his ascent mysteriously, abruptly ended. Coach Johannsen never made it to New York. In fact, he only got as far as Sillitoe when he pulled off the highway and found work as a number cruncher in the accounting department of the same mining company that employed my parents.

Why in God's name would someone forgo such fame and fortune? Coach Johannsen was an amiable sort, gracious and exceedingly easy to talk to, but on this subject he became what you might call warmly diffident. Whenever my parents tried prying into why he'd quit the game, he would just smile in a way that said he didn't mind at all that they were asking, but he had no intention whatsoever of answering.

I was stumped myself. Rejecting the NFL was like refusing the gift of flight.

By age twelve my pulse started racing at the oddest moments—whenever gym class ended and it was time to hit the showers, or when the warm weather returned and my male classmates resumed wearing T-shirts and shorts. A group assignment would be announced in biology and I would find myself in a lose-lose bind: if I was partnered with the boy I wanted to be paired up with, I would become unhelpably nervous when we worked together, thereby reconfirming my reputation as a weirdo; but if I wasn't partnered with him, I would fall into a quietly violent funk that ended only once I developed an obsession with a different boy. Then there were the magazines. I'd been keeping a collection of my favorite back issues of *Sports Illustrated* in a blue trunk in my bedroom since I was seven, and since that age I had happily spent hours alone in my room rereading articles about football's greats. But as I got deeper into middle school, the magazine's photographs took on a new significance, and now when I lay on my stomach in bed looking at, say, the photo of a tennis star whose shirt had lifted in mid-serve to expose bronze belly hair, I would start imagining the coarser hair that curled beneath the elastic band of his shorts.

My body's inner upheavals were compounded by outer ones. I had a tremendous growth spurt the summer before eighth grade, six inches and twenty pounds in just three months. This explosion coincided with daily weight-lifting sessions overseen by Coach Johannsen at our local YMCA, and by the end of the summer my body's soft meadows and gentle valleys had transformed into hardpan plains and sheer cliffs. My voice started changing, too, deepening in fits and starts like a 747 making its final descent through a nasty storm. My metamorphosis caused a dramatic reversal in my social prospects, making me someone boys wanted to befriend and girls wanted to date; and yet I knew that caution was paramount in a town where "faggot" and "fairy" were the epithets of choice. So rather than turn into some big man on campus, I became an amiable cipher: I was friendly with male classmates but didn't trust myself enough to develop any real friendships, and I went on enough dates with girls to avoid suspicion but used the Catholicism I bought less every mass as an excuse to squirm out of anything sexual.

Realizing I was gay placed me in better stead than many pre-teens like me, kids who also lived in little conservative towns in the heart of the heart of this country, but my self-knowledge only led me to face the next, even bigger quandary. I was indisputably gay and indisputably a football player, and yet all I had to do was look at the swimsuit editions of those same *Sports Illustrated*s, or listen to my teammates argue over which of our cheerleaders had the best tits, to know that "gay" and "football player" did not equate. It was like the transitive law I was learning about in math class, in which A=B, A=C, and so B=C—except that everywhere I looked, everything I heard, everything I was taught was telling me B could never, ever, equal C.

I hoped, prayed, that this irreconcilability would change—but for now I funneled all my passions into the game, and at thirteen I was rewarded with the glorious experience of seeing my talent for football catch up to my enthusiasm for it. I was the only freshman at Sillitoe High to make varsity that year, and by the fourth game of the season I earned a starting spot, the first freshman in a decade to do so. As the weak-side outside linebacker, aka Will linebacker, I led our team in tackles, sacks, and interceptions.

I capped that season with my favorite performance of my entire career. It was a Friday night in early November, blustery and biting cold, the sky low with thick clouds that glowed purple in the way they do when snow is imminent. We were down three points with eight seconds left in the fourth quarter, and our opponent had the ball. The offense and defense broke their huddles and trotted up to the line of scrimmage. The opposing quarterback grinned as he approached center, clearly preparing to take a knee and run out the clock. My teammates were resigned and halfheartedly got into their stances. But not me—as soon as the ball was snapped, I knocked the center ass-over-teakettle, and he in turn tripped the quarterback, causing him to fumble. I caught the ball on the bounce and ran away with the game, sprinting eighty yards down the field. I wasn't usually a demonstrative player, but I felt so exuberant, so invincible on that run that I flipped over the goal line, hugging the ball to my chest as I landed on my back in the end zone, feeling my body sink into the brittle, delightfully cold grass. I panted, staring up at the clouds—which at that exact moment started to pour down snow, like ticker tape.

Coach Johannsen and my parents waited in the school parking lot after the game.

—There he is!

Coach Johannsen ran up to me, draping his arm around my shoulders and telling my parents:

—You guys won't have to worry about college tuition. Not with this one.

On the way home, Mom and Dad wondered if he was right, if I *could* earn a full football scholarship. They had made this suggestion before, but in the past had mentioned it in the same offhand, head-pat way they would when, say, I brought home a miniature cabin made of Popsicle sticks and they said maybe I could be an architect. But there was nothing offhand in their voices now, only a plain, heavy need. Three months earlier, they had both been pink-slipped by the mining company after twenty years of loyal service. Since then Dad had hustled temporary gigs while he looked for a permanent job—stints at the nuclear waste project up in Rocky Flats, at the Coors Beer HQ in Golden—while Mom got hired as a phone wrangler at the Jefferson County Courthouse, forced to fend off the advances of a handsy district attorney so we could be on the state's health plan. I wanted to help my family but hadn't known how—it's not like my paper route was going to dig us out of our ever-deepening financial hole.

But that changed with Coach Johannsen's pronouncement about my prospects for a scholarship, and by the time we pulled into our driveway that evening I was resolved to win a full ride to college and take some of the weight off my parents' shoulders. Nor would I win just any scholarship—I would earn a ride from one of the country's elite programs, from a Division One school, like where Coach Johannsen had played.

14

. . .

The following Monday I returned home from school to find magic waiting in our mailbox: an envelope with the University of Colorado's address on its upper left corner and the school's leaping buffalo mascot beneath.

Dear Miles,

I was impressed by how you bore down and played your butt off in the fourth quarter against Highlands Ranch. That's the kind of heart we look for at the University of Colorado.

Sincerely,
Hank Woodruff

It was the kindest, most considerate, most eloquent, most genuine letter I had ever received. I rushed into the house and reread the thing at least a hundred times that afternoon, relishing the phrasing, admiring Coach Woodruff's blocky handwriting, and when my parents returned from work that night, I beamed as I handed over the letter. We celebrated by ordering a pizza—an extravagance for us back then—and as we ate and laughed, I had no doubt this was just the beginning of a flood of interest I'd be receiving from D1 programs.

That spring, I was nodding off in the back of my history class when I was slapped awake by a loudspeaker announcement summoning me to my head coach's office. I leapt out of my seat, knowing there was only one reason why this would be happening, and when I reached the coach's office at the back of the gymnasium, I found an overfed, hastily shaved white man in khaki pants and a polo shirt with the University of Utah's logo stitched to the right breast. The Utah coach extended his hand to greet me, and I knew to keep my whole body rigid for what came next: not merely a handshake, not only a greeting, but a sanctioned form of groping in which the coach would simultaneously squeeze my hand like a fruit he wanted to juice and use his other hand to pat me first on my right trap muscle, then on my shoulder, then encircle my arm with his fingers so he could touch both biceps and triceps. He was testing my musculature, seeing whether this boy was made of the man-stuff that's a must for this game. He nodded, but then asked the dreaded question.

—What's your weight?

I was beginning to appreciate the world-historic injustice of skipping the second grade. It had made me a year younger than the players I was competing against for a scholarship, made me a good ten pounds too light for an outside linebacker—and this regardless of the fact that under Coach Johannsen's supervision I was eating a daily fourth meal we called "superdinner" and drinking wretched sludgy protein shakes whenever my stomach had the slightest vacancy. In theory I could have lied to the Utah coach about my weight, but to have lied to a coach was unthinkable to me in those days. So I told him the truth and watched the light die in his eyes.

—Well, he said, trailing off. You still got some time to grow.

I did have time, and did grow over the next year—not to mention having another excellent season—and yet remained undersized and watched as the quality of the programs sending letters to my house and emissaries to my high school grew more obscure. By my junior year, panic began setting in. Now college coaches were allowed to call me on the telephone, one coach per program, but as fall turned to winter, and then winter to spring, I only received calls from programs from the lower divisions, 1AA and 2, places I wasn't interested in. That summer my parents pooled funds with Coach Johannsen to make a hundred copies of a highlight montage of my greatest plays, and when the tapes were ready, the four of us sat around our dining room's drop-leaf table and stuffed them into padded manila envelopes addressed to every D1 program in the country, as well as every football-recruiting rag that could be found in the Sports rack at Barnes and Noble. Yet all this did was get my okayness entered into the public record: I was described as a "small but promising" linebacker in those magazines, and I heard nothing from the schools.

Senior season was the best of my career. I was selected first team All-County and second team All-State. Letters arrived by the dozen, and I received calls from coaches almost every week, since they were unrestricted for seniors. But the only scholarship offers were from 1AA and 2 schools, and to the consternation of my parents I declared I would never consider anything other than a D1 ride and would attend college only when I was in possession of one. I knew my parents needed the financial help more than ever, but I also knew, *knew*, I was D1 caliber and was convinced that to choose a school in a lesser echelon would have been to deny my destiny.

At last, mercy. One of those highlight tapes we mailed landed on the right desk, and the night before the final game of high school I received a phone call that, while not ending with a scholarship offer, did end with an invitation to make an official campus visit that coming January. The call was from the King College Monarchs, about which I knew precisely three things: 1) King was in Blenheim, North Carolina; 2) it was one of the best academic schools in the country; and 3) it was the very worst football program in all of Division One.

King's first emissary was a chocolate chip cookie cake propped up on a tripod. The cake was shaped like a castle turret, and beneath the parapet were letters in alternating purple and gold frosting that spelled out

## WELCOME TO KING COLLEGE

I broke a chunk off the battlement and munched, still buzzing from my free cross-country plane ride, admiring a Marriott suite so large and lavish I could scarcely believe I had it all to myself: a top-of-the-line television twice as wide and half as thick as the one my parents had back home; a mini fridge stocked with snacks, which a sticky note welcomed me to gorge on; and two king-sized beds. The weather was miraculous, thirty degrees warmer than it had been in Colorado, and the sunlight streaming in from the windows was so strong I had no need to flip on a light.

After gobbling another three chunks of battlement I dove onto one of the soft mattresses and examined a purple folder that lay on the bedside table. The folder contained a letter saying I would be picked up by my player-host at 6 p.m., plus informational pamphlets about the college's departments and a history of the school. I slid out the history.

*Before King was King, it was Triune College, a denominational school founded in 1844 to train Methodist ministers. Many of Triune's graduates went on to have distinguished careers, but none more than Jedediah King, the scion of a prominent Blenheim planter family. An energetic, brilliant young man who served as pastor of Blenheim's First Methodist Church, Jedediah was known throughout the Piedmont for his ability to recite whole chapters of scripture from memory.*

*When the Civil War broke out, Jedediah volunteered to serve as chaplain for a newly formed North Carolina regiment, and the town of Blenheim sent him off to battle with great fanfare and even greater enthusiasm for the Confederate cause. But their optimism was to be rewarded with bloodshed, as Jedediah's regiment suffered one of the highest attrition rates of any in the Confederacy, and when its survivors finally returned home, the men were, as one contemporary letter noted, "wounded in mind, body, spirit." Jedediah was said to be nearly unrecognizable with his long black beard and a limp that required use of a cane. To the shock of his neighbors, he refused to resume his duties as the leader of First Methodist and instead took over his family's plantation.*

*He used the talents he had developed as a preacher to become a visionary businessman, transforming the King landholdings into one of the biggest manufacturers in the South. After he died in a railroad accident in 1880, his oldest son, Augustus, took King Tobacco's reins and elevated the company to still greater heights—an international force that, among other accomplishments, helped open the West's tobacco trade in China. Blenheim's fortunes rose in tandem: it went from the one-horse town Jedediah had known as a boy to one of*

*North Carolina's major commercial centers, home to state-of-the-art factories and stately neighborhoods built in the Victorian style.*

*But Blenheim's renaissance was not to last. At the turn of the century, King Tobacco was broken up by an antitrust ruling. What parts of the company weren't sold off moved overseas during the next fifty years. Having lost the engine of its economy, Blenheim gradually reverted to the sleepy southern burg it had once been. Augustus, set adrift by the court's decision, left the company's management to his sons and set sail for a tour of the European continent to decide how to spend his fortune.*

*For the next two years he immersed himself in Europe's rich cultures, and it was upon seeing the Gothic architecture of Germany's great universities that he had an epiphany: he would found a college in the South that could compete with the world's best schools. He booked passage back to America and bought Triune College, renaming it King College after his father. He hired the era's finest architects to oversee the expansion of the campus, clearing the forest on the western edge to make way for new buildings built in the same magisterial style Augustus had so admired in Germany—including a 200-foot chapel complete with a 70-bell carillon and three pipe organs. The chapel stood in the center of the new West Campus, while Triune's Georgian-style campus was renamed East Campus and became*

I blinked. The hotel room's air had gone grainy with evening, and I was so disoriented that I only belatedly realized that what had woken me was the sound of the door opening. A hulking figure stood in the doorway to my left, its big body limned by hallway light. It closed the door, merging with the room's dark air, still looking at me. I turned my eyes to the ceiling and dug my fingernails into my palms, hoping this was a nightmare I could wake myself from. But the pain in my hands told me I was already awake, that I had indeed watched a large black man slip into my hotel room. I knew he was going to walk my way. Knew he was going to sidle alongside my bed, breathe evenly, and . . .

The overhead lights snapped on. The figure was, somehow, Reshawn McCoy.

Reshawn played for Archerville High School, a powerhouse program in western Oregon famous for producing half a dozen, sometimes more, D1 signees every year. Reshawn was not only Archerville's captain but the greatest player in the pantheon of its great players—starting tailback, middle linebacker, kick returner, punt returner, even punter. He had on several occasions graced not just *USA Today*'s prep coverage but the front page of the whole paper, top of the fold, nestled between Davos updates and reports on arms trafficking in Khartoum. He was everything I'd failed to stop myself from dreaming I could be: an All-American, a glory of strength, size, and speed, a star who had received offers from every D1 program, some 120 schools. He was the type who kept his choice secret until National Signing Day, when TV networks would broadcast him dramatically donning a baseball cap featuring the logo of whichever program he'd chosen.

But what the hell was he doing here?

—Hey, he said.

I cleared my throat and sat up in bed.

—I'm Reshawn? he continued.

—Miles. Sorry. I didn't know I had a roommate.

He nodded and looked over the disfigured cookie cake.

—This was last minute.

He didn't say anything else as he unloaded the contents of his backpack onto the second bed. A pair of carefully folded jeans and two polo shirts, a ziplock bag tidily packed with toiletries, a notebook, a calculus textbook, and a novel I'd never heard of, *Cane*. The questions I wanted to ask were running into each other like harried office assistants sent in conflicting directions: What was he doing here? Did he know who I was? Was he upset I'd eaten some of the cake? *Did* he know me? But I didn't ask anything, too intimidated to initiate conversation as his presence—Reshawn McCoy!—continued to sink in.

He sat at the desk next to the windows and began work on a calculus problem set. It was the first time I'd been in a room alone with a black person.

Chase McGerrin was just this side of albino, his hair so light and buzzed so short that when I saw him from the opposite end of the hotel lobby, I initially mistook him for bald. He seemed bluntly big even from that distance, and to walk toward him and watch him take on his true dimensions was like spotting a boulder from afar that you know is huge but that, when you finally reach it, still surprises you with its sheer rocky immensity.

I was ready to be intimidated by the team's second-string Will linebacker, but Chase's face melted into a friendly smile when we shook hands.

—They still putting a giant cookie in the rooms? he asked. When I was on my visit, I thought I had to eat the whole cake or they'd take away my offer.

—I don't have an offer yet.

I wanted to go right back to my room and die. Chase nudged me.

—It'll happen.

It was kind of him to say so, and I continued to warm up to Chase as we talked. Meanwhile Reshawn awkwardly traded pleasantries with his own host, Devonté Sanders. Devonté was the starting tailback, black, on the shorter side, and formidably built. Even in long sleeves and pants I could tell he had the exquisitely detailed muscle definition that's common to smaller players. And yet Devonté was measly compared to Reshawn; from the way he kept looking over Reshawn's body, it was clear he understood this himself.

We walked out to Devonté's car, a 1991 Grand Marquis with a rattle in its throat and a heel-sized hole in the floorboard. The hole let chill night air stream into the car's interior, keeping us in our jackets, and when we pulled onto the highway, the air rushing into the car made a high-pitched whistle.

—What do you guys major in? Reshawn asked from the backseat, having to raise his voice to be heard.

—What, in school? Chase said.

Devonté glanced in the rearview mirror and saw Reshawn was being serious.

—Marketing, he said. Minor in kinesiology.

—Haven't declared, Chase said, and turned to Devonté. They let us major in female anatomy?

—Are there any English majors on the team? Reshawn asked.

—*English?*

—Like, literature.

—Hell no, Devonté said. Most guys can barely speak the shit.

—Well, I am, Reshawn said, looking out the window. I'll get a PhD, too.

None of us knew how to respond to such a strange, defiant declaration. Everyone was quiet for the rest of the ride.

We arrived at a sprawling corporate campus and parked in front of a cylindrical office building with a rounded glass roof. We rode the elevator to the penthouse and entered the most elegant space I'd ever seen—dimmed lights, gleaming stainless surfaces, floor-to-ceiling windows that gave views of the Blenheim skyline. Toqued servers stood behind steel buffet containers doling out steaming proteins and carbs, while above our heads flat-screen TVs played a King Football highlight reel on loop.

I sat with Chase at a table full of other recruits and their hosts. The King players talked among themselves, leaving us recruits to silently scarf our dinners and wait for one of the coaches to come over. But at the moment all the coaches were talking to Reshawn, a dozen grown men turned Beatlemaniacs for the first five-star prospect to have come through King in decades.

—This is like prom in hell.

So said a tall, sharp-jawed white boy in the seat next to me.

—I'm Charlie, he said.

—Miles.

—Got an offer, Miles?

Was everyone going to be asking me that?

—Me neither, Charlie continued, recognizing my stymied expression. I hear they call this Pity Weekend. They already made more offers than they have scholarships. So you got some long shots they wanna woo—

He lifted his chin at Reshawn, then added:

—But mostly you got players like us.

—I have a meeting with Coach Zeller tomorrow.

Charlie popped a roasted rosemary potato into his mouth and shrugged.

—Me too. Doesn't mean we're getting offered. They get a certain amount of money for these visits every year. They figure, hey, we got cash left over, let's give the no-hopes a weekend in lovely Blenheim before we reject them. Like I said, prom, and we're the girls nobody wants to fuck.

—Miles!

I turned to see Radon Hightower, the linebackers coach. Black and in his early forties, he was six foot four and the rare ex-athlete who'd gone lean rather than chubby after his playing days. I shot up from my chair to shake his hand.

—So you're the one who took the last flank steak, he said.

Hightower was born in low-country South Carolina, and I was so unaccustomed to deep southern accents that his words came in strange shapes I had to work hard to decipher.

—Flackstake, Coach?

—Huh?

—Sir?

—Steak, son. *Steak.*

—Oh. Do you want mine?

I'd have gladly cut it up and hand-fed it to him. Coach Hightower smiled.

—Fuckin' with you, Miles. You have a good flight?

—Yes sir.

—Don't have any mountains around here.

He leaned down and pinched Chase on the back of the arm.

—How's Miles doin'?

—Good, Coach, Chase said, rubbing his arm.

Hightower nodded absently and glanced over my head at the next recruit he wanted to talk to.

—Good good, he said, patting me on the shoulder. Get my man some pussy tomorrow night, hear?

I didn't sleep much back at the Marriott. I kept replaying my conversation with Charlie, and the thought of leaving Blenheim without an offer sent sour pangs ripping through my stomach. This would have been stressful enough, but in addition Reshawn slept only in his boxer shorts on top of the duvet cover, and even when I turned my face away from his body, I could still see the light from the parking lot outlining his pecs and ab muscles, the thick clefts in his quadriceps.

I was bleary when Chase and Devonté collected us the next morning. This time we took Chase's truck, a souped-up Ford with oversized tires that forced me and Reshawn to hop into the cab's backseats and a sound system so powerful the tinted windows shuddered every time the bass line throbbed with a blaring rap song. Small talk impossible, I leaned my head against the window and got my first sustained daytime views of town.

Blenheim was described as a "sleepy southern burg" in that history I'd read, and judging from the road we were driving down, the place didn't ever really wake up: rows of fast food signs like so many ships' masts, bail bonds and checks cashed, XXX and Jesus Saves, the buildings worn and weather-eaten, hunched and darkening in a way that the clean dull sprawl of central Colorado hadn't prepared me for. I would see a dead-eyed Laundromat and think the place was closed, only to then watch customers walk out of it, while places I assumed were open would, on second look, have chains strung through their door handles or neon condemned notices stickered to their windows. There were flashes of Blenheim's former glory—a grand Romanesque church, an art deco movie house—but these just served to emphasize how ramshackle and exhausted most of the town was.

The vibe changed the instant we passed beneath a high stone arch with King College's motto carved into it—*Virtus et Veritas*. A one-lane road wound gently through pristine pine forest, and among the trees I spotted King's cross-country team training on a dirt path, the runners' breaths smoking in the crisp air, the pale legs of the white kids splotched red by the cold. The forest dropped away and the landscape opened into the school's athletic region, scarcely more populated than the Blenheim we'd just driven through, and yet with an air of voluptuous indolence rather than abandonment. The empty baseball diamonds were manicured, the unused lacrosse and soccer fields immaculate.

Our destination rose into view: the Hay Memorial Football Center and the horseshoe-shaped football stadium downhill to the right. The Hay was a five-story brick fortress with Gothic stone accents. Two stern oaks flanked its façade, and a cold-looking flagstone path led up to the entrance. Chase parked at the bottom of the path and said they would pick us up here this evening to take us to a special party for recruits.

Reshawn hopped out, but I remained nailed to my seat, staring at the Hay. So long as I didn't enter, I wouldn't be rejected.

Chase saw me panicking in the rearview.

—All good, man. Remember all the offers you already got.

I blew out a breath and hopped down, walking with Reshawn into what was the Hay's third floor (the bottom two levels were underground, built into the hill). We took an elevator to the Hay's fifth floor, and by the time we stepped into the lobby, my throat was so cottony I could barely reciprocate the secretaries' hellos.

Reshawn was called back first. I waited on a purple pleather couch, right leg joggling fiercely in place as I examined the action shots of King Football players on the walls—glossy photos of wide receivers diving to catch passes, King defenders crunching opponents, godly bodies in glorious jerseys I would superimpose myself onto only to worry I was in danger of jinxing my chances. Five minutes later Charlie, the kid from last night, walked out of the open entryway I'd seen Reshawn disappear into. Charlie was alone, and there was a defeated cast to his face that told me his cynicism last night had been a front; he'd been hoping for an offer at his meeting and had just come from not getting one. I looked at the action shots again, pretending not to notice him as he despondently waited for the elevator.

An hour had passed by the time Coach Hightower led me through the back half of the floor. We walked down a hallway that smelled of fresh computer paper and stale coffee, passing coaches' offices, conference rooms, film rooms. Reshawn was exiting the corner office just as we reached it, and he looked even more downcast than Charlie had. But I couldn't linger on why that might be, not now. I only had room for my own nervousness, which was reaching such an irrational pitch that when my shoulder brushed against Reshawn's I hoped some of his magical luck rubbed off on me.

George Zeller, head coach of King Football, stood behind his desk. At twenty-nine, Zeller was the youngest head coach in Division One. He'd come to Blenheim two years earlier to work as defensive coordinator, and after King posted last year's winless season and fired its head coach, he'd been tapped for the top job. Sandy-haired, azure-eyed, and six inches taller than me, the man had a chest perpetually puffed by the muscle he'd retained from his defensive end days at TCU, not to mention the confidence of somebody who'd summited the sport before the age of thirty.

—Miles! How you feelin' today? Strong?

Zeller did the shake-and-squeeze, holding my biceps for an extra count.

—*Feelin'* strong. Feelin' like you're 'bout ready to take a receiver's damn head off!

We sat, Zeller behind his desk, Hightower and I across from him in unforgiving wooden chairs. The corner walls to my right were floor-to-ceiling windows that gave views of the stadium and practice fields.

—So how you likin' the Hay?

—It's beautiful, Coach.

Zeller smirked. I panicked that "beautiful" had given me away, somehow.

—Awful nice of you to say so, he said. I wouldn't call it "beautiful" myself. But we're gettin' there, Miles. We. Are. Gettin'. There.

He knocked on his desk.

—Enough of the lady-talk. I wanted to let you know we appreciate your patience while we get this recruitin' class in order. We're puttin' together a damn good group. Quietly the best this school's ever seen. And that's complicated, son. You got all these different facets you gotta address.

—Yes sir. Facets.

Zeller looked down at a manila folder splayed open on his desk. I saw my name on the top of a form.

—Grades are fine, he said, trailing his finger along the sheet. Test scores much better. Any idea what you'd want to study?

"Linebacking" was the real answer, but I wasn't sure how well that would go over.

—English, I said. With a minor in kinesiology.

He looked up, surprised by my ambition to be a literature devotee who also knew how to treat sprained wrists. He resumed reading, and soon I saw his eyes stick. He squinted, bringing the sheet closer to his face, and my heart pounded at the thought that he'd happened on something damning. He slid the sheet toward me and pointed at my birthday.

—That a typo? Sixteen?

—I turn seventeen in August, Coach.

Zeller looked at Hightower.

—You tell me this already?

Hightower nodded. Zeller's body relaxed as he leaned back in his leather chair, thumbs tapping the armrests.

—Sixteen, he said again, to himself this time. And you still don't have any D1 offers?

—No sir.

He leaned forward, energized.

—You know, most of our program's made up of players other schools overlooked. Grades on the bubble. Attitude problem. Forty time a little slow. Other people might call 'em misfits, scraps, what have you. But you know what I call 'em? Diamonds in the fuckin' rough. So tell me, Miles. You feel like you can be part of somethin' bigger than yourself?

Jesus Christ.

—Yes sir.

—You interested in makin' history?

—Yes.

He smiled. He was smiling, he was smiling and saying:

—Then we're ready to offer you a scholarship.

I was standing—when did that happen? I was laughing—but at what? Coach Zeller and I were shaking hands. I was fairly sure I was breathing.

I hugged Coach Hightower, hugged him as if the world had flooded and he was the tree trunk that had spared me.

I was so dazed I barely registered anything I saw during our tour of the Hay's lower levels, and I only settled down when the recruits were taken to the flagstone sidewalk outside the third-floor entrance. There we were placed in the care of an Athletic Department flack named Mary Sue Kim, a small Asian woman—I'd only recently learned not to say "Oriental"—dressed in blue jeans and a purple King College fleece.

Mary Sue was to give us a tour of King's academic region, which began with a dormitory shaped like a medieval fort. We walked beneath the Gothic arch cut through the dorm's center, and on the other side entered another world altogether: West Campus's main quad. There was a long lawn down the middle pillared with mighty oaks, and bordering both sides were more Gothic dormitories that mirrored each other for a good quarter of a mile, their gables and crenellations, towers and ramparts, parapets and finials so finely carved that the granite looked supple. On the quad's far end stood the King Chapel, more a stone ship than a church that plied the bright winter sunlight. Three-o'clock classes had just let out, and the quad was bustling with King students—*my* future classmates.

Reshawn walked at the head of our group. The downcast look I'd seen on his face had continued during our tour of the Hay, but he was alert now as he walked alongside Mary Sue.

—Through that arch is Kaledin Plaza, she said. Sophomore players live over there, in Mennee Hall. And you can catch the shuttle to the other campuses at—

—Where's the Rare Book Room?

Mary Sue pushed her face toward Reshawn, smiling.

—Rare what?

—*Books*, he said. Like manuscripts and letters? I read King owns Hawthorne's notes for *Blithedale*.

Mary Sue remained baffled. Reshawn's face darkened. I was beginning to realize how short his temper was.

—Where's the *library*?

—Oh! she said. Over there—it's on the itinerary. We'll go after dinner with the Coronets.

Reshawn tilted his head.

—Coronets? The fuck are they?

Mary Sue somehow managed to squirm without moving.

—You know, she said. The cheerleading squad?

Reshawn sucked his teeth and broke away toward the library, ignoring Mary Sue's calls for him to stop. She set off after him, seeming to forget there were fourteen other recruits she was responsible for, and we were forced to trail after her, dodging between King students amused by the sight of overmuscled boys straggling behind a tiny, determined woman. We caught up with Mary Sue at the entrance to the library, and she caught up with Reshawn in the Rare Book Room, a dim, musty, pin-drop space where he was leaning over a glass display case of illuminated manuscripts. He must have noticed us coming in, must have known he was being watched, and I doubted he could focus on whatever he was reading; but he stubbornly kept looking at the manuscripts. There was something performative about this I disliked, something false and pretentious, something—what's the word I'd heard my uncles use?—uppity.

Reshawn couldn't ignore us forever, and he was sullen the rest of the afternoon, blatantly ignoring the cheerleaders at dinner as he sat at the far end of the table and read pamphlets he'd collected in the Rare Book Room. After the tour of the library, Reshawn and I walked back across campus, neither of us speaking as we passed beneath the tall, curling iron lamps that lit up the darkening quad. But forget Reshawn: there was the Ford, idling in front of the Hay. I had my new teammates to talk to, and I was especially eager to see Chase, who'd been so kind to me, who could now welcome me as a D1 peer, a brother Will linebacker.

We climbed into the cab's backseats. Chase pulled away from the Hay.

—Heard you got offered, Devonté said to me.

I heard a foamy crack and watched a can of Natty Light rise up from Devonté's seat. I accepted it.

—Welcome to—

—Don't spill that shit, Chase snapped.

He didn't turn when he said this. Come to think of it, Chase hadn't looked at me once since I stepped into the truck.

—*Chill*, Devonté said, cracking open another beer and handing it to Reshawn.

—One of my tires is worth more than your whole shitbox, D. I don't need some retard pre-frosh stinking up my truck.

—I'll be careful, I said, but Chase ignored me.

Ten minutes later we arrived at Central Campus, forty hilly acres of tan-and-brown apartment complexes built in the 1970s to accommodate the expanded student population after King went coed. We parked on a sodium-lit street in front of one of the complexes and started up a small knoll. Chase hurried ahead of us and disappeared into the apartment.

—Did I do something wrong? I asked Devonté.

—*Nobody* knows how to read McGerrin's ass. He's, what's the word, volatile. He'll be all happy-happy when he doesn't think you're a threat. You're a Will? Yeah. He's probably tellin' himself you're his fuckin' enemy now.

It was imperative I find Chase, tell him this couldn't have been further from the truth. But I couldn't see him in the living room we entered, packed as it was with a hundred-plus players, loud as it was with all the drunk voices, heady as it was with warring smells—hormones, cheap cologne, Black and Tans, the faintly fecal scent of weed, alcohol breath of every variety. Reshawn and I were handed red Solo cups of huge-headed Natty Light and sat on two of the twelve wooden desk chairs arranged in a circle in the room's center. Reshawn sat to my left, bored again. Charlie settled unsteadily onto the chair to my right: out of sympathy for not being offered today, Charlie's host had gotten him drunk.

Bodies heaved and the temperature swelled, the room abuzz with the erratic electricity of too many waiting men. I started to hope the main event wasn't going to happen, that the night was going to be a bust, when a gush of cold air swept over me. Voices grew even louder now as the wall of players parted and a woman stepped into the center of the room. She was bigger and brawnier than I was, wearing heavy Timberland boots, baggy black cargo pants, an untucked red flannel shirt, and a purple King College baseball cap with the school's logo, a gold crown, glistening in its center.

Its owner's face glared from beneath the cap's unbent bill.

—The rules! she shouted, silencing everyone. You do not

*touch* my lady—my lady touches you. You give my lady words of *respect*—call her a bitch and we gone. You follow her instructions—

She looked straight at me.

—She tell you to jump? Jump. She tell you bark like a dog?

She flashed a smile, showing a front tooth encased in silver.

—Then *do* that, motherfucker! My lady is chief from now till we walk out that door.

She surveyed the recruits one last time.

—And tips is *more* than welcome.

The bouncer stepped away from the center of the circle and set up a boom box on the floor next to my chair. R&B started slinking out of the speakers. The overhead lights dropped, and now there was just a single bright beam from a standing lamp in the corner, used to illuminate the inner circle.

The dancer stepped into the center. Even in vertiginous heels she stood well under five foot, dressed only in a lime green G-string and matching bra. Her greased ass and hips and thighs shone in the lamplight; her tummy sported a long scar northeast of her navel. Braided hair extensions spilled all the way down to the top ridge of her buttocks, which I noticed had stretch marks running across each cheek—stretch marks that matched the ones I'd developed myself after I'd started lifting weights.

The lap dances commenced, the dancer moving clockwise along the chairs to ride each recruit, making Charlie third-to-last, me second-to, and Reshawn last. Bra still on, she pushed her cleavage into the recruit's nostrils while the players behind us whooped and laughed, and when she dismounted you could see the jean-clad erection left to long after her. She hadn't even settled onto Charlie's lap before Charlie slapped her ass so hard I heard it over the loud music. The boom box was paused and the bouncer scolded Charlie to keep his hands to himself. The dancer abandoned Charlie and moved onto me. I thought it wise to show her how assiduously I followed directions, so I gripped the underside of my seat to ensure my hands went nowhere forbidden as she slid up and down my lap.

Reshawn's turn. Only now did the dancer remove her bra, and in the first genuinely sexy moment of the performance she lowered her crotch softly onto his lap and paused her gyrating to make eye contact with him. She guided his hands to her nipples, rocking slowly, tilting her head back so her braids cascaded down to his knees. But was Reshawn smiling, licking his lips as the others had? No. He was more bored than ever. The dancer noticed this when I did, and her face registered, in lightning succession, confusion and sadness and rage, sealing it all off with a stony blasé.

She pushed herself away from Reshawn and retreated to the center of the circle. Up to then the music had been slow, smoky ballads, but now the mix turned to the apocalyptic sirens of a rap anthem. The dancer began making circles within the circle in the center, hard stepping mock-militantly in her stilettos, hand up in a salute. She dropped precipitously down into a crouch and, hands on knees, swayed from side to side while the bouncer stepped behind her to lay down a lime green beach towel. The dancer lay back onto the towel, writhing, wriggling, I swear to God working off her G-string without the use of her hands, scissoring her legs back and forth so that you saw everything—everything. With a final snap she spread-eagled, and I noticed a piece of silver wink out of her vagina. I assumed this was a piercing until she reached inside herself to remove a full set of handcuffs.

The darkness detonated, players leaping, shoving each other, screaming. The dancer laid the coruscating handcuffs on the towel and stood, making her way to Reshawn once again. She took his hand and tried to pull him toward the towel, looking coy, as if to tell him all had been forgiven. But Reshawn yanked his hand away and stood. He pushed through the crowd.

A couple players halfheartedly tried to stop him on his way to the door. As he stepped outside, the dancer placed her hands on her hips and shouted:

33

—Later, faggot!

For a moment she kept looking in Reshawn's direction, recalibrating. Behind her closed lips I could see her tongue contemplatively run over her top row of teeth.

—So, she finally said, turning to the rest of the recruits. Which one of y'all wants his money's worth?

She'd barely finished asking the question when two strong hands gripped my right biceps, trying to force me to raise my hand. I looked up to see Chase. His pale face was flushed, and the beads of sweat suspended in his blond hair rained onto me as he tried elevating my hand. He wasn't smiling. There was nothing playful in this. As I struggled to keep my hand down, I recalled that this was Reshawn's fifth official visit. No doubt the other schools had hired strippers, which meant there must have been good reason why he'd refused to get a special lap dance.

I was saved by Charlie, who glugged down the rest of his beer, threw the empty cup to the ground, and stood as tribute. Chase released my arm and reabsorbed back into the crowd while the dancer smiled at Charlie and beckoned him over with her index finger. Long-limbed, knobby-kneed Charlie obeyed, standing in the center of the circle while the dancer laced around him. She removed his polo shirt and then unbuckled his belt, dropping his khakis to his feet. She sauntered behind him and hooked her arms under his armpits, sliding her hands along his pale bare chest. Her fingers turned downward, bumping along his ribbed abdomen, fingertips kissing the waistband of his boxers and sliding beneath the elastic band . . . But just as her fingers seemed about to dive, she retracted her arms and shoved Charlie forward so he was kneeling on the towel.

She used the handcuffs to secure his hands in front of him, prayer-style, and pushed him over so he was resting on his elbows with his ass in the air. I hadn't noticed until now that on top of the boom box stood a tube of Vaseline, which the dancer must have rubbed onto herself before she started the performance. She coated

Charlie's body with the jelly as she circled him, streaking her hands across his back. Charlie closed his eyes, and though his torso was taut and his triceps flexed from taking all his weight, his face was placid—you would have thought he was receiving an unconventional deep body massage.

There was a ragged hunger in the voices of the players behind me, a collective urging for the dancer to do what it was clear she was about to. Standing to the side of Charlie, she laid the lubed heel of her hand on the top of his spine and skated it down the muscled half-pipe of his back. She plunged her hand beneath the band of his boxers, and I saw her fingers extend beneath the cloth. From how Charlie winced, I knew the fingers were working inside him.

An erection was rising from me, and to hide it I leaned forward in my seat, making it seem like I was trying to get a better view of the dancer.

Early the next morning I woke with a start and lay apprehensively in my hotel bed, staring at the ceiling. I waited to realize I hadn't been offered yesterday, that it had all been a dream—an experience I'd had more times than I could count over the past two years. But the details of what happened in Coach Zeller's office weren't crumbling in my mind's fingers, as those dreams had. The details remained, cool, firm, strokeable stones I could turn over as many times as I wanted without fear of them losing a gram of their materiality. I had my offer. I relaxed, my body drinking in the softness of the sheets, and soon fell back into a deep sleep.

When I woke again it was from my shoulder being shaken. Reshawn was standing above me, dressed.

—You need to leave.

I sat up and looked at the clock.

—Is the shuttle—

—Somebody needs to talk to me. Get breakfast and I'll be done by the time you're back.

35

No "please," no "can you do me a favor." I considered refusing just to show this kid I couldn't be ordered around; but Reshawn was still much too intimidating for me to dare something like that.

I dressed and entered the hallway, where housekeeping crews were wheeling pushcarts with fresh linens. The elevator bay stood catty-corner to our room, and when the doors parted I made way for a burly white man in a polo shirt with the King crown on its chest. With his build, clothing, and the purposeful way he stepped off the elevator, he resembled a coach, and yet all the coaches I'd met had stopped to introduce themselves, whereas this man swept right past me without looking and knocked peremptorily on our room's door. Maybe he *was* a coach? But then why would I have to clear the room for Reshawn to talk to him?

The restaurant downstairs was filled with hungover recruits. I sat at a table where the boys relived last night's strip show. Charlie sat at the head and pushed scrambled eggs around his plate, smiling faintly whenever someone mentioned the crazy shit he'd let the stripper do. His reddish hair was mussed into a kind of coxcomb, his face was a bit swollen, and he still smelled of booze and Vaseline. No one would have called him handsome, but because he was linked to the most extravagant sexual act I'd ever witnessed in person, I found him almost painfully attractive.

I returned upstairs at ten. Through our room's door I could hear Reshawn still talking to the man I'd seen step off the elevator. I sat on the carpet and leaned my back against the wall to the right of our door—and if you'd asked if I was eavesdropping, I would have insisted no, I just was nervous about missing the shuttle. But of course I could have just as easily taken a walk instead. And if I had done that, I wouldn't have heard Reshawn raise his voice to say, "Ten thousand," and heard the man respond with "We already said five."

Now: I had been devouring sports journalism for nearly as long as I could read, and I knew perfectly well that parts of the football world were corrupt—but that fact had registered as deeply as the civil war in a place called Yugoslavia, or that you took off your shoes before entering a house in Thailand, which is to say that while I believed such things were possible, I didn't think they were possible in *my* life; they happened, just not anywhere in proximity to me. That willed obliviousness alone would have made me resist the idea that I was listening to something untoward, but on top of it I was still basking in the glow of my offer, still marveling at the generosity and goodness of the program that had granted my life's greatest wish. I didn't want to compromise that feeling.

And yet I heard them repeat those numbers, and now heard Reshawn say, "Do you know how much more I could—?" It was useless to deny what I was hearing. The voices petered out, and I heard shuffles, prompting me to scramble upright and hurry in the opposite direction from the elevator bay. I heard our door open and close, and a few seconds later the elevator bell dinged. I turned to find the hallway empty.

Reshawn sat at the desk and didn't move his eyes from his calculus textbook as I went about packing. I wasn't intimidated by him anymore, in fact felt something close to superiority—but it was a hollow sort, knowing I was attached to the program that he had just successfully extorted. But that was something, wasn't it. Reshawn had been in the *position* to extort King, while my program, which was doing its best to climb out of the gutter, had been taken *advantage* of by this haughty, aloof, spoiled star.

And there, with that neat little trick, I forgave what my program had done.

National Signing Day was a few weeks later, and when Reshawn donned his King hat at the press conference, his shocking choice was carried live on ESPN. Over the next days prep recruiting gurus and spittle-lipped pundits dissected why he had chosen King. The most generous said he wanted a great education for free, since

King was at that time ranked the third-best university in the richest country on earth. But to this the more skeptical observers replied that he had received offers from several top-notch schools that also had top-flight football, that that combination had been the common denominator linking the programs people believed he was selecting from. King wasn't merely mediocre, it wasn't just bad—it was D1 pond scum and, lest anyone forget, *hadn't won a single game last season.* This disconnect led the least generous to wonder whether Reshawn hadn't experienced a medical event the moment he was choosing his school, a fugue state that caused him to place that purple cap on his head—or maybe he wasn't as smart as his high GPA and SAT scores led people to believe. But the theory I didn't come across, not once, was that some kind of corruption was involved. Nobody wanted to believe that the kid celebrated as the future of the game might have been compromised. Nor could I blame them. The more I thought about it, the more I wished I had gone for a walk when I'd heard Reshawn and the man still talking.

Back at Sillitoe High, the only official recognition I received on National Signing Day was a schoolwide PA announcement I didn't even hear because the loudspeaker in our homeroom was busted. I received attaboys from teammates, but these were tepid gestures from people who'd never known what to do with a team captain who actively prevented anyone from getting close to him. Really the only passionate responses at school were negative ones, dirty looks from fellow gifted-and-talented students who'd watched me sink into academic indifference only to now be enjoying acceptance—not to mention free tuition, room, board, and food—at a university many of them would have murdered their siblings to attend.

At least the people who loved me were happy, and the Saturday after Signing Day we had Coach Johannsen over for dinner. Mom, already nostalgic about me leaving for college, served dishes I would miss when I was away—beef stroganoff, potato and mushroom casserole seasoned with French onion soup powder, bread pudding with golden raisins. Dad talked nonstop about Reshawn, who I'd recently learned would be my roommate during the school year. When Coach Hightower had called to inform me of the assignment, my first impulse was to ask to room with somebody else; but I knew I'd have to explain why I didn't want to room with Reshawn, and it didn't seem a good idea to hint that I knew something unsavory about our star signee. So I'd be stuck with Reshawn for the school year, just as I was stuck now listening to Dad talk about how the two of us were going to become best friends.

Coach Johannsen pinged between Mom and Dad—alternately sentimental and ecstatic. Up to then, the fanciest outfit I'd seen him wear was a pair of faded blue jeans and a stretched-out polo shirt, but that night he was in dark slacks, a pressed white oxford shirt, and the gold Wyoming class ring he kept polished to a high shine. He hugged me more times that evening than he had in the decade I'd known him, and when hugging wasn't an option he would watch me with a pride so intense I'd have to look away. He'd brought three bottles of merlot, and over the course of dinner I watched his teeth darken with the wine.

My parents called it a night, leaving Coach Johannsen and me to sit at the table. Soon Coach drifted into the past, reminiscing about his own freshman year of college, how Laramie had seemed like the fanciest place on the planet. He told me playing-days stories I'd never heard, as well as about the thrilling, out-of-body experience of sitting in his off-campus apartment while he got the call about the NFL draft. I perked up, thinking I would finally learn why he hadn't played for the Jets; but when he finished talking about the draft he grew quiet and licked his lips, staring at the empty bottles arrayed on the table.

I didn't want him sad, not tonight. I thought I could cheer him up by telling him about the stripper party, which I'd kept secret since I returned from Blenheim. I cast the story in a humorous light, but it didn't have the intended effect. Coach Johannsen only got graver as I spoke, and when I told him what happened to Charlie, he stood unsteadily and asked me to drive him home.

A blizzard had swept through the state earlier that week, and though the strong Colorado sun had melted away most of the snow, the storm system wasn't quite done. Violent gusts lashed the long blond grass that lined the roads' shoulders, ripping tumbleweeds from their roots and sending them skittering across the pavement. The wind knocked my dad's small Dodge Colt from side to side, forcing me to white-knuckle the steering wheel. Coach Johannsen calmly watched the dark shape of the Rockies fill the windshield as we drove west.

I thought I heard him say something.

—Coach?

He used the hand crank to roll down his window. He lifted his face to the cold air, wind blasting through his thinning red hair.

—That black kid's got nothing on you, he said.

I might have disliked Reshawn, but I'd seen the highlights they'd shown during his Signing Day broadcast. He and I were two different species.

—He's pretty good, Coach.

—No, Johannsen said, pushing my arm, which was the last thing I needed while driving in this wind. You're going to show people when you get there. It's like Zeller said. You are . . . you're a diamond.

We pulled into his condo's parking lot, where leftover sand laid down for the blizzard whirled in little eddies. I parked in front of Coach Johannsen's unit.

—Were you listening? he said.

—Yeah, Coach. I'm a diamond.

He unbuckled his seatbelt, but only so he could face me more fully.

—You can play at King. And you can go to the League. But listen to me, Miles. People are gonna tell you college is when you're supposed to open up. That . . . that you can be the person you can't be at home. Bullshit. There are no second chances in football. You have one chance.

He was holding up his index finger to reinforce that number—*one*.

—Do you want me to help you get upstairs?

—*Listen to me, goddamn it!*

He paused, breathing hard.

—You got the rest of your life to be what you are. Life is long. Too fucking long. You just keep making football your love. And love—love can come after.

I realized I was clasping the steering wheel so hard my hands were starting to tremble. Every time I thought Coach Johannsen had intimated he knew I was gay—a glance, an oddly slanted laugh—I had dismissed it as wishful thinking. He would hate me if he knew, would never talk to me again, abandon me, scorn me. But he knew. He'd known. And understanding this now was at once exhilarating and dreadful. Exhilarating because he seemed to be telling me he wasn't disgusted, that he was willing to sit and breathe not eight inches from where I sat and breathed, that he had been my greatest advocate for years even though he'd known. And dreadful because I had been convinced I was an expert at hiding myself and was now being told I was anything but—that I was giving off signals that were invisible to me or, worse, had fooled myself into thinking weren't signals at all.

—Yes sir, I said.

I released the wheel and softly exhaled, hoping he would sit with me for a while. But he opened the door and gripped the top of the frame with both hands, clumsily hauling himself out of the car. He slammed the door and stuck his fists into his pockets as he hunched through the wind.

I remained parked there, trying to decide whether he had meant to slam the door.

# Two

That summer my parents surprised me with a used Saturn station wagon painted the color of butterscotch. They called the car my reward for winning a scholarship, but I knew the real reason they'd bought it was that a thousand bucks for a pending junker was much cheaper than flying me back and forth between Colorado and North Carolina over the next four years. Dad was still grinding away at temp jobs, while Mom had traded her harassing court gig for a daycare service she was struggling to get up and running out of our living room. But I didn't care why they'd bought it. I was just over the moon to have my own car.

I left for Blenheim at dawn on the first Sunday of August, and in one of those death-daring stunts sixteen-year-olds specialize in, I drove straight through the 1,600-mile trip, stopping only for gas, bathroom breaks, and fast food feasts. I didn't permit myself to drink caffeine in those days, but I didn't need the help staying alert—my mind was racing with thoughts of the three-week training camp I was driving toward, of the new teammates awaiting me, and especially of Coach Johannsen and the promise I'd made to him in February. About that: Our relationship was mortally wounded by the conversation we'd had that night in my dad's car, and after a series of increasingly sporadic Sunday dinners in which neither of us could figure out where to point our eyes, Coach Johannsen had stopped coming around altogether—no explanation, no goodbye, just silence that baffled my parents and humiliated me. I blamed myself, naturally, and the chief lesson I took from my coach's withdrawal was that I needed to short-circuit every gay signal I was sending out if I wanted to avoid getting abandoned by other people I loved.

And yet if Coach Johannsen made me feel monstrously insecure off the field, his belief that I could play professional ball also made me more confident than I'd ever been as a player, and as I sped through Kansas, Missouri, Indiana, Kentucky, and Virginia I became convinced that I would exceed expectations at my inaugural college training camp. Generally speaking, freshmen have one of two paths in camp: either they play well enough that they earn a role in games and use their first of four years of NCAA eligibility, or they struggle to learn the playbook and/or adapt to the power of the college level and sit out the season, "redshirting" so they can mature. Underweight by a good fifteen pounds for a D1 outside linebacker, I was expected to finish camp a redshirt. But size, I told myself now, was only a piece of what made a player great; far more important than poundage was your football soul.

And I knew I had soul to spare. Certainly more than Chase McGerrin, whose sweaty pink face had been appearing to me in nightmares—whose casting us as enemies felt exactly right—whose spot as the second-string Will linebacker I had every intention of stealing by the end of August.

I pulled into the players' parking lot just after ten the next morning, punch-drunk and back-sore from my epic drive. After living in my car's air conditioning for the past twenty-odd hours, it was a shock to step out of my Saturn and be engulfed by my first southern summer, the sun a heavy-breathing host with no concept of personal space, the air crazed by a strange insectoid chirring that radiated from the trees.

I followed the posted signs to the Hay building's first floor and entered a hallway raucous with players waiting to report for camp: daps, playful shoves, how's-your-mama, Minnesota honks,

43

Tennessee purrs, Bronx burls, tattoos so fresh they shone with Vaseline, bodies so big it was impossible to believe the oldest boys here were still in their early twenties. I wished to God I had changed out of the outfit my mom had bought me, a short-sleeved collared shirt and cargo shorts so new they still sported the store creases.

—Freshman? the black player ahead of me in line asked.

—Yeah, I'm—

The veteran was uninterested in introductions, and instead handed me a laminated card the size of a driver's license.

*Reign, reign, Monarchs,*
*Rule your realm with an iron fist.*
*Claim, claim, Monarchs,*
*All you see and all you wish.*
*Score, score, Monarchs,*
*Touchdown, field goal, try, and safety.*
*King, King, forever!*
*We'll fight and win, never "maybe"!*

—King's fight song, the vet explained. Every freshman has to sing it during camp.

—Sing it when?

—*When?* the veteran behind me asked. Yo, meat just asked when he's gotta sing the fight song.

The people around me found this hilarious. I smirked, as if I meant to make the joke, but I was more confused than ever.

—*How* do we sing it? I tried again.

They laughed even louder, and I knew better than to ask anything more. Blushing, I kept my eyes on the card and studied the lines, trying to get a feel for their rhythm, humming softly what seemed a plausible melody. I was starting to get the hang of them when I heard the first familiar voice of the morning, albeit the last one I wanted to hear: Chase's. He had just reported and was moving against the line of players in my direction, alternating between playfully nudging teammates in the arm and wickedly flicking

44

them in the balls. I pretended not to notice him, but I kept my hands at my sides, ready to fend off what I was certain would be a flick.

—Furling!

I flinched and clutched my hands over my crotch. This delighted Chase.

—Jesus, freshman! I thought guys *loved* touching sacks in Iowa!

—I'm from Colorado.

—Iowa, Coronado, whatever. Everyone west of the Mississippi eats corn and fucks sheep.

I shook my head and looked away.

—Lighten *up*, he said, pushing me. I'm your Big Brother.

It was tradition for every freshman to be paired with a veteran player who served as his guide during camp. Chase was not only responsible for getting me situated today, he would be rooming with me at the Marriott for the next three weeks. I didn't want to keep standing in line with the guy, let alone live with him for most of the month. But there he remained, cracking more jokes about bestiality in Colorado, and after I gave a graduate assistant my name and received my Marriott room key, Chase led me down the hallway to a counter that was built into the wall and resembled nothing so much as a bank teller's window.

A balding, frumpy, middle-aged white man named Cyrus Pyle greeted me from behind the counter. Pyle was from Atlanta, and would later tell me his ancestors' general store had been torched by General Sherman's troops on their fiery march south. He was in his own way a merchant of goods—the team's equipment manager.

—Come on back.

The counter he stood behind was also a door, one of those two-segmented ones, and Pyle swung the bottom half open to welcome us into his cavernous office. Directly in front of me was a scarred wooden workbench scattered with tools and the various plastic and metal doodads that cinch football equipment together.

To my left, industrial-sized washers and driers lumbered methodically and created a kind of ambient music for the space. And to my right, rows and rows of high metal shelves were packed with helmets, chinstraps, shoulder pads, cowboy collars, shock absorbers, practice pants, practice jerseys, game pants, game jerseys, girdles, tail pads, hip pads, thigh pads, and knee pads. After recording my size for each piece, Pyle set about fitting me with my helmet, first giving me a primer on my face mask options, then adjusting my helmet's tightness with a little hand pump whose needle he inserted into the helmet's bladder. Finally, to the very last row of shelves, home of the accessories: Gloves or no gloves? Wristbands or armbands? I feigned indifference in front of Chase, but inwardly I was thrilled by the cornucopia. Sillitoe High had only given us stretched-out old jerseys and sour-smelling equipment, zero bells and whistles.

Chase and I crossed the hallway into the locker room, which from a bird's-eye view was shaped like the head of a fork. The tines were three-walled spaces the players called cubes, and the cubes' walls were lined with consecutively numbered lockers that corresponded to jersey numbers. Chase led me to the cube where most of the linebackers were located, and there I was introduced to Phaedrus "Fade" Rawlings, our first-string, senior Will linebacker. I might have felt confident about stealing Chase's second-string spot, but I saw immediately there was no way in hell I was also going to displace Fade. First of all, he was black, which was no less intimidating to me now than during my official visit. Second, he was jacked, even more than Chase, from his thick calves to his bulbous ass to his swelled chest to a cannonball-shaped head so freshly Bic'ed I could smell the shaving cream. Fade's race and body seemed to feed off and inflate each other, so that his blackness made his muscles look all the mightier and his musculature seemed to deepen his blackness. But more intimidating still was the brand on his right biceps—a big omega symbol blistered a permanent pink. He noticed me staring.

—You gonna get yours on the same place? he asked.

—*That?* I said.

—Yeah, young'un. All the Wills get one. Night after camp's last practice we go to this old tobacco barn out in Blenheim County. Get a bonfire going, then lay your sweet self down on a bed of hay and—

He closed his fist and pretended it was the brand, twisting it hard into my left biceps while he made a hissing sound. I rubbed my arm, smiling uncomfortably, and turned to Chase to see where his brand was.

—Ass cheek, he said, patting his butt. Way less painful.

I was unnerved—but also, I have to say, stirred by the idea of the communal pain.

—I'm ready, I said.

Chase and Fade looked at each other. They burst out laughing.

—"I'm ready!" Fade yelled, clapping and throwing back his head. *This* motherfucker!

Chase flicked my ear.

—The brand's for Fade's *fraternity*, he said. You really think I'd let someone put a hot poker on my ass?

I dressed in a purple sweat-absorbing T-shirt, purple mesh shorts, and purple Nike flats and followed the herd of players up an unenclosed staircase that connected the Hay's first floor to the second. We filed into the Team Room, King Football's primary meeting space and a place that resembled a medium-sized lecture hall. Against the front wall was a long whiteboard with a mechanized projector screen hanging above it, and facing the board were 150 cushioned chairs arranged on an incline. The lowest rows were reserved for seniors and team captains, with the farthest right chair saved for Coach Zeller. The highest, rearmost rows were for assistant coaches. The seats between were a free-for-all.

I had just taken my seat when Reshawn walked in with Coach Zeller. The room's vibe shifted with our messiah's arrival, and whether players quieted down and stared at him or kept talking to their friends and studiously didn't look, everyone was tracking him, assessing him, orienting their bodies and talents in relation to his. Reshawn seemed oblivious to the effect he had, and as he listened to what Coach Zeller was saying he wore a pinched expression, the look, I thought, of someone holding his nose for the lowly team whose money he was deigning to take.

Coach Zeller, on the other hand, was the picture of excitement, compulsively patting his new star on the back. I knew Zeller must have been instrumental in Reshawn's bribe, and yet I found I couldn't hold that fact against him. And how could I, when this man had been the only D1 coach to offer me a scholarship, the only one who'd seen my youth as an asset rather than a drawback? If it weren't for Coach Zeller, I'd be at this very moment sighing in some janky junior college meeting room.

Reshawn found a seat while the last of the assistant coaches filed in. The door closed and Coach Zeller clapped his hands—a single hard clap that immediately silenced the room.

—Welcome back, men! And welcome especially to our freshmen. First day always feels like a family reunion, don't it?

—Yes sir!

—It does, it does. So before we do brass tacks, I got a question for y'all: What makes an army? I want some guesses. Yeah—Devonté.

—Guns, Coach.

—Uh huh. Cornelius?

—Technology.

—Technology. Right. Anybody else?

—The number of soldiers.

Zeller nodded.

—All of that matters. But that's what an army is *made of*, not what *makes* an army. You see? What makes an army, what binds all that together, is somethin' more—somethin' *spiritual*, you might say. You can look at some of the most important wars ever

48

fought and you'll see the victors weren't the biggest armies with the best guns. They were armies nobody bet on, scrappy little things. Revolutionary War's a great example. And why you think the Americans won?

My heart raced as I raised my hand. Coach Zeller's eyes brightened.

—Hey there, Miles.

—Hi, Coach.

—Good flight?

—I drove, sir. One day.

—*One day?* he said. Now *there's* a man ready to contribute!

Everyone seemed to be watching me. Do not smile.

—So what you think, Miles? Zeller continued. Why'd the Americans win the war?

—They won because they wanted it more, Coach.

Zeller snapped his fingers.

—Good, son. *Good.* That's exactly right. These little armies, they had somethin' to fight for—homelands to protect, causes to believe in. The big armies were fightin' just because they were told to, because they had the money. Y'all see what I'm gettin' at? We had a rough season last year—god*damn* do I know it. And I ain't saying it's gonna be peaches and cream this fall. But if we *believe* more than our opponents do, we're gonna shock folks. And that's what we're gettin' started on today—formin' those beliefs, *believin'* those beliefs.

He stuck his hands deep into the pockets of his khaki shorts.

—So what do y'all say? Y'all with me?

—YES SIR!

Players who brought cars to campus acted as shuttle drivers for the players who hadn't, and before I knew it six teammates were piling into my Saturn, a car decidedly not designed to accommodate some 1,300 pounds of sweating, bouncing, shouting humanity. Like a lifeboat captain trying not to capsize, I had to fend off another three players who somehow thought there was still room to squeeze in. Once they gave up, we were on our way to Training Table.

Training Table was the facility on Central Campus where we ate team meals. A drab hexagon that bore a suspicious resemblance to the maintenance sheds down the road, its roof was made of corrugated steel, its sides painted in sun-faded browns and tans, and its windows flecked with shredded grass that had been spewed out by a ride-on mower. The interior was no more impressive: faux-wood wall panels, a linoleum floor scored by generations of chair legs, and two dozen folding tables that were identical to the ones my family ate doughnuts on in our church's basement. At the far end of the room was a glass-roofed buffet, which for lunch today was offering iceberg salad you could slather with ranch dressing sweet as cake icing; a pile of overcooked spaghetti accompanied by a vat of red sauce burbling like lava; breaded chicken bricks stuffed with nondenominational cheese; and sweet potato pie topped by a molten wreath of marshmallows. The food here was always wretched, but that was compensated for by its utter freeness.

I sat at a table with three other freshmen, each of whom had already been renamed by the veterans. Jamal Winston and Jamal Reese were a black wide receiver and defensive back, respectively, best friends who'd attended the same high school in Alabama and had over the years developed uncannily similar ways of looking and talking, from their matching cornrows to their speedy southern mumbles. The vets had nicknamed them J1 and J2, less to help tell them apart than to surrender to their basic indistinguishability. The other freshman, Clarence Turrell, was also black, a pug-nosed, owl-eyed defensive end from Irvine whose name had been reduced to C.T. in the Team Room this morning and then immediately revised by a premed vet to Scan, as in the computerized tomography procedure the vet was planning on studying in medical school.

Scan dominated the conversation with a litany I was to learn was common among King players: he listed all the other, better D1 programs that had recruited him and then provided too-convenient explanations for why he'd chosen King.

—UCLA wanted me, *bad*, but I needed to get the hell out of California. Florida State was on my *nuts*, but Florida's just too damn hot. And Ohio State? They acted like my—

A great din rose up in the hall, vets striking silverware against their plates.

—SCAN! SCAN! SCAN!

We looked around, clueless. Devonté, the starting tailback and Reshawn's host from the official weekend, leaned over from the next table.

—Time to sing the fight song!

—SCAN!

Scan looked around, grinning, nervous.

—Stand on your chair, nigga!

A giddy jolt ran through me at hearing the first "nigga" that wasn't in a rap song. Scan was less excited. He climbed onto his chair, so nervous he didn't realize he was still holding his fork.

—Introduce yourself!

— I, uh, I'm Clarence Turrell.

—Don't you lie 'bout your motherfuckin' name!

—People are calling me—

—SCAN! SCAN! SCAN!

—Scan.

—So how 'bout a song, Scan?!

—Y'all just gave us that shit two hours ago.

—Goddamn right!

—I—

—Get to singin'!

Scan blew out a defeated breath. He squinted at the buffet, as if the lyrics might start inscribing themselves on the steam-smogged glass. Finally he began reciting in a flat, tuneless voice.

—Reign, reign Monarchs.

—Oh no. You *sing* that shit!

Bullets of sweat pushed out of Scan's forehead. He started again, now in a creaky, map-less falsetto.

—Reign, reign, Monarchs, give me your . . . iron fist?

Vets howled, slapping tables.

—I hope he buys you dinner first!

Scan belatedly realized what he'd said. He blushed, but had no choice but to continue.

—Score, score, Monarchs . . . All you see and all you—

—BOOOOOOOOOOOOOOOOOOOOOOOO!

Players jumped out of their seats, clapping and laughing. Our starting punter threw a dinner roll at Scan's head, leaving a faint floury imprint on his right temple. Scan stepped down from his chair, looking like he was considering committing hara-kiri with the fork he was still clutching.

The room calmed, conversations resumed, and now it was J1 and J2's turn to explain why they'd come to King. I was only half listening, having taken out the laminated card and begun furiously trying to commit the song to memory. I had a feeling I was next, and indeed not five minutes passed before silverware pounded plates.

—MILES! MILES! MILES!

Chase led the chant, his face glowing red as a hot coal. I set down my card and mounted my chair.

—Introduce yourself!

—I'm Miles.

—Giles?!

—*Miles.*

—Got a last name?!

—Furling.

—Hurling?!

This was all Chase.

—So what the fuck you waiting for?!

Over a childhood of churchgoing I had developed something close to a beautiful singing voice, to the point where our priest insisted I sing solos during Lent. But there had been a serious hitch—while my speaking voice lowered over the years, my natural singing voice had remained a clean, clear alto, which had been red meat to classmates who attended our church and who, come Monday in the lunchroom, would tell everyone else I sang like a girl. Over time, I had learned to force myself down to a baritone, which was still good but nowhere near my alto.

I would sing baritone now, no question, and after one last trembling breath I let the meter of the song guide my singing.

*Reign, reign, Monarchs,*
*Rule your realm with an iron fist.*
*Claim, claim, Monarchs,*
*All you see and all you wish.*

I could see the remainder of the song. But I could also see that not a single veteran was smiling—not at my agile voice, not at my memorization.

*Score, score, Monarchs,*
*Touchdown, field goal, try, and safety.*

—The fuck?! Fade yelled in disgust.

Not even Devonté, kind Devonté, was happy with how well I was doing. I realized I had already given Coach Zeller the correct answer in our meeting, and if I were to get through the song now without a mistake, I risked earning a reputation as a coach's pet—a reputation that would be hard to shake.

I looked up at the ceiling, as if suddenly stymied.

*King . . . sing? For . . .*

—BOOOOOOOOOOOOOOOOOOOOOOOO!

I stepped down from my chair. I never thought I'd be so grateful to be heckled.

The afternoon break lasted seventy-five minutes and was the longest stretch of free time we had all day. It wasn't quite long enough to, say, catch a movie, and most players just returned to the Hay to nap on the locker room's soft purple carpet until it was time for afternoon meetings. This made it so that every day, from 12:30 to 1:30, the locker room looked like a day care center for Brobding-nagian toddlers.

Exhausted though I was from the long drive, I lasted maybe twenty seconds lying in front of my locker. I was too agitated by Chase's antagonism, too nervous about our first practice this after-noon, too I-don't-know-what by the proximity of all these big bodies slumbering next to me. I stood and tiptoed between dozing cubemates, looking for something to do, and saw Reshawn was awake the next cube over. He was sitting on the floor, leaning his back against his locker seat and reading a book so thick I initially thought it was the Bible, a not uncommon object in a locker room. But on second glance I saw it was poetry, *The Complete Poems of Emily Dickinson*. I'd read Dickinson too, but that didn't mean I needed to announce it ostentatiously.

A group of vets were sprawled out on the floor in a corner. They waved me over and invited me to sit.

—Chase is *on* you, boy. That's good—means he's scared you're gonna take his spot.

This was said by a defensive back named Jimbo Jaredson, a tall, wiry veteran who wore a cumulus-shaped Afro. I was struck by how hairy Jimbo's body was: His forearms and shins were thickly scrawled with curls, and he had chest hair so extravagant it reached out of the top of his T-shirt collar like an invasive spe-cies. I hadn't known black men could have heavy body hair like white men did.

—You think? I asked.

—Fuck, yes. Coach Hightower doesn't want anything to do with his ass. Not after the spring game.

The other vets nodded sadly.

—Dude had a great winter, Jimbo continued. Workouts. Conditioning. Everything. You'd see Coach Bruz's eyes tear up whenever he watched Chase hang clean. Then spring practices start and he's playing better than ever. Everyone was convinced he was gonna take the starting spot from Fade. He was *on*, you could see that, that . . . I don't know, beatific—

—Be a what? another vet asked.

—Saintly, Jimbo said. That saintly shine on his face.

—Furling, you know Jimbo's got two majors? Philosophy and, um—

—Philology, Jimbo said. Anyway. So we get deeper into spring ball, and by now Chase knows he's riding something special. He starts the little routines you do when you don't want the universe fucking with your momentum. Starts coming into the locker room the same time every afternoon—and I mean the same *minute*, 1:54. If he got to the Hay early, you'd see him wait out in the hallway until the clock turned over. He gets dressed in the same order—strips ass naked, slides his pads into his girdle, slides his girdle on, right leg, left leg, pulls on his football pants. We'd go to meetings, and when we got back down to the locker room to finish dressing, he would slide on his shoulder pads and call his girl, Sadie. Sadie lived down the hall from us freshman year but then transferred to Georgetown. They did the long-distance thing. So like I said, Chase calls Sadie, Hi honey, love you honey, can't wait to see you sweetie, smooch. Sounded like he was chanting when they talked.

Jimbo paused, clamping his lips shut and pushing air out of his nose.

—We get to the week of the spring game. Chase keeps up the routine, but now when he calls Sadie, you can hear this tension in his voice. She doesn't answer sometimes. Or she will, and they bicker and she hangs up. You could see Chase trying not to let that shit disrupt his routine, and he keeps playing like a maniac. But I knew he was going to break.

—The hell you did. That's—what's the word? *Revisionism.* Revisionist history.

—I told y'all he seemed off! Jimbo exclaimed. But y'all didn't want to believe me. Talk to me about revisionism, *you* had observer bias.

I was lost. Jimbo saw it.

—Look, what I thought isn't the point. Point is, he'd been planning on marrying that girl. She wears this silver ring Chase bought her, pre-engagement shit. But their calls *stay* getting worse, until the day before the spring game I come into the locker room and see Chase on the phone, face stained from crying. He leaves this *looong*-ass voicemail, saying some of the saddest shit I ever heard. Next day's the spring game. Chase gets on the field with the two defense and lines up for his first play, and you could see it in how he was standing—guy had left his heart sitting in his damn locker. He blows his first assignment, lets Devonté run for a touchdown. Shit happens, right? Maybe he'll snap out of it. But then the next play, O'Connor pancakes him to the ground. It was fucking catastrophe. Chase has somebody wrapped up for a tackle? They shed him and leave him facedown on the grass. Chase supposed to cover that tight end? Dude covers the *tailback* and gives up another touchdown. And Hightower is *screaming* the whole time. Screaming shit I hadn't heard before. I didn't know what an anal bead was before I heard him call Chase one.

—Yo, Chase's parents were in the stands. Mom's face went like—

—After the game ended, Jimbo continued, Hightower marched Chase to the practice fields and made him run sprints until he collapsed. And here's what gets me—to this day, Chase *stays* trying to win Sadie back. My girl fucks me over before the biggest scrimmage of my life? I'll boot her ass to the curb, let the garbage truck take her away. But I bet you twenty you'll hear him on the phone with her at the hotel, begging her to return his goddamn manhood.

The break ended, and I followed Jimbo and the others to numbered cubbies built into the hallway wall next to the equipment room entrance. Jimbo explained that, after finishing a practice or a workout, you stuffed your dirty clothes into a purple laundry net and slid the net into your cubby, which communicated with the other side of the wall. By the time of the next activity, a warm purple net would be waiting in your cubby, your clothes having been washed and dried during the break.

Along with my clean clothes, I found a white practice jersey waiting for me, number 42. Jimbo lifted his chin at the jersey.

—Coaches use your cubby like a mailbox, he said. You make it onto first- or second-team defense, you'll keep getting a white jersey. But if you're kicked down to the threes, it'll be red. That's how you know you're redshirted.

—When do they start handing out red jerseys? I asked.

Jimbo shook his head.

—Don't worry about that yet, rook. One practice at a time.

After meetings I fetched my helmet and cleats from my locker and walked to a tall Gothic arch embedded into the wall of the first-floor hallway. I sat on a metal bench just inside the arch to tie on my cleats and then walked down a dark, cool, gently declined tunnel. The tunnel emptied into an open-air stadium that was built in the mid-1920s, with whitewashed concrete benches instead of modern metal bleachers. The game field's grass was roped off for preseason pampering, and we had to walk on the straightaway of the running track that ringed the field. Past the Jumbotron scoreboard at the far end zone lay three full-sized practice fields bordered by forest. Groups of vets stood scattered on the fields, gossiping, idly stretching, but I wasn't brave enough to join one uninvited. So I stood alone near the punters and watched them warm up their legs—thud, a football sailing into the blue, nicking the brutal sun, descending into the arms of a kick returner who ran for a five-yard burst.

Following team stretch was Individual period, in which each position group and its coach ran drills to hone technique. The linebackers started a drill in which a linebacker would crouch in his stance across from another linebacker, who pretended to be an offensive lineman, while Coach Hightower, standing behind the lineman, pretended to be the quarterback. At each Hightower "Hit!" the lineman would simulate either a running block, upon which the linebacker should step up to meet him, or a pass block, upon which the linebacker was to drop back into coverage and catch a ball Hightower threw his way. This was to practice the "read step," the first, most crucial step a linebacker takes.

Each time it was my turn, I read the lineman correctly. Whenever Coach Hightower threw me the ball, I caught it and returned it at a sprint.

—Good shit, Furling!

Chase, on the other hand, could do nothing right in Hightower's eyes. He got no word of encouragement when he made a correct read, and if he did anything that had even a whiff of a mistake about it, Hightower pelted him with vitriol.

Chase's turn again. I acted as the lineman, with Hightower standing behind me. Hightower barked:

—Hit!

I stood for a pass block. Chase correctly dropped back. But when Hightower threw to him, the ball was much too high. Chase had no chance of catching it.

—Get your fucking head on straight! Hightower yelled. Do it over!

We all reset.

—Hit!

I stood once more, Hightower threw the ball, but this time the pass was much too low, forcing Chase to dive to the ground.

—Same cunty shit I saw during spring ball! *Again, McGerrin!*

I could have watched this all practice.

Chase continued bullying me the rest of the day, right up to when we entered our Marriott room a little after nine-thirty. He acted like he had the place to himself, taking his sweet, smelly time in the bathroom, leaving his shoes and clothes strewn on the carpet. I knew he was trying to get a rise out of me, but I was too exhausted to take the bait. After brushing my teeth I slid between the soft, almost erotically cool bedsheets and fell asleep.

I was out only forty minutes before the sound of a closing door woke me. The room was black, and stars burned steadily in the window to my right. I looked left and saw light seeping from the space beneath our bathroom door—Chase had locked himself in there. He must have been talking to Sadie, and as I lay listening to him murmur, I wondered what kind of girl would want to be with Chase. I conjured a petite, peroxided blonde, dumb and kind, the type who doesn't like contradicting her boyfriend in front of others. Did Jimbo say they lived in neighboring houses growing up, or was I just sleepily imagining that? I buried my head beneath my pillow and passed out again.

It seemed like I had just fallen asleep when I was startled awake, this time by the sound of the room's phone ringing. Now the air was a watery blue and the moon was in the window, fading in the dawn sky. Not twenty seconds after the wake-up call, there were loud knocks on our door—graduate assistants trawling the hallways, making sure we didn't fall back asleep. Chase and I got up. He was wearing only maroon mesh shorts with a faded high school mascot on the right leg. I found something tender about the thick clusters of freckles on his chest and shoulders.

—The fuck you looking at? he said.

—Were you on the phone last night?

—No.

We didn't talk again as we took the elevator downstairs and walked to our respective cars, teammates who needed rides trailing each of us like zombies. Once my car was full I pulled out of the parking lot and joined a two-lane road that was slowly coming to life: day laborers gathering in strip mall parking lots, greengrocer deliverymen unloading wooden crates of vegetables from the backs of their trucks. At a stoplight, a father and his daughter passed in front of me at the crosswalk. The father was a morbidly obese man in a sagging tank top and baggy swim trunks, and the daughter was about ten years old, wearing a polka-dotted bikini and matching flip-flops. They were holding hands, and the girl had to skip-walk to keep pace with her big dad.

At breakfast I sat with Jimbo and some of the other vets I'd met during the afternoon break, the only players who'd been willing to talk to me without mocking me thus far. Training Table had been a zoo during yesterday's lunch and dinner, but it was quiet now, the spirits of the players still snuggled comfily in their Marriott beds while their bodies grudgingly scarfed down rubbery eggs and gooey cheese grits.

—Least we got one day down, said a wide receiver named Pedro.

Jimbo shook his head.

—You have played here too damn long to be saying stupid shit like that. You know you can't just multiply yesterday by twenty and be done with it. You gotta *weight* that shit. Gotta account for how sorer you're gonna be every morning. The sleep you'll lose every night. The names the coaches are gonna call you. Today's gonna feel twice as long as yesterday. *Tomorrow*'ll feel three times as long as today. Extrapolate, motherfucker.

Everyone fell silent as they crunched the numbers. Devonté walked into Training Table, wearing a sunken expression that was different from the tired faces of the rest of the team.

—McCoy is *looming* over D's ass, Jimbo whispered.

—He ran with the ones yesterday, I said.

Jimbo shrugged.

—That was a courtesy, coaches thanking him for his service. Dead man walking right there.

He was right. At practice that morning, Reshawn did continue running with the second-string offense while Devonté ran with the ones, but there was no mistaking that everything was being catered to Reshawn's edification. If Devonté carried out an assignment correctly, Reshawn would be asked by several different coaches whether he understood what had been done right; when Devonté made a mistake, Reshawn was always told why. Devonté was clearly devastated by his impending demotion, and yet he didn't slack off during his reps, didn't mouth off to coaches, didn't refuse to give Reshawn advice that guaranteed his own redundancy. Instead he helped Reshawn every chance he got, talking him through assignments during water breaks and helping him with his alignments after practice. I already liked Devonté for how kindly he'd treated me during my official visit, and now I admired him for his selfless desire to help our team.

But Devonté also couldn't have failed to see just how continental the differences were between his talents and Reshawn's. Devonté was a small, wily tailback, excellent speed, good instincts, decent strength, the kind of player whose greatest asset is understanding his shortcomings better than his opponents and finding a workaround to those flaws. But Reshawn had no need for back doors—he came dominating through the front one positively spoiled with options: he could use his size or his speed, strength or quickness; he could use the intelligence that was allowing him to pick up the offense at an alarming pace or rely on his preternatural instincts.

When Reshawn ran, his feet barely skirted the grass. When he spun, his planter foot didn't plant so much as tap the ground; and yet that tap was decisive, perfectly timed and calibrated to redirect a body that, notwithstanding its 224 pounds, moved as lithely as a bantamweight's. His mistakes could be miraculous. In one play during Team period he took a handoff for a dive and tripped over a defensive tackle's foot at the line of scrimmage, sending him tumbling to the ground. For even an elite athlete like me that tumble would have been it, the whistle blowing and me looking up at the morning sky. But Reshawn somehow transformed his trip into a somersault in the midst of twenty-one hustling bodies, and half a moment later he was back on his feet and sprinting to the end zone, barely having lost a step.

Reshawn's talent had an affirming, energizing quality. It inspired our teammates to elevate their own level of play, and after only a few practices I noticed how much harder everyone was working. And yet the rest of Reshawn had the opposite effect, to the point where the goodwill he generated during a rep could be undone totally by how he acted after that rep was over. Take the trip-and-sprint I just described. As he jogged back to the offensive huddle, he ignored the praise everyone shouted his way and then shrugged off the arm of Kendrick, the starting fullback, who tried hugging him.

His unpleasantness extended far past the practice fields. The few grudging words he'd given Coach Zeller in the first meeting were virtually the only ones I'd heard him speak so far in camp. He was a mute in the locker room; at meals he kept his head down and shoveled food into his mouth so he could get out of there quickly; and during the afternoon break he read his fat book of Dickinson, sighing if people in his cube dared disrupt his concentration by horsing around. Bighearted players like Devonté excused Reshawn's prickliness by saying it was the inevitable result of being burdened with the fame this kid had already lived with for four straight years. Reshawn was painfully shy, they claimed, and was so modest he hated praise. But most people just thought he was an asshole. White players called him a prima donna, while black players mocked his voice—an Oregonian non-accent. Jealous rumors began to proliferate. He used steroids, was why he was so big; he was actually twenty-five and was lying about his age. But just as had happened with the commentators who tried guessing why he'd committed to King, I didn't hear anyone here suggest corruption had played a part in why he'd come. Even at King, the players took great pride in their team, and nobody wanted to entertain the possibility that the only way someone like Reshawn would have joined our program was by receiving tens of thou-

sands of illicit dollars. If anything, players made the opposite inter-
pretation and took Reshawn's presence as a sign that our program
was more attractive than people thought, that it had a secret value
detectable by the most discerning sensibilities.

There were also more quotidian reasons why people didn't
suspect Reshawn. A player receiving under-the-table money was
expected to show that off in some flashy way, but Reshawn was
ascetic, wearing faded T-shirts, walking-around shoes with soles
worn down to the soft sub-rubber, no necklaces or rings or ear-
rings that I ever saw. And wouldn't a player who received bribes
own a car? Reshawn decidedly did not, and it was his constant
need for a ride that led to our first conversation during camp.

It was the third day, Wednesday, and I was walking to my
Saturn to drive to lunch when I found Reshawn standing next to
my passenger side door. For all the superiority I felt toward him,
for how morally bankrupt I thought he was, he was still the best
football player I'd ever been around, and it was exciting to see him
silently ask to sit in my passenger seat.

We got in, along with four more players who piled into the
back. Reshawn looked out the window at the forest that separated
West Campus from Central as we started for Training Table.

—My parents brought us a mini fridge for the dorm, I told
him. Pyle's letting me stash it in the equipment room.

He nodded, still looking out the window.

—Are you in all English classes this semester? I tried again.

—And Math 103.

That was the highest math level a freshman could take.

—I'm in Computer Science, I said.

—Bet you are.

—What?

He didn't respond, but I wouldn't let him off so easily.

—What's that supposed to mean?

—It means it's a jock class, he said. It means you're taking the
same shit everyone else is.

Fuck him. I could have said I was sixteen because I'd skipped a grade. Fuck him. I could have said I'd been in the gifted and talented track since I was in elementary school. *Fuck him.* I could have taken Math 103, if I'd wanted to.

I parked in the Training Table lot, and before I'd undone my seatbelt Reshawn slammed out of the car—no "thanks for the ride," nothing. I trailed him across the parking lot and marveled at how much extra effort it must take to be a prick every waking moment.

When I entered Training Table, the veterans were chanting. Reshawn sullenly climbed onto a chair.

—Say your name!

—Reshawn McCoy.

—Speak UP!

—Reshawn McCoy, he repeated, not raising his voice one bit.

—You got a song for us, McCoy?!

Reshawn looked down at his shoes.

—What you lookin' there for?!

—Thought you was supposed to be a genius! Can't memorize ten damn words?!

Reshawn sighed and raised his eyes to the ceiling.

*The Brain—is wider than the Sky—*

Players squinted and tilted their heads, looking at one another to make sure their ears hadn't malfunctioned. The room was so silent you could hear the cicadas outside.

—This motherfucker memorized the wrong thing!

—The *fight song*, McCoy. Not some fucking poem!

Reshawn had stopped. Maybe he'd gotten it out of his system, maybe now he would do what he was supposed to, what every veteran in that room had himself done freshman year. When he launched into the second line, there was an exasperated groan.

*For—put them side by side—*

As if the words weren't odd enough, Reshawn was pausing at

64

odd moments, sometimes at the end of a line, other times right in the middle. At first I thought he was struggling to remember the poem, but his voice was unhurried, his face still. Other players were sunk in their own puzzlement, and to look around the room was to see the collective momentarily reduced to its parts, each player trying to figure out by himself what Reshawn could mean by doing this, not to mention what the words themselves actually meant.

*The one the other will contain.*

It was enough. The parts cohered once again into sum, and before Reshawn could continue there rose up a

—BOOOOOOOOOOOOOOOOOOOO.

This was nowhere near the satisfied booing Scan and I had received. This booing had an irritated edge to it, and as soon as Reshawn climbed down from his chair the boos ended with a grumpy peremptoriness, as if the vets were eager to begin forgetting the whole unpleasant episode.

Reshawn and I got in line for the buffet behind J1 and J2, who'd ridden with us in my Saturn.

—McCoy, J1 turned to say. That was a poem?

—Yeah.

—You write it?

—It's by Dickinson.

—Man, I *thought* that shit sounded familiar, J2 said. We read *Tale of Two Cities*.

—Not Dickens, Reshawn said. *Dickinson.*

We returned to the Hay for the afternoon break. I decided to look up the rest of the poem, see whether the remaining stanzas clarified what he'd been trying to say. I went to the training room and used one of the desktop computers to search online using "brain" and "sky" and "Dickinson" as search terms. What I found was shorter than I'd expected, only three stanzas, but I still could not for the life of me understand why he'd chosen this particular poem. Or was I overthinking things and he had just randomly chosen it, knowing one Dickinson poem would be as jarring and strange as another? That was probably the answer. Probably the poem's content wasn't the point, probably the point was him showing us he was perfectly capable of memorizing the fight song and chose not to—the point was to remove himself another degree from the team, to keep extending the distance between us and him.

What made this so galling was that, while he was trying to get as far from us as possible off the field, he was becoming more integral to our offense with every practice. He continued to play superlatively, and by the next morning he was promoted to starting tailback.

We gradually wore more pads to practice as we acclimated to playing in the punishing heat, which meant we were edging toward tackling and the advantage was tipping toward Chase. He was a nasty, physical player and took every chance to face me in drills so he could use his extra twenty pounds to crack, slap, yank, jerk, and generally manhandle me. Also, the defensive packages we were installing were growing more sophisticated than anything I'd ever seen. Chase already had everything memorized and moved through his assignments confidently, but I was carrying my playbook everywhere to try and learn its hundred-plus pages, and whenever I got onto the field for reps during Team period, there was a crucial delay between thought and action.

Yet there was one way in which I maintained an undeniable edge—Coach Hightower. On Thursday morning, we practiced our fits during Individual period. The "fit" is when you punch your hands into the breastplate of your blocker's shoulder pads and grab his jersey, the move necessary to gain control of that blocker and move him wherever you need. To practice it, the linebackers paired up, with partners kneeling across from one another on the grass. The hitter then lowered himself into a four-point stance (hands also on the ground) and on the whistle cocked his arms and shot them upward, exploding his hands into the breastplate of the hittee, grabbing his jersey and jerking him backward. The hittee, meanwhile, stayed on two knees and was totally pliant, absorbing the shock and falling back onto his haunches.

To get a good fit you had to thrust your hips in a single fluid motion, and to help us visualize how we should be doing this, Coach Hightower said we should move our hips like we were fucking a girl from behind. For a couple of reasons this particular pedagogical tool fell flat for me, and when Coach Hightower saw me struggling to get it right, he took a fatherly knee to the side of me while I was on all fours. Without warning he grabbed the back of my running shorts with his left hand, grabbed the jersey cloth covering my breastplate with his right, and proceeded to guide my body upward in the quarter-circle motion he was looking for. The knuckles on his left hand pressed into the small sweaty patch of hair just above my tailbone, which made me so tense that I went even more awkwardly rigid.

—Relaaaaaax, he whispered into my helmet's earhole. Just keep thinking about that sweet thing you took to homecoming.

—Yes sir.

—All right. Go again.

Thrust, thrust, thrust—Hightower lifting me, guiding me, making it feel like I was being helped to practice flying as much as fucking. Eventually I relaxed in his hands and started to get the motion down.

—That's what I'm talking about! he said, patting me on the helmet and rising to his feet.

He moved down the line of players and stopped at Chase.

—McGerrin, stop moving like some dude's fucking *you* in the ass. Go again!

Chase did, and though I couldn't find any fault with his form, Hightower grew exasperated. He butted Chase's partner out of the way, positioned himself on all fours across from Chase, and proceeded to use his old linebacking skills to show Chase his errors, striking Chase's breastplate full force, jamming him hard over and over again.

—Like *this*!
—Like *this*!
—*LIKE THIS!*

When it came time for the afternoon break, I took the elevator up to the fifth floor, thinking I would visit Coach Hightower and keep pressing my advantage. Though I wouldn't have admitted it back then, I was also hungry to establish Hightower as the mentor who'd fill the hole Coach Johannsen had left.

He was in the middle of typing an email when I knocked on his open door. He left his hands resting on his computer's keyboard as he turned to me.

—Furling! Take a seat.

I sat in the chair across from him while he finished the email. Hand-annotated scouting reports were scattered across his desk, many of them patterned with brown coffee mug rings or yellow grease stains. On a bookshelf to my left, videotapes of last season's games stood in unflush stacks, while more tapes stood on the floor, highlight films of high school hopefuls like the one I'd sent to King. On the windowsill behind him were two framed photographs. The first was a studio shot of his toddler daughter, a cherub crawling on a faux-sheepskin rug who was naked save for her diaper and a white bow in her hair. The professionalism and gloss of that photo accentuated the amateur roughness of the other, a fading Polaroid of a Sunday-best bunch assembled in front of a rickety wooden house somewhere in the woods. Hightower was young in the picture, maybe seventeen, tall and gangly in the back row. A scowling matriarch sat in a wheelchair in the center of the large group. She wore a cornflower-patterned cotton dress and a ziggurat-shaped church hat, clutching her purse to her lap in a way that suggested the relatives standing around her weren't to be trusted.

Hightower swiveled toward me.

—So, how you settling in?

—Good, Coach.

—When I was a freshman, a vet put it perfectly to me: you

show up to camp and it's like someone hands you three balls and says, "Juggle, asshole," and you never juggled in your life, but you gotta do it anyway. Getting homesick?

—Not really, sir.

He turned to that Polaroid.

—I grew up three hours away from here and still got so lonely I'd call my grandma every night. That's her. Raised me after she already brought up nine kids.

I was learning smiles were rare with Coach Hightower. If he was pleased by something, he'd do a little shoulder shake, as if the laughter had snagged on something inside him.

—So, what? he said, turning back to me. You just come up to shoot the shit?

—No, sir. I wanted to see what else I needed to do to make the twos.

He nodded.

—You're gonna find I ain't sentimental—I don't put someone on the field because I've known them all these years. Fade's got the best physicality and the best grasp of the defense, so he's one. Chase has the physicality, but he's shaky as shit on execution. Two. I know you're a smart player, Miles, that's why we brought you here. So now I need to see how physical you are. Especially since you're a little lighter than we'd like.

He stopped to think.

—Oklahoma is Saturday morning. You show me you can hold your own with the big boys, I'll start getting you some reps with the twos.

"Oklahoma" was the first full-contact drill of the season. It would be the first time I tackled as a college player, and on Saturday morning the tunnel that led to the practice fields was nothing less than a birth canal, with me inching through the dark of preexistence toward a blinding light.

—Meat!

Fade and Chase were a few steps behind me in the tunnel. I didn't turn around.

—Meat! Chase repeated. You getting nervous?!

—Yo, Fade added. I heard every freshman goes against seniors today. Scary shit right there.

Oklahoma was a high holiday for King Football. Down at the fields, waiting for the stretch whistle, players talked over one another about cataclysmic tackles from Oklahomas past, speculating on who would go against whom today. The whistle blew, and players hooted and hollered as they found their partners and formed stretching rows. I fell onto my back and raised my right leg for my partner to stretch, the seat of my football pants soaking up the cool dew. I draped my forearm across my brow to block the sun.

—Your balls dropped, Furling?

I slid my forearm away and squinted up at Coach Hightower.

—Sir?

—Well, don't worry if they haven't. One hit today and you'll feel them plunk right on down!

I tried to laugh. Hightower's voice turned serious.

—I'm expecting you to impress me today, son.

After stretch, we sprinted over to Coach Zeller and three sets of cones that had been set up behind him. Linebackers and running backs formed two lines facing one another; same for the defensive linemen and offensive linemen; same for defensive backs and wide receivers. The first linebacker and running back would step up from their respective lines, crouch into stances three yards apart, and on the whistle sprint at an angle toward a cone placed to one side. The running back, ball in hand, had the goal of passing that cone, while the linebacker's goal was to bring him to the ground before he did so. Following the linebacker–running back collision, the linemen would face off, then the defensive backs and wide receivers. Whistle, CRACK, on to the next group—whistle, CRACK, on to the next. Many drills in football are nuanced, some even delicate, but not this one. In Oklahoma, the one and only goal is contact. Running-start, bone-jostling violence.

You counted your place in line and then counted the players in the opposite line to see who you were going to face. I was toward the back of the linebackers' line and saw I was set to go against Kwame, a walk-on tailback. It was a fantastic draw: I was bigger and faster than Kwame. I was on scholarship and he was not. I would definitely overmatch him. Better still, Chase was second in line and would face Reshawn—would get obliterated by Reshawn, humiliated by a freshman who'd never taken a college snap.

First up were Fade and Devonté, two captains. Whistle, sprint, CRACK—Fade wrapped up Devonté, chopping his feet in the grass, lifting and upending Devonté well short of the cone. The team sprang into the air at the sound of the collision, screaming and shoving each other, and when Fade pushed off Devonté and stood, he was mobbed by the team—helmet slapped, shoulder pads shaken, heavy body lifted into the air while players drummed his elevated ass. Hightower stood to the side and snarled approvingly, making excited jabs in the turf with the toe of his right cleat.

Linemen were up, and we all watched big Tapps, a one defensive end, face off against big O'Connor, a starting offensive tackle, both well north of six foot six and 300 pounds. The whistle was blown, and their collision put me in mind of two grizzlies grappling over a mate.

Defensive backs and wide receivers were next. This was usually the least impressive group—not only the smallest but also the most contact-averse in the game. But when the whistle was blown our starting Y receiver, carrying the ball in his right hand, took only a single step forward before he caught a cramp in his left hamstring. The drill seemed to go into slow motion: the wide receiver's body sinking, on its way to collapsing on the ground in pain, his helmet lowering, allowing the charging defensive back to strike him with his own helmet, face mask to face mask, CRACK, a brutal hit that sent both the ball and the receiver's helmet flying.

The team erupted. Players sprinted over to slap the defensive back's ass or stand over the wide receiver and whinny into his naked, woozy face. I was part of the pandemonium, jumping, laughing, my blood fizzing furiously through my veins, and when I felt a hand grab the back of my jersey, I thought it was just one of my ecstatic teammates seeking something to hold on to. But then a second hand grabbed me, and now I was being shoved forward against my will, toward the cones, and as the team settled down I found myself standing face-to-face with Reshawn. Chase had taken advantage of the frenzy to swap our places in line.

—Fuck yeah, Furling! Coach Hightower yelled, thinking I'd voluntarily stepped up to slay our star freshman.

My heart slammed in my chest, like the fist of a karate novice trying to clumsily break through a sheet of particleboard. I had no choice but to crouch into my stance. You should want this, Miles. If you're going to play D1, if you're going to achieve the greatness Coach Johannsen saw in you, you're going to have to take down backs like him.

Reshawn stared back at me. His eyes were cold, indifferent.

The whistle shrilled. One moment I was lowering my shoulder, and the next I was being sucked backward, breath fleeing my body.

Overall, I did quite well in my first collegiate Oklahoma. I got to go two more rounds, and in them I managed to bring Devonté to the ground before the cone, then gave Kwame a concussion that forced him to sit out the rest of practice. But nobody cared about those. All people talked about at lunch and in the break was what they referred to simply as "the hit," and when the linebackers gathered for afternoon meetings, everyone was eager to watch my unmanning on film. Coach Hightower arrived through the door in the back of the linebackers room. He was silent, and pointedly didn't return my desperate stare. He turned the lights off, lowered the projector screen, and cued up the film.

When the team had exploded at Reshawn's hit in real time, it had been with a happy, chaotic clamor, but the film we watched was silent, making it look like the players who were slapping and pushing each other were rioting. Reshawn was indifferent to what he'd just instigated and calmly walked to the end of the running backs line. All the while Miles lay sprawled on the grass, and I didn't realize until now that Coach Hightower had been standing less than a foot behind me. He looked down at me with his arms crossed, like someone who'd been wandering through the forest when he happened on a badly wounded doe.

—You surprised, Furling? he asked me now. You come at someone like that and a retarded girl's going to truck you.

—Yes sir.

He rewound the film and sent me and Reshawn into slow motion.

—You're crossing your feet . . . your hips are high . . . your fucking head is tilted *backward*. Did you pay attention at *all* during fit drills?

—Yes sir, I said, voice shaking.

—Sure as *fuck* don't look like it!

My body was meeting Reshawn's again on screen, rippling upward, tilting inexorably from vertical to horizontal.

—That is a goddamn disgrace.

I dragged myself downstairs to dress for the afternoon practice. Did I know there would be a red jersey waiting in my cubby? Yes, I did, but that made me no less disappointed to find it, and no less embarrassed to walk into the locker room holding it.

Fade and Chase were dressing. Chase smiled, knowing full well that if I blamed him for swapping places I would just come off as trying to make excuses for what Reshawn had done. Fade saw the red jersey in my hand.

—Chin up, young'un, he said. I got redshirted. Chase did, too.

I sucked my teeth like I'd seen the black players do.

—Coach Hightower was on my nuts until Oklahoma, I said.

Fade smiled—not cruelly.

—You gotta understand, he said. Hightower wasn't really talking to you. He was talking to Chase.

—What's that mean?

Fade slid on his shoulder pads, fastening the elastic straps around his armpits.

—Look. Chase had a bad spring game, but he had a great *spring*. Everyone knew that. Hightower knew that. So . . . it's like you and your girl are in love, right? Everything's great, birds singing. Then y'all have a fight. Big fight. You say things you don't mean. You break up. You still got feelings for your girl, but you just don't know whether y'all can get back together again. Then one night you find out your ex is heading to a party. You decide to go too and bring *another* girl with you. You make it so the three of you are in the same room at the party, and you kiss on the new girl, tell her she's the prettiest thing in sight. It's win-win—either you make your old girl crazy with jealousy and she realizes she wants you back, *or* you leave the party with your new girl and fuck her like the world's fit to end.

I was now firmly third string for this season, or, in team parlance, was now a bottom feeder. My campaign to grow close with Hightower stalled. He'd warned me he wasn't sentimental, but I hadn't realized that that meant he would essentially forget I *existed*. His in-practice encouragements ceased, as did the happy joshing in film rooms, as did the gossiping during pre-practice stretch. The two of us would go on to have exactly one substantive conversation for the rest of camp, and it revolved around the fact that I needed to gain, at minimum, ten pounds of muscle before next season.

I was a tackling dummy for the first- and second-string linebackers during Individual period, after which I was banished with the other red jerseys to serve as a blocking dummy for the offense. The latter drudgery meant I was lining up across from Reshawn on snap after snap, and whereas in that film session with Hightower I had been torn at least two new assholes for not hitting Reshawn hard enough, if I collided with him at full speed now, the offensive starters would shove me and the offensive coaches would shout:

—Don't be a fucking hero!

I could not escape Chase. He was in my cube, in my meetings, in my practice drills, at my meals, and in the hotel room every single morning and every single night. He was as cocky as you'd expect, and often when the linebackers met for film, he would have gotten to the room early so he could cue up Reshawn's hit. He would pause the film the moment after the collision, so that when I walked in I would find myself on the screen, suspended in midflight.

This all would have been torturous enough, but as we started the second week of camp I developed a deep, confounding obsession with looking at Chase's body.

It had taken me the length of my high school career to grow comfortable in locker rooms, to use a surface sangfroid to chill the innermost heat and confusion, and by the time I came to King I was so at ease that the only reason my eyes rested overlong on a teammate's naked self was out of aspiration—I wanted this one's pecs, I wanted that one's thighs, I'd always wished my calves had the heart shape his did.

But during camp's second week my eyes started straying toward Chase every time he was dressing or undressing in the cube. I had the urge to look not just at his cock but at the pale buttocks speckled with red welts, at the thighs streaked with blue bruises and raspberry turf burns, even at the forehead rubbed raw by the strip of rubber at the front of his helmet. My compulsion was horribly circular. I would tell myself not to look at his body, which would increase my need to see, which need would only make it that much more important not to look at him for even one moment.

Was this sexual in nature? I couldn't tell. It's not like I worried about getting an erection whenever I struggled not to look at Chase, and yet there was something about his relentless, gleeful urge to dominate that found in me an answering submissiveness, a desire to *give in* to the bullying, and so maybe why I kept looking at his body was to puzzle over why exactly he was bringing this out in me, what it was about him that affected me the way it did.

My obsession spread to the point where Chase didn't even have to be undressed for me to need to look at him. If he was sitting in front of me in film, I had to stop myself from staring at his nape or the crinkled dry skin on his elbows. If he was snoring in the hotel room, the only way I could not watch his lips softly putt-putter was by keeping a pillow clamped over my face. Even his voice stirred me, and whenever he hid in the bathroom to talk with Sadie, I would have to turn on the television and crank the volume in order to drown him out.

The volume got higher and higher over the course of the second week as Chase and Sadie's fights grew worse. He would yell and plead, banging his fist against the bathroom's countertop to punctuate whatever words he was angrily saying. By Saturday night his voice was so loud and our television so blaring that Fade, staying in the next room over, knocked on the wall our rooms shared to quiet us down. Chase ripped open the bathroom door and stuck his head out to glare at me, thinking I was the one who'd knocked; but when he saw the sounds were coming from the wall, he realized how loud he was being. He closed the door, said a few final words to Sadie, and hung up and came to bed.

I turned onto my stomach and laid my pillow over my head. A few seconds later I heard a weird whine, as if a mosquito had somehow gotten trapped in the goose down, and when the whining turned into a keening I realized what was going on. I uncovered my head and looked over to see Chase leaning his back against his bed's headrest, clutching his cell phone with both hands while snot streamed from his nose. My first feeling was joy, and I considered just sitting there and watching him weep. But his sobbing was getting wild and starting to make me uncomfortable. Purely out of the urge to stop my own discomfort, I testily asked:

—You okay?

He slapped himself across the face—a hard, vicious slap. There was a pause, red creeping into his cheek, and just when I thought that would be it, he hit himself again, then again, the strikes harder each time. I thought he was doing this to stop himself from crying, but even as his sobs subsided and a taut silence took over the room, he continued to slap himself. Then he made a fist.

I leapt out of bed and grabbed his wrist before he could punch himself, holding his hand down at his side. He struggled, trying to push me away with his free hand, but I kept holding on until he gave up. He broke out in sobs again. I sat next to him, leaning my back against the headboard, still holding his wrist, and we stayed that way for what must have been ten minutes. Slowly his breathing began to even. He cleared his throat and nodded to me, signaling I could let go of his hand and he wouldn't hit himself again. I released him and crawled into bed. I was exhausted, but forced myself to stay awake until I heard his breathing downgrade into snores.

At the sound of the next day's wake-up call Chase was out of bed like a shot, not bothering to brush his teeth before hurrying to the elevator. He didn't say anything to me at breakfast or in any of our day's first meetings, but I would catch him watching me and would see him become as flustered by being caught staring as I had been when I'd been caught watching *him* over the past week. At morning practice he was manic, sometimes changing places in drill lines so he wouldn't have to face me, other times striking me viciously. Once, he tackled me so hard he broke off one of the plastic clasps that held my face mask, so I had to get a loaner helmet from Cyrus Pyle while mine was fixed.

Chase couldn't come down on whether the carrot or the stick was the best way to prevent me from telling the team what I had witnessed, but he needn't have worried: I had no appetite for embarrassing him in front of the others. If anything, I was grateful for what had happened. It had been thrilling to hold his wrist, to feel his strength surge beneath his skin, to feel his adrenaline make mad fast laps around his thick, warm body.

# THREE

Camp ended and the team's freshmen were given Sunday afternoon to move into Stager Hall, a red brick and white marble dormitory perched at the top edge of East Campus's main quad. The room Reshawn and I were to share was small, irregularly shaped, and old, outfitted with cast iron doorknobs, painted-over water pipes that ran along the ceiling, and a pair of creaky wood-framed windows we had to shove open because this building in the heart of North Carolina didn't have central air. I found the place unimpressive—if our school was so rich, why couldn't it afford to put freshmen in a new building?—but Reshawn seemed energized by the genteel dilapidation, and he set about nesting so thoroughly you would have thought he planned on living here for the next ten years: carefully arranging photographs of his parents and two little brothers on the windowsill next to his bed, alphabetizing on our built-in bookshelf the hundred-odd volumes he'd packed into a large wheeled suitcase, and showing an indecisiveness I'd never seen from him before as he vacillated over where to hang a collage print—the name in the corner said Bearden—depicting three sad-eyed, snub-footed musicians jamming on a country shack's porch.

He finally settled on placing the print above his bed, and he was standing on his mattress and tacking it up there when an Asian girl knocked on our open door. She was tall and bob-haired and wore a lemon-colored sundress.

—Football players? she asked, seeing the logos on my T-shirt and shorts.

—Yeah, I drawled proudly.

I noticed the armpits of her dress were dark. With a wilting smile, she asked:

—Would you do me the biggest favor?

Her name was Michelle. We followed her to the parking lot behind the dorm, where an elderly man was laboring to haul a heavy wooden futon frame from the trunk of his minivan. Michelle took him by the elbow and said something not-English, pointing at us.

—My grandpa really shouldn't be lifting this stuff.

We carried the frame up for her, as well as the unwieldy futon mattress, and in thanks for our help she insisted we stay in her room while she ran downstairs to buy us water from the vending machine. Her grandfather remained stoically upright while she was in the room, but the moment she left he plopped down onto a bare striped mattress, pulling a crinkled handkerchief from his pocket to dab his forehead. He offered me the rag, and though I tried to wave him off he impatiently shook the thing at me until I gave in and dabbed some of his sweat onto my own.

Reshawn, meanwhile, was looking over a stack of books on Michelle's desk, bending nearly perpendicular as he read the spines. Michelle returned with an armful of frosty Dasani bottles and handed them out. Her grandfather started rising, but she laid a hand on his shoulder to keep him resting.

Reshawn gestured at the AP Biology textbook in her stack.

—Premed? he asked.

—Yeah maybe, she said in an excited rush. Or PhD. Or maybe MD/PhD? I don't know—I just want to study neurology.

—Do you like Oliver Sacks?

She didn't know who he was, and with that Reshawn set

down his water bottle and jogged to our room, returning with his copy of *Awakenings*.

—I also have some of his essays, he said.

She read the back cover.

—Are you premed, too?

—Nah. I just like stuff about the brain.

She looked up from the book, and her expression suggested she wouldn't have minded a back cover for Reshawn, *something* to summarize why this bruiser owned a personal copy of a 1970s medical memoir.

Michelle invited us to meet her at the freshman carnival being held tonight on the quad. Reshawn practically shouted yes and then rushed back to our room to get ready. He took a long shower and returned brushing his hair in short, vigorous swipes, which confused me: his hair was maybe an inch high, and I didn't understand what good all the brushing did. He proceeded to try on half a dozen different outfits in front of the mirror that hung from the back of our door, even more indecisive now than he'd been with the Bearden poster as he paired this polo with those shorts, these khakis with that T-shirt, at last settling on cargo shorts and a white oxford he buttoned down to the wrists. It was much too warm for long sleeves.

The sun was sinking behind the library's white marble dome by the time we arrived at the quad that ran between the Georgian buildings. I was unimpressed by the carnival. A student rock band fumbled its way through a cover song on a makeshift stage; two perky upperclassmen stood in a tent handing out free T-shirts commemorating move-in day; a cafeteria employee in a chef's uniform tried not to get too much of his sweat on the appetizers he was reheating on a propane grill. The one genuinely carnivalesque touch was a row of glittering rent-a-fun structures, but few people were playing the games of skill—we were too close to being children to want to be seen doing childish things like shooting water into a clown's mouth.

Michelle stood with a motley group, girls and boys, white and Asian, some in stylish outfits and others in mishmashes that made it clear they were at sea without their mothers here to dress them. The girls were instantly taken with Reshawn, this statuesque boy asking them informed questions about AP credits, majors, and double majors who barely gave them time to respond before asking the next question. Yet there was none of his usual abrupt haughtiness, only ingenuous, slightly gawky enthusiasm.

I had no opinion on double majors myself, and stood off to the side with a shy boy who wore an Afro to rival Jimbo's and a gold necklace with Hebrew characters. A girl named Josephine belatedly noticed the King Football insignia on my clothing.

—I *knew* I knew you from somewhere! she said, playfully pushing Reshawn. My dad is the *biggest* Michigan fan.

—That right? he asked, trying to pretend like this was a happy turn in the conversation.

—*Oh* yeah. When you visited Ann Arbor, he acted like the pope had come to town.

—We have a football team? another girl asked.

—I think they're intermural.

—We're on full scholarships, I broke in, too annoyed to remain quiet.

The girls paused to look at me, but no one thought my comment worth responding to. Josephine continued to Reshawn:

—You'd have thought the pope *died* when my dad found out you were coming here. I said, "Dad, you remember that's the school *I'm* going to, right?" He said I didn't get it—you coming to King was like me going to community college.

Reshawn smirked.

—Tell him I wanted to use my brain cells before I killed them all off.

The girls looked at each other to confirm this kid had mocked himself in a way they'd have only done behind our backs. Reshawn was emboldened to shock them again.

—Don't get me wrong, he continued. I love wearing spandex. Almost as much as I love watching linemen piss their pants because they're too afraid to ask coaches for a bathroom break.

—They *do not*.

—Sure do. And I don't blame them. The coaches command absolute respect. Brilliant men. *Geniuses*. You know why coaches use Xs and Os to draw plays? 'Cause those are the only two letters they know.

It was repellent, our best player abasing his team for the sake of amusing some girls. Yet Reshawn wasn't only mocking our team, was he? He was mocking the entire enterprise of football, and it was now I realized I'd been wrong about something. His aloofness didn't stem from the disdain he had for playing for a losing team. He hated the game itself. But was that really possible? Could you be the football miracle he was and despise the game?

The girls wanted their free T-shirts at the tent, but Reshawn begged off. He was riding high from his first conversation with regular King students and wanted to find another group to charm. I stayed with him, and once we were alone I mustered the courage to say:

—My parents went to community college.

He pretended not to hear me. This made me even angrier.

—Why would you say that shit about the team?

He sighed, turning to me.

—What shit?

—Oh, I forgot. I'm a football player. I must be a moron, too.

He was angry now.

—Anyone forcing you to be out here, Miles?

—I—

—And if you're going to keep walking with me, go change out of those fucking clothes. I don't need these people knowing I'm a football player.

—You think my *clothes* are the only way people are gonna know you play?

Before he could respond, I added:
—Fuck you.
I headed back to the dorm.

I was asleep by the time Reshawn returned to our room, and when I woke the next morning he was already gone, off to a seminar on African American folktales—which, like all the classes he'd be taking this semester, was so abstruse none of the veteran players had even heard of it, let alone enrolled in it. My classes, on the other hand, were golden King Football oldies chock-full of teammates: a biology course about dinosaurs with one graded assignment the whole semester; the aforementioned computer science survey, which satisfied the undergrad math requirement without requiring me to do any actual math; a sports marketing course taught by an athletic department official who had allegedly never given out anything below an A+; and an intro-level public policy seminar taught by a Methuselah known to doze off in the middle of his lectures.

Easy as my classes were, they still took up half of my day, while football consumed the other half, and before I knew it Friday afternoon had arrived and I was standing on our game field's freshly painted sideline, watching the starters walk through their assignments one last time before tomorrow's game against Virginia Military Institute.

Everybody traveled for home games, and following the walk-through we returned to the locker room to change into purple windbreakers and matching pants. Players called this the "silence suit"—for as long as you wore it, there was to be no grab-assing or gossiping, only focus for tomorrow's game. We boarded the charter buses that idled next to the stadium's wrought iron gates and drove down the same roads we'd taken during camp, pulling into a Marriott parking lot that by now felt as familiar as my parents' driveway back in Sillitoe. But this wasn't a disappointment, not at all: off-loading the buses in our identical gear, encased in our monkish silence, the hotel lobby transformed into a hallowed staging ground, the drunks at the bar and the bored front-desk folk morphing into solemn witnesses to our heroes' procession.

The food at dinner was the same boiled/broiled fare we ate at Training Table, except now it was being scarfed under the high coffered ceilings of the Marriott's grand ballroom, lending the activity a new gravity, making the food inexplicably taste better. Following dinner we had one last round of film in a conference room, and now the coaches transformed into different men. Sunday to Thursday they used film to name and shame players who didn't know their assignments, but tonight they were engaged in a conspiracy of optimism, and as we watched film of VMI, they only asked easy questions, directed to players who they knew knew the answers. The meeting felt less like a tutorial than a catechism.

We were in the locker room by ten the next morning. Players stood before body-length mirrors and meticulously drew eye black beneath each eye, or tied on durags so their helmets didn't muss the cornrows they'd gotten special for today. Fade wore sound-canceling headphones and paced around the carpet as he rapped along to a 50 Cent song, while Cornelius used a permanent marker to draw names, numbers, and symbols on the white athletic tape on his wrists. I had the option of wearing pads, too, but I decided to save that for when I'd actually put the pads to use. I slid my purple home jersey over a plain white T-shirt and tucked the jersey's long tails into my best pair of jeans.

We formed a half circle in the middle of the locker room, which was beginning to resemble church in the moments before mass. You had your notable parishioners, the ones and the captains, who enjoyed the best places at the front. Twos and vets—your dutiful, every-Sunday churchgoers—knelt behind the ones. Bottom feeders stood at the back of the group like the family that doesn't arrive in time to get seats, while bustling around the room's edges were mass's supporting cast, the scripture readers and altar boys and deacons (trainers, student trainers, assistant coaches) who made their final, hushed preparations.

Here came the celebrant. Coach Zeller's vestments were a

purple polo shirt, pressed white khakis, and unscuffed tennis shoes he reserved for games. He took his place at the head of the half circle, and once the last people squeezed inside and the doors closed he began his first pregame speech as King's head coach.

—You don't stay the same in this game, fellas. Every down— every play—you got two directions. Either you rise, or you slide. You get better, or you get worse. You gotta *choose* which direction, every single time.

Devonté was kneeling in front of Zeller. Zeller paused and fondly rested his hands atop Devonté's shoulder pads.

—And those choices build, men. They accumulate. You elevate one play, it's just the littlest bit easier to improve the next. You get a first down, you're that much closer to a score. Each one of you starters is gonna play dozens of reps today. And on every goddamn one, I want you to *choose* to get better. Want you to play a little harder'n you did the play before. Run a little faster. Tackle a little cleaner. We do that, I guaran*tee* VMI won't have a fuckin' prayer.

He popped his palms against Devonté's shoulder pads and stepped aside, creating a hole into which players rushed like whitewater, leaping to feet, raising arms, overlaying hands. Devonté stood in the center and screamed the team's twist on the King College fight song:

> *One one two three*
> *Who the fuck you came to see?!*

and the rest of us responded:

> *King King motherfucker!*

We paired up and held hands, forming a long line that lockstepped down into the dark tunnel. The frontmost players, Fade and Devonté, stopped at the tunnel's bottom, fidgeting as they waited for the announcer's call, while the rest of us bunched up behind them, rocking in place, waiting (unbearably), needing (excruciatingly) to be released, to be shot out into . . .

A void of poured concrete, smattered by a crowd of maybe 2,000 people in a 35,000-capacity arena. What fans were here weren't exactly rabid: somnolent good ol' boys who dribbled tobacco slime into empty beer cups; King students who'd used the game as an excuse to flirt with alcohol poisoning before 1 p.m.; cheery VMI family and friends and live-in-the-area fans who sat behind the visitor's bench; and the pleasantly bustling parents, siblings, and girlfriends behind ours.

But I was still overjoyed to be running onto my first game-time D1 field, and as the starters readied themselves to play, I paced up and down the sideline carrying out the two jobs I had today—staying out of the way and cheering my lungs bloody:

—Let's go!

—Atta boy!

—WoooooOOOOooo!

My palms stung as I slapped helmets and shoulder pads, my voice rang with the name of every starter I passed. We won the coin toss and elected to receive, and I hurried over to where the kickoff return team huddled so I could lean in to listen to the call.

Clap, break, our kickoff return jogged to their positions on the field while VMI's kickoff squad fanned into formation. There wasn't enough of a crowd to create that otherworldly buzz of anticipation you hear in elite stadiums, and to try and compensate for that our PA system blared a Guns N' Roses guitar solo while the teams settled into position. The music was mercifully cut off when VMI's kicker placed the ball on the tee. He backed up three careful steps, raising his hand. The whistle shrilled and he strode forward, the rest of the kickoff team stalking a step behind, slowly, slowly, until the ball was lifted high and long, the VMI players accelerating, lowering their shoulders on our blockers, angling toward Devonté, our returner, who caught the kick on the 5-yard line, sliced through the first wave of attacking players, and was brought down at the 37.

VMI was a D1AA program, and if we were generally imposing compared to them, Reshawn in the backfield showed you what it must have looked like when Apollo descended into human battle. The ball went to him on the first snap, a dive, and one moment he was on my right-hand side, behind the line of scrimmage, and the next he was on my left, having passed through the roil of bodies without losing a step. He spun away from a lunging linebacker, and now it was just him and a VMI safety. Reshawn lowered on the defender, ran *through* him.

—WOOOOOOOOOOOOOOOOOOOO!

Our sideline shifted leftward to track him, leaping onto one another and screaming as my roommate scored a 63-yard touchdown on the very first touch of the first game of his college career.

You wouldn't have known that by looking at him. Reshawn carelessly dropped the ball in the end zone and turned immediately for the sideline, once again avoiding the linemen and wide receivers sprinting over to hug him. He took a seat on the bench, snapping off his helmet and obliviously accepting a water bottle from a moony student trainer. I knew he wasn't going to be one for celebrating after scores; yet that still hadn't prepared me for how, like, *misanthropic* he acted.

Judging from the irritated looks on our teammates' faces, nobody else knew what to do with him, either. So instead we sought inspiration from Coach Zeller—the energized, enlivening, exhilarating man pacing the sideline as he chattered into the headset clamped over his ears. When someone made a great play, Zeller would slide the headset down his neck to call out that player's first name—which, in a game where family names are the rule, was a sign of great intimacy. If a player made a big mistake, Zeller made sure to catch him as he returned to the sideline—not to browbeat, but to reassure him he knew the player had gotten that error out of his system and would henceforth be on the straight and narrow. In the rare times he stopped moving, Zeller's hand sought the back collar of the nearest player's shoulder pads and hung from there, as if this was the best way to keep himself anchored.

Had I ever seen a more natural leader?

· · ·

88

We beat VMI by twenty, Reshawn rushing for 226 yards, receiving for another 55, and scoring all four of our touchdowns. But the most important number by far was one—it was King's first win in almost two years.

The locker room was all sweaty effervescence. Coach Zeller's big face beamed as he wandered from cube to cube to relive his first victory, recounting his favorite plays so vividly I would remember his recountings much longer than the plays themselves. Veteran players who'd trudged through a desert of losses looked like they'd just bathed in a cool, clear oasis pool, the color restored to their faces, the worry lines erased from their foreheads. No one was eager to break the spell, and long after the players had showered and dressed, they were still sitting on their locker seats happily arguing over the best bits of the game.

Fade and Chase toweled themselves off in the cube and talked logistics for the party being thrown tonight at the Football House.

—Got plenty of cups, Fade said. Eli's getting the Natty Light.

—Do we have balls?

Fade stopped to think and shook his head. He turned to me.

—Buy some Ping-Pong balls on your way over.

I wanted badly to go to that party, but I knew Coach Johannsen would have told me to keep myself at home, stay clear of the risks.

—I've got a lot of homework, I said.

—Homework?!

—Bull*shit*, Chase said. I saw that hundred you got on the PubPol quiz. You don't need to fucking *study*. And we need at least three packs of balls. I swear to God these motherfuckers eat them when they get shit-faced.

My odd crush on Chase had lingered since the end of camp, and I thrilled to be ordered around by him. Coach Johannsen hadn't specifically told me to avoid parties, had he? And wouldn't I become a better player if I got to know my teammates, if they got to know me? I just wouldn't get too drunk.

—Okay, I said. Three packs.

I returned to the dorm room, finishing what scant homework I had as a way to kill the rest of the afternoon. At sunset I dressed, bought the balls at the East Campus Union, and started across the lawns that gently undulated off the main quad, passing baroquely branched magnolia trees and an ancient gazebo rumored to be the spot where Jedediah King renounced God. I walked through a gap in the low stone wall that bordered East and entered a neighborhood of rundown bungalows with children's toys scattered on lawns, a few rusty cars up on cinder blocks, more than a few windows covered by Confederate flags. The faded green bungalow Chase had described was at the end of a cul-de-sac, and when I mounted the porch and tried the front door, the handle turned but the door itself didn't budge. Someone inside shouted, "Lower your shoulder!" and that's when I noticed a concave, discolored patch in the door's wood about two feet above the handle. The door swelled in the warm months, and the patch was from a decade's worth of players butting the thing open.

Two violent rams and I stumbled into a front room that could most generously be described as spartan: unpainted walls speckled with off-white spackle that covered holes made by fists and elbows; window blinds hanging askew, if they hung at all; and a few pioneering ants busying along the baseboards. The only thing that amounted to a furnishing was the beer pong table, which had been fashioned from two overturned plastic garbage cans and a slice of particleboard that bridged them.

I'd arrived early, and only Fade, Jimbo, and Chase were here, busy arranging red Solo cups into triangles on the table and filling each cup a quarter full with foamy Natty Light. Chase waved me over to his side of the table. I admitted I had never played.

—Pong virgin! Chase said, cracking open a can of Natty Light and handing it to me. Pong virgins have to chug a can before every game.

—Since when? Fade said.

—Since today. Drink up!

This wasn't in line with my plans to stay sober, but I didn't want to resist Chase. I closed my eyes and glugged down the warmish, bitter beer. The Solo cups were ready, and we started playing the first game.

—Where's McCoy? Jimbo asked me. Wait wait, let me guess. All-night poetry reading. Or, no, particle collider.

—He's with regular students.

Jimbo landed his shot in the cup at the top of our triangle. I plucked the ball out and downed the beer. Devonté also made his shot, and Chase simultaneously downed the beer and rolled the ball back to Devonté, leaving a foamy trail along the length of the table.

—He'll learn, Jimbo continued. I was the same way freshman year—thought coming to King meant I was coming to *King*. Then I found out regular students think we're all losers and they're all winners.

He adopted a snooty white voice.

—"*I graduated the top of my high school class.*" "*I boarded Phillips Choate Andover Exeter.*" Yeah? Well I got a 3.9 *and* can run a 4.3.

—So why can't you fuckin' talk and shoot? Chase said.

Jimbo took his shot, missing. He resumed his lecture.

—I mean, there *are* differences. King's the only place I've ever been where you get snow blindness in the summertime. I was moving into my dorm sophomore year? Neighbors came by and said they needed a lightbulb replaced—thought I was the fuckin' janitor. *And* they're all rich as fuck. Most of the cars parked on West are worth more than your daddy's salary.

—Reshawn was making fun of us at the carnival, I said.

I'd been waiting all week for the right moment to tell people. The game was paused.

—Us who? Chase asked.

—Players, I said. Reshawn told them we piss our pants and only know the letters X and O.

It was Jimbo's turn to shoot, but he just contemplatively bounced the ball against the table.

—Is there a name for a football Uncle Tom? he asked.

—How about Cousin Shawn, Fade said.

—There you go, Jimbo said, raising his ball to shoot. Cousin fuckin' Shawn.

I missed nearly all my shots, and my percentage only worsened in the second game. Chase groaned every time I missed, and groused the few times I did make it ("About fuckin' time"). Yet despite the heckling he remained my partner. After I cost us our second game in a row and some newly arrived players tried to claim our spot, Chase put his arm around me and announced Will linebackers would stay here as long as they fuckin' liked.

Midway through the third game, Chase's cell phone rang. Sadie was calling, and without further ado he dropped his ball into the cup of water to the side of our triangle and walked outside. I was left to finish the game alone, and lost. Without Chase by my side, I didn't dare to stop J1 and J2 from claiming next.

By now the front room had filled with players and the women they'd invited—perfume, beery burps, the shush and rattle of another abused window blind. People were moving in and out of the house so often that the front door was left open, which is how I saw Chase sitting on the front porch stairs, holding his phone between his legs. I stepped outside and took a seat next to him. He seemed sobered by his conversation.

—Stubborn, is all he said.

Mosquitoes bit at our ankles. Chase dug his wallet from his pocket, removing a photograph and handing it to me. The porch stairs were too dark to make it out, and I had to lean back and rest on my elbows on the porch floor to catch the light coming from inside.

—She's pretty.

Sadie wasn't the thin blonde I'd conjured during camp. She seemed to be Mexican or something, short and curvy with dark brown eyes and a loosely tied ponytail that rested on her right shoulder. She stood on a riverbank next to a weeping willow. I guessed it was her portrait from senior year of high school.

—Sadie's a nickname, Chase said, reclaiming the photo and returning it to his wallet. Her parents gave it to her when they moved from Guatemala. Her real name's Soledad.

He talked about her at length for the first time. She'd been a walk-on field hockey player at King, and they met at a Sunday night Fellowship of Christian Athletes meeting freshman year in the basement of the chapel. At the end of the meeting the FCA group formed a circle around a men's lacrosse player whose father was dying of cancer, and Sadie and Chase held hands while the prayer was said. She squeezed Chase's hand before letting go— then found him after the meeting and asked him out—then kissed him at the end of their first date—then told him she didn't believe in waiting until marriage to have sex. She loved Chase but hadn't liked King, and transferred to Georgetown. They tried long-distance, but by last spring she had tired of the arrangement and called to say she thought they should break up—a decision Chase had been trying to reverse for five months now.

—You a virgin, Furling?

I laughed.

—Only in beer pong.

—Uh huh. When you *do* start fucking, get a girl like Sadie. She looks all holy in that picture, but she used to beg for me to come on her tits. She wouldn't move after I did it, either, she'd stay right there with her eyes closed, letting the come roll down. You don't let someone like that just . . . leave. I told her we could meet at the hotel when we travel to Maryland next week. She said it's not a good idea.

Chase sighed and returned inside. I waited a moment before joining him, which allowed me to stealthily tuck my erection beneath my boxers' waistband.

Not only was Maryland away, but so were the Clemson and Georgia Tech games that followed, leaving bottom feeders in Blenheim three straight Saturdays. I found this humiliating, like I was the little brother too short to ride the roller coaster, and I hated, *hated*, the period that stretched between when the team left for the airport and when we convened at the Hay to watch game film on Sunday. Hated walking around campus and knowing people mistook me for some regular student. Hated sitting in my dorm room and doing homework I had all these spare hours to concentrate on. Hated antsy unnecessary jogs around East Campus in which I obsessed about how far my life was from the bulb-blinded, crowd-roared fantasies I'd had of Division One.

During game time on Saturdays it was tradition for bottom feeders to meet at Stefan Knows, a bar within walking distance of East Campus. The place had been founded in the 1950s, and who Stefan was or what he'd known was lost to history. At night the bar was a shitshow of late adolescence, wall-to-wall with King undergrads drinking cheap liquor from plastic cups and fondling each other in barf-scented bathrooms. But during the day the place was peaceful and drowsy, mellow afternoon light slanting in through the small old windows, solitary alcoholics playing Keno at high-topped tables—the perfect setting in which to belly up to the bar, watch better D1 programs face off on the TV that hung above the well drinks, and keep an eye on the news ticker at the bottom of the screen, where the score for our own game periodically scrolled.

My first two outings to Stefan Knows were disheartening—we lost to both Maryland and Clemson—but we were cautiously optimistic the third weekend, since Georgia Tech was down that year. We filed in at one o'clock and were greeted by the bartender, a young guy named Enrique who claimed to have been a star tight end in high school. In exchange for us listening to his inconsistent explanations for why he'd missed a D1 scholarship, Enrique didn't ask baby-faced types like me for ID.

As a graybeard biker down the bar got increasingly restless

about his Keno results, we watched the Iowa-Nebraska game and called out whenever we spotted the King score scrolling.

| King College | 3 | Georgia Tech | 0 |
|---|---|---|---|
| King College | 10 | Georgia Tech | 7 |
| King College | 10 | Georgia Tech | 13 |

Scores could tell us only so much about how the game was actually proceeding, and I noticed that how your imagination filled the gaps depended on how long you'd been on the team. Veteran bottom feeders were saddled with deep pessimism after years of losses; if the score appeared and we'd fallen behind, they shook their heads and said nothing had changed, while if we tied or pulled ahead, they'd say don't get your hopes up, we still have plenty of time to blow it. Rookies like me were eternal optimists, convinced King Football's darkest days were over.

| King College | 13 | Georgia Tech | 13 |
|---|---|---|---|
| King College | 19 | Georgia Tech | 13 |

But no matter how old you were, you sooner or later came to feel a dark antagonism for that goddamn news ticker. We'd watch the thing ten straight minutes, waiting to see our score, and just when the numbers seemed on the verge of appearing, the programming would cut to commercial. By the time the game returned, our score would have been skipped, leaving us to wait *again* with no guarantee our score would appear before the next commercial break. There seemed to be some invisible force deciding which scores appeared, and it was difficult not to believe this force was spiting us, mocking us, toying with us.

| King College | 19 | Georgia Tech | 20 |
|---|---|---|---|

Only a minute remained in the game. We stopped watching Iowa-Nebraska altogether, ignored the biker screaming gibberish at his Keno screen.

—An exciting finish in Atlanta, Steve, the announcer said.

Suddenly our team appeared. Our offense was on the field, the ball was snapped, and Reshawn caught a screen pass at the line of scrimmage. A defensive tackle dove at his knees, but Reshawn hurdled him with an elegant lift of the legs, regained his feet, and lowered his shoulder on a linebacker, trucking him as he'd trucked me during Oklahoma. He was deep in the secondary now, facing a final defender, a strong safety Reshawn froze in place with a stutter step. He was off—43 yards, untouched, touchdown. We toppled our mugs of beer as we jumped off our stools, gripping each other's biceps and hands, and when the final score appeared we high-fived Enrique and happily accepted smelly bear hugs from the biker who'd gotten caught up in our exultation.

After making plans to meet back at the Football House, we went our separate ways for the rest of the afternoon. Tired from the beer, I intended to take a long, sweet nap; but when I got to Stager Hall and was approaching my room, I spotted a boy at our door. He was reading the whiteboard with the names Miles and Reshawn written across the top.

—That's Reshawn McCoy? he said.

—He isn't here, I said. Just to warn you, he doesn't like giving autographs.

The boy laughed.

—Jesus. Autographs. Would you mind if I left a note?

He walked in with me. I tore a sheet of paper from my Public Policy notebook and loaned him a pen, sitting on my bed while he bent over Reshawn's desk and scribbled. The boy was white and on the smaller side, with a tie-dyed T-shirt, a thin brown starter beard, and a ponytail that showed off a dagger-shaped widow's peak that could only plausibly be called not-balding for another couple years. His note took up both sides of the sheet, and when he was done he folded it in half and left it propped on Reshawn's desk, like a table tent. He returned my pen.

—So he's where, at a game? he asked.

—Are you in one of his classes?

—No no, we met at Brown.

—In Cleveland?

He laughed.

—Not the Browns. *Brown.* University? We were on the same campus tour. He was obsessed with how you didn't have to declare a major. We learned we were staying at the same hotel in Providence and spent the weekend hanging out.

The more he talked, the less I understood. Ivy League schools like Brown were not just D1AA and consistently boasted the division's worst teams, but they gave you no money, none, for athletic scholarships. Whenever one of the programs had contacted me, I felt offended they would dare to even *think* I would consider playing for them. So it would have been confusing enough to learn Reshawn had let it cross his mind to humor one of these schools, and I don't quite know how to convey the disorientation of hearing this kid say he thought Reshawn was planning on *attending* one.

—We lost touch last year, the kid continued. I assumed he'd gone to Brown, but a girl at lunch today was talking about this football player named Reshawn who lives in her dorm. I'd thought it was a different kid, but then she says this guy brought like five hundred books for his dorm room, so I knew it was him.

—You didn't know Reshawn was a football player?

—I saw he was muscular, but this was a guy who kept talking about the history of Anne Hutchinson he was reading. You really lucked out—my roommate's an asshole. I'd give anything to have someone nice like Reshawn.

—You sure you've got the right person?

He paused, miffed by the suggestion that Reshawn was himself an asshole.

—One hundred percent.

I read the note as soon as he left. The kid's name was Jesse, and the note referred to people, places, and events I had no context for. But that didn't matter. What did was the warmth in Jesse's writing, the exclamation points, the insistence they catch up.

I lay down for my nap, but I couldn't manage to fall asleep, restless with all the paradoxes. Reshawn was taking bribes on top of his full scholarship, but had considered attending a school where they didn't even pay for your textbooks. He despised football, and had just played yet another dazzling game. But I think what unsettled me most was the idea that the Reshawn Jesse had met and the one I'd known at school could be so antipodal, that Jesse had grown fond of an eager kid, an excitable literature nerd, while I was living with someone who smiled so seldom I couldn't have said with certainty that he possessed all his teeth.

You had to go back six seasons to find the last time we started with a record as good as 2–2, and more than a decade for our last victory over Georgia Tech. But for all that, the Hay was sedate during Sunday film and grew even glummer as we entered the next week. Short-tempered players were liable to snap at the slightest provocation, while whole cubes that were usually riots of pranks and howling laughter went silent. I was at a loss until I overheard Devonté and Fade talking during afternoon lift: midterm grades were out on Wednesday.

King's system was in the process of transitioning from paper to digital, and this was the last semester in school history when you first learned what your grades were when you held a piece of watermarked paper. After breakfast on Wednesday I walked with Scan, J1, and J2 to the mail room in the basement of the East Student Union, a low-ceilinged, windowless space whose walls were honeycombed with metal post-office boxes.

—Fuck, J2 muttered as we squared up.

On the count of three we inserted our keys and removed our envelopes. Scan let out happy little noises at the sight of his grades. J1 and J2 both squinted at their sheets, as if to blur the Ds into Cs and the Fs into Bs. I winced at my own report.

| Intro CompSci | A |
| Sports Market. in Mod. Age | A |
| Whose Public Policy? | A |
| Dinosaurs | A |

I took no pleasure in the grades, and not only because I'd gotten them in the easiest classes I had ever taken. They signified how much spare time I had, no new defensive packages for me to memorize, no punishing games to recover from.

—Furling, what'd you get?

—Doesn't matter, I said, tossing my report in the trash.

The coaches also received copies, and before afternoon film we convened in the Team Room to hear Coach Zeller's impression of the team's academic status. He ambled in just after two-thirty, wearing an inscrutable smile.

—How're y'all's asses? he asked. Sore?

—Yes sir.

—I bet they are. One of my TCU coaches use to have this sayin'. He told us academics come first.

Zeller held up two fingers.

—And football comes second.

Now he held up one finger.

A few players chuckled, but most people, including Zeller himself, weren't amused.

—That was funny at TCU, he continued. But we can't fuck around at a school like this. I need y'all *eligible*, or else this whole thing goes to shit. So listen up: anybody below a 2.5 has study hall the rest of the semester. Get your hand down, O'Connor, I already know what you're gonna say. I don't give a good goddamn if you're fifth year or freshman. You're below 2.5, your ass is in study hall till December. And do not test me. You miss a session and you'll be running a stadium at six a.m. Reshawn, Miles.

—Yes sir, we both said, sitting up in our chairs, exchanging confused looks.

—Y'all got some osmosis shit goin' on in your dorm room?

—Sir?

—Darren says y'all are the only roommates we ever had who both got a 4.0.

The whole room turned to glare. Reshawn kept watching me, not bothering to hide his surprise. I wanted to disintegrate.

—This is a team, Zeller said. I expect people like y'all to take the lead in makin' sure the rest of your teammates stay in school. So get with folks and get to tutorin'.

—Yes sir, we both said again.

Nobody was going to ask Reshawn for help—the guy gave you a murderous look if you so much as asked to borrow his pencil—which left me all the more mobbed. In class teammates bickered over the desks near mine that gave unobstructed views of my quizzes, and after team dinners I attended study hall so as to float from table to table seeing what help I could provide. The desperate paid me some of their stipend or Pell Grant money in exchange for writing response papers, added income I gladly accepted. The death-by-a-thousand-cuts repairs I already had to make to my Saturn took a huge bite out of my own Pell funds, while the negligible walking-around cash I received as part of my scholarship barely covered the after-hours calories I devoured to try and gain Coach Hightower's extra ten pounds.

A few evenings after Coach Zeller's come-to-Jesus, Chase found me in study hall and asked if I'd come to his apartment for one-on-one tutoring. He'd received an especially bad midterm report, which didn't surprise me. He was in three of my four classes, and for over a month I'd watched him snore through whatever lectures he hadn't skipped.

I followed his truck to Central Campus, and when I entered his apartment I recalled how uncomfortable he'd grown during Jimbo's rant about the wealth of King students. At the time I'd thought maybe that was because Sadie was rich and Chase was offended on her behalf; but now I understood Chase was the rich one, the rare player who could have afforded to attend King without a full scholarship. He lived alone, which you could only do if you paid an extra housing premium the team wouldn't cover. There was a leather couch with cushions as soft as pork belly, a new flat-screen television, and a mighty sound system with cabinet-sized speakers that had been professionally mounted. Other details I'd observed about Chase clicked into place: that he wore a different Abercrombie and Fitch outfit every time I saw him (I'd learn his mother sent care packages once a month); the tricked-out truck he drove (his second since coming to King); and, more generally, the wide-stanced entitlement with which he approached life.

He was surprisingly gracious as we sat on the couch, offering me a beer and asking if I wanted to order some late-night pizza, his treat.

—Want to start with PubPol? I asked.

—Fuck yes. I didn't know who the fuck those liars were Professor Wilson keeps talking about.

It took me a second. Outliers.

—It's easy, I said, opening the textbook.

I'd been tutoring teammates since freshman year of high school and quickly recognized the telltale signs: Chase's inability to sit still, his impatience with explanations, the unfunny jokes he cracked about his stupidity. After I explained outliers, we moved on to the homework that was due tomorrow. Halfway into my explanation of standard deviations, Chase asked if I'd finished the assignment yet. I knew what he was getting at and handed him my finished answer sheet. Now all the focus he'd been lacking snapped into place, and the apartment fell silent as he concentrated on copying my answers in such a way that the TA would have trouble matching his answer sheet with mine.

Idle, I finished my beer and went to get another. The refrigerator was decorated from top to bottom with photographs of Chase and Sadie: standing at the beer pong table at the Football House, sitting on the flagstone steps that led up to the King Chapel, Sadie smiling for the camera while Chase was too cool to do anything but stare. I thought, for the thousandth time since he'd told me, about him ejaculating onto Sadie.

A knock at the door. Chase took out his wallet and handed me a fifty-dollar bill to pay for the pizza. It only cost twenty, but when I returned to the couch and tried to give him the change, he waved me off.

—Keep it.

Thirty dollars would cover gas for my Saturn for two weeks. And yet I didn't want to accept money from Chase like I had from other teammates, didn't want tonight to amount to nothing more than a transaction. I insisted he take the money back.

A better payment by far was sitting next to him on the couch as he finished copying my homework.

To balance out the three consecutive away games we had at the beginning of the season, we played several games in a row at home. But though I was happy to have my weekends full up with football again, the streak of home games also made it painfully clear how right Jimbo had been—King Football meant nothing to King College.

When we played the University of Virginia, there were just as many seagulls picking through the trash in our stadium's stands as there were people sitting in them. During Kent State, the only kids in the student section were frat boys who'd made the mistake of getting drunk before they painted King's letters onto their torsos, spelling out KNG FOTBALL. And by the Navy game, word started spreading among players of the unsavory tactics the athletic department was using to boost the crowd count: instructors in King's half-credit gym classes were talked into making attending games a course requirement, while members of the Blenheim Boys and Girls Club were bused to King on the pretext of exposing underprivileged kids to an elite college when really it was a way of adding a hundred-odd fans.

During Navy I could look at the family section behind our bench and easily pick out individual faces—which is how I saw that Reshawn's parents and little brothers had come to town. Mr. McCoy was a big, fit man, youthful looking but for the silver at his temples. From a *Sports Illustrated* profile I knew he owned a sporting goods store back in Oregon, and the simultaneously relaxed and authoritative way he had of crossing his arms and talking to the parents surrounding him made it easy to imagine him chatting up customers on the floor. Reshawn got his build from his dad, but his face and bearing were his mother's. They shared the same high, strong cheekbones, and the look of intense concentration his mother wore as she watched the game was the same expression I saw on Reshawn. His little brothers Morris and LeDale were identical twins, made even more matching by replica King jerseys with their big brother's number.

Family and friends waited outside the stadium gates to greet players coming out of the Hay's third floor, and thanks to our win today (we were now 3–4) the scene was happy. Younger siblings hyper with candy chased each other around; parents doled out compliments about other peoples' kids and made subtle one-ups about their own; girlfriends from back home tried to seem mature beyond their years as they fussed over infants dressed in floppy purple King Football fishing hats. My own parents wouldn't be here—we agreed it was better they save their money until they could actually watch me play—but I received collateral love on my way to the parking lot, saying yes sir, I know my time will come.

—Miles.

Reshawn was hailing me. He stood with his parents, and as I redirected toward them I was surprised to see his mother leaning on two metal walking sticks, the kind that clasp around your forearms for stability. She must have been keeping them down by her feet during the game. Had she been in an accident?

—This is my dad, Reshawn Senior. My mom, Ali. They wanted to meet you.

Reshawn looked none too happy about that request. We shook hands.

—Your folks here, Miles?

—No sir.

—Colorado?

—Yes sir.

Mr. McCoy clapped me on the shoulder.

—Call me Senior. What do your parents do?

—My dad owns a restaurant.

I'm still not sure why I lied. Maybe I was embarrassed by the truth, which was that my old head coach had set my dad up with janitorial shifts at Sillitoe High to help supplement his temp work.

—Small business owner! Mr. McCoy exclaimed, rolling his shoulders back proudly. I'm in sporting goods, myself.

As Senior and Ali continued asking about my family, I noticed that what I'd initially thought was Reshawn's annoyance with me was in fact a nervous vigilance about the crowd bustling around his mother. He was watching his brothers, who were slaloming between adults' legs as they chased Cornelius's eight-year-old sister and Devonté's nine-year-old brother. I had never seen Reshawn look so solicitous, so vulnerable, and in spite of myself it made me like him just a little bit more.

—after the diagnosis, Mr. McCoy was saying.

—Sir? I said, refocusing. What diagnosis?

—I have MS, Ali said. Primary progressive. Reshawn didn't tell you?

Of course he hadn't. And I didn't understand what any of what she'd said meant, other than that it was bad enough that the mere mention of it sapped Senior of his energy.

—I'm sorry, I said.

—You give me these genes? Ali responded. The sharpness, the barely bayed sarcasm, were exactly what I would have heard from her son.

—Great game, Reshawn!

Devonté's father pulled Reshawn in for a hug, and at that exact moment the kids were running by us again. Reshawn's brothers knew to keep far from their mother, but Cornelius's sister didn't, and when Devonté's father and Reshawn blocked her path with their hug, the little girl dodged toward Ali, in danger of colliding with her. I caught her just in time and sent her running in a different direction.

Ali went protectively stiff. Senior was smiling nervously, looking weak. Reshawn let go of Devonté's father and said angrily to his parents:

—I told you this was a bad idea.

We walked to the handicapped spot where the McCoys' rental was parked. Reshawn helped Ali into the passenger seat, her arm around her son's shoulder, wincing.

—We should get back to the hotel, Senior told me. But, rain check? We'll take you out to dinner next time we come for a game.

—I'd like that, I said, shaking his hand. I waved goodbye to Ali, who was wriggling in her seat, trying to get comfortable. She forced a smile.

I wouldn't own a laptop until the next year, and in order to use the Internet I had to sit in a computer cluster on Stager Hall's ground floor. I looked up primary progressive multiple sclerosis and learned about the prognosis. Affecting nerves in the brain and spinal cord, it manifests initially with a weakness of the legs and worsens over time, expanding to affect vision and speech, causing fatigue, incontinence. Ali's body was attacking itself, and would continue to do so for however long she lived. I also looked up Senior's store and found an article from five years ago in a local Oregon paper. The article described Mr. McCoy's plans to add two stores to the one he already owned, and it quoted Senior as saying one day McCoy's Sporting Goods would challenge corporate behemoths like Sports Authority and Dick's. But a second article from a year and a half ago—just a paragraph, really—served as a postmortem for his gambit: all his businesses had filed for Chapter 11.

I could now piece together a rough timeline. Reshawn at some point had fallen out with football and decided to attend Brown. That would have coincided with the implosion of his father's business—and, judging from Ali's symptoms, would also have happened around the time she got her diagnosis. But knowing this ultimately frustrated me, since it just raised questions to which I had nothing like an answer.

The more time I spent with Chase, the more I realized there wasn't a single him. There was Public Chase and Private Chase, and seldom did the twain meet.

Public Chase was the one I'd long known: the brash, boorish, cocky, obnoxious man-boy prone to pranks he alone found funny, who snidely called me "Brain" when I sat next to him in a lecture and who came up with gems like "Cunthole" to substitute for my real name when he, say, was ordering me to grab him a water bottle during Team period; the veteran who went out of his way to strike me brutally in tackling drills; the beer pong partner who gloated over my continued badness at the game even though I was, you know, *his partner.* One day I went to use the toilet in the locker room, and when I returned to our cube Chase was spraying Old Spice cologne on my street clothes, the stink of which three separate trips to the laundry room in Stager Hall couldn't remove. And then there was Private Chase: the kid so shy about his love for his estranged girlfriend he would only ever talk to her in a separate room if she called while I was tutoring him; the kid who pinched the inside of his wrist in punishment as I explained this or that quiz answer he'd gotten wrong; the kid who apologized for ruining my clothes with Old Spice by insisting I take a couple of the new Abercrombie shirts his mother had mailed him. The whiplash could be exhausting, but I continued spending much of my free time with him, and I think there were two reasons. One, I believed Chase's split personality was beyond his control, as if the cruelty wielded him, rather than he it. Two, and probably more important, Chase was far from the first crush I'd had who treated me like shit. In fact, by now I had come to almost want such poor treatment, the punishment I deserved for my feelings about men.

One weekend in late October, Chase invited me to have dinner with his father. He said Mr. McGerrin wanted to meet me, which I happily took to mean Chase had talked about me with his dad. So after our home game against Missouri (which we lost) I showered in the locker room and dressed in the slacks, collared shirt, and sports jacket Chase told me to bring. We took his truck to a remote part of Blenheim I'd never seen, nothing but skinny roads weaving through heavy forest. When we turned onto a narrow driveway marked "Private" and began winding downhill, the tree cover thinned and water began to shimmer in the gaps between the trunks. At the bottom of the hill the forest halted abruptly, like a crowd held back by an invisible rope line, and from then on the ground proceeded as a level, pristinely maintained lawn that led up to a nineteenth-century Italianate mansion. A lake lay behind the club, turning a molten gold as the sun set behind the far shore.

The lobby of the King Club was done in dark mahogany, with white marble flooring that had lilac-colored veins. Business-casual men sat on wing-backed settees and frowned at laptops propped up on their knees, while bellhops in purple uniforms steered golden luggage carts. At the dining room entrance, which had the same Gothic archway you saw on West Campus, a penguin-suited maître d' greeted Chase by name and led us through the opulent dining room filled with parents dipping baguette crusts into buttery escargot slime, undergrads sitting primly in long dresses or navy sport coats, liver-spotted husbands with King College lapel pins and their bepearled wives.

At a table toward the back I saw a man I recognized—and immediately wished I didn't. It was the same man I'd mistaken for a coach when he stepped out of the Marriott elevator during my official visit, the man I'd heard haggling with Reshawn over the bribe money that would secure his commitment to King.

—Lucas McGerrin, he said, shaking my hand.

Mr. McGerrin spoke with a heavy southern accent, but whereas Coach Zeller had never met a *g* at the end of a word he couldn't dispense with, Mr. McGerrin's own speech was what you might call melodiously precise. Chase had mentioned his dad had played linebacker at King, and now that father and son sat side by side, I saw just how close the resemblance was, down to the slab bodies and blond hair that seemed to vanish under strong light.

—First time at the club?

—Yes sir, I said, trying to seem calm.

—This is the President's Room, he said, pointing at the large oil paintings of white men that hung on the walls. Only people allowed to hang here are past King presidents.

A waiter materialized.

—Scotch? Mr. McGerrin asked us.

—I'm not twenty-one, sir.

—*Christ,* Chase said, and with that one word made clear I was going to be getting Public Chase tonight. Mr. McGerrin smiled indulgently.

—Drinking age is a little lower at the club, he said. Bring us three Glenmorangies, rocks, and three filets, medium rare.

The waiter left to place our orders. Mr. McGerrin snapped open his napkin.

—Chase says you've got straight As?

—Yes sir, but—easy classes.

—Not *that* easy, Chase said.

Mr. McGerrin laughed softly at his son.

—Well, I'm just glad Chasey found someone smart to cheat off of. That Ritalin doesn't work for shit.

Two undergrad girls walked by, dressed in skirts and form-fitting cashmere sweaters. Mr. McGerrin subtly watched their asses sway beneath the skirts. Once the girls passed, he grinned and patted Chase's arm.

—Miles, is this boy still moping about Sadie?

Chase warned me off with a killer stare. Mr. McGerrin noticed.

—There is a *lot* of pussy in this world, son. But remove thine own beam, I guess. McGerrin men want what they want. Chase's mom is a King alumna, Miles. Graduated second in our class. We lived down the hall from each other sophomore year, and she would not give this jock the time of day. But I asked and asked and asked until she finally gave in.

The waiter returned with our drinks.

—King Football, Mr. McGerrin said, raising his drink and taking a long, thirsty pull after we clinked our glasses. Who knew I'd be so happy with three damn wins? We lost two games—*two*—the entire time I played. Four All-Americans my senior year. But then the slide started. Gradual, like frogs in water. In the eighties we'd make bowl games, but the bowls kept getting worse. The nineties were Dark Ages—winless seasons, losses against 1AA teams. FSU beat us by eighty points in 'ninety-eight. A lot of alums threw up their hands and said we should just go full U Chicago and cancel the program. But that was fatalism, Miles. *I* knew there was a cause.

Mr. McGerrin had clearly recited this history a hundred times, and it was his great talent as a speaker that you didn't hold it against him that what he was saying was canned. He was also proving to be a prodigious drinker, and without being asked the waiter replaced his empty glass with a fresh scotch.

—Augustus King founded this place to be the South's premier school, he continued. When people hear that, they focus on the word "premier." But you know what's the really important word? "South." *That's* what makes King special. *That's* what makes it different from the other elite colleges. We have a culture we can draw from, like a natural resource. I'm from Jacksonville. Born and bred. The South is *in* me, and that was true for just about everyone else in the program when I played here—most of the normal students, too. But a couple years after I left, something called the Porter Commission was set up to evaluate how King could stay competitive into the twenty-first century. They came out with a report saying the school was in danger of becoming "regional." That was code for the school being "too southern." Does anyone at Yale say it's "too northern"? Hell no. But people from the South, we're taught to carry this shame with us, and the commission exploited that. The college started aggressively recruiting students and professors from around the country, and every year what made this school special, what made King *King*, got diluted a little more. The culture here started to be no different from what you'd find in Massachusetts, for God's sake. I'd come back to campus and hardly recognize the place. Antiapartheid idiots chaining themselves to chapel doors. Boys holding hands like we're at some San Francisco faggot parade. *Women's Studies.* It wasn't one bit of a coincidence King Football started slipping around the same time. We got infected by the university and hired coaches outside the South, men who had no way of valuing what made King Football stand apart. We started saying our graduation rate was as important as the number of bowl games we'd won, if you can believe that.

—Count it: the last thirty years, we've had twelve head coaches, and ten of them haven't been from the South. When we fired the last doofus, I had the chance to give input into the search for the next coach, and I came right out and asked each one of the candidates: "Where are your people *from*?" I knew Zeller was our man when I heard him go down the line: South, South, South. He's got a framed letter Stonewall Jackson wrote to his great-great-granddaddy. *He's* the foundation, right there. And now that we've got that—that *base*? I'm happy to use materials from anywhere to build the rest of the program. I mean players from Colorado, like you, Miles. Players from Oregon, like Reshawn.

Our food arrived. The scotch had sharpened my appetite, and the buttery scents flooding my nostrils made me light-headed. Mr. McGerrin sawed off a slice of steak and dipped it into his bowl of creamed spinach, leaving a little blood on the greens.

—How's Reshawn? he asked me, chewing.

—Fine, sir.

—Just fine?

—He's got good grades, too.

—But are you saying he's having trouble adjusting?

Mr. McGerrin hadn't taken his second bite; he'd rested the tips of his knife and fork on the edge of his plate, watching me. I realized that I hadn't been invited to dinner because Chase had spoken so glowingly of me. Mr. McGerrin knew I was Reshawn's roommate and wanted to use me as a way of checking on his investment.

—Well, sir, I began, not sure how honest to be. He's got a lot of responsibilities.

—He's got a lot of fucking attitude is what, Chase said. I was walking to class with a group of players on Thursday and we passed him on the sidewalk. He didn't even *look* at us, Dad.

—You think he's unhappy? Mr. McGerrin asked me.

—I don't know, sir. We don't talk much.

—*Unhappy?* Chase said. Come on. What could he be unhappy about? Coach Zeller would give his right nut if Reshawn asked for it. I want to tell him, "*You* chose to be here, asshole."

Mr. McGerrin still hadn't taken another bite.

—Do me a favor, Miles, and get my cell from Chasey. You think there's anything, *anything* out of the ordinary wrong with Reshawn, I'd appreciate you letting me know. We want to make sure he's happy at King.

—Yes sir.

We finished the main course, and when Mr. McGerrin learned I had never eaten crème brûlée, he insisted on ordering one for each of us. I'd always wanted to try the dessert, but by now I was ready to leave. I was coming to dislike Mr. Lucas McGerrin, whose faux-innocent questions about Reshawn nettled me, and whose theory of King's sullied southerness became more incoherent the more I thought about it. The man said he'd made his fortune in "plastics"—what the hell did that even mean?

If anything good came from dinner, it was the confirmation

that Chase didn't know the role his father had played in bringing Reshawn here. Seeing Chase duped by his own father made me feel all the more tender toward him.

Spirits were high as we entered November. Our record was 3–5, which might not sound like much, but keep in mind this was already a three-win improvement over our total from last year. Meanwhile our losses had all been by respectable margins, and a few so close we could tell ourselves that, were it not for this unlucky gust of wind or that unfavorable ball-bounce, we could right now have a winning record. Reshawn's superlative play already guaranteed he would be the first Freshman All-American from King born after Jimmy Carter was in office, while Coach Zeller's admiring mentions in the press were becoming so regular that one day J1 asked me the meaning of a word used to describe Zeller in the latest issue of *Sporting News*: wunderkind.

Yet our optimism was also prophylactic, since we knew it wasn't just the days that were about to get colder and darker—we were staring down our final, most vicious stretch of the season, in which we would be facing three consecutive nationally ranked teams. Our ninth and tenth games were massacres: Boston College and Boise State both deployed defensive strategies with the sole aim of pulverizing our running game, and here I use "pulverize" with the highest definitional fidelity, in that our offense started out a solid, single unit that was pounded into eleven pitiful particles, the defenses stacking the line so that two, three, sometimes four defenders would have already flooded our backfield by the time Reshawn took the handoff, buffeting, broadsiding, and barraging him, leaving his body decorated with shining rug burns and crisscross cuts from fingernails and face mask corners. We were forced to pass, and since our quarterback was so bumbling I'm not even going to ask you to memorize his name, those passes either fell fruitlessly to the ground or found their way into the hands of defenders. Before we knew it, our defense would be jogging back on the field, and though Coach Zeller in his time as defensive coordinator had made this unit considerably stronger than our offense, they were still emasculated—a term that, again, I'm using more literally than you might think, as the offensive lines of both BC and Boise State had sadistic predilections for punching, slapping, and yanking their enemies' genitalia. In the game film, you'd see the refs' shoulders hunch empathetically before they reached into their back pockets for flags.

| Boston College | 48 | King College | 3 |
| Boise State | 61 | King College | 16 |

Up to now, we had managed to play well enough to keep the King student body's sneering impulses in check. But all bets were off after the blowouts. On the Monday following the Boston College game, the student newspaper, the King *Herald,* featured two large photographs that could only have been featured to embarrass us. One showed our Y receiver, JaMarcus Stephens, upside down in midair, arms extended helplessly beneath him like a bungee jumper whose cord has snapped; the other depicted our punter, Gunter Atkinson, as a kind of gridiron Tantalus straining to reach for a fumbled ball while a Boston College player was holding on to the back of his jersey. We faced Boise State at home on a blasting-cold afternoon, and our student section was empty save for an anarchic undergrad improv troupe called the Court Jesters who'd come armed with signs mocking our team and belittling chants whose cruelty was rivaled only by their cleverness. We did our best to ignore these kids, but by the middle of the fourth quarter Graham Robbins, one of our graduate assistants, finally lost his composure and ran into the bleachers to assault a flat-footed sophomore trouper. It was the best part of the game, watching Robbins pummel that kid, but even this modest solace was spoiled when *SportsCenter* featured footage of the assault in that evening's broadcast. It was the first time we had appeared on that program all season, and the last time Robbins coached in Division One.

It seemed the worst was yet to come. Our final game was away at the University of North Carolina, a rival we hadn't beaten in sixteen years, currently ranked number 8 in the country. I have to admit I wasn't totally excited to learn that, because UNC was an eighteen-minute drive from Blenheim, bottom feeders got to travel. I wasn't sure I needed to witness our asses getting handed to us a third time in a row.

Yet there I was on Friday, dressed in my silence suit, taking a seat in one of the shuttle buses that would drive us to the Marriott. The shuttle was quiet as we pulled away from the Hay, but that lasted all of thirty seconds before Fade blurted:

—The *fuck*?!

We were driving down a little West Campus road that served as the unofficial border between the school's athletic and academic regions—passing, in fact, the same castle-shaped Gothic dorm that Reshawn and I had walked through during our official visit. I looked right and saw what Fade had seen: a bedspread suspended from the windowsill of one of the dorm's second-story rooms, these words handwritten in thick permanent marker:

Go King Football! Beat (the Spread Against) UNC

The whole bus turned to look, players leaning over seatmates to see if they could spot the student who'd hung the fucking thing. But the only students in sight were the ones standing in front of the dorm pointing at the sign and laughing.

At dinner that night in the Marriott ballroom, the players at my table talked of nothing else.

—Maybe a UNC student hung it, Cornelius said.

Jimbo blew a raspberry.

—That's someone in your fucking *class* who did that. Same somebody who asked you to help move their couch.

—People look gloomy as hell, Fade said, surveying the room. Zeller needs to bring that shit up.

This was the consensus opinion, and in every meeting and film session that night we waited to hear our head coach give marching orders to the elephant in the room. But Zeller didn't say a word about the bedspread, and so superstitiously routinized were these meetings that for a player to have broken pregame protocol and brought up the subject himself would have been as unlucky as smashing a roomful of mirrors, walking under a city block's worth of ladders, having a whole pack of black cats run across your path. The elephant stayed right where it was.

On Saturday morning our buses pushed into UNC's campus, where the parking lots were already teeming with tailgaters and the sidewalks astream with fans eager to get to their seats. Our buses were unmarked and the windows tinted, but we didn't get far before fans realized who we were. I looked down to see a ten-year-old boy dressed in a Carolina blue replica jersey, a dimple-faced kid who raised both of his little middle fingers to us.

We dressed for warm-ups in the small visitors' locker room, and I followed Coach Hightower and the linebackers to a corner of the sold-out stadium's end zone. This placed us spitting distance from a group of what are, objectively speaking, the very worst group of fans: middle-aged men untethered from their wives, lives, responsibilities.

—I fucked your mom's hairy asshole last night!

—No calculators in football, faggot!

—Look at that one—you're supposed to take your tampon out *before* you get on the field!

The last was directed at me, and I made the mistake of looking at the man who said it. Up to then, the men had been shouting generally, but now they latched onto me for tailored abuse.

—Nice jeans, Mary!

—Look how small that fucker is. You get lost on the way to the soccer game, sweetheart?!

Back in the visitors' locker room we knelt in a half circle, waiting for Coach Zeller's speech. Players looked defeated already as they listened to crowd-throb that seemed to get louder, more tactile, the longer we waited. And that wait proved unusually drawn out. The clock signaled we were getting close to kickoff, and yet there was no sign anywhere of Coach Zeller. Assistant coaches shared concerned glances, while Devonté and the other captains looked impatiently toward the doors. Was Coach Zeller puking in a bathroom stall? Was he hiding, terrified of the humiliation we were about to undergo?

I felt a tap on my shoulder. It was Coach Zeller, and as he passed me, the rolled-up bedspread he was carrying brushed against my forearm.

—Help me with this, he told two student trainers as he took his place at the head of the half circle.

The trainers each took a side of the spread and unfurled it, showing us the same banner we'd seen hanging from the dorm window. Zeller scowled and sunk his hands into his khaki pockets.

—Somethin' has been naggin' at me ever since I moved to Blenheim. Somethin' about this school. First I thought it was the way students treated you. How these people acted like they were fuckin' royalty and y'all were peasants. But over time I realized that wadn't the problem. Not the real one. It was just the *symptom*. The *real* problem was that students were *allowed* to treat you like that. They were *allowed* to say, "We're royalty, and you ain't." They were *permitted* to beat that idea into your minds, into your *hearts*. . . . It's a head coach's job to protect you. And I'll just come out and say it—your old head coach failed. Didn't protect you, not one bit. I remember thinkin' to myself: I ever get the privilege to lead these men, well, I'd see to that.

What, exactly, Zeller meant by "see to that" I can't say. What I can tell you is that the image that entered my mind—Zeller bursting into that King student's room and tearing that banner from his windowsill—is probably what a lot of other players were envisioning.

—Now it's your turn, Zeller continued. Your turn to show these motherfuckers how wrong they've been. Your turn to show them how they should be grovelin' at your feet. I want y'all to stay right where you are for two minutes. I want you to just *look* at that thing.

One of the uncanniest experiences of my life was standing in that silent locker room for the next 120 seconds. I could hear the plastic squeaks of players angrily masticating mouth guards. The creaks of shoulder pads shifting. Even, I swear to God, the sound of sweat slowly pushing out of pores. Finally, Coach Zeller lifted his chin at Devonté to signal it was time to bring it up. With a gush we converged on him, laying arms onto one another and screaming:

*One one two three*
*Who the fuck you came to see?!*
*King King motherfucker!*

We played our best game of the whole season, going score-for-score with UNC into the fourth quarter. With two minutes remaining in the game, our long-snapper snapped the ball high above our punter's head. UNC recovered the fumble and shortly thereafter scored what figured to be the winning field goal. We received the kick and Devonté was tackled at our own 31. Sixteen seconds left in the game, UNC leading by three.

What most coaches would have done next was send every receiver and back we had downfield for a Hail Mary pass. But before Coach Zeller surrendered to fickle fate, he wanted to make sure Reshawn touched the ball at least once. So we threw Reshawn a short out route ten yards down the field. The play was designed for him to sprint to the sideline, get out of bounds, and stop the clock. What he did instead was stop dead and, with rat-a-tat juke, tangle the ankles of the linebacker who'd been covering him, which freed him to sprint at an angle toward the middle of the field, and though a cornerback and safety both were closing in on him, he kicked into an even higher gear and outsprinted them to the point

117

of convergence, breaking free—40, 50, 40, 30, 20, 10, crossing the goal line as time expired, touchdown.

We ran onto the field to mob Reshawn, with a flushed, screaming Coach Zeller leading the charge.

The shuttles that had felt like hearses on the drive to Chapel Hill became Mardi Gras floats on the ride back to Blenheim, players laughing and dapping and jumping out of their seats, breaking into round after round of our team chant while keeping time by banging their palms against the windows.

I was sitting in the back and only belatedly noticed Chase on my bus, sitting at the very front and leaning his forehead against the window to watch the dun forest bordering the highway. I picked my way through my raucous teammates and took the empty seat next to him. When he saw it was me, he handed over his cell phone.

Fuck off. Never contact me again.

The shock I felt wasn't from the text's expletive so much as from seeing Sadie's words on the screen. Anything I'd ever heard from or about her had been secondhand, and because of that she had come to feel as silent and one-dimensional as the photographs I'd seen on Chase's fridge. But here were words straight from the source, blunt, harsh, slightly formal, indubitably final.

I was electrified by the idea of getting Private Chase all to myself. But I kept my excitement hidden, just as I knew better than to ask him what happened while we were in front of teammates. I lent him my presence for the rest of the ride, dressed with him in the cube, and rode with him to his apartment, where we sat on the couch while he explained:

After our dinner at the King Club, Chase had taken his father's words about indomitable McGerrin men to heart and gone on a campaign to bombard Sadie—expensive flowers and chocolates delivered to her Georgetown dorm, phone calls five, ten times a day, an impassioned handwritten note he sent via Priority Mail. He knew it was risky to be so overbearing, but he had already tried the giving-her-space thing to no avail, so he figured he might as well spill everything that was in his heart, leaving it to her to sort through the detritus and decide whether there was enough to make a second relationship.

It had seemed like the strategy was working. Sadie acknowledged his gestures with short, grateful texts, and more often than not replied with an "I love you, too" at the end of their phone calls. Then, last night in the Marriott, Chase made the leap he'd been working toward all this time, texting to ask if he could fly to D.C. after today's game. No pressure, he said, she wouldn't have to meet him at the airport or put him up in her dorm room; everything would be on his dime and her terms. She hadn't replied before he fell asleep, nor this morning, and by pregame his anticipation had gotten so distracting he forced himself to turn off his phone—which had left him to return from our miraculous victory and find waiting the most damningly definitive text she'd ever sent him.

Tears were streaming down his face by the end of the story, and I helped in the only way I knew how—getting him drunk. I raided his refrigerator for the four beers in it and found an eighth of a handle of vodka buried in the freezer under a stack of DiGiorno pizzas. When we finished the vodka, Chase walked to a liquor store down the road to buy a twelve-pack of Natty Light while I turned on the oven to make us two of the pizzas. We'd finished another three beers each by the time the food was ready, and I felt so exceedingly adult, sitting there across from him at the dining table, eating off nice Crate and Barrel plates, sipping beer with dinner like my mom and dad sometimes did. Chase's face was bright with all the booze, and he seemed to be feeling better. Things were perfect, and I saw no reason why we'd need to leave this apartment—not tonight, not ever.

Then Fade texted, saying some vets were meeting at Stefan Knows. I was disappointed to abandon our domestic idyll, fast-stepping with Chase down the building's zigzagging outdoor staircase and walking through the clear, chilly night to the bar. A long line had formed outside Stefan Knows, with ten of our teammates standing in the middle of the line. We joined them, ignoring the angry sighs and eye rolls of the regular students we'd cut in front of.

—You faggots wearing lipstick? Chase asked.

I'd noticed it, too: our teammates' lips were stained red.

—Devonté said Jell-O shots.

—Motherfucker, don't blame me!

—So he runs out, buys Everclear and Jell-O boxes, makes that shit and puts it in the fridge. He was too damn drunk to think how it needed like twelve hours to set. When we ran outta beer, we just started drinkin' this shit. It ain't half bad.

They'd brought a water bottle filled with the stuff and passed it to us. Chase drank first, which meant I got to place my lips on the same part of the rim his had touched. I chugged until I reached the sweet silt of undissolved Jell-O powder floating at the bottom.

The bouncer was checking IDs, and I started to get nervous. The players ahead of me were all veterans, either twenty-one or so much bigger than the bouncer they were getting waved in.

—Fuckin' kiddin' me? the bouncer said at the sight of my ID. You ain't even eighteen.

—What?! Chase said as he was waved into the bar. Y'all hear that? Furling can't vote!

The bouncer laid his forearm across my chest. I called for Chase to wait, but he was talking to Jimbo and didn't look back as he disappeared inside. The King students we'd cut in front of smirked.

I hurried away, telling myself to keep it together until I passed the last person in line.

—Whoa whoa whoa.

Devonté grabbed the back of my jacket. He saw I was on the verge of tears and put his arm around me, leading me back to the door.

—You gotta learn to speak *up*, rookie.

He convinced the bouncer to let me pass. The bar's lights were dimmed and the hip-hop cranked, the parquet floor alternately sticky with spilled drinks and slick from where puke had been mopped up. Our teammates were posted at the bar, but we couldn't reach them via a straight line. Two steps forward brought us up against a shoal of sorority sisters we had to skirt, and then we had to navigate the heavy swell of the dance floor, where I stumbled over a dreadlocked white boy on all fours searching for the tab of acid he'd dropped.

When we finally reached our teammates, I stared at Chase, waiting for him to apologize, to acknowledge that I'd listened to his sob story all evening, comforted him, just for him to abandon me. But I'd been too successful in getting him drunk, and his already small attention span shrank down to nothing as he talk-shouted at Fade.

—Yo, Jimbo said. You think the A/V guys recorded the pregame speech? Aristotle would have been proud of that rhetoric.

—That's Zeller's daddy's name?

Jimbo snatched the beer Cornelius was holding and pointed at him accusingly with the bottle neck.

—I tutored you a whole semester for Intro to Philosophy.

—The fuck's that got to do with my beer?

Jimbo shook his head and took a long pull.

—What did he call normal students again? Jimbo asked us.

—Royalty.

It was the perfect word for the people swaying in front of us, dressed in their North Face fleeces and limited edition jeans, wearing teeth they'd probably gotten whitened as high school graduation presents, people who didn't see us as the victors of a historic rivalry game, just as a row of irritatingly big bodies blocking access to the bar.

As I was looking out at the crowd, I noticed something that made me wonder if I'd accidentally ingested the acid that dreadlocked boy had lost. I saw a black kid on the dance floor who was a dead ringer for my roommate, grinding on a girl. The crowd was so thick the kid bobbed in and out of view as heads shifted right and left, and I had to keep staring at the spot, waiting for the next glimpse.

Jesus, it *was* Reshawn. I recognized the girl, too, though I didn't know her name. She had been coming to our dorm room the past couple weeks. Light brown skin, curly brown hair, a white tank top that glowed in the low light.

This was shocking, but nowhere near as shocking as the two boys I realized were dancing alongside them. The boys weren't grinding on each other as the girl and Reshawn were—if anything they were moving circumspectly—and yet the way their eyes met, how their hands rose in tandem and momentarily interlocked before separating once more, made it clear they were dancing together. Reshawn and the girl looked over at the two boys, and the four of them slowed down for a moment to dip their heads and talk.

My teammates saw what I saw. Cornelius started laughing, but Jimbo glowered.

—What, Jimbo said to Cornelius. You got people pointing at you and whispering, "That's Cornelius Belkins"?

—No.

—No, you don't. What about you, Fade? No? Well, they do with Reshawn. He's the only player any of these royals know. He represents our *team*, you assholes.

Jimbo downed the last of his beer and set the bottle on the bar.

—Cousin fuckin' Shawn, he said. I'm outta here.

One of the boys was petite and white, with sweaty red-blond hair that he could sweep back from his forehead with his fingers and the hair would remain standing, a wet flame. The other boy— the other boy was gorgeous. Almost as tall as Reshawn and Asian of some sort, he had buzzed black hair and taut skin displayed by a loose tank top. He raised his arms, closed his eyes, and snapped his fingers to the music, thin triceps flexing, dark nipples peeking out. With his eyes closed, the Asian boy lost the rhythm of the crowd and accidentally brushed against Reshawn. And did Reshawn recoil in disgust? Did my roommate mouth the words "Watch it, faggot," like my teammates would have? No, he just kept dancing.

Tabs paid, we snaked along the edge of the crowd toward a side exit past the end of the bar. Chase finally deigned to acknowledge my existence.

—That's what my dad was talking about! he said, grabbing my sleeve and pointing.

—So?

—So come *on*! Why are *we* the ones leaving?! Why are fags allowed to stay?!

—Leave them be, Chase.

He made a pouty face.

—Oh, are those your *friends*, Cunthole?

I ignored him, done with him, done with my stupid fucking infatuation. I kept following the group to the exit.

—Don't do anything stupid! Cornelius yelled.

I turned and saw Chase had broken away from the group. He was pushing through the crowd toward the two boys.

I was drunker now than I'd ever been, I had the liquid courage of my convictions, and so, without knowing exactly what I planned to do, I pushed into the crush of dancers myself, my shirt collecting strangers' sweat as I kept Chase's bullish blond head in sight. I was infuriated by the idea that Chase was going to take out his disappointment with Sadie on a couple of kids who'd been brave enough to go dancing.

Seeing Chase almost within reach of the boys, I gave up politely maneuvering around the crowd and pushed straight through, arriving just as Chase was leaning down to scream at the smaller of the two boys while Reshawn, who wasn't nearly as strong as Chase, tried to pull him off. The crowd opened a perimeter around them, which gave me the space I needed to grab Chase by the back of his collar and slam him against the sticky floor, cracking the back of his head against the parquet.

It says a lot about who I was back then that the very first thing I did was stand up and look back to the edge of the dance floor, checking to see whether my teammates had been watching. Devonté and the rest were indeed looking our way, but the crowd was too thick for them to know what I'd done. I looked down at Chase—dazed from hitting his head, struggling to sit up—and turned to look at the two boys. The smaller one, the redhead, was holding his hands over his face and sobbing. The Asian boy hugged him protectively to his side and gave me a wary look.

Reshawn gestured for us all to walk to the front of the bar, to the exit opposite the one our teammates were blocking.

I didn't realize how much I'd been sweating until my body flashed cold in the brisk autumn night, nor quite how drunk I was until I stumbled over a curb in the neighborhood of bungalows separating Stefan Knows from East Campus. Nobody noticed me trip; their attention was focused on the boy who continued to let out hiccupping sobs that prompted every dog in the neighborhood to bark. The girl and the Asian boy tried to comfort him, while Reshawn fell back to walk alongside me. He explained that the girl's name was Jamie, the redheaded boy's name was Henry, and the Asian boy's name Thao. All three were enrolled in his African American folktales class.

Henry and Thao were juniors who lived on Central Campus, and we agreed it wasn't a good idea to go there when Chase might be heading in the same direction. We walked to Jamie's. She was a senior who lived off-campus in a neighborhood called Carsonville, ten square blocks of historic homes that had been owned by King Tobacco's middle management during the company's heyday and were now King property rented to upperclassmen, grad students, and professors.

Jamie's house was a three-story Victorian, concord purple with soft pink detailing. We mounted the porch, and Jamie led Henry inside while Thao remained outside with us.

—Is your boyfriend okay? I asked.

—When he gets like this, he won't sleep for two days straight. And he's not my boyfriend.

Jamie returned outside, breathless.

—He locked himself in the bathroom. My roommates are going to shit when they find out he's here again.

Thao sighed.

—Give me a minute? I'm not ready to put on my nurse's uniform yet.

Jamie took Reshawn's hand and led him to the porch swing that hung from the portico's roof. They whispered as they rocked. Thao noticed me watching.

—Hell of a first date, he said.

The bulb over the front door had burned out, and only the moon lighted Thao's face. Had he meant he didn't have a boyfriend, period? Or just that *Henry* wasn't his boyfriend? I'd never said "boyfriend" out loud like that, at least without it being a joke.

—What's your name? he asked.

—Miles.

—Thao.

We shook hands.

—Thao . . . Am I saying that right?

—No, but that's how everyone says it. You're a football player?

I nodded, and without warning Thao slid his hand onto my right arm and squeezed it in a dozen different places, like a pool toy he couldn't figure out how to deflate.

—You *feel* like a football player, but you don't act like one.

We heard a commotion inside, roommates waking at the noise Henry was making in the bathroom. Jamie kissed Reshawn goodbye, rising from the porch swing. Then there were lips on my cheek, too, light stubble pressing against my hairless jaw. I froze in place as Thao pulled back from me, smiled, and followed Jamie into the house.

Reshawn and I took a sidewalk in the direction of East Campus. Thao's saliva was cold on my cheek and fading much too fast.

—Sorry, Reshawn said, meaning Thao's kiss. I came to pick up Jamie tonight and they were both at the house. "We're you're chaperones!"

Reshawn was impersonating either Henry or Thao and had added a sibilant *s* to the word "chaperones." It wasn't a cruel impression, not quite, and thanks to it I was able to more closely calibrate how Reshawn felt about gays: fine dancing next to them, fine talking to them, fine that the girl he liked was friends with them, but still far from comfortable.

I would be lying if I said I wasn't disappointed, but it was a disappointment I was well accustomed to. I focused instead on what was thrilling about this moment with Reshawn. He had felt the need to apologize, sincerely apologize, which he'd never done before. Moreover, how he was talking to me, how he *walked* next to me, seemed to welcome me to share in his delight at being kissed by Jamie. Here was the kid I'd seen making his happy rounds at the freshman carnival; the bright soul who'd entertained regular students in our dorm room all semester; the good heart who'd made such a lasting impression on Jesse during his visit to Brown. Brown—I was brimming with questions, hunting for the right moment to tell Reshawn I knew why he'd come to King.

—I couldn't believe it was you throwing Chase, he said. I thought—no offense, but I thought you were another drone. I mean, I always knew you were smart.

I'm not sure I believed this. But I was happy to hear him say it, regardless.

—But there are a lot of smart kids on the team, he continued. And they're the worst of the whole fucking bunch. Jimbo *knows* he's following the herd.

He laughed and started impersonating me at the bar, grabbing an invisible Chase's collar and slamming him to the ground. I can't tell you how much pleasure it gave me to have Reshawn impersonate something physically impressive *I* had done.

—Bam! he said. Chase's eyes all googly when he tried to sit up.

—What did he say to Henry?

Reshawn shook his head.

—I couldn't hear over the music.

We passed through a gap in the stone wall that bordered East Campus. The moon spilled light across the brown lawns. Reshawn impersonated me again.

—Bam! he laughed. That was the best hit of the whole season. I've fucking *hated* that kid since I met his ass back in January.

Here it was.

—Even more than his dad?

I didn't like watching the good energy drain out of Reshawn, and for a moment I contemplated leaving it alone. Knowing about the bribe hadn't changed my life in any important way, had it? But I could sense a possibility for a deeper connection with Reshawn; I just needed to push through the awkwardness.

—Don't know him, Reshawn said, and tried to change the subject. Did you see—

—I was outside the door at the Marriott. During our visit.

He stopped.

—You were fucking *eavesdropping*?

He was trying to intimidate me out of asking anything else. This would have worked before, but now I knew he was trying to cover his vulnerability with anger. I had the advantage.

—I didn't hear that much, I said. Only the part where you told McGerrin other schools were offering you more.

He watched me a moment, then continued walking.

—That's not how it happened.

—Then how?

—Why do you care? You want to blackmail me, too?

—Reshawn—

—*What?*

—Wouldn't everything be easier? Couldn't I—I don't know. Couldn't I help?

He laughed, which I thought was the final sign he wasn't going to say anything more. We reached the bottom of the main quad, and I was about to turn left, toward Stager Hall, wondering if I'd spoiled the first good moment I'd had with him. But then he said:

—Let's keep walking.

We turned right and walked to the far end of East Campus, where we joined the gravel jogging path that ran just inside the stone wall. Reshawn was quiet. I knew he was going to tell me his story, and I sensed that what had made him angry wasn't only that I knew his secret, it was also the idea that I was trying to coerce him into talking. So I think why we walked the next five minutes in silence was that Reshawn wanted to make it perfectly clear that he, and only he, was in control of the telling.

Finally he started to speak.

For the first half of high school, he had loved being the game's messiah and all the fanfare that came with it. His mailman carried a special bag for the dozens of handwritten letters coaches wrote him every week, the glossy school brochures, the personal testimonials from famous football alumni who wanted Reshawn to know their alma mater was the perfect fit. Ali had kept a scrapbook to hold the umpteen magazine articles and newspaper clippings, while Senior maintained a collection of VHSs on which he recorded every TV interview Reshawn gave. A simple walk through the Archerville mall would end with teenagers and grown men alike stopping him for autographs, photographs, recommendations-qua-interrogations for which programs he should consider. Growing up a black boy in Oregon had meant a childhood of unwanted stares, but now the attention seemed overwhelmingly of the good variety. The eyes no longer stopped at his skin but seemed to see right into the core of him, into his deepest, best self.

He had never given much thought to his schoolwork. He took easy classes he aced, and when his teachers told him he could be applying himself more, all he'd heard was that his brain was yet another of his preternatural muscles. Then, the summer before junior year, he contracted mononucleosis and was bed-bound for the better part of two months. It was the longest stretch he'd ever gone without playing some kind of sport, and the only thing he had the energy to do was read. First he read whatever was in the house, and when he tore through that, Ali started bringing home books from the library, novels she'd enjoyed when she was at Oregon State. He kicked the mono by late July and resumed training for the coming season, but to his parents' surprise the reading didn't stop. He said it was like a fever that replaced the fever. He read everywhere. During meals with his family. In between sets in the weight room. He was fascinated by how each book set its own borders, its own rules. One's idea of what made a book great, or even what a book could be about—this got reinvented every time you started a new volume. Freedom, is what I think he was getting at.

Junior season started and he noticed a strange new feeling while he played. It was as if his body was leading the rest of him around—like his body *wasn't* him but was in control of him. He hated the sensation, and he started to lose his taste for the attention he'd once adored, became impatient with people who asked for autographs, saw how rote the words were in the coaches' letters. He was close with his parents, always had been, and was honest about his sudden cooling toward football. When his junior season ended, they talked through his options and agreed he would play his senior year and start putting together college applications separate from football. If he still felt that inner distance by the end of next season, he would be allowed to quit the game and apply to schools as a regular student.

Ali and Senior made this promise because they believed they could afford it. Senior had a few years earlier opened branches of his sporting goods store in two more towns, while Ali, who had served as both comanager and bookkeeper for the original store, became so overwhelmed by the added business she brought in a woman named Diane to help manage their finances. But the next ten months saw twin disasters. Diane proved to be a crook who

siphoned money from the stores, and by the time the embezzle-
ment was discovered, all three business were in harrowing financial trouble. Diane fled to Canada. While the scandal consumed
the McCoys' lives, Ali hadn't thought to mention the strange tin-
gling she had started to experience in her right leg. When she finally got around to seeing a doctor, the family had already traded the
good private insurance they'd had for a much cheaper package, a
cost-cutting measure that they'd been forced to take as their businesses drowned, and that now made their medical costs astronom-
ical. Nor could they afford to get back on their old insurance, since
Ali's illness qualified as a preexisting condition.

By that fall there was no question Reshawn's passion for the
game was gone—and no question his family needed him to attend
college on scholarship, despite Ali and Senior's lukewarm assur-
ances that it was still up to him. He wanted Brown, yet felt he had
no choice but to visit the football juggernauts that had been recruiting him, places that, yes, had good academics but, more important, would put him in the best stead to play professionally.
Ali's medical bills would be rising every year, and he needed to
make whatever money he could for her by playing in the NFL.

Enter Coach Zeller, the newly crowned head coach of King
College, who came to Archerville High last December to make
what he knew was a long-shot pitch to the country's best recruit.
When Zeller arrived at the school that afternoon, Reshawn had
just returned from spending his lunch break at the physical thera-
pist with his mother, a session that had been especially horrible.
The PT had told Ali she would need help walking soon and would
eventually require a wheelchair. Reshawn was in a state when he
met with Zeller, and they hadn't been talking five minutes when
Reshawn broke down and told the King coach far more than he'd
admitted to any other recruiter—that he'd burned out of football,
that he needed the sport more than ever. Zeller encouraged Reshawn to get everything off his chest.

Later that week, an unmarked envelope was pushed through

the mail slot in the McCoys' front door, ten thousand dollars in cash. Coach Zeller called that evening and said there was only one string attached, and a thin one at that. In exchange for the money, he'd like Reshawn to take one of his official visits to King. The visit alone would boost King's profile, and if at the end of it Reshawn decided the school wasn't for him, he could consider the money a get-well gift. Nothing more.

Reshawn hadn't liked King, just as he'd hated all the other schools he'd officially visited, and he was planning on declining Zeller's offer at the end of the weekend. Zeller surmised as much during the meeting he and Reshawn had on the same Saturday morning I was offered, and the last thing he asked Reshawn was that, before he made a final decision, he meet with Mr. McGerrin, the source of the money. As arranged, Mr. McGerrin had stopped by our hotel room the next morning, and yet this visit was anything but rote. McGerrin marched into the Marriott room and told Reshawn that as far as *he* was concerned, the moment the McCoys deposited his money into their bank account Reshawn had accepted King's offer. By taking the bribe, Mr. McGerrin said, Reshawn had broken NCAA regulations, and if that came out, Reshawn wouldn't be eligible to get *any* kind of scholarship, not from any school. Reshawn saw he was trapped, and was convinced this had been the plan all along—that Coach Zeller would play the good cop and Mr. McGerrin the bad. But who meant what was moot, and in the meeting with Mr. McGerrin, Reshawn realized the only thing left to do was haggle for more money.

—Camp, Reshawn was saying now. Film. Yes sir. No sir. Pretending like the game *means* a goddamn thing to me. I'm used to that. I can kind of turn my brain off while the body does the work. But going to school here? Sometimes I wish I'd just gone to one of those big bullshit programs. Here the professors, classmates—everything's what I'd been wanting, but it's like I'm being held back from having it. Like this place is being kept just out of my fucking grasp and all I can do is stare.

By now we'd walked three full laps around East Campus. Sad as his story was, I noticed Reshawn had relaxed while he talked; he *had* gotten some relief from telling me his story. I'm not saying he was hanging his arm around my shoulders. I was still a teammate, after all, still someone who adored the game he loathed, and I could sense the hesitance he still felt around me, a skepticism about whether I could ever truly understand what he was saying.

I had my own reservations. The me that Reshawn had liked tonight, the player who'd been willing to break from the herd to stop Chase from bullying Henry, he was half fiction. Reshawn didn't know the real reason I'd thrown Chase, and I wasn't sure it would ever be safe to tell him.

What I'm saying is, we finished that night as allies, not friends.

# FOUR

Winter break was lonely and long—no childhood pals to catch up with, no old flames to rekindle, just solitary lifts in Sillitoe High's weight room, wind sprints up the hillside of a municipal park, and marathon viewings of bowl games on my parents' old corduroy couch. Every night at dinner Mom and Dad tried to make up for not visiting me at school by asking endless questions about it, and the difficulty I had in describing even the simplest events showed how the canyon gap that already existed between us when I left for college had only widened. But the main reason the visit was misery was Coach Johannsen. I'd been obsessing over the details of my encounter with Thao every day, every hour, every minute of the past month, feeling his whiskers on my cheek, his fingers squeezing my biceps, two kinds of touches I had never received from a man who wasn't father, coach, or teammate, two touches that brought me to climax even quicker than the picturesque jocks in my back issues of *Sports Illustrated*. But the vigor of my fantasies was matched by my guilt for indulging them, and all break long I was convinced I'd run into my old mentor—at the King Soopers or JCPenney, Sunday mass or the Chevron station—as if my sort-of violation of the pact we'd made would summon him so he could deem me unworthy of the game.

I didn't run into Johannsen, thank God, and by the first week of January I was speeding away from Sillitoe, heading east on I-70 and watching my rearview mirror for the moment the Rockies dissolved into the horizon. I drove straight through a day and a night again, and when I pulled into East Campus on a mild gray Sunday, it felt like I could take my first full breath in weeks.

I entered Stager Hall intending to sleep off the afternoon, and I was so woozy from the long drive that when I opened our unlocked door and stepped inside, it took me a beat to understand what I was looking at. A naked Jamie was sitting at the far end of Reshawn's bed, hands clutching the top sheet, nipples erect and ribcage coming in and out of view as she cycled shallow breaths. A naked Reshawn had his face sunk into her lap, back muscles working under his hairless skin as his ass cheeks puckered—

I slammed out of the room and hurried to the elevator bay, punching the button so hard it got stuck in the recessed position. I worried the two seconds I'd watched them had cost me all the goodwill I'd earned from Reshawn last semester.

—Hey!

Jamie's head poked out of our doorway. She held a bath towel against her body.

—That's okay! I said, punching the button again, *hating* how long this fucking elevator took.

She laughed.

—No! We'll be decent! Come baaaaaack!

The elevator dinged open. I sighed and let it close, slowly retracing my steps. When I walked into the room, Jamie and Reshawn had switched places: he was leaning his back against the headboard, wearing sweatpants and no shirt; she was leaning her back into his chest, nestling her butt into his crotch and laying her palms on his thighs, like you would the arms of a love seat. She was wearing King Football running shorts rolled up at the waist and one of Reshawn's long white tees.

—Good break? she asked me brightly.

—Sure.

—You're from Utah, right?

—Colorado.

Reshawn brought the back of his hand across his lips to see if anything was still on them. I was relieved to see his expression was more embarrassed than angry. Jamie, meanwhile, was neither. A senior who must have had practice shrugging off walk-ins, she carried on conversation as if sex-fug wasn't still hanging in the air.

—I was in Atlanta, she was saying about her own break. I grew up there.

—You don't have an accent.

—My parents are both from Brazil, she said. They got transferred to Coke's headquarters when I was little.

—She speaks fluent Portuguese, Reshawn added.

Jamie rolled her eyes, which Reshawn couldn't see.

—Just enough to get around. Anyway, *this* guy found out he gets to RA for Grayson . . . What are you taking this semester, Miles?

Another suite of joke classes I cared nothing about. I felt ashamed to admit this to serious students, and changed the subject back to what Jamie said.

—What's an RA?

—Research assistant, she said. Professor Grayson is the one who taught our folktales class last semester? Right. Well, his research is on this North Carolina poet, and he hires somebody to help him with database searches and logistics. I've been his RA the last two years, but now that I'm graduating, he needs someone to take over. I'll show Reshawn the ropes.

She squeezed his knees.

—Grayson is this *star* in American Lit. If I get into half the schools I applied to for my PhD, it'll because of his recommendation. Reshawn's going to have his pick of programs when he applies in three years.

Reshawn told me he was planning to play in the NFL for at least five years to make money for his mother's medical expenses, which would mean he wouldn't be applying to grad school for almost a decade. This alone made it clear he was keeping his reason for playing football secret from Jamie, but just to ensure I didn't contradict him now, he gave me a long, meaningful stare over the top of Jamie's head.

I stayed mum. She slept in Reshawn's bed that night, and the next morning the three of us rode to West Campus together for the first day of classes. In the players' lot Jamie broke off toward the English building for an independent study while Reshawn and I went to the Hay to retrieve our textbook vouchers from the team's academic advisor. We walked to the bookstore in the basement of West's Student Union, traveling from aisle to aisle. I didn't really need the plastic basket I was carrying, my courses required so few books, while Reshawn looked like someone on a shopping spree, his first basket full after just three shelves. He didn't comment on the disparity between our baskets, but I still felt like I was being judged for taking easy classes again.

We arrived at his last shelf, for a class called The *Other* Rebel Yells: Dissent in Antebellum America. The label said Professor Grayson was the instructor, and I impulsively took copies of the class's books.

—You sure? he asked. Grayson doesn't fuck around.
—Definitely.

The first lecture was that morning, and when we entered the classroom in the English building I wasn't feeling so definite. All four of my courses last semester had been in the college's biggest lecture halls, academic hangars that fit four hundred where I could happily disappear, but this was a seminar room that only seated fifteen. I wanted at least to sit in the back row, but Reshawn led us to the center of the front row.

And then there was Professor Grayson, who strode purposefully into the room and unloaded the contents of his leather satchel onto the wooden lectern without greeting Reshawn or anybody else. A grave-faced black man in his forties, Grayson was dressed in a beautiful houndstooth suit and a blue oxford shirt left open at the throat. A real professor, rather than one of the genial dupes King Football had cultivated to give its players passing grades. A man who commanded such respect that the room fell silent as soon as he raised his eyes from his lecture notes.

—You are born in 1830, he began in a low, level baritone. You are the property of one Jonathan King, gentleman planter. Master Jonathan is your sun. Your moon. Your stars. He is your *god,* just as he is the god of your mother, three older half brothers, and four younger sisters. He is the god that taketh away—when you are six, he sells your father to a man in Tidewater Virginia who needs a good buck for breeding.

—And what is it that god giveth? He gives you the *privilege* of being the playmate of his oldest son, Jedediah King. And as you grow older he gives you the *honor* of serving as the young master's valet, rather than working in the fields. You are quiet and you are obedient, with an unusually strong memory, and the year you turn nineteen you are allowed to walk with your young master the two miles to Blenheim, where Jedediah will begin training for the ministry at Triune College and you will be allowed to sell fruit on the college's campus. You make a pittance off the fruit. What you cherish about these days are the walks you take with Jedediah through virgin forests and along the edges of tobacco fields—walks in which you remain a few steps behind your master and listen to him practice for his classes by reciting passages from the Gospels, Aquinas's *Summa*, Milton, Coleridge, Wordsworth. And it is from listening to him that you discover you have a love for what you will later call "melodious meter."

—You do not know the meanings of the words you hear him recite, but you are resolved to learn them. You search the floors of open-air markets and the shoulders of roads for wordy trash, for ripped pages of spelling books and mud-stained glossaries. With these you cobble together a primer to teach yourself your ABCs. You prize above all anything with verse on it, and one of your dearest possessions will be a bloody page of newspaper used to wrap your master's mutton. Printed on it is Jaques's speech in *As You Like It*, "All the world's a stage." This will be the first verse you commit to memory.

—You stash these materials beneath your pallet in the slave quarters, and on Sabbath afternoons you use what few hours of free time you have to carry them to a lonesome spot under an ash tree. It is during these fugitive afternoons that you discover your memory is not just strong, it is prodigious, and in only four years' time you will go from teaching yourself your ABCs to composing original verses of your own. You must memorize whatever you compose, since it will be another decade before you learn how to write.

—At Triune, "pranking" slaves is a favorite pastime of the students. They trick slaves into accepting counterfeit coins in exchange for precious fruit; or they invite a pickaninny to take a bite out of what they insist is a delicacy but turns out to be prettily shaped offal. Most hilarious is to tease the black brain, and one day some friends of Jedediah hand you a love poem they have composed and ask you to judge its quality. You are expected to smile, shuffle, and stammer out your ignorance. But instead you stun them by reading the poem word for word, a spectacle one of the boys will later remark was "akin to watching a mule give a sermon." It is a violation of North Carolina state law to teach a slave to read, and what you have just done has gotten other slaves whipped, beaten, strung up. But Triune is a place of higher learning! And just as in the name of science you do not kill a dog with two heads—not immediately, at least—so too must a slave's freakish reading talent be humored.

—Your skull is measured by Triune scientists, your diction examined by a professor of rhetoric. You become known throughout the Piedmont as the Spouting Darkie, and soon the time you once spent selling fruit is occupied by reciting original poetry for undergrads. Students in search of a novelty for their sweethearts ask you to compose a poem. You charge a quarter, sometimes as much as a half dollar, for an original composition your customers transcribe. A few weeks after you turn twenty-five, a local newspaperman offers to publish your poetry. You will later write in an essay that the day you first saw your name in print—Carmichael Stewart King—was when you first felt the name truly belonged to you.

As students packed up, Grayson asked Reshawn to stay behind to discuss their research plan. I went to wait out in the hallway and found Jamie standing there—her independent study was a few rooms down.

—I was in Rebel Yells sophomore year, she said. Amazing, right?

Professor Grayson *was* amazing, but class wasn't what I wanted to discuss right now. This was my chance to ask about Thao without Reshawn present.

—What were the names of your friends I met last semester? At the bar?

It took her a moment.

—You mean Thao and Henry?

Breathe. Nod.

—Only Thao's my friend, she continued. To be honest, I've never gotten used to Henry. He can be a little . . . high strung. More than a little. He had another break in December.

—Doesn't everybody at King?

Jamie laughed.

—No, like a *psychotic* break. He had to go to McLean. He's out now, but Thao's taking the semester off to care for him in Massachusetts.

—Oh.

Disappointment was inseparable from relief.

The rest of my schedule remained as planned, three joke courses awash with teammates—including Chase. Now, though, Chase and I made sure to choose seats far apart, avoiding eye contact during lectures and keeping our distance as we filed out of the rooms.

I worried my rift with him would become a rift with the wider team, that the vets would take his side against mine. But I was safe—not just because a player drunkenly slamming another to the ground at Stefan Knows was far from unusual, but because many of my teammates were happy I'd done so. The first one to tell me as much was Cornelius Belkins, our starting Mike linebacker and Chase's roommate freshman year. Cornelius was born to two heroin addicts in Oakland who'd schlepped little him from one shelter to another until they were arrested for killing a store clerk during a botched armed robbery. Both were sentenced to life without parole when Cornelius was three, leaving him to bounce around aunts', uncles', and grandparents' houses, school to school, a strong-bodied, stronger-willed child who flipped from wary silence to destructive outbursts without warning. By nine he'd run out of relatives and was made a ward of the state, and his life would surely have gotten more difficult had it not been for the loving foster parents who adopted him. His new parents were social workers who moved him to Sacramento and enrolled him in an alternative school, an oasis of patience that taught Cornelius how to sequester his anger and use it only in sanctioned places, like the football field. His outbursts gradually subsided, and his quiet, watchful side gained the upper hand, so that by the end of high school he was captain of his football team and a speaker at graduation.

Radically self-sufficient, Cornelius was the worst possible match for the needy, spoiled Chase, and the two of them made horrendous freshman roommates. If anyone could tempt Cornelius into his old anger, it was Chase, and to prevent himself from backsliding Cornelius spent the majority of his first year in the East library, giving Chase and Sadie free rein to fuck, study, and watch movies on Chase's big-screen TV. The rare times Cornelius was in the room, he'd grit his teeth listening to Chase's passive-aggressive digs about Cornelius's habit of leaving wet towels on the back of his desk chair, or oblivious cavils about the souped-up truck Chase wanted to trade for a newer, even more expensive pickup.

By the end of that year Cornelius declared he would rather pitch a tent on the quad than room with Chase McGerrin again, and sophomore year the only person willing to live with Chase was our punter, Gunter Atkinson, and that only because Gunter had just transferred from the University of Richmond and didn't know what a nightmare Chase was. Gunter spent his first year at King listening to Chase argue on the phone with the girlfriend who'd transferred to Georgetown—often at one and three and five in the morning. Gunter told me he fantasized about smothering Chase with a pillow while the asshole was asleep, and come that spring he laughed in Chase's face when Chase asked if he wanted to room together again—as had everybody else in their class, which is how Chase came to pay the extra money to live alone in his Central apartment.

Learning all this might well have led me to feel for Chase, knowing his behavior was a compulsion he couldn't really control, knowing there was decency beneath all the posturing—*might* have, had it not been for the fact that, along with hearing these stories, I was also hearing the rumors he was spreading about me, such as the one that depicted me as a homesick little bitch during camp who had begged him to hold my hand while I cried in bed. So, no—no reconciliation, no forgiveness, only a resumption of our rivalry, which had higher stakes than ever now that Fade had graduated and we were competing for the starting Will linebacker spot.

My first order of business in beating out Chase was gaining weight, and as the spring semester got under way, breakfast and lunch and dinner ceased to be three separate meals and combined into a single, massive ordeal I shoveled down daily: fried eggs, slab bacon, link sausage, buttermilk pancakes, buttermilk biscuits, Belgian waffles, cheese grits, bacon ranch cheeseburgers, coconut chicken fingers, garlic knots, garlic fries, whole red velvet cakes, whole pecan pies. There were appetizers for my appetizers, snacks between snacks. My cholesterol shot through the roof and my bathroom visits became the stuff of horror films, but I was gaining another pound every couple weeks.

The next task was strength, and at team workouts I sacrificed my body upon the altar of my Body: bench press, incline press, decline press, military press, squats, cleans, hang cleans, dead lifts, biceps curls, lat pull-downs, triceps pull-downs, box jumps, suicides. My skin swelled so tight with angry muscle I felt at once like a water balloon and like the crazy-eyed kid who'd attached the balloon to a full-blast spigot, and I became so sore so perpetually that the act of rising from a chair in class, of climbing a solitary flight of stairs, of *sneezing* could leave me breathless. But, again, I was seeing progress: my lift maxes and vertical leaps rose, while my 40-yard-dash and shuttle times dropped.

And then there were the "fitness games," periodic strength contests that brought the coaching staff down from the fifth floor to watch. Our inaugural game fell on the last Friday of January. After my group finished its regular lift and conditioning, we were told to return to the weight room, grab two matching dumbbells weighing not less than forty pounds apiece, and form a circle that wound around the perimeter of the room. Like a train of circus elephants we were to march clockwise, doing a "lunge" every step. Lunging involves keeping your back straight and, weights hanging off each arm, touching alternate knees to the ground as you advance. But we noticed something troubling as we approached the rack to choose our weights: King Football had acquired a brand-new set of dumbbells, and the scored handles of the weights we were to pick up weren't yet worn smooth by hands. They appeared, in fact, to be made of a kind of metallic sandpaper.

—GO!

As we started lunging, I looked over at the floor-to-ceiling windows that formed the back wall of the weight room and saw every coach on staff watching us from the hallway, including

Coach Hightower's scowling self. The feeling of Hightower's eyes on my body seemed every bit as heavy as the two fifty-pound weights I was lugging forward. Knee-floor, up, knee-floor, up.

The dumbbell handles scraped back and forth against the thick calluses on my palms, creating blisters around the edges of the calluses. Sweat trailed down my fingers, making the handles slippery and forcing me to continuously re-grip—creating a second set of blisters on the insides of my thumbs' knuckles. My hamstrings went the way of cottage cheese. My forearms glowed hot orange. Knee-floor, up, knee-floor, up.

Fifteen minutes into the game a groan was torn from the throat of J1, and what followed was the sound we'd all been waiting for, the thud and ping of two dropped dumbbells knocking against each other. An invisible cord was cut—you could release your weights without the shame of being first.

But while several players immediately quit, I continued lunging. I passed J1, who stepped out of line and sucked air between clenched teeth as he examined the electric pink fissures that ran down his thumbs. Knee-floor, up, knee-floor, up. I thought about how you can't see wounds on black players as easily as you can on white players. Knee-floor, up, knee-floor, up. But when you *did* see them on black players, the wounds looked that much more horrible. Thud, thud, another player dropping out.

My blisters tore, sweat stinging the open wounds, and I soon lost track of who remained in the game, lost track of *anything* that fell outside my seared, aching body. I didn't notice that Chase had come up right behind me, and was caught completely unaware when, just as I was touching my right knee to the floor, he stepped on the heel of my left shoe so that when I rose the shoe slid halfway off my foot. I stopped, looking down at the shoe.

—The fuck, McGerrin?! Devonté yelled.

—Fuck you! Chase grunted, lunging past me.

Heckles from players who'd dropped out, calls for me to be allowed to set down my weights so I could reaffix my shoe. But

Chase knew what he was doing. If I set down the weights now, I'd lose the last of my momentum. The only choice I had was to keep going and hope my shoe remained mostly on my foot.

I resumed marching—slowly, precisely—and three minutes later I had the satisfaction of watching Chase kneel and fail to rise again, stuck in that position like an homage-paying knight. Knee-floor, up. Knee-floor, up. One by one, players continued to surrender, some with a bang of hastily dropped dumbbells, others with a whimper that got them mocked by players who'd already forgotten their own excruciations, until the only people remaining were me and Kendrick Slocum, our starting fullback and the odds-on favorite to win. Kendrick was a quiet, shuffling type from northern Louisiana, and his street outfit of choice was a pair of baggy jeans and a humongous white T-shirt, clothes he could disappear into. But beneath the loose wardrobe was a body that would have made Rodin proud: Kendrick's traps rose a good six inches above his collarbone, and his thighs were as muscle-marbled as what you see on thoroughbreds, while his triceps and biceps appeared flexed even when there was no way they could be. He was not merely the pound-for-pound strongest player on the team, he was the strongest in the absolute sense. I have no idea whether this was true, but word was Kendrick made walking-around money by modeling naked for anatomy classes at the medical school.

He was carrying two seventy-pound dumbbells to my fifties, and yet his steps were even, his tread light.

Knee-floor, up, knee-floor, up.

The handlebar steel grated across my weeping blisters. My grunting had started out as a he-man sound, but by now the grunts had become unselfconscious, were just how I was breathing.

Knee-floor, up, knee-floor, up.

By the time I reached the next straightaway, my whole body started to tremble. I clamped my cramping hands harder around the handles, knee-floor, but when I rose from this latest lunge, I took a slightly bad angle on my badly shod foot and felt the loose shoe crumple beneath me. The slightly bad angle was exacerbated into a majorly bad one by the weight in my hand, dragging my body rightward. I didn't want to let go of the weights. My left foot was slipping, my left foot would slide beneath my body and my shinbone would crack . . .

I dropped the weights and stumbled away. A cheer rose for Kendrick as he placidly set his dumbbells on the rubber floor. I stood looking at my fingers, which remained curled in the shape of the handles, my palms resembling haphazardly peeled fruit.

And yet I was elated. Players patted me on the back and congratulated me on finishing second despite Chase's sabotage. When I looked over at the bank of windows, Coach Hightower nodded from behind the glass.

In no time Reshawn and Jamie became an if-then couple—if one was present, then you could be sure the other was somewhere close. They slept together, ate together, walked hand-in-hand from class to class. Reshawn was forever carrying one of the theory books Jamie had loaned him, while she could be relied on to idly wander over to the shelf next to his desk and slide out a novel of his own. The sex was constant, which I knew because I would return to our room to find a little checkmark in the lower right-hand corner of our door's whiteboard, the signal Reshawn and I developed to stop me from walking in on them again.

Jamie's acceptance letters to grad programs began appearing in mid-February, and after a week in which she was accepted by Princeton, Northwestern, and UC-Berkeley she threw a celebratory party at her Carsonville house. Reshawn and I drove to her neighborhood together, and when we walked into the house, we found Jamie holding court on the banistered stairway that led up to the second floor. She was in a triumphant mood, and at the sight of Reshawn she quickly cat-footed down the stairs to plant a long kiss on her boyfriend. She took his hand and led us into the kitchen, retrieving a bottle of cheap chardonnay, a corkscrew, and three

Solo cups, and led us back to the funky (both senses) green couch in the living room. The couch was crammed with friends, senior English majors ababble about acceptances and wait-list notices.

One of these friends was Monique, a black girl who'd brought a box of Trivial Pursuit cards. We made up a game using the cards, taking turns asking each other questions from them and downing a slug of tequila whenever we got an answer wrong.

—What's narwhal tusk made of?

—What's Spain's most famous epic poem?

—What amphibian did Pliny the Elder suggest be tied to the jaw to make teeth firmer?

— Monique already asked that!

—Wait wait. What did she say?

We looked at Monique, who started laughing, looking up at the ceiling to avoid ruining her eye makeup.

—What Renaissance master sculpted the *Pietà*?

This one was for me.

—Um—

—Michelangelo, Reshawn jumped in.

—It's not your turn!

—It is now, Jamie said, reaching for another card. Okay, what US state has the lowest elevation at 60 feet?

—Delaware.

—Right! Okay, on what date in 44 BC was Julius Caesar assassinated?

—March fifteenth.

—What country did Rhodesia become?

—Zimbabwe.

—How many moons does Mercury have?

—None?

Jamie kissed Reshawn on the cheek

—I *told* you guys he's the smartest football player you'll ever meet.

Reshawn had been riding so high. Proud of his girlfriend,

delighted to share a couch with future leading lights of English scholarship. But now, though he continued smiling after Jamie made her compliment, I saw his eyes go dull.

Jamie didn't notice his change and read the next question.

—Okay, she said, easy one. What's Samuel Clemens's nom de plume?

Reshawn shrugged. She lowered her card and nudged him.

—You've got like *five* of his books in your room? Samuel. Clemens.

He shrugged again. Now Jamie couldn't help noticing the mood shift.

—What's wrong?

—Nothing.

—Samuel . . . Clemens . . .

—I heard you. I really don't know.

To preempt her from pushing anymore, Reshawn picked up the tequila bottle and took a shot. Jamie was still holding the card, at a loss.

The group became awkward, and after a few limp attempts at restarting the game, we stopped playing. Several people rose to refresh their drinks. Jamie finally sensed she'd done something wrong, and to make up for it she told us:

—Reshawn found something amazing this week.

He shrugged.

—It's not that big a deal.

—*I'll* tell them, then. He found this newspaper article about a mansion owned by Eula Bigmore, an old lady in Savannah. Eula is this *epic* hoarder. Every floor of her mansion is filled with junk, receipts from the fifties, a room with nothing but umbrellas. Dementia or something, and her younger sisters have been trying to move her to a nursing home for years. The only reason they haven't gotten a court order is because Eula's a millionaire and they don't want to endanger their places in the will. But a couple months ago the sisters got her to at least clean out her place, and that's how they found the old newspapers in the attic. *Thousands* from as far back as the 1870s, preserved beautifully. Turns out her father, and *his* father, were hoarders too. Reshawn learned the newspapers got donated to Savannah State, and he contacted a scholar there who he knew had coauthored some papers with Grayson before, see if the guy had discovered anything interesting. And he had—an essay by an ex-slave signed with the initials CSK.

—Your guy!

—Yes! Jamie said. Have you ever heard Professor Grayson laugh? I didn't think he knew how, but this week when he was telling me about Reshawn's discovery, he was like a giggly little kid. The three of us are driving down to Savannah next month to authenticate the essay.

—Can you do that? I asked Reshawn.

—It'll be fine, he said quickly.

—What—

—*Really,* he said, shutting me down. It's fine.

Attending that party meant I got to revisit the porch where Thao kissed me—a cumulative ten seconds walking over old wood that were enough to sustain fierce fantasies for the next week. The fantasies were alternate-reality branchings of the night back in November, and in them Thao's lips didn't meet my cheek but my own lips, and I didn't walk with Reshawn back to East but went inside the house with Thao, holding his hand as we entered a bedroom on the second floor, laying his lithe body onto a mattress, lifting the tanktop he'd worn at Stefan Knows and running my tongue around the nipples I'd seen flash out while he danced. Really, I told myself, it wasn't so bad he was gone—our brief encounter could remain unsullied by real-life sequels in which, say, he ran into me on the quad and failed to remember who I was, or I saw him in a café and pretended I didn't want to do to him the things I knew Reshawn was doing to Jamie.

Only the first week of the Rebel Yells course was dedicated to Carmichael Stewart King, and we had since moved on to other antebellum upstarts, Olaudah Equiano, Harriet Jacobs, Henry David Thoreau, Margaret Fuller. The content was as challenging as Reshawn said it would be, and rewarding for that—but what nudged me from respecting the class to outright loving it was the section on Walt Whitman.

> I see a beautiful gigantic swimmer swimming naked through
> the eddies of the sea,
> His brown hair lies close and even to his head, he strikes out
> with courageous arms, he urges himself with his legs.

It was a shock, reading this for a class; it seemed a miracle, a man publishing such language 150 years ago. My Whitman collection became the first textbook I read more from than I'd been assigned, and I tore through the collection's seven hundred pages in just three days.

I came upon a poem that is, on the face of it, one of the least remarkable things Whitman wrote, yet is the tenterhooks that have held me fast to the study of literature ever since.

> Lover divine and perfect Comrade,
> Waiting content, invisible yet, but certain,
> Be thou my God.
>
> Thou, thou, the Ideal Man
> Fair, able, beautiful, content, and loving,
> Complete in body and dilate in spirit,
> Be thou my God.

Thou was Thao, Thao-Thou. With that poem Whitman became a portal to my crush, and no matter how laughably unrelated a poem might have been to the King College junior who kissed me on the cheek, all of Whitman's words became imbued with the warm, pit-of-stomach sensation Thao made me feel last autumn. Thao-Thou, Thou-Thao—the simple act of *holding* the collection was enough to put me in a good mood.

—Yo, is Reshawn lookin' a little pale to you?

—Yeah, man. Shit is concerning.

I smiled but didn't look up at Devonté and Jimbo, who were teasing me as I sat on the floor in front of my locker, reading a last few lines before I dressed for morning workouts.

I throw myself upon your breast my father,
I cling to you so that you cannot unloose me,
I hold you so firm till you answer me something.

Kiss me my father,
Touch me with your lips as I touch those I love,
Breathe to me while I hold you close the secret of . . .

—The fuck is *this* faggot?

Chase snatched the book from my hands. The "faggot" he was referring to was the image of Walt on the cover of my paperback, a daguerreotype circa 1854. Walt is about thirty-five, with a shaggy beard and a roughhewn haircut in which his bangs are trimmed all the way up to his hairline but the sides hang loose over his ears. He wears a white smock whose left collar is flipped upward, as if badly ironed. His lips are sensuous and a little small, his eyes a pellucid color—blue, maybe gray-green—and stare at you with unapologetic frankness. The collar, the lips, the eyes come together in an almost disconcerting eroticism, which I presume is why Chase chose "faggot" to describe it.

—You're creasing the cover, I said, rising to take my book back.

He made a pouty face and ripped the cover off, tossing it at me like a Frisbee. I stepped forward to grab the rest of my book before he did more damage. As I reached for it, Chase dropped the book and swung his fist. The punch wasn't clean, more a chip than a punch, but his knuckle still struck the top of my cheekbone and it hurt like hell.

When Chase stepped up to punch me again I wrapped my arms around his knees and drove him back, upending him onto the purple carpet. I pinned him against the floor with my hips and jammed the heel of my hand under his chin, hearing his teeth clack. I wanted to keep pushing until his head popped off his neck, and I very well might have, had our cubemates not pulled me off.

Chase sat on the floor grinning at me, having finally gotten in a sucker punch to return the favor from Stefan Knows.

I could already feel the bruise forming. And yet I felt giddy, nearly victorious, as I stared back at him. No way could I have held my own had I not gained so much weight and strength.

Reshawn, Jamie, and Professor Grayson started their five-hour drive to Savannah after classes ended the second Friday of March. They had the whole weekend to authenticate the newspaper essay signed "CSK," and there was no question in my mind Reshawn had structured the trip such that he'd be back in time for Monday workouts. So when I didn't see him in the dorm room Sunday night, I thought he must have simply slept over at Jamie's. And when I found his locker undisturbed at 6:35 the next morning, I figured he would show up any minute. But twenty minutes passed and still there was no sign of him, and after another round of calls and text messages I gave up waiting and followed the rest of the players to the second floor where, in lieu of normal workouts, everyone would participate in a fitness game based out of the Terrarium.

The working image you've probably had of the Hay's second floor is a warren of hallways dotted by meeting-room doors. That's accurate enough, and all you need to do now is add one more room to your mind-map. Next to the staircase to the first floor was an enclosed, warehouse-sized space that featured a 50-yard field made of the artificial turf just then being popularized: green rubber blades molded to look like grass and ground-up black material simulating soil. A King Football alum before my time had nicknamed the room the Terrarium, and the term suited this place perfectly. It really did remind you of a gigantic version of the cages elementary school students use to house class pets.

While the players spread out on the Terrarium's turf to stretch, the strength and conditioning staff finished arranging five huge tractor tires along one end of the field and, at the other end, five steel sleds, each bearing two 45-pound weights and equipped with harnesses.

We finished our stretch and separated into groups of five. I was in the first group.

—Go!

Each of us flipped a tractor tire over and over, the length of the Terrarium. Next we were harnessed to the steel sleds and had to sprint back across the room dragging the sleds and their extra 90 pounds of weight. After that, we sprinted across the room once more and ran down the open staircase to the weight room, where we completed 25 unassisted pull-ups on the squat racks, 50 push-ups, and 100 sit-ups. For the last task—by now I felt like I was sweating blood and bleeding sweat—we picked up two 50-pound dumbbells and lugged them up the staircase, then lunged the weights the length of the Terrarium.

While the strength and conditioning coaches kept track of each runner's time, punching their stopwatches once we collapsed across the finish line, the rest of the coaches were again standing behind glass—this time a long window that looked into the room from the second-floor hallway. Coach Hightower nodded to signal his satisfaction with my performance, but the coach I was monitoring closely this morning was Coach Zeller. I held out hope the room was too chaotic for him to notice a single player missing, but that wasn't likely when the absent player was the most important on the whole damn team.

After Devonté led us in the team cheer, Coach Zeller stepped inside the Terrarium to ask me in front of everybody:

—Miles, where's your roommate?

—Not back yet, Coach.

—Back? From what?

—He went on a research trip with his professor.

—A research trip.

No interrogative edge, no question mark. It's like I'd handed my coach a dead pigeon and told him it was a live ostrich.

—Yes sir, I said, tense. He went to Savannah.

—He back today?

—Yes sir.

—When you see him, tell him he's got a stadium at six tomorrow mornin'.

I showered and crossed West Campus to the English Department. What had passed for winter in Blenheim was already in retreat. There was a sweet dampness in the air, and the oak branches on the main quad were knuckled with buds. I spotted Reshawn and Jamie approaching the English building from a different direction, each holding a coffee cup.

—The essay's real, Reshawn said in a rush, not giving me a chance to speak. It was—God, you should have come with us. . . . So there's this gap in what we know about CSK. He started publishing poems in the 1850s, but then around '57 the publications stopped, and there was nothing more until the '70s. We knew the war accounted for part of that, but not everything. The essay in the newspaper fills in the rest of the time.

The three of us walked into the English building.

—There was a young woman who lived in Blenheim, Mary Anne Wilmton. Her husband was a Triune professor, and they'd moved from Boston a year before CSK started publishing. Wilmton came from a family of abolitionists. She was more moderate, but still uncomfortable with the South. So she reads CSK's poems in the paper and seeks him out, and together they come up with a plan to publish a collection of his poetry, thinking they could use the subscription money to buy CSK's freedom. CSK starts composing at this amazing clip, thirty poems a week, with Wilmton transcribing, and they choose the best for the collection. Wilmton uses her network up north to sell subscriptions, and it's a success. By 1857 it looks like CSK can purchase his freedom.

—That's great, I said, dully.

—Jonathan King had died a few years earlier, Reshawn continued, and Jedediah inherited his slaves. By now Jedediah's famous for giving secessionist sermons around the state, and when CSK approaches him and says he wants to buy his freedom, King is furious. It would be humiliating if people learned the preacher promoting the dominance of the white race had been tricked by his own property. So King refuses to free CSK, saying the money CSK and Wilmton earned with subscriptions didn't account for all the time CSK had spent composing his poems. King says that *that* time equated to lost work hours that needed to be paid for, too. CSK could have just sold more subscriptions and paid off the extra money after another year, but to prevent that, Jedediah put him to work in the fields. CSK had spent his whole life doing indoor work, and going out to the fields almost killed him. He thought he could at least keep composing poetry, but when King caught him, he whipped him and said he'd kill him if it ever happened again. CSK returned to where he started, composing poems in his head, and he was still in Blenheim when the Union Army arrived in 1865. When Jedediah returned from the war and took over his father's tobacco business, CSK traveled north with a regiment to Trenton, where he started composing again.

We were standing outside the classroom. Reshawn was beaming.

—Zeller says you have a stadium tomorrow, I said.

—A what? Jamie asked.

—Nothing, Reshawn told her. Just football bullshit.

I could see that Jamie didn't like being put off, but she dropped it.

Spring ball started Friday, initiating four weeks of practices that would be capped by an intrasquad scrimmage called the Purple and Gold Game. Traditionally that scrimmage was even more sparsely attended than our regular-season contests, to the point where only our parents would be in the stands, plus maybe a few stray sunbathers. But this year Mr. McGerrin led a group of rich alums calling themselves the Crown Committee in sponsoring an all-out public relations campaign to boost attendance and more generally start regenerating King Football's fan base. A new AM radio show called "Talk to the Throne" was launched, and for two hours every week you could listen to Coach Zeller take calls about King Football and talk shop with guests about the coming season. Our stadium received a badly needed coat of whitewash; renovations began on the Hay's third floor to turn the level into an all-purpose football palace; and advertisements featuring an action shot of Reshawn appeared in wider Blenheim. Reshawn is in profile in the photo, running rightward in his purple game uniform. The ball is squeezed between his bulged forearm and biceps, his right leg is crooked and sweeping over the head of a diving defender, while his left leg is poised on the ball of his foot as he leans forward to take on the next, out-of-frame opponent, aka The Future.

There wasn't going to be an advertising campaign dedicated to me anytime soon, but I was still resolved to turn heads as we started spring practices. It was intoxicating to feel how much bigger my body was, how much more my biceps stretched the elastic bands on my practice jersey's sleeves, how differently my football pants contoured to my thighs and ass, how much better I could absorb the shocks of contact and how much more violently I delivered shocks of my own. My mental game was stronger, too. I had a grip on our defensive packages, a solid understanding of both the logic and the mechanics of good linebacking technique. The speed of the college game was still dizzying, but for now the key was to just throw myself into the maelstrom and knock the shit out of anyone who crossed my path.

One afternoon the second week of spring ball, the linebackers were settling into our seats in the linebackers room for film when Coach Hightower strolled in.

—McGerrin, he said. You get your head checked after Furling knocked you out at Stefan Knows?

For all the time we spent together, players and coaches fundamentally occupied separate worlds, and there could be a considerable delay when it came to a coach learning about something that happened among players. This explains how it had taken Hightower until the end of March to pick up on the enmity burning between Chase and me since the middle of November.

Chase's face reddened.

—He didn't knock me out, Coach.

—Ain't what I heard. Furling, you got anger issues?

—Sometimes, sir.

—Sometimes, Hightower repeated, doing his delighted shoulder shake as he turned off the lights.

From then on, Hightower took every opportunity to pour gas on the flames of our rivalry. And though I'm sure he told himself his heckling was equal opportunity, he bullied Chase far more than he did me. Evidently Hightower was still angry about Chase's debacle in last year's Purple and Gold Game.

—Hips *down*, McGerrin! *Furling* ain't playing like a fucking retard!

—God*damn* I bet your mama wishes she just went with the coat hanger.

During Team period, there was one phrase all second- and third-string players longed to hear from their position coaches: "Stay close." If a coach called out the magic words, you were to sprint over and stay clipped to his hip as he paced back and forth on the sideline, at the ready for the moment he grabbed you by the back of your jersey and shoved you onto the field to spell whatever player was ahead of you on the depth chart. By rights, Coach Hightower shouldn't have told me to stay close until Chase had gone through the majority of his reps with the starting defense— but Hightower was telling me to stay close from the very start of Team period, making it so that whenever Chase looked over at our coach he would also see me.

At first I thought this was no different from what Hightower had done in camp—that I was just being used as bait to motivate Chase. But Hightower's patience wore thinner every practice, and by the third week of spring ball he was regularly grabbing the back of my jersey to send me out to run with the ones. I would usually get only a snap or two before Chase replaced me. But when I returned to the sideline, Hightower would pat me on the helmet and say:

—Like what I'm seeing out there, son.

On Wednesday night of the last week of spring ball, Reshawn and I were sitting in the computer cluster in Stager Hall when Jamie called Reshawn's cell. He stepped out to take it, and fifteen minutes later he hurried back in, sitting at his desktop computer and opening the webpage for the Obituaries section of the *Savannah Morning News*. I read over his shoulder.

> **Eula "Lala" Bigmore** died April 2nd at the age of 75. She earned her undergraduate degree from Georgia Southern University and her JD from the University of Georgia School of Law. After graduation she went to work for her father at Peach Holdings, LLC, and following his death took over management of the real estate company. Eula was responsible for changing the company's focus to owning and managing low-income units, a decision that would make Peach Holdings one of the most profitable businesses of its kind in the Southeast. Eula never married and was fond of saying she was "wed to her past," as she had a great enthusiasm for collecting Bigmore family heirlooms and other relics. She is survived by her three younger sisters, Clyburne Holt (and husband Gary), Lucinda Smythe (and husband Moses), and Faye Anne Whiting (and husband Francisco), as well as nine nieces and nephews and eleven great-nieces and great-nephews. In lieu of flowers, donations may be made to the Georgia Historical Society.

Reshawn gave me the substance of Jamie's phone call. "Lala" turned out to be only one of Eula Bigmore's nicknames. Another was "Queen of the Slums," and the real insight of her decision to go into low-income housing was that there was tremendous money to be made building, buying, and running rathole housing developments with the help of state funding. She would keep those developments an inch above liveable so they could be rented by Savannah's poorest, and her company would evict many of those tenants with a ruthlessness born of the knowledge that Georgia state law fell squarely on the landlords' side. The profits she reaped allowed her to buy not only the grand Regency-style house where CSK's essay was discovered but houses in Savannah's historic Victorian District, Ardsley Park, and the Thunderbolt neighborhood, three additional mansions Lala had used as little more than annexes to store her idiosyncratic collection. Her younger sisters had had no idea about the other houses, and were now engaged in a battle over them—because, for all the maneuvering they'd done to remain in good stead for the will, and for all their big sister's legal acumen, Lala died intestate.

Jamie had called Reshawn from Palo Alto, where she was on a visit to Stanford's English Department, and before her call with Reshawn she'd been on the phone with Professor Grayson, who was himself away at a conference at the University of Texas. Lala's other estates were stuffed with old newspapers, letters, books privately published or long out of print, advertisements dating to the Civil War, and legal documents all the way back to when Georgia was a colonial dumping ground for criminals and the insane. But here the thrilling news came with the bad, as the fight between Lala's three sisters was putting the accessibility—indeed, even the continued existence—of many of those artifacts in doubt. Clyburne, the eldest of Lala's sisters, was in real estate herself and of the opinion that her older sister's belongings were so much junk cluttering what was really valuable, the mansions, and thus should be disposed of posthaste. On the other hand Lucinda, the next oldest, viewed those artifacts as assets that could make their departed sister's magnificently rich estate worth even more money, and she was of a mind to sell the artifacts to private collectors. Into this fray had stepped the Savannah State professor who'd made the original discovery, and he convinced Faye Anne, the youngest and most ambivalent of the sisters, that scholars should at least have a chance to look over everything and see what might be relevant for historical purposes. Faye Anne prevailed on her older sisters to give the Savannah State professor and his researchers access to the materials for a quick and dirty sifting-through, and the professor had called Grayson to ask for assistance. But, like I said, Grayson was away, as was his longest-serving research assistant, and the question Jamie had called Reshawn to pose was this: Could he drive to Savannah and sort through the materials, look for anything that might be of interest to the project? Reshawn answered yes, absolutely yes, he'd be on the road tomorrow evening.

It was as exciting an assignment as an aspiring scholar of American literature could hope to receive, not to mention the latest sign of the extraordinary trust Professor Grayson placed in Reshawn. We left the computer cluster and rode the elevator to our room, where Reshawn began packing a duffel bag.

—Can I borrow your car? he asked.

—What about spring ball?

—Don't worry, he said, not looking up. It's . . . when I agreed to come here, Zeller promised I could take whatever classes I wanted during the off-season.

Getting to take whatever classes he wanted and skipping one of the last days of spring ball didn't seem to align; but I'd never seen Reshawn this animated, and I knew better than to threaten his mood. And besides, if anyone was in a position to ask our head coach for a favor, it was Reshawn. He had put on six pounds of muscle and yet was somehow even faster than he'd been in the fall; he had mastered the offensive package to the point where Coach Donato, our new running backs coach, sometimes asked *Reshawn* for clarification on a package; and, in a nod to how completely he'd dominated spring ball, players had started calling Team Period "the McCoy Show."

Reshawn and I got to the Team Room early the next afternoon. As soon as Coach Zeller walked in, Reshawn popped out of his seat to explain the CSK discovery, so eager (and nervous) that he jumbled the story. Coach Zeller got the gist, though, and quizzically cocked his head.

—You bein' funny with me?

The pause that followed was torturous. I rose from my chair, thinking I should let them talk in private. But Devonté and a few other players arrived, making my departure moot. I sat back down.

—We don't have practice tomorrow, Coach.

—Still got meetings. And team lift. Spring game's *Saturday*, son.

—I know, Coach.

—On Sunday you can fly to fuckin' Timbuktu for all I care.

—But they need my help *now*. You promised I could take any class I wanted.

I could see Devonté and the other players were intrigued by the mention of a "promise." There was only one promise any D1 player could expect—a full scholarship in return for doing whatever the coaches ordered.

—No, son, Zeller said. *No*. You need to start thinkin' like a leader. A leader don't skip town just 'cause some biddy dies in Savannah.

—Coach—

—*Enough*, Reshawn.

That was that. When Jamie called at eleven that night and Reshawn said he couldn't go, I could hear her voice coming through Reshawn's earpiece, lecturing him on making promises he couldn't keep; on hurting their project by losing access to potentially groundbreaking materials; on making her look bad in the eyes of her mentor. And this is merely the part of the conversation

I heard. I'd been pretending to work at my desk while Reshawn was on the phone, and when he and Jamie began to get truly heated he put his hand over the mouthpiece and told me to go for a walk. *Told*, not asked, not requested or suggested. With that, Reshawn reverted to the angry, aloof asshole of old.

I tried not to hold it against him, knowing there was a sad subtext to all this. Jamie had loved Stanford and would be moving to Palo Alto for her graduate studies that fall.

My eyes snapped open just after daybreak. It was the second Saturday of April, but the dorm was already so warm we'd left our window open overnight. I lay in bed listening to the song of birds hopping around the blooming cherry branches down on the quad, the tired laughter of two security guards approaching the end of the night shift, the rumble of a wheeled trash can over a sidewalk. I tried to make myself fall back asleep, but it was no use. I was too nervous for the Purple and Gold Game.

The locker room was the same solemn place it was before any home game, with the key, thrilling, historic distinction that rather than me dressing in my civvies and trying not to envy too much the players around me, I was preparing to play myself. I dressed in my girdle and white game pants and went to the training room next door, hopping onto one of the high purple-cushioned chairs and not saying a word while I got my ankles taped, hypnotized by the expert swoops and loops and toothy tears. I returned to my locker and pulled on white knee socks, ensuring the stitching ran perfectly flush from ankle to patella, and then locked myself in a bathroom stall, where I sat atop the toilet lid and quietly recited an Our Father, a pregame ritual I had started back when I used to believe there was a God Who Art in Heaven and had continued long after the loss of my faith, still enjoying the rhythm of the words, the solace of speaking to myself in a narrow stall.

My routine's next stage was carefully lacing my cleats, but when I went to do so, I saw my shoes were missing from the bottom cubby space of my locker, where I always kept them. Maybe I'd just placed them in a different cubby yesterday? But those cubbies were already filled with my other shoes. Had I taken them back to the dorm? Of course not. We were fifteen minutes from Coach Zeller's pregame speech, and every second I failed to find my shoes, another layer of luck fell away.

Chase. He was sitting in his locker, tying on his own cleats and not-looking at me in a way that suggested he was only pretending he wasn't watching me freak out. It had taken me eight months to break in those cleats the way I liked them; if I were to wear my second, unused pair, I wouldn't get ten minutes into warm-ups before my feet developed blisters. He'd sabotaged me. Again.

I stomped over to his locker and looked over his shoulder into his locker's cubbies.

—You lost, retard?

—Where'd you put them?

—Put what? Your tampons?

—My *cleats*, you faggot.

The word just leapt out of my mouth. Chase was caught off guard, too, and was more surprised than angry when he responded:

—I don't have your shoes.

—Well, they *were* in my locker, I said, pointing back at it. And now they aren't. I'm not fucking around, Chase.

—And *I* don't have your fucking *cleats*!

—Yo, settle down.

This was Cornelius, whose locker was three spots down from mine and who'd been disturbed enough by our bickering to pause in writing ritualized runes onto his wrist tape. I admired Cornelius as much as I did anybody on the team and wouldn't dare disobey him. I stalked back to my locker and stewed, resigned to the new cleats. Just as I'd feared, they pinched my heels when I slid them on.

—Can't win anything fairly, I muttered.

—*What*, retard?

I looked directly at Chase.

—I said, you have to fucking *cheat* to get anything you want.

—Fuck you.

I was standing again.

—Couldn't get Sadie on the phone, Chasey? She tell you to fuck yourself again, *Chasey?*

Chase hurled his helmet at me, missing my head by inches. I rushed him, ready to punch him in the throat, but Cornelius stepped between us.

—Chill, Furling! Go dress in another cube . . . God *damn.*

I snatched my new cleats, shoulder pads, and helmet, walking past Chase, staring at him, daring him to hit me. But he didn't move, and I sat in an empty locker in a cube on the opposite side of the room, so furious I didn't acknowledge the jokes players were cracking about my newfound temper. I was thinking about Chase, not the game or my assignments, which is exactly what he must have wanted.

A minute before Zeller was to come in for the pre-scrimmage speech, Cyrus Pyle, the equipment manager, walked up to me. He was holding my shoes.

—I noticed they were down to the nubs, he said, handing them over.

They had new three-quarter-inch cleats screwed in. Embarrassment welled, but I pushed it back down, needing to regain focus.

I took Scan's hand and followed the line of other paired-up players down into the tunnel. The structure trembled as we waited to be introduced, the steel vibrating in a way it never had, and when we sprinted onto the game field we were met with a roar I hadn't expected to hear in Blenheim. The Crown Committee's advertising campaign had worked, and the lower third of the stadium, from one end of the horseshoe to the other, was filled with fans, some 12,000 people. That left two-thirds of the stadium empty, of course, but to me, dressed in full pads, blood still boiling from the locker room episode, it seemed like the entire world had come to see us play.

The scrimmage would proceed in phases, the one offense facing off against the one defense, then twos versus twos. The one defense stood in a huddle on our sideline, listening to last instructions from our defensive coordinator. I stood nearby and caught Chase looking at me—and at my cleats.

He ran out with the starting defense, and if he didn't play as poorly as he had last spring, he also was nowhere near his peak. "Mushy" is a good way to describe it. The ball would be snapped and he'd step into the gap he was supposed to fill, but he'd get stuck there and not make the tackle; or he would wrap up a ball carrier, but not well enough to bring him down by himself, having to wait for reinforcement defenders to finish the job.

—Remind me never to fuck with you, Jimbo said, standing next to me on the sideline. Bringing up Sadie was some cold shit.

Guilt tried staking another claim, but I wasn't going to let it, not now. I focused on Coach Hightower, who was growing impatient with Chase, pointing out to me all the things he was doing wrong. Chase mistakenly blitzed instead of dropping back into coverage, and Hightower had enough. He threw his call sheet into the air.

—Get his ass out!

There it was, the shove, and here I was, sprinting on the field, passing Chase as he dejectedly trotted to the sideline. I joined the defensive huddle and clasped hands with the starters, ducking my head to hear the call, and when the huddle broke I clapped so hard my palms stung.

I lined up, crouching into my stance, fingers suspended above my knees and wriggling like I was making nervous notes on an invisible piano.

The ball was snapped, the linemen rose in their stances, pass. I dropped back into coverage, head swiveling, telling myself to murder the first purple jersey that crossed my path . . . but the quarterback's protection broke down and he was sacked by Cornelius.

I wouldn't have admitted it, but I was grateful not to have been tested on the first play.

Call, clap, I lined up again, hamstrings springy and fresh as I crouched into my stance. Wheeler, the tight end, went into motion. I pointed and yelled, adjusting my alignment. I'd watched my idols point on TV as I was pointing, and though there was no need to yell I did so anyway—I knew Hightower *must* be watching me, must be nodding his head at how natural Miles looked out on the field.

The ball was snapped, the handoff went to Kendrick, the Adonis from the lunge game in the weight room that winter. I beat the pulling guard to the hole, and when I hit Kendrick the tackle was so hard the collision felt downright soft, and when I drove him into the grass my nostrils were flooded with a wonderful, nearly cloying scent.

I stood up in the April sunlight, listening to players on the sidelines call out:

—All right, Furling!

I returned to the huddle, scarcely able to hear the call over my heartbeat.

The point where the tunnel emptied onto the game field was a large arch with benches lining its top rim. On a good day last season there would be a handful of fans waiting to congratulate players, maybe a kid with a team T-shirt he was too shy to ask us to autograph. But following the Purple and Gold Game a heave of people were waiting, shoving arms between railings in the hope of high-fives, tossing balls to be autographed, the crowd swelling so dangerously the security guards caught a couple people by the backs of their shirts to save them from taking spills onto the running track below.

At least half those fans wore number 23 replica jerseys, and when Reshawn approached the tunnel, the security guards strained to contain the surge, the railings digging into their backs so many fans were reaching down to touch Reshawn, have him sign something, or just get a closer look at the genius who'd rushed 190 yards on thirteen carries. But Reshawn didn't look up when they called out to him, letting balls and programs and T-shirts rain onto the track as he disappeared inside. He was hurrying upstairs to shower, dress, and then hustle to catch the campus shuttle to Carsonville. Jamie had returned from California that morning.

I drove to the house around nine o'clock. By now all of Jamie's roommates had finalized their postgraduation plans—consulting firms, law schools, backpacking odysseys—and as a result the Carsonville house had become the site of a near-perpetual party. Two teams of drunk students were playing croquet on the front lawn, using rusted equipment someone had discovered in an old woodshed behind the house. The dark porch was constellated by the ghostly green glows of blocky Nokia phone screens and the orange ends of cigarettes, while the chains of the porch swing groaned under the weight of six people. The house's interior was even more hectic, with people resorting to sitting on coffee tables, in the deeply recessed wooden windowsills, on the stairs leading up to the second story. When I entered, Jamie was standing at the foot of the stairs, dressed in a fresh red T-shirt with the Stanford tree in the center.

—Where have you *been*? she asked me, wobbling.

So she could hug me, she placed the Solo cup with her beer on a chest of drawers next to the front door. But once she released me and went to retrieve her drink, she found two Solo cups standing side by side, each filled with beer. She shrugged and grabbed them both, handing one to me.

—Congratulations, I told her.

I raised my drink after we toasted and noticed a long strand of hair floating in it. I set the cup back on the chest.

—Let me ask you, she said after gulping her beer. Is there any law saying football players can't change schools?

—You mean transfer?

—*Transferring*. Is there?

—No. That's allowed.

Her eyes widened.

—I *told* him. Stanford would take him. They would. He *hates* this place, Miles. He says he doesn't, but *I* know.

—Okay.

—Okay! So that's the plan. You and me. We'll get him to come to Palo Alto, and all this *sadness*? Poof.

It was painful to realize how much more I knew about Reshawn than this girl who loved him, to see how good Reshawn remained at keeping his secret.

She led me into the kitchen to get another round of drinks, and there we found Reshawn talking to some girls near the refrigerator. Reshawn wasn't the sad boy Jamie had described—he was laughing, swaying, flirting, even drunker than Jamie. He saw us approach and arrayed Solo cups on the sink counter, pouring shots of Aristocrat vodka.

—To royalty! he said, and everyone repeated after him even though they didn't know what he was talking about. I couldn't tell whether he was he mocking them or himself.

Jamie left to use the bathroom, but after twenty minutes she still hadn't returned. The keg was dead, the fridge's alcohol raided, but Reshawn would not be denied. He rummaged in the cabinets until he found a tall brown bottle of something called Suze, an aperitif whose label was in French. He uncorked the bottle and passed it to me to sniff. The liqueur had a pleasantly strong scent of orange peel. He poured us each a shot, and it was only when Reshawn threw his back that we learned Suze is bitters.

I hustled him to a swinging door, through a mudroom stale with the smell of running shoes, and out onto a short flight of wooden steps built into the side of the house. He puked on a patch of ivy next to the stairs—once, twice, retching so hard he would wake up the next morning with burst blood vessels in both eyes.

Once he finished, we sat on the steps. We faced a tall wooden fence that separated this Victorian from the one next door.

—I'm taking an independent study with Grayson this summer, he slurred.

—See? I told you he wasn't mad about Savannah.

Reshawn shook his head.

—That was pretense. Pretext. Jamie being Jamie.

I didn't know what he meant. Reshawn pressed his thumb against his nostril and shot out a chunk of vomit lodged in his sinus cavities.

—She was right, he continued. We should have gotten that stuff from Eula's. I have this theory, Miles. I'm gonna tell it. Carmichael? A slave who teaches himself to *read*? There's no evidence, but I know it happened.

—"It"?

He looked at me, confused, then raised his eyebrows, remembering.

—We don't have anything saying he ever tried to escape. He was born here, in Blenheim.

Reshawn made his left hand into a kind of fin to mark the beginning of CSK's life.

—He died in Trenton.

He made a right fin-cum-gravestone.

—Blenheim, then he leaves with the Union Army. No mention, *none*, of him trying to escape. Not in the poetry, or the essays. But *I* know he did it. If he didn't already attempt before King time-tricked him, he *must* have after. I bet there's another essay out there, saying he did. You can't be him, in that world, and just . . . accept it. You gotta run.

After he puked a third time, I helped him inside. I led him past people sitting on the first staircase, then up another set of stairs from the second floor to the attic. The ceiling lowered dramatically. We entered Jamie's bedroom, which must have once been servants' quarters: The ceiling was sloped on both sides by the gable the room fell within, so that the only place we could stand up straight was the exact center of the room, where the two sides of the ceiling met. Every decoration was some form of King paraphernalia—King pennants pinned to the wall; photographs of Jamie and her friends in King College–branded picture frames; a quilt on her bed featuring a woven King Chapel. I laid Reshawn on the bed, and he was asleep before I removed his second shoe.

I was drunk enough myself that I held fast to the banisters as I descended the staircases. I walked outside toward my car, passing the abandoned croquet mallets, balls, and wickets. An old minivan pulled up in front of the house, the van's sliding side door banged open, and a surprising number of students spilled out, like a clown car, everyone heading toward the porch.

—Miles!

I dug the fingernail of my index finger into my thumb.

—Thao? he continued, prompting me.

—Yeah, I managed to say. I remember.

I had imagined this conversation countless times, and at this point in each fantasy Thao was already immobilized by my charm. Now I was just hoping I didn't puke on his Pumas.

—Jamie told me you're in Massachusetts, I said.

Thao gasped and looked himself up and down.

—I *am*? But then where are *you*?

It's not that he looked different from how I remembered him, it's that he hummed with the strangeness of being right there, in front of me. I loved his voice. Loved how it could sound at once so airy and strong, like lightweight metal that can support thousands of pounds. I didn't have a clever response to what he'd said.

—I guess I'm still mostly in Massachusetts, he continued. I'm just visiting for the weekend.

—Your friend's still sick?

—He is.

Thao didn't seem to be willing to expand on the subject. Say something, Miles.

—So what's this summer? I asked.

—What?

—I mean, what *are* you this summer?

Thao's face grew serious, and he said in a low, stern tone:

—Sir, I'm going to have to ask you to walk this line.

He pointed to one of the edges of the path. I stepped onto the border and closed my eyes, centering myself. Then I opened them and started to walk, finger on my nose, accessing what athleticism hadn't been shorted out by the alcohol. I stayed on the line ten straight steps, then turned around and managed the feat again as I walked back to him.

—Okay, he said. I'm going to let you off with a warning.

—Thank you, officer.

I couldn't believe I'd flirted like that. Now he was the one to get slightly shy, and I got a little more confident.

—What are you *doing* this summer? I finally succeeded saying.

—Summer school, he said. I need to catch up on credits I lost this semester.

—I'm here this summer, too.

He smiled. I smiled. The friends he'd arrived with were calling for him from the porch.

—Well, he said, squeezing my biceps. Maybe I'll see you around.

# FIVE

King College transformed into an immaculate husk. Sumptuous buildings went dark and manicured quads emptied as students departed for internships, jobs, and family vacations; professors and administrators migrated to conferences, field research, and retreats; clerical and maintenance staff were dismissed to work even worse-paying gigs until they were needed again in the fall. You would see the occasional grad student emerge from the stacks looking as stunned and pale as a surfaced deep-sea creature, or a group of ulcerous premeds worrying flash cards in advance of an Organic Chemistry quiz, but by and large what life there was on campus was athletes—football players staying in Blenheim all summer, taking classes and training for August's camp.

The only school housing available was on Central, and on a Sunday far hotter than a late-May day had any right to be, Reshawn and I lugged our stuff up three flights of an outdoor staircase and moved into a dim, spider-haunted, two-bedroom apartment. I was perfectly content to be here instead of Sillitoe, but Reshawn was sullen as he sweated up and down the stairs, clearly missing his newly ex-girlfriend. After final exams he had lived in the Carsonville house with Jamie until graduation, the idea being that without the stresses of football or class they could enjoy a sweet valediction. But they bickered most of the time, Jamie unwilling to drop the idea of Reshawn transferring to Stanford and Reshawn just as stubbornly insisting he had no interest in doing so.

I was surprised that he continued to keep the secret. Jamie was leaving King, after all, and telling her didn't seem to risk the secret spreading to the wrong people. But when I said as much to Reshawn, he just shrugged and asked what difference it would have made.

As it happened, the next morning we saw both of the men responsible for Reshawn's stubborn silence. We had finished our first team workout and were undressing in the locker room when Mr. McGerrin and Coach Zeller walked in with the fifteen members of King Football's newest class in tow. It was a historic group, universally considered our best-ever recruiting class. Each kid was at minimum a first-team All-State honoree, and several were All-Americans, their bodies so much bigger and brawnier than, say, those in my own freshman class that were it not for their baby fat and overcompensating coolness you would have thought they were seniors rather than pre-frosh. My teammates saw the recruiting coup as the latest sign of our program's steady ascent, not to mention yet another confirmation that our head coach was as talented a recruiter as he was a strategist. Though both things were undeniably true, I also knew Mr. McGerrin had played his own quiet, crucial role—some, if not most, of these players must have received extra enticements to commit to King.

Ironically, though, the best player among them was also the one recruit I knew for certain hadn't been bribed. He was the white kid standing at the head of the pack, six feet five inches of muscled lank, with buzzed hair the color of graphite and the whitest teeth I had ever seen. Errol Machen, a transfer student three years older than I was. He'd been the number two quarterback prospect in the nation my junior year of high school, and in contrast to Reshawn he'd lapped up the limelight during his prep days, glad to mug on magazine covers, comfortable chatting with reporters on postgame fields, happy to gossip with superfans during an ESPN-carried Signing Day ceremony in which he'd chosen Auburn over dozens of other top schools. But things had quickly gone downhill. When he arrived at Auburn, Errol went from being the savior of his team to just one of its many prophets, and his ego was ill equipped to handle the demotion. He threw water bottles and started fights, talked back to coaches and badmouthed his team to whatever reporter would listen. And yet even this was par among immature star recruits, and Errol rose to proper infamy only when, in the celebratory locker room following Auburn's bowl win that December, he had been so bitterly jealous of the starting quarterback that he shoved the QB in front of the whole team, claiming it should have been *him* out on the field. This starter, who had taken Errol's shit for the better part of four months, finally had enough and slammed the kid's face against a locker seat, breaking his nose.

By then Errol had burned so many bridges that players and coaches alike blamed him and only him for the fight, and he was dismissed for violating team rules. The football world gorged itself on the scandal for the next few weeks, while Errol and his parents, who owned a string of liquor stores in a suburb north of Los Angeles, publicly and repeatedly threatened to sue the school. The threats made Errol so non grata that no other elite D1 team was willing to take him on as a transfer, and he was forced to retreat to a junior college in southwestern Arkansas to wait until he was picked up by a program. The elite coaches continued to stay away, and his anger over this snub made him so petulant that even coaches from lower-rung programs, men who should have been delighted to take Errol, said no thanks as well. Months passed, National Signing Day was approaching, and Errol realized he was staring down the barrel of life in limbo for another year, if not of becoming a cautionary tale about football hubris that coaches use to admonish their coltish players. And so when Coach George Zeller from the King College Monarchs visited to preach the from-the-margins gospel he'd given me when I was recruited, Errol kept an open mind.

—Hold up a minute, fellas.

A dozen of us were heading for class when Coach Zeller beckoned. He and Errol were standing next to the locker room's Gatorade dispenser.

—Y'all meet Errol yet? Zeller asked.

—What's good, Errol said, lifting his chin.

Though Errol had been raised in an all-white suburb, he affected what he thought was a black pattern of speech. He came off sounding like a hill person from West Virginia.

—Errol's takin' French with y'all, Zeller said, and turned to Errol, patting him on the shoulder. These guys'll set you up.

We started across a dewy, steamy West Campus, heading for the Romance Languages Department. Reshawn hung toward the back, trying to avoid talking to Errol, but Errol found us anyway.

—Yo, you go to USC's summer camp? he asked Reshawn.

—Nope.

—I *swear* I saw you there senior year.

—Must have been some other black kid.

Errol's laugh was surprisingly high-pitched.

—McCoy's got jokes. . . . You sealed the deal for me coming here. I figured someone like *you's* at King? This place can fuckin' *win*.

Reshawn walked even more slowly. But Errol took no notice, enamored of being seen walking alongside Reshawn, the one player on our team he was willing to consider a peer. When Reshawn didn't give him help continuing the conversation, Errol just did it himself.

—Not gonna lie, he continued. I'm straight nervous 'bout these classes. At Auburn you didn't have to study for shit.

—You'll be fine, I said. Players take French every summer. It's the easiest language here.

That's why the other players and I had enrolled. But Reshawn was taking French on Professor Grayson's recommendation. It was a mark of Reshawn's esteem for Grayson that he agreed to take the class despite knowing it was to be filled entirely with football players.

Though my drunkenness had brought me dangerously close, when I saw Thao at Jamie's I'd managed to stop myself from asking for his phone number or where he was living that summer. I told myself to be grateful for at least that much self-control. King was a big place, three separate campuses, hundreds of buildings and thousands of rooms, and chances were that I wouldn't run into him, that I would reach the far side of these seventy days without temptation.

But fate intervened the second week of classes—or, to be more precise, Jamie. She and Reshawn still talked on the phone, and she was concerned about what he would do for companionship now that she was gone. Reshawn's friends had largely been hers, seniors who had graduated and left Blenheim, and she understood Reshawn was as isolated as he'd been at the start of freshman year. She had some younger friends, though, and in fact knew one who would be at King this summer. He had taken Professor Grayson's folktales class with Jamie and Reshawn the previous fall, one of the boys who had come dancing with them at Stefan Knows last November, the smart, generous, half-Vietnamese kid who Reshawn seemed to get along with and who could maybe serve as a conduit to another non-football group at King.

Friday night, Reshawn knocked on my door while I was doing French homework in bed.

—Do you remember Thao? he asked.

The top layer of my skin simmered. I kept my eyes on my textbook.

—Maybe?

—You met him at Stefan Knows. The gay kid.

He seemed to land especially hard on the *g* in "gay," but maybe I was overthinking it.

—Right, I said.

—He and his friends took over the place in Carsonville. He texted asking if we wanted to come to a party.

—Do you want to go?

Reshawn sighed.

—Isn't shit else to do around here.

The Carsonville house's windows were dark, and rather than enter through the front door we took a path around the side, passing the ivy patch Reshawn had vomited on. We entered a spacious backyard where a fire blazed in a pit dug into the grass, with a ring of mismatched lawn chairs around it. I spotted Thao. He sat on his haunches next to a red cooler, removing beers from a cardboard case and burying them in fast-melting ice.

He noticed us and walked over, wiping his wet hands on his khaki shorts. He leaned in to hug Reshawn hello, but Reshawn preempted this by sticking out his hand for an awkward handshake. If that was awkward, though, I'm not sure what word to use for how I said:

—I'm Miles. I think we met last fall.

Thao didn't miss a beat.

—I *thought* you looked familiar. I'm Thao.

We shook hands. His palm was cool from handling the beers.

Reshawn and I took two of the chairs and cracked open our Heinekens. We were introduced to six boys sitting around the fire, one of whom wore jean shorts that stopped high up his smooth, evidently shaved legs. Reshawn saw me see this boy and leaned over to whisper:

—We don't have to stay long.

I gave him a what-are-you-gonna-do shrug. Thao finished unloading the beers into the cooler and took the chair on the other side of Reshawn.

—Jamie told me Professor Grayson's thinking about adopting you, Reshawn.

—It's just an independent study.

—Riiight. I wish *I'd* found a mentor when I was a freshman. Do you mind?

Thao took out a pack of Marlboros. Reshawn shook his head and Thao lit up, cranking his head back and blowing smoke. His Adam's apple jutted wonderfully from his slender neck.

—Don't tell Jamie, Thao said, waving his cigarette. Bad habit I picked up in Massachusetts.

—We don't talk very often, Reshawn said.

—Oregon's not so far from California, you know.

Reshawn stood to get himself another beer. Thao looked over at me.

—So what about—sorry, what's your name again?

—Miles. What about me?

—Oh, I don't know. What are you going to declare?

Reshawn sat back down. I had started thinking I would study English too, but I didn't want to say so in front of Reshawn. It might seem like I was imitating him.

—I'm not sure.

—Have you taken any dance classes?

I smiled.

—No.

—Why's that funny? I had two football players in my class last year. They enrolled because they thought it'd be easy, but they ended up loving it. They said dance helped improve their balance. Kerry, what were their names?

Kerry was the boy with shaved legs.

—James and Phaedrus.

Reshawn and I looked at each other. Phaedrus was Fade, but James was . . .

—Jimbo, I said.

Thao laughed.

—Do all you people have nicknames?

—Not me, I said.

—I'm Cousin Shawn.

I looked at Reshawn. I had no idea he knew what Jimbo and the others called him. Thao waited for an explanation, but instead Reshawn excused himself to go to the bathroom.

Once Reshawn disappeared inside, Thao took his chair. Thao's right hand lay on his armrest, my left hand on mine, separated only by a few inches of warm night air.

—You'd think I invited him to an orgy, he whispered.

—He's okay. He's better than most players.

—Well, *that's* a high bar.

There was asperity here; he was referring to Chase and what happened at Stefan Knows.

—So you're in dance classes now? I said, trying to change the subject.

Thao flicked the butt of his cigarette into the fire and lit another. He didn't ask if I minded, which I found encouraging.

—One class and one internship, he said. I'm working for the Columbian Dance Festival. It's stapling, mostly, but they let me perform.

—I've never seen dance.

—Where are you from again?

—Colorado.

He tilted his head in condolence.

—Well, I'd be proud to break your cherry.

—Thao, *stop*, Kerry said from the other side of the circle. I can see that boy blushing all the way from here.

Thao leaned in toward me, peering into my face.

—*Are* you blushing?

—It's just the fire.

The group laughed. I had never allowed myself to imagine there might be a place like this at King. Or, I guess I had imagined such a place, but not that I could ever be present at it. I could have sat next to Thao, surrounded by the other boys, mesmerized by the fire, for the rest of my natural life. I wouldn't have needed food. I could have just lived off the occasional sip of cheap beer and the smell of Thao's Marlboros.

The porch door slammed. I looked up to find Reshawn standing over me.

—Ready? he asked.

"Skellie" was short for Skeleton and referred to a passing drill that pitted offensive players (quarterbacks, wide receivers, tight ends, and running backs) against defensive players (linebackers, cornerbacks, and safeties). It was an ideal drill for the summertime, since it required neither pads nor coaches—the second fact being especially pertinent, since the NCAA technically barred coaches from making us practice during this stretch of the off-season.

Errol ran with the one offense during our first Skellie. Though his athleticism was undeniable—he moved with a loping grace, and his throwing motion was simultaneously fluid and powerful—he was badly out of synch with receivers, lobbing gorgeous arching spirals that died useless deaths five steps ahead of the intended recipients, or bullets that bounced off hands unaccustomed to such drilling velocities. His grasp of the offensive package was shaky at best, and for every play he got right, there were three he flubbed, taking too many drop-back steps or too few, throwing to a receiver he thought was doing a button route who was actually running a hook. All the while he spoke aloud in a feverish stream of consciousness, castigating himself ("*Fuck*, Errol! Let's go!"), haranguing other players ("Gotta look that shit *in*!"), praising the rare successful play ("What I'm talkin' about, son!"), and then when the next play failed acting like all hope was lost ("God*damn* it, y'all!"). He was equal parts impressive and insufferable, but there was one unequivocal good thing about him—he loved being the leader.

In the shower stalls, Errol asked Devonté when the next scrimmage would be.

—Next Monday? Devonté guessed.

—Can't, Jimbo said. Got an Ethics exam.

—How about Tuesday?

—Nope, Cornelius said. Goin' with my girl to Wilmington.

—So let's do that shit tomorrow, Errol said. I need to get up to speed like a motherfucker.

Players laughed.

—And run the same plays we did today?

—Skellie gets *boring*, young.

—So what, Errol said. Y'all gonna be happy with another four-and-seven season?

I'm still astonished Errol had the gall to say this. He'd been on the team less than a month.

—Try speakin' on some shit you know, Cornelius said, grabbing his towel and heading back to the cube.

The other vets quietly finished up their own showers. Errol was embarrassed, but persisted.

—So ain't *nobody* tryin' to get better?

—I'll come, Chase said.

—Aight, McGerrin. That's what I'm talkin' 'bout. And I *know* my boy McCoy is ready to put in work.

Reshawn had been showering in a stall on the other end of the room. I didn't think he'd been paying attention, and was surprised to hear him say:

—Hell yeah! I can *never* practice enough. Same time tomorrow?

—*Hell* yeah! Errol said. There's a man who wants to win!

Jimbo and other vets exchanged uncertain glances. Was Reshawn making fun of Errol? Or was he being sincere?

—Fine, Jimbo said. But I'm serious. Summer's boring enough without having to run the same damn plays every afternoon.

Errol buttered up more volunteers as we dressed, then enlisted more in the weight room the next morning during workouts, and by that afternoon the offensive and defensive sidelines were full again. Coach Zeller and the other coaches came down from the Hay to watch us, standing at the edge of the practice fields and pretending like they'd just happened to be strolling here at the same exact time we were scrimmaging.

But Reshawn hadn't shown up. He had never intended to. Of *course* he'd been mocking Errol to his face.

• • •

The Blenheim Mall was state of the art when it opened in 1984, home to an indoor water park, three-theater cineplex, and upscale stores you couldn't find anywhere else south of the Mason-Dixon. Designed by a grad of King's architecture school and pitched to the city council as the panacea that would cure the city of its economic ills, the mall had inspired such optimism that the ribbon cutting was presided over by the Honorable Senator Jesse Helms and featured a taped message from none other than President Ronald Wilson Reagan. But the people of Blenheim would have needed jobs that paid enough to let them shop at those designer stores, while residents of the wider Piedmont would have needed easier access than a two-lane country highway bombed out with potholes, and over the last two decades the mall had devolved into an unwilling microcosm of Blenheim. The water park's reputation never recovered from an *E. coli* outbreak, the movie theater became a feeding ground for bedbugs, the high-end stores gave way to bargain-bin joints that gave way to military recruiting centers, and the parking lots grew so notorious for gang activity that Fade and Devonté were once detained by security guards for wearing team-issued clothing, purple being the color of Blenheim's biggest gang, the Diadems.

Yet it was still the only mall within a twenty-mile radius, the best available shopping option if you were, say, a seventeen-year-old who wanted to look extra nice for the first dance performance of his young life, and on the third Saturday of June I drove there to buy a pair of long jean shorts, a red-and-white-striped Tommy Hilfiger polo, and Old Spice cologne the color of a blue mai tai. I didn't want Reshawn to see me getting dressed up, so I drove straight from the mall to the Hay's locker room, shaving carefully at the bank of sinks next to the showers, nervously practicing witty repartee with myself in the mirror. A little before seven I crossed West Campus to an auditorium near the chapel and found a seat in the very last row, scanning the crowd to make sure Jimbo hadn't loved his dance class so much he'd decided to take in a summer performance.

The house lights dropped and a single lamp above the stage snapped on, casting a cone of light onto a floor mat. Thao stood directly beneath the lamp, dressed in black tights, no shoes, and no shirt, every twitching torso muscle, every smooth sinew hungrily delineated. I had been expecting something along the lines of the ballet I'd seen on television or in movies, *Swan Lake* or *The Nutcracker Suite*, but what I got was something far stranger, something that seemed the very antithesis of football's motion. Whereas a player's movements were concrete and linear, Thao's were abstract and proceeded with no discernible rhythm; whereas I was to keep my body as coiled and compact as I could, Thao's seemed to want nothing more than to stretch itself in all directions, to kiss and caress maximum space. In the middle of the performance he transitioned to dancing with an invisible partner, reminding me of players in pregame warm-ups; but rather than trying to fool or truck or flee the invisible, Thao coaxed it, desired it, embraced it. I could not get enough—of the irregular patter of his feet on the mat; of how, when he stepped into the light, he seemed to escape the darkness surrounding the stage; of how, when he retreated from the light and disappeared for a moment to chase after his partner, I held my breath until he reappeared.

At the end of the show Thao and the rest of the dancers grabbed their duffel bags from backstage and exited through the auditorium with the audience. I shuffled down my row to meet him in the aisle, running my hand through my hair, worrying I had put on too much cologne. Thao smiled and stepped into my row. I could smell the dried sweat on him.

—New shorts? he asked.

—No. Why?

He peeled the size sticker off my left pant leg. I had been *surrounded* by mirrors in the locker room and still somehow missed it. I wanted to evaporate, to run back to my car and drive it straight into the Atlantic. But then Thao did something wonderful. He folded the sticker in two and slid it into his shorts pocket, as if for safekeeping.

—I've never been to ballet, I said.

—You told me that already.

—Right.

—That's okay, I've never seen a football game.

The witty words I'd practiced in the mirror rose into my throat, but it felt like my pulse kept pounding them back down, like the hammer in whack-a-mole. Another dancer, a young straw-blonde woman who'd tied her hair into a hasty bun, was passing our aisle. Thao stopped her.

—Can you hold on to this? he said, handing her his duffel bag.

He led me outside, behind the auditorium, down a little hill and across a little campus road into the Alice M. King Gardens. We entered through the arboretum, taking a gravel path past trees with placards pinned to their trunks that gave the trees' common and Latin names. The gravel became flagstone and the landscape opened into a meadow adorned with frog-songed lily ponds, wooden trellises hung with gourd vines, lanes of cherry trees and rose bushes, Italianate fountains whose white marble figurines had taken on a bluish cast. We climbed a knoll and sat on its flat grassy top, looking down on a moon-dimed lake and the woods lining its shore.

Thao hugged his knees to his chest and caught me looking at his bubbles of bunched-up quad muscle.

—Does your family know? he asked.

I shook my head.

—Colorado, he said, stretching out the *a*.

—Colorado, I agreed, shortening the *a* the way most natives do.

—My dad was still a teenager when he fled Saigon. He got resettled in Saginaw. My mom was his caseworker, and they say they fell in love over failing to get him to pronounce the difference between "Saigon" and "Saginaw." She still works with refugees, and my dad opened an Asian grocery in Lansing. He's pretty— well, he's *really* fucking traditional. Sometimes it's like he never left Vietnam.

He took out a pack of cigarettes, lighting up. I was learning to love the smell of freshly ignited nicotine.

—They drove me here for freshman orientation. I'd decided I was going to be out at King, and I practiced what I was going to say the whole ride, this elaborate, passionate confession, like my big number. But we got here and I clammed up. Didn't say anything while we were moving in, or at dinner that night. They stopped by my dorm room the next morning to say goodbye. It was now or never, and so I blurted it out. I'm gay! My dad's face looked like a boiled tomato. He ranted for like twenty minutes, switching between English and Vietnamese, saying he was going to stop payments on my tuition, I was a disgrace, he didn't have a daughter he had a *son*, blah blah *blah*. Mom kept tugging at my dad's shirt cuff, telling him to lower his voice. They left without hugging me, and it became this saga the rest of the year. My dad didn't follow through on his threat, but I still try not to go home. Every time I do, there's another girl he wants me to meet.

He tried to blow a smoke ring, but it just came out like a bad cloud.

—Your turn, he said.

What was there to say about my own parents? When I'd been home between spring semester and summer, Dad had made a crack about King's cheerleaders and Mom invited our church's priest over for dinner, the same man who the previous Sunday had focused his sermon on the brain-busting hypothetical of whether any of us would be here if Abraham had married another Abraham instead of Sarah. Mom and Dad were hopeless, and I loved them, and I assumed it would always be thus. But Coach Johannsen and the promise I'd made to him, that was different, that didn't feel static or settled one bit, and "talk" doesn't do justice to the speed of the words that gushed out of me as I told Thao about my old mentor and the promise he'd extracted.

Thao lowered his cigarette while he listened, not once taking his eyes off me. His Marlboro was more ash than tobacco by the time I finished.

—*Fuck* Coach Johannsen, he said—which maybe doesn't sound like the most eloquent response but was precisely what I needed to hear.

The ash fell from Thao's cigarette and landed on the tip of his right shoe. I reached down to brush it off, then kept my hand on Thao's foot and, heart juddering, slid my palm over his bare ankle, up his bare shin bone, working against the grain of his fine black leg hairs. Now it rested on the quad muscle, my thumb pressing into his taut, responsive flesh. The only way I managed to do any of this was by keeping my eyes on my hand, and Thao brought his thumb under my chin to raise my face to look at him. He slid his other hand around the back of my slightly sweaty head and brought his lips to mine. His tongue was stale from the cigarettes, but then again my mouth was cotton-dry from my nervousness, and soon his saliva became my own and the staleness became anything but.

My hand had been resting on his quad, and I slid it down the inside of his thigh to his crotch, but he caught me by the wrist and pulled his face back.

—Sloooow down, he said. Buy a girl a meal first.

—Are you hungry now?

He laughed.

—We should go. The gardens supposedly close at dusk.

We stood, and he reached his hand into his pants to tuck away his erection. He looked down at my shorts and saw I needed the same thing. He bit his lip and stepped up, plunging his hand into my shorts, maneuvering my cock to twelve o'clock. I'm shocked I didn't come in his hand.

—The festival ends on Thursday, he said. How's Friday?

—Friday is . . . Friday.

—No truer words have *ever* been spoken.

We padded back down the knoll and returned to the arboretum path. I wanted to hold his hand, but I was happy enough with the music of our shoes on the gravel.

. . .

185

—So she smiles and I turn to Chase, like ask him with my eyes and shit, "Did she just say what I think she did?" And Chase is so sauced he straight up turns to *her* and says, "You sayin' you want us to run a train?"

—Buuuuuullshit.

Errol held his hand over his heart, looking to Chase for back-up.

—It's true, Chase said.

—All right, so what did *she* say?

—What did she say. Bitch looks me straight in the eye and goes, "All aboard."

Players leaned back in their swivel chairs, laughing, embarrassed.

—The whole damn campus is in a pussy *drought*, Errol continued. So I'm tellin' myself, share what wealth there is, son. But then I thought about what that shit actually requires. I'm fuckin' her from behind, *while* I'm looking at Chase getting blown? I just couldn't do it. I told her that and thought the deal was off. But this girl was a slut, yo. Bitch shrugged and said we could both still hit it. I went first, Chase after.

—McGerrin, you took sloppy seconds?!

—*You* get any pussy last night, O'Connor?

We were sitting in a lab in the basement of Romance Languages, a windowless space that resembled a telemarketing center. There was a carrel for each student, and each carrel was outfitted with a desk and desk chair, a desktop computer on which to take our exams, a headset for listening to verbal sections, and high walls on either side to prevent us from seeing others' work. Mademoiselle Carter arrived just before the exam was set to begin. She was a young lecturer in the department and the crush of many teammates, with honey-brown hair she wore in a long braid down her back and a predilection for summer-battling tank tops and form-flattering skirts. She said *bonjour* and handed out sheets of scrap paper for us to use when, for example, we wanted to outline an essay. The clock turned to two, and we logged on to our computers to begin the test.

Reshawn and I sat in neighboring carrels. As always, he finished his exam first and exited the lab. I finished second, about ten minutes later. Walking out, I passed Errol and noticed he was looking through the contents of a little blue cloth pencil case he'd brought with him.

Reshawn waited for me in the quad's spongy heat. We started for the Hay.

—Did you see Errol's pencil case? he asked. He had a slip of paper in there with vocab words.

I shrugged.

—It's not like he's the only player who cheats.

—That's not the point.

He didn't elaborate what "the point" was and fell quiet for the rest of the walk. I noticed he was doing this more lately, falling into unexpected silences, and when he resumed talking, what he said wouldn't necessarily bear any relation to whatever he'd broken off saying.

We reached the players' parking lot and I handed him my car keys—he was taking my Saturn back to the apartment, and I was heading to the locker room to dress for Skellie. We were about to part ways when he said:

—"Sealing the deal."

—What?

—Those posters they have with my picture on it. It's like they're using me for bait. Fucking *bait*. And if I was bait for Errol, what kind of player do you think Errol's going to be used as bait for? We could have a whole *team* of Errols by junior year. I heard Errol's dad used to feature him in TV ads for his liquor stores when Errol was in high school.

—What's that got to do with anything?

Reshawn didn't seem to know, either.

—I just can't, Miles. I can't.

—Can't *what*? Are you okay?

He didn't answer and walked to my car.

I entered the Hay. We had forty-five minutes before Skellie, and as usual I went to the training room. It was quieter than the locker room, and I could lie on my stomach on one of the large cushioned examining tables with my French textbook propped in front of me and get a head start on homework.

—What's good, Furling?

Errol was one of those athletes who needs something to be on the verge of escaping his hands at all times in order to remain moored to the earth, whether that was a football he spun on the tip of his index finger or a tennis ball he kept in his backpack so he could fidget with it during class. Now, before he could settle onto the table next to mine and continue talking, he had to search the drawers built into the table's underside for something to play with. He found a dense little blue rubber ball that players used to work out plantar fasciitis. He sat on the edge of the table and tossed the ball from hand to hand.

—You think Mademoiselle Carter has a boyfriend?

Errol used his normal voice whenever it was just the two of us.

—No idea, I said.

—She is pretty as hell. Thinking I'll ask her out after finals.

He lost control of the ball and it bounced across my textbook. I caught it before it fell, tossed it back.

—Probably shouldn't hold my breath about McCoy coming today, huh? he asked, fidgeting with the ball again.

—Probably not.

—I mean, I get it. Reshawn's a competitor. Doesn't like someone like me rolling in and threatening his touches. That's how I used to think. *Everybody* was a threat. *Everybody* wanted something that belonged to *me*. But that kind of thinking got me in all the bullshit down at Auburn. It only ends up burning you. McCoy and me can *help* each other, you know? Become a dynamic duo. Motherfuckers won't know *where* the ball's going.

He stopped tossing the ball, squeezing it with his right hand.

—Look, he said. I know you're cool with McCoy. Just tell him I'm here to help him. All right?

—All right.

—*Cool*, he said, hopping off the table and patting me on the back. Good lookin' out, Furling.

When Thao suggested we get something to eat on Friday, I assumed he meant for dinner, and I spent my free time over the next days creating a dossier on off-campus places we could safely visit, restaurants on the outskirts of Blenheim or neighboring towns where I knew my teammates wouldn't show up. But then Thao texted saying to meet him for lunch at the Stone Grill, a restaurant in one of the long, low Gothic buildings that flanked the King Chapel, in the dead center of West Campus. I hated the idea, but I was so nervous about displeasing him and blowing my first, maybe *only* shot at having something like a boyfriend that I didn't dare suggest a different time or place. It was fine, I told myself. It was just lunch.

I drove to West early on Friday, and despite the unrelenting heat I took a long walk around campus to work out my nerves. A group of Japanese high schoolers strolled on a flagstone sidewalk cutting across the main quad, all the girls wearing long-visored caps, long-sleeved shirts, and cotton pants to protect their skin. Another group of tourists, speaking French, were standing around the base of an oak tree and photographing a squirrel that had climbed halfway up the trunk. I picked up every fourth word they said, enough to glean they were either commending the squirrel for its bravery or saying it was holding a stick. I walked, and walked, dark sweat stains spreading on my short-sleeved collared shirt.

The Stone Grill had two entrances, a main door that faced the quad and a second, less-frequented door in back. I entered the second entrance and saw Thao already waiting for me, his chair facing the front. He wore a white cotton shirt in the same style as mine and was pulling at the armpits, tenting them and trying to cool off. Really, this place couldn't have been a better choice, empty save for a professor sitting alone in a booth and a waitress leaning languidly against the hostess's podium. But in that moment the emptiness seemed a guarantee that, the second I sat down, a crowd of my teammates would come rumbling in. I couldn't do it, and left the way I came.

I could have lied and claimed some emergency prevented me from showing, and yet a big part of what made that night in the gardens so seismic was the honesty Thao had drawn out of me. I wanted to be honest with him about everything, and I forced myself to text and admit I had freaked out, the Stone Grill was just too public—could we meet tonight instead? He texted back with a single word, "Sure," that I tried not to read too much into.

On my way to Carsonville that evening, I stopped at a little market and bought a yellow rose the woman behind the counter told me would "make her very happy." Walking to my car, I half-consciously snapped off the thorns—laying my thumb widthwise across a thorn, careful not to prick myself, feeling a click calmer every time I made another clean break.

Thao waited on the front porch's swing. The night was even hotter than the day had been. He smiled at the rose.

—I think there's a vase in the kitchen.

Inside, his roommates were playing a board game in the living room. Their voices lowered when we passed, and they clocked me in a way that made it clear they knew what I was doing here, why Thao was holding a rose.

He searched the cabinets above and below the kitchen counter. When he couldn't find a vase, he filled a glass pitcher halfway and placed the rose in it. The dark green stem was speckled with the lighter green wounds I'd made.

We returned to the front porch and sat on the swing.

—You know I wasn't going to suck you off in the middle of that restaurant, he said.

—I know. I'm sorry.

I reached over to take his hand. He let me do it, but he didn't apply much pressure back.

—I like you, Miles.

—Me too, I said too quickly.

He released my hand to dig a pack of cigarettes out of his pocket. He lit up. I waited for him to take my hand again.

—I really do, he said. But I don't need a boyfriend who can't sit in a restaurant with me for lunch.

—Was that like a test, asking me to meet you there?

—You're not listening.

I was confused, clammy. He saw this and put his hand on my knee, lightly, anonymously.

—We can be friends, he said. I *want* to be your friend, Miles. I'm not the only gay boy at King.

—But I don't want anybody else.

—I—, he began.

And then he saw my face.

— Oh, sweetheart, don't cry.


A row of stationary bikes stood against one of the shorter walls of the weight room. The bikes were technically intended for walking woundeds who weren't allowed to run and needed some form of cardio, but they were used primarily by Coach Zeller and his assistants. While the coaches sweated and pedaled, they would bullshit with players they were fond of and stare hard at the slackers, taking micro-measurements of the temperature of the team and, when necessary, making interventions to adjust it.

Zeller was riding one of those bikes on Monday morning when we walked in for team lift. He was already deep into his workout and raining sweat onto the rubber mats under the bike.

—Mornin'! he said as we split up for our stations.

—Mornin', Coach.

—Heard you got after it Saturday night, Jimbo.

—Lies, Coach. You know I was home doing needlepoint.

—Mm-hmm. Kendrick, how's your daddy?

—Good, sir.

—You tell him I'm prayin' for him, hear?

—Yes sir.

Coach Zeller looked at Reshawn and watched him a moment.

—Hey there, Reshawn.

—Hey, Coach.

—What you up to this afternoon?

Players sliding weights onto their universal bars glanced at Reshawn. By now it was public knowledge that Reshawn had skipped every scrimmage since he'd blown off Errol the month before. The latest Skellie was scheduled for three o'clock today.

—My professor's giving a talk in Chapel Hill.

—Talk? Zeller said. Like a presentation?

—Yes sir.

—That a part of your class?

—It's . . . no.

—Well, good. Then he won't mind if you come to Skellie instead.

—I thought Skellie was voluntary.

—Sure is. But so's that talk, from the sound of it.

—You're saying I have to go?

Zeller laughed, pinching the sweat from his eyes.

—Time is yours, Reshawn! NCAA says so. But I know your teammates sure would appreciate one of their leaders showing up to a team activity.

The talk in Chapel Hill meant more to Reshawn than he let on. Professor Grayson was presenting a paper on CSK that Reshawn had been helping him with all summer. Reshawn was listed as coauthor, the first academic citation he ever received. But he knew that Zeller was still sore over his incredible request to skip a spring practice to drive to Savannah, a soreness that hadn't been alleviated one bit by his conspicuous refusal to attend Skellie. Despite Zeller's lighthearted tone now, it was clear our coach was at the far edge of his patience, and Reshawn knew better than to risk finding out what awaited him beyond that edge. So he responded with a sullen "Yes sir" and finished sliding weights onto his universal bar.

Come 2:45 that afternoon, Reshawn was back in the Hay with the rest of us, dressing for Skellie. He was quiet as we walked down to the practice fields, quiet as we stretched.

Errol was stretching near Reshawn. He saw Reshawn's face and tried to cheer him up.

—McCoy, he said. What's that talk in Chapel Hill about?

—Hermeneutics.

It wasn't really. Reshawn had just reached for the most abstruse word he could think of to baffle Errol.

—Herman Who? Errol said.

—You wouldn't understand even if I explained it.

Players yelled out, "Ohhh!" and waited to see what Errol would say.

—Shit, Errol said, laughing drily. I guess that's my bad.

—What's your "bad"? Reshawn said.

—Huh?

—What do you mean by that phrase?

—It means . . . it means I'm sorry.

—Then why didn't you say, "I'm sorry"? Why'd you say it was your "bad"?

—Look—

—You from Compton, Errol? Inglewood?

—LA.

—LA like the *city*?

—Huh?

—*Huh?* You say that a lot, don't you, you fucking retard. Maybe when I need something from you I should call out "Huh!" and your dumb ass will—

—*McCoy*, Devonté said. Be easy, man.

The ones lined up for the first play. What added insult to injury about Reshawn's being pressured to attend was that tailbacks had a minimal role during Skellie. Like I said, the drill was geared toward the passing game, and the most Reshawn would be doing was run little routes and then stand idle in the near field while passes sailed to wide receivers and tight ends. Which is why, when the ball was hiked and Reshawn ran a button route, he didn't expect the pass. But Errol didn't even glance at other receivers before he threw Reshawn the ball. No, not threw, *launched*, and not at Reshawn's chest, either, but straight at his face. Reshawn was lucky he got his hands up in time to punch the ball away, or it would have broken his nose.

Huddle, clap, another short throw to Reshawn. This was somehow harder than the first, and low this time, drilling straight toward Reshawn's balls. Had Reshawn missed the catch, he'd have fallen groaning to the grass.

Errol threw to Reshawn every other play that scrimmage, and he made each throw a little more unwieldy than the one before. On top of the difficulty of wrangling the ball, you have to appreciate how painful this was for Reshawn. He didn't wear gloves, and his bare hands were nowhere near accustomed to catching Errol's blazing passes.

But he caught them, and I and the rest of the players watched in queasy suspense as Errol threw to Reshawn again and again, hurling balls at Reshawn's eyes, his crotch, at the dead center of his sternum.

Incredibly, we were only now reaching the hottest days of summer. The last week of July topped out at a skin-bubbling 105, while the nights never dropped below 90. Heat that made the blacktop gummy, that turned my Saturn's pleather steering wheel into a torture device, that kept Blenheim children in swimming suits all hours and killed four nursing home residents when the building's central air failed.

If I wasn't in workouts or in class I was back in our apartment, shades drawn and AC cranked, an icy cave where I sat in bed and lamented my stalled relationship with Thao. We had been trading text messages since that night on the porch, half-flirty things I both relished and dreaded receiving. He invited me over, but I was unsure I wanted to spend time with him if we were only going to be friends, unsure I could stand to look at him, smell him, if that's all I'd ever be allowed to do. I tried telling myself I was lucky, that I had dodged yet another bullet. I had been cycling in with Chase for starting Will all summer in Skellie and was looking forward to a camp in which I stood a real chance of becoming the one for my first season. But this gave me less consolation than I would have expected.

By the time the heat relented on Sunday, I was more than ready to escape the apartment, and when Thao invited me to come over yet again, I forced myself to go. Final exams were Monday, camp started Tuesday, and as painful as I knew it would be to see Thao, I liked even less the prospect of not seeing him again until fall semester.

We sat in his kitchen, an AC unit droning from the window above the sink. The de-thorned rose I'd bought was still there, dried out and sitting in the vase Thao had finally found. He poured two glasses of cheap white wine, took a sip, and winced. To make the stuff drinkable, he chopped up some watermelon from the fridge and mashed the fruit at the bottom of our glasses.

—Jamie said you asked about me last semester, he said.

—She did?

—Don't worry. She knows not to say anything to Reshawn.

He was right that that's where my thoughts immediately went, and there was a slight edge in his voice, suggesting that this, here, was why we couldn't be together. I could feel him pulling away, that we were reverting to being strangers, and to try and stop this slide I said:

—Did you know Walt Whitman wrote a poem about you?

—Oh?

—"Thou the ideal man. Fair, able, beautiful, content, and loving. Complete in body and dilate in spirit."

The next part was "Be thou my God," but I didn't think it wise to recite that. Thao smiled.

—He recites poetry, too. What's the last part again?

—"Complete in body and dilate in spirit."

The front door opened, and we listened to two boys walk inside, laughing. They hurried up the stairs to one of the bedrooms on the second level, steps reverberating loudly on the house's wood floors.

—What do you like about me? Thao asked.

—Your knees, I said, trying to flirt.

—What else?

—Everything. I like everything.

—Everything? he repeated, skeptically.

—You don't understand. If my teammates find out, they'll crucify me.

He stood and poured us each another glass of wine. I could tell he was considering something. He sat back down and handed me my glass.

—That's the same shit Chase used to pull with Henry.

Thao had never said Chase's name—I hadn't even known Thao knew who Chase was—and the shock of hearing him say it now put me a step behind what Thao told me next. It was like that for the following hour: me scrambling to process what he'd just said while also trying to hear the next part of the unbelievable— the very believable, the *inevitable*—story.

The day after Thao came out to his parents, he attended an informational session at the office of King's LGBT association. That's where he met Henry Bryte, a gay freshman who lived in the dorm next to Thao's on East Campus. Thao's parents' terrible re-action to his news only made Thao that much more resolved to be out at King. Henry, on the other hand, had been raised by a bipolar single mother in Natick, Massachusetts, who used to whip him with the metal end of their dog's leash whenever she thought he was "talking wrong," so that Henry was now deeply, often paranoically, circumspect about how and to whom he signaled. The simple act of walking into the LGBT meeting had led him to have a low-level panic attack. Thao noticed Henry's state and made sure to walk out of the meeting with him, helping Henry calm down as they rode the campus shuttle back to East—a preview of the dynamic that would drive their friendship throughout freshman year.

With Thao's help, Henry grew somewhat more comfortable in his own skin over the next ten months—enough, at least, not to hyperventilate when he walked into the LGBT association—but the true breakthrough occurred the following summer, thanks to a fellowship Henry received to work at a cancer research lab in San Francisco. Henry lived in the Tenderloin, attended his first pride parade, lost his virginity to a postdoc at UCSF, and by living on the opposite coast from his sick, abusive mother got the perspective he needed to realize he didn't have to be tyrannized by her anymore. Thao barely recognized the boy who returned to West Campus for their sophomore year: vivacious, funny, *risky*. Henry wore outfits Thao wouldn't have dared and flirted with anyone who struck his fancy, including the big, blocky, blond football player who lived down the hall. Henry made a point of smiling at the player whenever they saw each other, of saying hello even though the football player never said it back. Thao thought Henry was taunting the type who'd tormented him in high school, but Henry insisted that he sensed a secret receptivity in the blond boy, who seemed alone, withheld, in a way Henry recognized. And sure enough, late one night the player returned drunk to their dorm and knocked on Henry's door. Henry lived in a single, which Chase must have known, and which was why, when Henry sleepily opened up, Chase pushed him back inside and locked the door behind him.

Rules were established. They would see each other only in

Henry's room, and only late at night, when Chase's roommate, Gunter, would be sleeping. They wouldn't acknowledge each other outside the room, and when they called or texted, it would be using a special code Chase had come up with. Freshman year, Chase had dated a Guatemalan girl named Sadie with whom he had amicably broken up when she transferred to Georgetown. Chase would tell his teammates he and Sadie had decided to keep dating long-distance. Chase saved Henry's number under the name of his ex-girlfriend in case a teammate happened to pick up his cell, and whenever Chase took a call from Henry around the others, he would call him Sadie. The secrecy, the arcane rules, all ran counter to what Henry had become over the summer—but he couldn't stop falling for Chase, this boy whose beloved father would have cut out his son's heart if he knew what was going on; this boy who was flourishing and free when he was safely locked in Henry's room; this boy who was funny, sweet, gentle, goofy, and far smarter than he acted. Chase and Henry started seeing each other during the football season, and Chase was so tired when he came to Henry's door that they just as often fell asleep as fucked. Chase always set an alarm for 5 a.m., waking in time to tiptoe back to his dorm room and be there when Gunter woke.

Henry didn't expect the main parts of Chase to change, but he had hoped for the edges to soften—for Chase to at least sometimes *look* at him when they saw each other in public. But Chase was as disciplined here as he was in football. Nothing of their inner world seeped into the outer. It was when the outer world started to invade the inner that Henry started to rethink what he was doing. Because Chase would sometimes joke and call Henry "Sadie" when it was just the two of them in Henry's room, when there was no reason to use the code they had developed. Though Henry didn't think it funny, he at first played along, attributing it to Chase's odd—and oddly intense—sense of humor. But this just encouraged Chase, until one night Chase called Henry "Sadie" while Henry was going down on him. Henry pulled his mouth away and told Chase to never do that again, and this sent Chase into an embarrassed rage. He kicked the little plastic dorm trash can and hissed that Henry had no right, no fucking right at all, to tell him what to do. Chase hadn't hit Henry, but he had frightened him, had shown he *could* harm him if he wanted, and when a few nights later Chase called Henry "Sadie" again during sex, it seemed like Chase was daring Henry to say something. Meanwhile, outside the room, the stress was leading Henry to revert to his old, closeted, paranoid self. He started dressing conservatively again, tried not to speak, and when he did speak tried not to give off signals.

Thao had been hesitant about the whole arrangement between Henry and Chase from the start, and once he saw what was happening to his friend, he came right out and told Henry this relationship was poison, that it was erasing every good bold thing about him. Eventually Henry came to see this himself, and the first week of April he sat Chase down on his bed and told him it was over. Chase cried until the sun rose, when it was time for him to return to his room.

Fall of their junior year, Thao worked hard to reclaim his friend, listening to Henry talk and talk about Chase, assuring him he'd done the right thing. Meanwhile Chase was obsessively texting and calling Henry, apologizing, promising he'd change, saying they could try again, he had gotten a room to himself on Central just so they could start over. If Thao was around, Henry would ignore Chase, but when Henry was alone he would sometimes give in and take the calls, answer the texts, and in this way encouraged Chase to keep pursuing him. Then came Chase's all-out campaign in the last weeks of the football season, the gifts, the handwritten letter. Thao could see it was working, that Henry was considering giving Chase a second chance, and he became so concerned for his friend's safety that he finally snatched Henry's phone and typed a text telling Chase to fuck off and never contact him again.

Henry was relieved that Thao did what he hadn't been able to, and they went out that night to celebrate, the first time Henry had gone out all semester. They decided to meet at Stefan Knows with Thao's friend Jamie. The three of them took shots at the bar to get Henry relaxed, then ventured out to the dance floor. Henry was still nervous as he danced with Thao, but that he was dancing at all was in itself a feat, a victory, an important step toward recovering his old confidence. Then Thao saw Chase pushing through the crowd. Chase confronted them, screaming at Henry, getting in Thao's face and accusing him of trying to keep Henry for himself—which is when I arrived and slammed Chase to the floor. The scare led Henry to have a breakdown the next week, and he was checked into McLean at the end of November. Thao had been hoping Henry might try to return to King for the coming semester, but that was looking unlikely. Henry was living at home with his mother again, and Thao wondered if it was just a matter of time before he had another, even worse break.

Thao finished talking and we sat listening to the air conditioner. I knew Thao was giving me time to absorb everything, but it was impossible, naturally, there was too much to take in, and in the days afterward I would be going about my life and suddenly be stopped in my tracks as I recalled yet another strange thing Chase had said or done that now made sense—such as Chase's infamous breakdown during the Purple and Gold Game, which I saw had been caused by Henry breaking up with him.

—I'm not putting myself through something like that, Thao told me.

—That's not the only way we can be together.

—Then how? You couldn't sit with me in an empty restaurant, but you think we can date?

—I—I don't know.

—Well, you *need* to know. You need to prove it.

He didn't explain what "prove it" meant. I was too cowardly to ask.

Chase still lived on Central, two blocks away from the place I shared with Reshawn, and I parked outside his apartment on my drive back from Carsonville. On the façades of all Central units the front door and a sliding glass door stood side by side. The drapes were pulled over Chase's glass doors, but I could see the living room light burning around the drapes' edges. He was home, likely sitting on his big leather couch halfheartedly flipping through the French textbook for Monday's exam. All those times I'd sat close to him on that couch. All the times we'd walked together to practice. All the times I'd stretched him, or he me. His almost rapacious need to annoy, to prod and goad, to simultaneously push and pull whoever was around him in public, and the deep, pouring shyness and delicacy he was capable of when it was just the two of us. What if I knocked on that door right now? He'd stare, doubtless, ask me what the fuck I wanted, but it probably wouldn't take much effort to get him to let me in. And what would I want to do, what could I say, once I was?

I didn't knock on his door, and didn't see him again until Monday afternoon, when our class met in the language lab for the final exam. Chase arrived with Errol. The two of them were growing thick as thieves, and as they settled into neighboring carrels I recalled the story Errol told here a few weeks earlier, the one in which the girl asked the two of them to fuck her at the same time. Assuming the episode actually happened, how could Chase have felt while the negotiation was happening? Was he hopeful, sick to his stomach, both? I remembered thinking it strange that, when Errol said they fucked her separately and Errol had had her first, Chase hadn't been embarrassed by having her second. I wondered if Chase had been *happy* it happened in that order. Had he liked knowing Errol had just been inside her? Had that seemed like the closest he could ever come to touching Errol in that way?

Thoughts like these kept breaking my concentration during the exam, and when Reshawn finished the test I was only halfway through my questions. He tapped me on the shoulder and whispered:

—Give me your keys.

—You're not coming to Skellie?

—*Messieurs*, Mademoiselle Carter said from her desk. *Ne parlez pas pendant l'examen.*

—*Pardon*, I said, and handed Reshawn my keys.

I ended up staying with the rest of my teammates for the full three hours. Mademoiselle Carter finally called time, I reviewed my essay for any stray missing accents, then hit the Submit button. As we filed out of the lab, Mademoiselle Carter said:

—Errol, stay behind a minute?

Errol smirked. The summer session was officially over, and it seemed like his talk about bedding Mademoiselle Carter might not have been as idle as we thought.

We left the Romance Languages building, standing in the useless shade of an oak tree on the quad and asking each other about this or that exam question. We kept an eye on the door for the moment Errol triumphantly walked outside.

—How old you think she is? Cornelius asked.

—Like thirty, thirty-five.

—Yo, O'Connor said. Her pussy's probably so dry he's gonna get paper cuts on his dick.

—Nah, Chase said. That's the best pussy. . . . *What*, Furling?

—Nothing.

Errol walked out through the double doors, the expression on his face anything but triumphant.

—What happened, Machen? Cornelius asked, grinning. Mademoiselle tell you she needs a *real* man? You give her my number?

—She asked to see my pencil case.

We went silent.

—*Fuck*.

—Yeah, "fuck," Errol said. She opened that shit and emptied it out. I made my sheet this morning and everything, but then I did the math and I thought, I can get a D on that exam and still get an A-minus for the summer. So I left that bitch at home.

—So, wait, she didn't catch you?

—Nope.

—How'd she know, then?

Errol looked at me.

—I didn't tell her shit, I said.

—But what about your boy? I *told* you Reshawn was a jealous motherfucker, but I didn't know he'd be on some Judas shit.

—No way, I said.

—How else would Carter know? Tell me *one time* she got up from her desk during an exam.

—Maybe a different player snitched.

—*Who?* Errol asked, gesturing incredulously at the players standing with us.

I didn't have an answer, and my case wasn't helped when we entered the Hay and everyone else learned that Reshawn was skipping Skellie for the first time since Zeller made him attend. Now Errol was convinced Reshawn snitched, convinced he was skipping Skellie because he was too afraid to face him. As we dressed, Errol kept repeating that he was going to knock Reshawn the fuck out when he saw him tomorrow for the first day of camp.

I knew Errol wouldn't be so stupid, but what did worry me was the reaction the rest of the players had. They weren't finding it difficult to imagine Reshawn's disdain for the team tipping over into something as unconscionable as snitching on our new starting quarterback. In fact, that's *precisely* the kind of shit Cousin Shawn would pull. I continued to speak up for Reshawn, saying he was going to be on this team another three years, and there was just no way he would do something to guarantee everybody despised him for the rest of his time here.

After Skellie, I got a ride from Devonté back to the apartment. When I walked inside, I found Reshawn sitting on our scratchy living room couch reading a paperback edition of *Mumbo Jumbo*, which Professor Grayson had bought him as a thank-you gift for all the work he'd done this summer. Reshawn set the open book on his thigh when I appeared, and the hopeful look on his face made it clear I'd made an ass of myself in front of the team.

—She didn't find anything, I told him.

—What? he said, the book falling to the floor as he sat up.

—Are you *trying* to make your life miserable? Is this, like, *intentional*?

He stood and picked up the paperback, twisting it with his big, strong hands like the neck of an animal he was strangling. His eyes were glassy and shallow. He dropped the book on the couch and walked past me, slamming the door to his room. I heard him on the phone with someone—Jamie, I assumed.

I sat on the couch, angrier with Reshawn than I'd ever been. This was *my* team, Devonté's team, Jimbo's team. We had put thousands of hours toward a season that Reshawn had so impulsively, insanely endangered. From these thoughts my mind jumped to Thao, to Reshawn's lazy, knee-jerk bigotry toward him, and by extension toward me. How could I ever have thought this kid wasn't the biggest asshole I'd ever known?

Twenty minutes later Reshawn's door opened. He was holding a duffel bag. I could tell immediately what was happening.

—Please don't.

—Professor Grayson's in Savannah until school starts. He said I can stay with him. I'll take out loans and apply for financial aid next year. My parents are going to have to learn to take care of themselves.

He snatched my car keys off the kitchen table.

—No, I said. You're not taking my fucking car.

—Miles.

—Don't give me—

—You know what I see every time I walk past the chapel? Every single time? My body, falling from the top of the tower. I swear to God I can feel the air against my face.

Was he being serious? Or was he trying to manipulate me? His eyes seemed even shallower than before.

—*Please*, he said, voice cracking.

# Six

Spiderwebs hung between the iron handrails of the outdoor staircase, big as window screens and bedizened with thick beads of dew. We had nothing like this in Sillitoe, and all summer long I had liked opening our front door to find the webs waiting for me, harvesters of the heavy southern light, strange devices that never failed to revivify the fact that Blenheim was the most exotic place I'd ever been. And yet this morning the sight of the webs drained me, almost sickened me, and I hated having to break through one after another with my body on my way down the stairs, hated how the sticky wet strands clung to my arm hairs and nape, wisped off my elbows, knuckles, nose, and fingertips. I decided to walk to the Hay rather than get a ride from a teammate and risk him asking why I wasn't driving myself, and as I made my way through the hot, overripe day I kept ruffling my hair and brushing my body, half crazed by the thought that the one strand of web I hadn't gotten off yet was the very one being ridden by a brawny brown spider.

When I arrived at the Hay's first-floor hallway, a long line of players had already formed to report to camp. Everybody seemed to be gossiping about Reshawn's snitch on Errol, distorting details of the story like taffy, one-upping each other about what they would have done had Reshawn tried pulling that shit on them, *I'd a choked him the fuck out, I'd a given him the pencil case with a*

*bow on top, I'd a—goddamn, I don't know* what *I woulda done.*
But for all the disgust in people's voices, I also heard relief. They
might not ever manage to surpass Reshawn on the field or in the
classroom, but they sure as hell would never have snitched.

Listening to all this just worsened my anxiety, and I decided
to get it over with. I was going to have to break the news about
Reshawn one way or another, and it would be better to tell Coach
Zeller one-on-one rather than take him by surprise in the team
meeting at eleven. I left the line and rode the elevator up to the fifth
floor, which was first-day festive: secretaries tan and recharged
from Outer Banks vacations, assistant coaches jolly after enjoying
the longest stretch they'd have with their families all year, phones
ringing off the hooks, staplers giving off satisfying smashes. Miss
Gemma, the head secretary, waved me back to Zeller's office.

The door was open and Zeller was sitting behind his desk.

—Miles! How you feelin' today? Been meanin' to tell you
how happy we were with you in Skellie.

—Thanks, Coach.

I closed the door and sat in a chair across from him.

—Somethin' wrong? he asked.

—Did you hear about what happened with Errol yesterday?

—Some kinda misunderstandin' in y'all's French class.

—Yes sir. Reshawn got upset after, and—he left. He took my
car to Savannah to meet his professor. He quit the team.

Zeller watched me a long moment, as if hoping there was
more to the story, a better ending coming. When he saw I had
nothing else to say he closed his eyes and used his index finger and
thumb to smooth his eyebrows.

—This was this mornin'? he asked.

—Last night.

He opened his eyes.

—Last *night*? Why'm I only hearin' about it now?

—Coach—

—You tell anybody else?

—No sir.

Zeller leaned back in his seat and continued to stare, though now he was just using me as something to rest his eyes on while he thought things through.

—All right, he said finally. All right. You keep it that way, hear?

—Sir?

—Miles, *nothin'* we just said leaves this room.

—Yes sir.

—I trust you.

His tone seemed to imply the opposite. I stood, palms wet from how hard I'd been clenching my fists.

—Yes sir.

I boarded the elevator, furious with Reshawn. I needed every ounce of coach goodwill I could get if I wanted to steal Chase's spot this August, and I was worried I'd just tainted myself in Zeller's eyes.

The first floor's line had shortened, and soon my name was checked off the reporting list and I was walking to the second floor. Errol was seated in the Team Room's front row, looking uncharacteristically serene, comfortable wearing the martyr's mantle. People perked up at the sight of me, clearly expecting to see a disgraced Reshawn in tow, and I hated to see how undisturbed they were when Reshawn failed to appear, hated that they assumed Reshawn would be arriving shortly. But worst of all was the man I saw sitting in the second-to-last row. In his mid-forties and underfed everywhere except the small paunch that drooped over his belt buckle, he had skin so translucent you could see the turquoise veins bisecting his temples and crisscrossing the male-pattern bald crown of his head. His name was Arnold Duffy, and he covered college football for *USA Today*. I had forgotten Duffy was to spend the next three weeks in Blenheim covering camp.

The digital clock turned to eleven and the assistant coaches filed in. Teammates watched the door for Reshawn, certain they were about to enjoy the sight of our star walking into the room with his tail between his legs. Meanwhile I was watching for Coach Zeller. And here he came, taking his place at the front of the room, looking sepulchral.

—Morning, Coach!

Players were showing off for the reporter. Their enthusiasm seemed to catch Coach Zeller off guard.

—Aaah, mornin', men.

He cleared his throat.

—Got a lot to cover. But before we start, I got some news. Some of y'all might know Reshawn's mama is sick. Real sick. Multiple sclerosis. She took a bad turn last night and Reshawn's had to go on home to Oregon to be with her.

Duffy scribbled furiously on his steno pad. My teammates looked whiplashed. Now they were being asked to *feel bad* for this kid?

—How long's he gone? Jimbo asked.

—Don't have that information, Zeller said. But obviously his priority's gotta be with his family. And we gotta move forward. Devonté, you'll be takin' over at one tail. Errol, time for you to step up.

—Yes sir, they said simultaneously.

Zeller gave his opening speech, which I can't recount because I couldn't focus on his words for more than a few seconds at a time before returning to the questions bouldering through my brain. Had Zeller lied to buy himself time? That seemed likely. Reshawn could conceivably take anything from a day to a whole year to be with his mother, and while he was away people like Duffy wouldn't think to question the decision of a son to go be with his sick mom. But what was Zeller's plan to get Reshawn back? *Did* he have a plan? And what the fuck would happen when it failed?

Besides, while people outside our program might have been willing to take Zeller's story at face value, many teammates were skeptical that Reshawn's failed snitch and his sudden departure for

Oregon were mere coincidence. Their suspicion only grew when we walked to the parking lot to drive to lunch and they saw my Saturn was missing.

I asked Devonté for a ride. Jimbo always rode shotgun with Devonté, and as we pulled out of the players lot Jimbo asked me:

—Broken down how?

—I don't know. My steering wheel's been shaking.

—And when did McCoy leave again?

—Yesterday.

Jimbo turned in his seat, staring at me.

—What? I asked.

—His mom's really sick?

—Goddamn, Devonté said. You ain't seen her in those crutches after games? Have some respect, J.

Jimbo sucked his teeth and faced forward.

That afternoon Arnold Duffy stood on one of the practice field sidelines, waiting for the stretch whistle like the rest of us. It was 91 degrees, blisteringly bright, and barely any of the man's sun-allergic self was left uncovered. He wore a long-sleeved oxford shirt and blue jeans, one of those neck-caped caps you see on movie-star colonialists riding camelback through the Sahara, and an oily Coppertone coat on his cheeks and nose.

Later on in camp Duffy would roam from field to field to observe different position groups and units, but today he remained with the offense the whole time, more specifically with the quarterbacks, watching Errol adjust to being the team's new lodestar. From the first snap, it became evident Errol's adjustment would be anything but smooth. The self-satisfied serenity I'd seen in him before the team meeting had vanished, and the petulant boy we'd known during the summer, the neurotic self-narrator, was back in full force, castigating himself in the third person when he flubbed drop-back steps, telling wide receivers they weren't hustling hard enough, slapping himself on the helmet after a mistimed throw, remonstrating with Devonté to give him more room during hand-offs. The spectacle was embarrassing, and I wanted to yank Errol aside and remind him he was doing this in front of a man who had the power to elevate or sink our program's reputation. But as practice continued, I noticed Errol himself was obsessively checking to see where the reporter stood, and I came to understand Errol was trapped in a vicious feedback loop in which he'd do something bratty, remember he was being observed, and get so flustered his brattiness only worsened. And what more could I have expected from him, really? The kid hadn't played a single game-time down of D1 football, let alone borne the future of a whole program on his back.

Errol's behavior and Duffy's silent observation put me and the rest of the team in a foul mood, and our grumpiness seemed to get sucked up into the sky and seed the weather. Slate-colored clouds were gnarling themselves above the fields by the time we ran end-of-practice conditioning sprints. We heard the first thunder rip while we were showering, and at dinner the rain hammered Training Table's roof so fiercely it was difficult to hear what people said. Flash flood warnings were issued, and the coaches decided it was too dangerous to drive back to the Hay for the last round of meetings, so we separated into our position groups right there in the dining hall, talked a few minutes, and then broke up for the night.

We bunched at Training Table's open double doors and looked out at the rain falling in wind-ruffled sheets. In groups of six or seven, players at the front of the bottleneck girded themselves and sprinted out to the parking lot, and when it was my turn I ran for Devonté's car. He had been giving me rides all day, and I took it for granted he was saving me a seat now. But as I stamped into the flooded lot I saw his Grand Marquis already pulling away.

I ran over to the driver's side window of Chase's truck and knocked frantically. He rolled down his window, and I saw that Errol was sitting in the passenger seat.

—Can I come with you? I asked.

—Sure! Chase said, smiling. Got plenty of room in the bed.

The truck's bed had two inches of standing water. I shook my head and turned around, hunching in the downpour as I tried to see who else I could ride with.

—Come on, Errol told Chase. You gonna give my man pneumonia.

I turned back around. Chase was annoyed, but I could see he wouldn't contradict Errol.

—Fine, he told me. Ride bitch.

"Bitch" meant sitting on the middle of the back bench seat, squeezed between Scan and J2. Chase pulled out of the parking lot, and despite the dangerous conditions he sped through Central Campus, delighting in the high fins of water his oversized tires made in the flooded street, music blasting at its usual aneurysm-inducing level.

—I can't with that shit, Errol said, turning down the music. My nerves are already on edge like a motherfucker.

I had never seen someone touch Chase's stereo without Chase acting like the honor of all McGerrin men had been challenged; but not only did Chase not turn the music up again, he sought to comfort Errol.

—You'll be good, he said. Just remember, they brought you here for a reason.

Errol shrugged, looking out the window.

—I fuckin' *hate* that Duffy bama, he said.

In the Marriott parking lot we sprinted one last time through the storm. The front desk folks had fresh towels waiting, and we dried ourselves as we rode the elevator upstairs. I got off on the same floor as Errol and Chase.

—You want anything from the vending machine? Chase asked Errol.

—Nah, I'm good.

Chase opened his mouth, then closed it again, checking himself for some reason. He walked past the door to their room, toward the alcove at the end of the hall that housed the vending machine.

Reshawn was supposed to be my roommate during camp, which made me the only player on the team who would be sleeping alone. In the room I stripped off my clothes and left them in a wet heap on the carpet, and as I got a fresh towel from the bathroom I wondered whether Chase was going to buy Errol something from the vending machine anyway, in case he changed his mind. That's the kind of thing I'd done all the time with my own crushes, and the thought of Chase standing in front of the vending machine, agonizing over whether Errol might prefer a Snickers or a bag of Cheez-Its, filled me with a tenderness I hadn't thought I would ever feel toward that boy again. I had spent the past nine months whittling Chase down to the enemy I'd needed him to be, the gay-bashing bully, obstacle to my football dreams; but thanks to Thao's story he was regaining a roundness, a three-dimensionality, I knew I'd never be able to banish.

I wasn't a saint, though, and while my hatred for Chase might have been in retreat, my competitiveness with him decidedly was not, and as I finished toweling off in the bathroom I felt a sudden, hot urge to do something I knew Chase wouldn't be able to. I walked back to the main part of the room and dialed Thao.

—Where are you? I asked him.

—We just got back from dinner. It's biblical out there.

—No, where are you *right now*?

—In my room.

I was nervous, terribly nervous, that what I was about to ask would blow my door off its hinges, knock down the walls, allow my teammates to come streaming in here to murder me. But my urge was much stronger, and it was only mounting as I kept thinking of Chase and his hopeless crush on Errol.

—I'm naked, I said, starting to fondle myself.

—Oh?

—What are you wearing?

There was a pause, background rustling. I worried I'd gone too far, disrespected the boundaries Thao had drawn these last weeks. But then he returned to the phone, slightly out of breath.

—Sorry, he said. I needed to lock my door.

The world was renewed when I stepped into the Marriott lot the next morning. The two orgasms I'd shared with Thao had allowed me to sleep like a nursed infant, and my thoughts ran clear. The storm had passed and the leaves on the trees surrounding the lot glinted like washed coins as they flipped back and forth in the breeze, while the temperature balmed at a miraculous, an almost unbelievable 76 degrees, making this by far the coolest morning I would ever know at a training camp. It couldn't be coincidence that how I felt and how the day felt were in perfect alignment, and I knew, *knew*, the universe was telling me it was time, I was ready to start my final ascent toward starting Will linebacker.

I was 211 pounds of muscle, after all, my mind an encyclopedia of techniques and assignments, and in practice that morning—and in every practice that week—I experienced a new confidence that melded body and mind, transformed me into a single, inexorable football *thing*. Need me to collision that fullback? I'd strike him so hard he'd walk away shaking his arm from a stinger. Need me to cover that tight end? I'd go step for step, and if the quarterback was foolish enough to throw in his direction, I would slap the ball away like the impertinence it was. *Attaboy, Furling! I see you, Miles! That's my man right there!* Coach Hightower cheered, acting like he hadn't treated me like scenery most of the last year, while Cornelius would ask *me* to clarify something about the newest defensive package we were installing, as if I was the senior and he the redshirt freshman.

What made this even sweeter was that while I was only just beginning to realize my potential, Chase was slamming up against the outer limits of his. Now that our physical sizes were equivalent, the weaker aspects of his game came into stark relief—his slowness, his choppy footwork, his tendency to get trapped inside his head after a mistake. I was showing him up in every meeting, every drill, every scrimmage, and he knew this, could not *stop* knowing it, couldn't stop from obsessing about it. Such self-consciousness was blood in the water for Coach Hightower, and whenever Chase fucked up again, our coach seized the chance to marvel at how impressive it was that a retard like Chase could have fooled the coaches into giving him a full scholarship, to exclaim he had *no idea* a clitoris could grow legs and run around a football field. *Get your fuckin' head on straight, McGerrin! We got a goddamn season to prepare for! Is that the best you can fucking do?!*

Everything built toward Saturday, the first day of full contact, when we would run the Oklahoma drill. I had dreamt for a year straight about redeeming last August's performance, and in the lead-up to that morning's practice I was concentration incarnate. I kept separate from the gossip and grab-ass in the locker room so I could visualize myself making the perfect tackle. I walked down to the practice fields alone, chanting under my breath that today was the day, today was the day. And down at the fields I moved far from the crowd, facing the chirring woods that bordered the fields, and crouched in my stance to rehearse my read step again and again and again.

Team stretch ended, and three hard whistle bleats sent the team stampeding toward Coach Zeller and the orange cones set up behind him: running backs versus linebackers, offensive linemen versus defensive linemen, wideouts versus defensive backs.

First up for the linebackers and backs were Cornelius and Devonté. Cornelius jumped up and down bellow-yodeling, hands convulsing at his sides. Devonté turned toward the running backs behind him in line so they could scream hype into his face and slap his helmet—not your usual nominal slaps but hard, painful strikes that turned the palms of the white running backs bright red.

—Ready!

Cornelius and Devonté crouched into their stances, and on the whistle the sharp sound of their collision was like a piece of sheet metal falling onto a sidewalk from a great height, THWAP! The sound of the collision was a credit to Devonté, who was thirty pounds lighter than Cornelius; but Cornelius dominated, lifting Devonté off his feet and ramming a shoulder pad into his stomach so that when they landed, a spurt of Gatorade-orange bile was forced from Devonté's mouth, staining the back of Corny's jersey.

Next for the linebackers, Chase faced Bellum Darcy, a freshman fullback who'd already won the starting spot and looked like a steroidal cherub—five foot ten, 245 pounds, with pinchable pink cheeks and corn silk curls that frothed out of the bottom of his helmet. Bellum was nicknamed Slo-Mo for his inching Ozarks accent and the fact that he brought up the rear of conditioning sprints, but the flipside of Slo-Mo's molasses speed was his power, and when the whistle blew and he and Chase collided, you had an unstoppable force meeting an immovable object. The speed Chase had as an advantage was neutralized by Bellum's extra weigh, and they stopped where they met, their Clydesdale legs chugging in place. Coach Hightower ran up and screamed:

—Push, McGerrin! Puuuuuuushhhhh! Don't you fuckin' quit now!

They were stalemated, and you could see their bodies start to tire, standing up straighter, hands sloppily grappling as their legs continued to churn. Technique was giving way to pure mass, which tilted the advantage to Bellum, and with a final roll of the hips Bellum knocked Chase off balance and pancaked him to the grass. The team cheered, helping Bellum to his feet, hugging him. Chase pushed off the ground and punched himself in the helmet as Coach Hightower's stare escorted him to the end of the linebackers' line.

My dance partner was Kendrick. This was my moment, now was my chance. Hightower was watching me with his arms crossed, the whole team, all civilization, was waiting, and as I crouched into my stance I did something I had never done before on the field—I prayed. And though I was praying to my talent rather than to Christ, the feeling I experienced was the same: I was addressing something that, though mute, could hear me perfectly; something that, though invisible and intangible, had the power to destroy me.

Coach Zeller blew the whistle.

I collided with Kendrick.

Resplendence pealed through me: I made a clean, a perfect tackle, drilling Kendrick into the earth.

When Reshawn was happiest with Jamie, I could go days without hearing a word from him. Text messages wondering where he'd put the laundry detergent, calls asking for advice on a term paper would go unreturned, and once I finally did see him, he would admit he hadn't even had his phone. He'd done this on purpose, wanted to quarantine his non-football life to prevent contamination by me or anyone else on the team. So it didn't surprise me that a whole week of camp passed without a word from him: he was in Savannah with his hero Professor Grayson, tracking down more evidence of the extraordinary life of Carmichael Stewart King; he was enjoying the first August in more than a decade in which he wasn't sweating his weight during practices; he was getting to *own* the King student's life as he'd dreamt of doing.

I couldn't say any of this to Arnold Duffy, who on the second Monday of camp received permission from Coach Zeller to interview me in the Team Room during the afternoon break. I tried to not appear nervous as I took the seat next to him in the front row.

—Been in touch with Reshawn lately? he asked.

—I want to give him some privacy.

—Right. Of course.

Duffy took a tape recorder from his pocket and balanced it on the armrest between our chairs. I stared at the back of his pale left hand and its convoluted, colorful veins. It looked like a map of hell's subway system.

—I've talked to some of your teammates about Reshawn as a

player, he said, pressing Play on the recorder. But I haven't heard much about the rest of his life at King. I was hoping you could tell me about that.

—Okay.

Duffy expected me to go on, but I decided staying as close-mouthed as possible was safest. He smiled.

—Maybe I'll start. Coach Zeller shared Reshawn's schedule from last year. Pretty impressive stuff.

—Yeah.

—I could hardly understand the *titles* of some of his classes. But on top of that, Coach Zeller tells me Reshawn takes time to tutor guys on the team?

—Reshawn does?

Had Reshawn been doing that and I just hadn't known? Duffy tilted his head.

—You didn't know?

—No, I . . . It's hard to keep track of everything he does.

—Right. *Right.* I guess that's what I'm getting at. There's this team he's dedicated to. Then his classwork. Tutoring. *And* his mother's health issues. Seems like a lot of pressure for an eighteen-year-old. Has he . . . I don't want you to betray his confidence here, but has he ever hinted the pressure can get to be too much?

—No.

—Never?

—He—, I began. He has ways of keeping everything balanced.

—Right. Like the Fellowship of Christian Athletes.

That Reshawn had tutored people without my knowing was barely possible, but when Duffy mentioned Reshawn's membership in the weekly prayer group of King's Christian jocks, it took all I had to stop myself from laughing. Reshawn referred to the FCA as the "Fund for Christ's Automatons." He'd have sooner downed a bottle of Drāno than attend an FCA meeting.

—I didn't know he went, I said.

—Coach Zeller says he attends every week. He said the group leads prayers for Reshawn's mother.

I got my bearings. Coach Zeller had curated a heroic version of Reshawn for Duffy, one in which Reshawn was the hardworking star of the team, the devoted son, the devout Christian. I saw a safe way out of the interview: just hew close to Zeller's lies.

—It makes sense he wouldn't tell me, I said. Reshawn's pretty humble when it comes to that stuff.

—Right. "Humility" is a word Coach Zeller uses a lot. How do you account for that in somebody who's got so many talents? I'd be the cockiest man in America if I was him.

I nodded, like I'd wondered this myself.

—Maybe it's the Christianity? I said. Like, he knows he has God to thank for all the gifts he's been given.

—Right. Great.

I became a Reshawn alchemist, transforming all the base metals of my roommate's reality into print-worthy gold. In my hands, Reshawn's passion for literature no longer stemmed from his need to escape football, but was a natural extension of a love for language rooted in his passion for the Bible's teachings; his disappearance from the team wasn't a desperate, angry escape, it was an anguished, righteous choice to nurse his beloved mother. The deeper we got into the interview, the more fun I had. It was like a game: take whatever Reshawn did, said, believed, and present Duffy with the opposite.

We moved on to Reshawn's relationship with Errol.

—They're kind of an odd couple, Duffy said. I covered Errol when he was at Auburn. He's got this *big* personality. Reshawn seems so private by comparison.

—I think that's why they work so well together, I said. It's too bad you weren't here this summer. I've never seen chemistry like theirs.

He nodded, checking his recorder to make sure we weren't in danger of running out of tape.

—Is that maybe why Errol's struggling a little in practice now? he asked. Because he's missing Reshawn?

—Maybe. But nobody's worried about Errol. We know he can lead us while Reshawn's away.

Errol, of course, was a fucking mess. Violet bags hung off his eyes; a dripping sack of ice was secured to his throwing shoulder whenever he wasn't in pads; and his breath stank perpetually of the chocolate-covered espresso beans he was popping to keep his tired self alert. The caffeine only managed to put him even more on edge, and seldom did a conversation pass without him reminding you he was the first player down to practice every day and the last to leave, just as he bitched ad nauseam about how while all of us were nuzzling our faces into our warm laundry nets during the afternoon break, he was upstairs in the quarterbacks room watching extra film.

He was learning to stop the outbursts in front of Duffy, but that just forced his anger to flow through more passive aggressive channels. And though everybody on the team was in danger of setting him off, the person who suffered most was Chase. When life had been good that summer, when Reshawn was in Blenheim and Errol had a long runway to develop as a leader and starting quarterback, he had clearly loved having someone like Chase worship him. But now he was exhausted and irritable, and more and more he needled Chase at team meals, withered Chase over his trademark stupid jokes. Chase tried to laugh it all off, as if Errol's increasingly nasty ragging was a sign of deepening intimacy.

Reshawn's disappearance put a damper on veterans' usual hazing spirit, and in the first week of camp nobody had the heart to bang on their plates and make freshmen sing the fight song at Training Table. But we couldn't stay in mourning forever, and as we got into the second week the old hazing energy returned. By lunch Thursday we were chanting Errol's name, and the chanting only grew stronger when we saw his baffled reaction. Busy as he'd been cramming plays and audibles, he had forgotten to memorize the words on the laminated card he and the rest of the freshman class had been given.

—What's your name?!

—Man, y'all *know* my name.

—Motherfucker, I asked you a question!

Errol paused, surprised by the anger in J1's voice.

—Errol Machen, he said.

—Well, come the fuck on, *Errol Machen*. Our food ain't getting any warmer!

Errol blew out a breath and looked up at the ceiling.

*Reign, Monarchs . . .*

He stopped, knowing that wasn't how the song began. J1 resumed taunting him, but then was shushed by other vets. This wasn't done, I realized, to give Errol the silence he needed to recall the words of the fight song; it was done so our quarterback felt every second scrape through him like a rusty rake; it was done to shrink back down to size this whining, wheedling leader who had managed to make our wretched situation even worse than it needed to be.

Errol started over.

*Reign reign, Monarchs*
*Rule your realm with—iron fists*
*Claim, claim . . . a . . . Monarch*

Errol punched his right fist into his left palm, muttering self-reproaches. The silence in the room continued, and I have to admit there was something nourishing in watching Errol suffer.

—BOOOOOOOOOOOOOOOOOOO!

We turned to look at Chase. He alone was booing, banging his table with his palms. Players tried to shush him, but he kept booing, and then surprised everyone further by plucking a baby carrot from his salad and throwing it at Errol's crotch. There was an astonished pause at what he'd done, and then laughter. Now a hail of carrots flew at Errol, a dinner roll, a slice of Salisbury steak that left a greasy slug's trail on our starting quarterback's shorts. The boos built into a vicious, an overwhelming sound, and they only ceased when Errol climbed down from his chair.

Lunch resumed, the mood in the room noticeably lighter and more playful. As usual, Errol and Chase had been sitting next to each other at a table. Chase picked at his food and glanced repeatedly at Errol, hoping for a sign that his friend understood the boos had been done out of merciful love. But Errol ignored him, the blush on his cheeks slowly subsiding as he sullenly shoveled food into his mouth.

. . .

Miles: What are you doing?
Gwen: Late lunch. You?
Miles: Lying in the dark.
Gwen: Mysterious.
Miles: I have a hard-on.
Gwen: Around all those boys?

"Gwen" was an inside joke between us, referring to the first time I'd mangled the pronunciation of Thao's last name. All camp long we had traded texts like this during the afternoon break, using them as preludes to our nightly phone sex sessions. After I returned from my last meeting of the day I would lock, bolt, practically board up my door, draw the drapes, and crawl into bed, where I arranged the pillows so I could lay my phone next to my ear in a way that allowed me to keep my hands free. Sometimes Thao and I came together almost immediately; other times we drew out the ritual as long as we could stand, talking dirty until one of us suddenly swerved out of sex talk altogether to discuss a mundane part of our day. Something as neutral as what we had for breakfast would get imbued with unbearable sexual intensity, our anticipation all the while ratcheting as we waited to see which one of us would make the swerve back into the explicitly erotic. Once the change was finally made, we'd be so achingly ready that we'd come before getting through the first filthy sentence.

But this afternoon flirty text messages didn't feel like enough. Watching Chase's desperate dynamic with Errol at lunch had made me horny again, and I didn't want to just lie here and squirm on the locker room carpet for ninety minutes. Steeling myself, I typed the invitation I had been contemplating since the beginning of camp.

Miles: Do you want to share it with me?
Gwen: What? Your hard-on?
Miles: Yes.
Gwen: And where would we do that?
Miles: A big comfy bed at the Marriott.

He said yes. I tiptoed out of the locker room and snuck into the smothering day, walking to a rotary on the far end of West Campus nobody on the team would have occasion to use at that hour. Thao picked me up in his Honda Civic and we held hands across the center console on the drive to the hotel, talking about everything except what we were about to do. We parked in an obscure corner of the Marriott lot, and Thao waited in the car while I went inside. I wanted to make sure the coast was clear, and also to buy my first-ever package of condoms from the little lobby store.

Thao knocked softly on my door ten minutes later. I was prepared for some awkwardness, maybe another serious conversation about his reservations regarding dating a football player, but as soon as he closed the door he kissed me with his tongue, running his palm down the front of my shorts. This caused the condoms in my pocket to let out a telltale crinkle. He stopped kissing and shoved his hand into my pocket, pulling out the string of condoms.

—Sorry, I said.

—For what?

He switched off the lights and led me to bed, dropping the condoms on the bedside table. I hadn't closed the drapes completely, leaving a sliver of sun to blister through the gap. As he laid me down on the mattress and kissed my neck, I became hyper-attuned to my surroundings—to the sunlight so strong it seemed to emit a sound; to the drone of vacuum cleaners and voices of housekeepers in the hall. Footsteps were approaching my door, the door would fly open, Coach Zeller would be here, staring. The footsteps continued past.

Thao reached down and felt I was only half hard.

—Sorry, I said again.

—No. More. Apologizing.

He took off my shirt and moved his mouth down my chest, letting the back of his tongue trail along my belly hair. He slid off my shorts and boxers, and as he took me into his mouth I closed my eyes and tried to focus on the warm hum of his tongue, the hand cupping my balls. That didn't work, so I opened my eyes and looked down at him, but I saw past the top of his head the reflection of us caught in the dark television screen opposite the bed. I couldn't bear to look at the image, and now I was losing what erection I had. How could this be happening? Since turning twelve I'd had, what, a hundred thousand erections that served no purpose whatsoever? And now that I finally had a man in the same bed as me, sucking and fondling me, I was going limp as a piece of overcooked spaghetti?

Thao took his mouth off and looked up—and saw I was on the verge of tears. He slid back up my chest, but when I tried apologizing yet again, he hushed me. He lay on his back and stroked himself, inviting me to watch, to see how naturally and unselfconsciously he could get hard with me alongside. It was the sexiest thing I had ever witnessed, the steady fleshy beat of his hand, the faint moans slipping from his thin, perfect lips. By watching him I could forget myself, and by forgetting myself my mind could leave my body alone to want what it wanted, do what it had always needed to do, and now I was the one moving down on him, breathing in the slightly sour odor rising from his pubic hair, taking him into my mouth. I had no idea what I was doing, at first taking in too little of his cock and then way too much, but he was turned on anyway. Thao came in my mouth, and I onto the duvet cover.

I spat into the trash can next to the desk and crawled up the mattress, lying next to him. His eyes were closed, and he smiled when he felt my hand stroke his hair. He looked relaxed, and contented, and while we might not be out on the West Campus quad holding hands, I knew he appreciated the risk I was taking by being here.

This, I understood, was what he'd meant last month when we'd talked in his kitchen and he'd told me to "prove it."

Much has been made of Reshawn's intelligence, and for good reason. I've never known anyone else who has lived the life of the mind as ardently, as purely as him—have never known someone who has come closer to making the life of the mind his actual *life*.

But if we're talking about sheer intellectual horsepower, there's a good chance Jimbo ran on even more cylinders than Reshawn. Jimbo was to win a college-wide award at the next spring's graduation ceremony for his honors thesis on how the nicknames football players bestow on one another reflect the intersection of African American life and corporate culture, and in that paper he coined a word—"gridonym"—that's now a term of art in academia. He could have had great success studying language as a career, but so remarkable was his brain that, after he graduated summa cum laude in philology and philosophy, he decided that actually his true field of interest was chemistry. He changed directions vocationally just as skillfully as he had changed them as a free safety and went on to obtain a post-bacc degree, then a PhD. Last I heard, he was a senior researcher at a major pharmaceutical.

So no wonder I had a minor panic attack every time he asked how the repairs on my car were coming. If there was anybody on the team capable of sussing out the truth from the lies Coach Zeller and I were peddling, it was Jimbo. I decided to firm up my story about what was wrong with my car, and one morning I woke early and took the elevator down to the Marriott's business center, using a desktop computer to figure out what might keep a 1997 Saturn station wagon in the shop for a prolonged stretch, and also to find the name of an auto body shop in nearby Cary, where I could tell Jimbo my Saturn was being repaired. And yet, even after I gave Jimbo this information, he still didn't seem satisfied. He was becoming something of a conspiracy theorist, insisting Reshawn was somewhere other than Oregon for reasons that had little to do with his allegedly sick mom.

We were eating dinner the second Saturday of camp when Wheeler came hurrying into Training Table.

—Yo, I just saw a black guy driving a station wagon.

—So?

—A Saturn. It's Furling's.

—You sure?

—Shit is gold, ain't it?

The whole room turned to look at me.

—My mechanic's black, I said. He's probably taking it out for a test drive.

—You told me the shop's in Cary, Jimbo said.

—It is.

—That's two fuckin' towns away!

He banged his fist against the table.

—McCoy is back, and not from Oregon. I will keep the Football House stocked in beers the whole fucking *season* if Furling's station wagon isn't in the Hay parking lot.

—That's a bet!

People gobbled what was left of their dinners and left in droves to speed to the Hay. I rode with Devonté, listening to Jimbo crow from the front seat.

—Y'all just never learn, he was saying. Seen with your own eyes that we have the most spoiled player in D1, somebody we call

*Cousin Shawn*, and you *still* insist everything about him isn't one long lie.

—Like you don't want him back, Devonté said.

—Oh, I do, I do. I've been dreaming about that motherfucker every night. I'm just not under the illusion the rest of y'all are.

—Which is?

We never found out what Jimbo meant. We pulled into the players' lot, and the only cars in sight were those of the teammates who'd outraced us from Training Table. We stepped out into the night and watched Jimbo walk from one end of the lot to the other, looking for the car, muttering.

—Let's switch to Coors this season, Jimbo!

—Nah, let's do fancy shit! Make it Heineken!

Arnold Duffy was already in the Team Room as we filed in for the day's final meeting, and the journalist's presence made people mock Jimbo even more mercilessly, everybody hoping their jibe might be the one Duffy chose to publish in the part of his story about the failed resurrection of our star. I laughed along, but underneath I was still disturbed by what Wheeler had seen. I knew that just because my car wasn't in the lot didn't mean Reshawn hadn't returned.

And I was right. After the last players sat and the assistant coaches trailed in behind them, we watched Coach Zeller enter the Team Room with Reshawn. Reshawn's hair was longer than I'd ever seen it, a starter Afro scraggly at the hairline. His body looked slightly reduced in the way you would expect of an elite athlete who'd gone without intensive exercise for two straight weeks. He looked miserable, and blew out a heavy breath as Zeller hung his arm around his shoulders and said in a low, emotional voice:

—Let's welcome our boy home.

We clapped. Coach Zeller pulled Reshawn toward him, squeezing him. Reshawn's body gave in—he even draped his arm around Zeller's shoulders—but his face was in full recoil. The applause died down and Reshawn took a seat in the front row.

—Prayers work, Zeller said, nodding. Don't let anybody ever tell you different. Mrs. McCoy's got a long road ahead, but the recovery—how'd they put it, Reshawn?

—Unprecedented, he said.

—Unprecedented. And we are just so damn grateful.

Zeller smiled, sinking his hands into his pockets.

—You know, the night after Reshawn went back to Oregon, I had a dream. Strange dream. I was standin' in my kitchen and starin' at this wooden table. But it wadn't the table my family eats on. It was a new table. A *strange* table. And what made this table strange was it had legs and legs, more legs'n I coulda ever hoped to count. Like an insect, or trees in a forest . . . That was it, a table, then I woke up. Don't know about y'all, but I don't usually put much stock in dreams. Thought women were the only people who did that kinda thing. But this dream, it kept naggin' at me. Kept demandin' I figure out its purpose. I thought and thought, but just could not get an answer. And then tonight, soon as I walked in here and saw y'all, the table appeared to me again. I understood. God had given me a vision.

Zeller's eyes widened, hands levitating out of his pockets.

—With most tables, you knock out a leg and they're easy to tip over. But that table in my dream? You take out one of *those* legs?

He held out his flattened right hand.

—Steady, men. Unshakable. You see what I'm gettin' at?

—Yes sir.

—We ain't a player, men. We're a team. We ain't a leg of that table. We're the fuckin' table itself. Reshawn goes back to help his mama? We stay standin'. Errol breaks his arm tomorrow? Same goddamn thing. Nobody, ain't *nobody*, can knock us down—not if we don't let 'em.

—Fuck Savannah, Reshawn said. Fuck every fucking inch of it.

He said he despised the city's poor outlying districts, which

227

like all such places in the South seemed simultaneously cramped and empty, overgrown and barren. He hated the city's wealthy, touristed center, too, with its iron-grilled mansions, its avenues of live oaks draped with Spanish moss, the old brick buildings and sparkling new shops and everything else that sat so contentedly on foundations where concrete and stone mixed with slaves' bones. At first I thought he was being hyperbolic—it seemed impossible he could have felt such hatred for a place he was visiting for only the second time—but as he kept talking, I came to understand he wasn't really referring to Savannah but to the hellish mental space he'd thrashed around in for the entirety of his stay.

—Everyone pretended to act all understanding. Zeller. My parents. "You're overwhelmed, Reshawn, we get it." "It's okay to take a break, sweetie, we understand." They told me take a week, call when you're ready.

He told Professor Grayson he had come simply because he had burned out of football, and Grayson had been good enough to take him at his word and put him to work sifting through the latest tranche of materials they'd gotten from Lala Bigmore's collection. One of the pieces was a newly uncovered poem by CSK, printed in a Greensboro paper in the late 1850s. The poem was written in off-kilter meter that was unusual for CSK, closer to the kind of verse Emily Dickinson was that same year composing in her bedroom up in Amherst.

> Rain, rain, my lady,
> Fell o'er my heart and o'er my soul.
> A floodplain, my darling,
> Like Noah's storm the waves did roll.
> But like the prophet I heard a voice
> Sweet and mild, a clement zephyr,
> And I built an ark for two, my love,
> On which we shall sail safely, forever.

Reshawn immediately marked the similarities between the

poem and the fight song—"Reign" and "Rain," the same jouncing music of the lines, the use of "forever." He spent the next days researching the fight song's origins and learned its author was one Samuel Ginty, a King professor of rhetoric. Ginty was an old man by the time he published the song, old enough that his alma mater had been known as Triune College when he attended it, old enough that he had been in the same graduating class as Jedediah King. It was difficult to imagine Samuel not knowing about—if not interacting regularly with—CSK when the slave accompanied his master to Triune's campus, and Reshawn believed the King fight song was an appropriation of the love poem written by CSK, which in turn meant our team's chant "King King motherfucker!" was a bastardization of a bastardization.

It was precisely the intellectual adventure for which Reshawn had so yearned, whole mornings and afternoons and evenings doing nothing but reading scanned newspaper articles and searching for more clues to Carmichael King's life. And yet no matter how far his dark library room might have stood geographically from King's sun-blasted practice fields, Reshawn still hadn't been able to stop football from coming into the library with him, couldn't stop the game from sitting down in the chair next to his and restlessly tapping its foot, waiting for him to acknowledge what he was supposed to be doing, where he should be.

Arnold Duffy might have been respectful about giving the McCoys their space during their time of need, but he was far from the only journalist to learn Reshawn had left camp. The phone rang repeatedly at the McCoy house in Archerville, and though Senior and Ali said no, they didn't want to comment, the journalists had succeeded in interviewing the McCoys' neighbors, Reshawn's old high school teachers and coaches. And this wasn't even the biggest source of stress. The McCoys had been receiving two checks a month from Mr. McGerrin, one on the first and one on the fifteenth. Reshawn had fled Blenheim on July thirtieth, and as a show of good faith, as a sign he believed this was just a temporary blip, Coach Zeller had allowed the first August payment to go through. But the fifteenth was fast approaching, with Reshawn still in Georgia, and the night finally came when Zeller called to say his patience was at an end; the next check would remain unwritten until Reshawn returned to King. Reshawn knew Ali and Senior had come to structure their whole lives around those checks—grocery runs, mortgage payments, Ali's physical therapy and her medications—and when Reshawn told them the next check wouldn't be coming and they should start making a contingency plan, his mother had had to get off the phone, she was so upset, while Senior stayed on the line and, for the first time since Reshawn had come to King, lost his temper. What, exactly, is so hard about your life in Blenheim, son? Is it the free tuition? The complimentary food and clothing? Or is it the free housing and textbooks? Are your grades a single point lower than they've ever been? Do you really think you could get those things—that you can get *anything* in this world—without working for it?

—I couldn't stop crying after I got off the phone.

You're not half as smart as they say, Reshawn—you fucking idiot, you fucking fool. His bedroom was next door to Grayson's, and Reshawn sobbed so hard Grayson came to check on him. Reshawn confessed everything: his falling-out with football, his father's business failure, his mother's diagnosis, the bribes, his hatred for Coach Zeller and the team. It was good to get all of this off his chest, but Reshawn knew he wasn't confessing merely for confessing's sake, it was also a last-ditch attempt to escape the game. He hoped Grayson would interrupt and tell him there was still a way out, some academic scholarship Reshawn could get from King. But Grayson did no such thing. When Reshawn finished talking, Grayson told him about his own time as an undergraduate at Williams College, another elite, expensive school where he had taken out the same loans Reshawn would have to take out, loans that had led to two decades of crushing financial stress before Grayson managed to pay the last of them off. And though he made the point more gently than Senior, Grayson also came down on the side of staying in football, of viewing the game as just a job—and not even a permanent one, at that. Only, what, eight or so years? His mother would be taken care of, Reshawn would still be a young man when he left, he could count on a superlative recommendation from Grayson whenever, forever. Reshawn nodded and dried his face, thanked Grayson for talking, and spent the rest of that night in bed wondering if he should sneak out and drown himself in the Savannah River. But by the next afternoon he was on the road again, driving north.

—Zeller told me McGerrin's sending the check tomorrow.

That was the last thing Reshawn told me that night. We had been in our Marriott beds the whole conversation, lights off, and when Reshawn finished he lay on his back and stared at the ceiling. I wanted to ask where the hell my car was; but that could wait.

It doesn't matter how great an athlete you are, if you miss two weeks of training in the torrid August heat it's going to show, and when Reshawn made his return to practice the next day he must have felt like he was running through hell with a thick winter sock duct-taped over his mouth. He moved sluggishly through drills. During water breaks he would stand on the sideline, chest heaving, hands hipped, tributaries of sweat running down his forearms and draining into his soaked football pants. Rusty on the plays he knew and at a loss when it came to new offensive packages installed in his absence, he made more mistakes in that first practice alone than I'd seen him make all last season.

A few teammates—Jimbo chiefly—took open satisfaction in the sight of his suffering, but for the most part the players encouraged him, bringing him water bottles, putting their arms around him so he could lean on them in between conditioning sprints, yelling out that he'd return to his old self soon enough. Some did this because of genuine compassion for the boy who'd fallen out of shape while standing next to his mother's hospital bed, but others—people I knew for a fact hated Reshawn—cheered him on simply because they understood we needed him to return to form if we wanted to make a real run at our first winning season in decades. Errol fell squarely into the latter camp. Off the field he would harp on the Intro to French snitch and studiously avoid talking to or even *looking* at Reshawn, but on the field there was nobody who encouraged our starting tailback more vociferously.

*USA Today* was delivered to Marriott guests' doors, and on the last Friday morning of camp Reshawn and I stepped out of our room to discover that Arnold Duffy's article had been published. Front page, above the fold, it featured a large photo of Reshawn and Coach Zeller returning from practice. They are entering the game field tunnel that leads up to the locker room, player and coach centered in the mouth of the tunnel. Reshawn is on the left-hand side and still wearing his shoulder pads, face mask dangling from the fingers of his left hand. Sweat beads his nape, and his body is slumped, head down. Coach Zeller is on the right, vigorous yet nurturing, his left hand resting on Reshawn, fingers gripping the back collar of his star's shoulder pads.

Players were poring over the article when we arrived at Training Table for breakfast. They bragged about how swoll they looked in the background of other photos accompanying the story, boasted about how insightful they sounded when they were quoted. Duffy described me as a "rising star in Reshawn's recruiting class." It was the first time my name had appeared in the most important college football newspaper section in the country, and I had been dreaming of being described like this for, well, pretty much all my life. But I couldn't derive any satisfaction from his words, and in fact wasn't even able to bring myself to finish the article. I knew the thing was a sham, and I didn't like how it prompted me to wonder how many of the other articles I'd cherished as a kid had been fiction.

By camp's last practices Errol finally started getting the hang of our offense, while Reshawn recovered his old brilliance. The gamble Coach Zeller had taken in lying about Reshawn's disappearance was going to pay off, and the man was in raptures whenever you saw him, humming the fight song as he hurried from one meeting room to another, lying down on a bench press during team lift to show us he still had some of his old college strength.

On Saturday afternoon, the penultimate day of camp, we were falling into formation for team stretch when Coach Zeller mused:

—Feels like I've lived 'bout a hundred years the last three weeks. How about y'all?

He strolled between the lines of stretching players.

—Coach Armando, what we got planned tomorrow?

—Normal schedule, Coach.

—That's it?

—Yes sir.

—Seems kinda anticlimactic.

Zeller stopped.

—At the end of camp every year at TCU, we had us a freshman talent show. One of the best damn days of the whole season. What we got planned tomorrow night, Coach?

—Just move-in.

Zeller broke into a big smile.

—What do y'all think? he asked us. Freshman talent show tomorrow? Start a new King Football tradition?

—YES SIR!

Sunday happened to be my birthday. The team checked out of the Marriott that morning, and when Thao picked me up at the rotary during the afternoon break we drove to his house in Carsonville so he could give me his gift. I thought the "gift" was his body, which had to be the loveliest body in the history of the world, in particular the muscles that descended from either side of his belly button, twin grooves of hard smooth flesh called the iliac furrow, the Apollo's belt. My hands rested on those grooves as I went down on him, gripping them when I felt his body lock into climax, and after he'd gone down on me and we lay on our sides in bed, facing each other, I trailed my index finger across those grooves again, skating along the hard, sweat-slicked surface.

—Do you want it now? he asked.

He didn't wait for me to respond before jumping out of bed and hurrying downstairs. I felt so happy, listening to him bustle around the kitchen below, hearing his careful footsteps as he ascended the wooden stairs, and though I knew what I was about to see, when he nudged the door open with his hip and walked in carrying a small Black Forest cake with eighteen burning candles, I couldn't stop myself from crying. Thao laughed gently and blew out the candles himself. He set the cake on his dresser and sat next to me in bed, rubbing my back.

That moment alone would have made this the best birthday I'd ever had. But then Thao drove me to West Campus, and when I followed the other linebackers into our meeting room I found a tray of homemade chocolate cupcakes waiting on the back desk. The number 18 was written on the cupcakes' tops in white icing.

—You getting into baking, Coach? Cornelius asked Hightower.

—Bet you'd like to see me in an apron. No, a little bird told me it's Furling's birthday.

Hightower turned to me.

—Why didn't you tell me last year, son?

I had been a bottom feeder this time last year, when Hightower had done his best to pretend I'd never *been* born. But I couldn't hold that against him now.

—You're only eighteen? Cornelius asked, holding up a cupcake. Been sleepin' on you.

I took a cupcake. Everybody was enjoying themselves, chatting and scarfing down the treats—save for Chase, who sat alone at a table at the front, his back to us.

—McGerrin, you allergic to chocolate? Hightower asked.

—No sir.

—You too good for my wife's baking?

Chase grudgingly stood, took one of the cupcakes, and returned to his seat. The rest of us took our second (or third) cupcakes and sat at our tables. Coach Hightower walked to the white board, sucking icing off his fingers. I could tell he was nowhere near done with Chase.

—What'd you get Furling for his birthday, McGerrin?

—Nothing, Coach.

—*Nothing?* Seems kinda rude. You gotta get your fellow Will *something* on his birthday. We're a team, ain't we?

Hightower pretended to think, and then snapped his fingers.

—I got it. What about the starting spot?

Players laughed. Chase tried to force a smile.

—That's okay, Coach, he said. I'll get him a card.

—Shit. Eighteen's a big birthday. No one's gonna remember a fucking *card*. The one spot, though, I feel like he'll remember that. What do you think, Furling? If Chase gave you his spot, would you take it?

—Yes sir, I said, laughing.

—Settled, then. Furling with the ones today, McGerrin with the twos.

Coach Hightower was notorious for flogging a joke far past the time of death, and I saw the other linebackers couldn't tell, either, whether we were supposed to still be laughing.

—Are you being serious, Coach? I asked.

—What, you not interested in running with the ones?

—No! I mean, yes sir. I am.

—Well, good. Make it count.

I didn't entirely believe he meant it until we went down for the last practice, and even when I was sent out with the starting defense, I waited for Coach Hightower to laugh and admit he'd been fucking with me. But that didn't happen. I ran with the ones, and not for just a few snaps before Chase was subbed in—for every rep that practice.

By the time we returned to the locker room, everybody had heard about Chase's humiliation. Vets agreed it was the worst way a King player had ever been demoted.

Practice ended early to give us time to move into our housing for the school year—on West Campus now for Reshawn and me—and the team reconvened at Training Table at seven. Once dinner ended, Training Table staff set up a long folding table at the head of the room, arranging six chairs behind it, while the chef emerged from the kitchen pushing a two-tiered cart displaying six warm apple pies, which he laid on the table, one before each chair.

Vets were on guard for any talent show performance that wasn't sufficiently humiliating, and we booed at the sight of the pies, thinking the first group was trying to get away with a boring eating contest. Then, to further stoke our annoyance, the six performing freshmen—and, strangely, the sous-chef Judy—locked themselves in the men's bathroom.

We grew restless, stamping our feet.

—Getting blow jobs from Judy isn't a talent!

—Let's *go*!

The door opened at last, and our wait was rewarded with the sight of six freshmen stumbling out of the bathroom in high heels, black cocktail dresses, blonde wigs, and the lipstick and rouge Judy had helped them apply. Players fell to the floor laughing. They rushed over to slap the freshman asses so prominently hammocked in the tiny dresses. A fight was only narrowly averted when Jimbo yelled to Cornelius:

—Orin looks like Sandra!

Orin was a six-foot-seven, 323-pound freshman defensive end, and Sandra was an All-American shot-putter on King's track and field team, as well as Cornelius's longtime girlfriend.

The dresses turned out to be an ingenious twist on the eating contest. The freshmen took their seats, gripping the bottoms of their chairs to prevent themselves from using their hands, and on the count of three pounded their faces into the pies—wigs flailing, lipstick smearing, globs of cinnamony filling jumping into breast cups. By the time the winner was called, the room was shaking with stomping feet.

The following two groups were a mixed bag. The second group was made up of four freshmen who'd evidently waited until the last minute to figure out what to do. They walked to the front of the room holding plastic sacks of water containing live goldfish and explained their talent would be swallowing the fish alive. But while it was indeed entertaining to watch them hesitantly dip their hands into the bags, tip their heads back, and gullet the fish, the routine was spoiled when one of the freshman, a cornerback from Santa Fe named Alfonso Carpentier, dropped his sack and clutched his throat. Luckily there was a trainer in the audience who could Heimlich him, and after three heaves the mangled fish fell to the floor with a pathetic little plop, while Alfonso was escorted back to his chair sniffling like the scared child he was. The next group was a trio dressed in khaki pants, polo shirts, and King Football hats—coachwear. They proceeded to rap, in alternating Beastie Boys style, a clever original song dense with inside jokes about the team. The song was good, but most of us were distracted by Alfonso, who was struggling to get hold of himself after his brush with death.

The show was saved by the fourth and final performance. It featured Slo-Mo, our cherubic starting fullback, and Errol. Slo-Mo carried a cardboard box filled with props and announced they were going to do a series of impressions. This alone got a chuckle, since the idea of marble-mouthed Slo-Mo doing an impression of anybody was amusing. But Slo-Mo turned out to be little more than a sidekick. Errol was eager to redeem himself after his disastrous recitation of the fight song, and what we got now was the Errol Show.

The first impression was of Kendrick on a date. Errol played Kendrick by stuffing hand towels into the chest and sleeves of his T-shirt, and then more towels into the front and back of the compression pants he wore beneath his mesh shorts. Slo-Mo played the girl, wearing a blonde, pie-matted wig one of the freshman had worn during the first performance. The gag was that Kendrick was too packed with muscle to go on a normal date. First, he and the girl sat in chairs across the table from each other, pretending to have dinner. But when Kendrick picked up his plastic wine glass he accidentally crushed it to smithereens, just as when he tried to use his metal fork he bent the thing against his plate. Next, Kendrick walked his date home, but when he tried to kiss her at the doorstep his gigantic pecs got in the way and, try as he might, he couldn't make his lips reach the girl's. The girl wasn't deterred, though, and for the final bit she invited Kendrick inside her place. They tried to have sex doggie-style, but Kendrick's quads were so big and bouncy that his first thrust sent the girl flying. We howled. Even the stoic Kendrick formed something resembling a smile.

For the next impression, Errol and Slo-Mo were joined by a special guest, Cornelius, dressed in the coach gear from the Beastie Boys performance. Slo-Mo and Errol sat in two chairs side by side, pretending to be players in a meeting. Cornelius stood in front of them and said:

—Good morning, fellas!

—Morning, Coach Hightower!

I laughed: Cornelius had nailed our coach's wry scowl.

—Special day, Cornelius-as-Hightower said. Special *day*! You know what day it is?

—My birthday! Slo-Mo yelled out.

—That's right, Miles. Happy goddamn birthday.

If Slo-Mo was me, Errol most definitely was Chase. I looked two tables over at the real Chase, who was fidgeting in his chair, his grin doing little to hide his unhappiness.

—Chase, Cornelius said. What you get Miles for his birthday?

—Oh, the *best* present, Coach! Errol-as-Chase said in a ditzy voice.

He reached under his chair and presented Slo-Mo with a small box done up in bright wrapping paper.

—What is it?! Slo-Mo asked, shaking the box next to his ear.

—Now, Miles, that's from me too, Cornelius/Hightower said.

Slo-Mo tore off the wrapping paper and gasped when he saw what was inside. He turned to Errol.

—For me, Chasey?!

—For you!

Slo-Mo reached into the box and removed two pink squash balls and held them up for the room to see.

—It's Chase's balls!

Let's pause a moment to consider why Errol would have done this. One possible answer is he wanted to humiliate Chase in front of the team as Chase had humiliated him when he'd booed him down during his freshman song. Errol was too narcissistic to register anything other than the humiliation, and too petty to blame that humiliation on anybody but Chase. Another, related answer is Errol wanted to put a hard stop to the friendship with Chase that Errol had been growing tired of during camp, and was using this impression as the nuclear option to kill off the relationship. A third answer, which I think is both simplest and strongest, is that Errol wanted to strike while the iron was hot, to use a piece of team gossip that couldn't have gotten any fresher for his skit, so he could maximize the laughter.

And maximize he did. The players lost their minds when Slo-Mo held up the two squash balls—shouting, stamping feet, cooing at a blushing Chase as Chase rose from his chair and fled Training Table.

The talent show ended and the players started for the parking lot, everyone heading to the Football House to celebrate the end of camp. Meanwhile I lingered, eating another slice of tonight's coconut cake and watching the Training Table staff clean the mess we had made. Once I was the only player left, I started walking across Central Campus to carry out the plan. When Reshawn was driving to the Hay to turn himself in last week, he had seen Wheeler see him driving my Saturn. Reshawn realized that if he parked my car in the players' lot, the lie about taking care of his mother was in danger of being exposed; so he had changed direction and driven my car to a parking garage on the far end of Central Campus, where he knew no players would be going during camp. And because Jimbo had continued to insist that in my car lay the real explanation for where Reshawn had gone, we decided it would be best to put a week between the time Reshawn returned to the team and when I started driving my car again, so that the two didn't seem in any way connected. Enough time had passed for me to fetch the car.

Royalty had returned to campus, and as I walked across Central I passed juniors sitting on the concrete porches of apartments they had recently moved into, barbecuing burgers and hot dogs and brats on small Coleman grills, slouching in beach chairs as they caught up on each other's summer break. These people felt like my classmates in a way they never had, and I knew this was thanks to the regular student who was at that moment waiting for me to drive to his off-campus house in Carsonville, the boy I was starting to think of as my boyfriend even if I hadn't yet dared to say the word out loud, the warmth with whom I would spend the night and who would be there smiling when I woke the next morning.

I passed Chase's building, where he would be living for another year. The lights in his sliding glass window were on behind the drawn shades, and I knew there was no way he would go to the Football House tonight, not when every player would ask how painful it had been to remove his own balls. I'd be lying if I said the spectacle of him getting humiliated at Training Table hadn't stirred the same strange, strong horniness I'd been experiencing all camp when it came to Errol and Chase; but that feeling had passed, and now, seeing Chase at home, knowing how crushed he was by his crush, left me feeling ashamed for what my endless competition with him had brought out in me. I should at least make sure he was okay.

—What?

Chase gripped the door, preparing to slam it in my face. His eyes and cheeks were clear, but I knew his face wasn't the prime casualty when he was upset. And sure enough, when I looked at the knuckles on the hand holding the door, they were fat and red from whatever he'd been punching.

—Errol's a prick, I said.

—Feeling guilty? I *knew* you gave him the idea.

—Are you gonna let me in?

He watched me a moment, then turned back inside. He left the door open.

I hadn't been in the apartment since the night we went to Stefan Knows last November, and I saw that in the past ten months he'd replaced much of his perfectly good furniture with newer, even pricier stuff. This saddened me, but not half as much as the photographs of Sadie, which still hung on his refrigerator.

I took a beer from the fridge and sat on the couch next to Chase. He was watching the last NFL exhibition game of the pre-season, San Francisco versus Chicago. The Bears had Brian Urlacher, a six-foot-four, 258-pound sneer with a barbed wire tattoo on his right biceps. The second quarter was beginning, and Urlacher was subbed out of the game so his backup could get some reps. The camera followed Urlacher as he jogged to the sideline and took off his helmet.

—I might get one like that, I said, meaning the barbed wire tattoo. Cornelius says the guy he got his from would give me a discount.

—Who, Fabrizio? Chase asked.

—I don't know his name. Corny just said the parlor was downtown.

—That's Fabrizio. There's a lady named Rouge in Hillsborough who charges half as much. She's the one who did Devonté's.

Devonté's tattoo was the consensus best on the team. It was modeled on the Gothic cross that thrust up from the nave of the King Chapel, and was so finely drawn I would find myself standing behind him in the shower line and discovering details I hadn't noticed before, like the exquisite shading that fell on the right side of the cross, or how the top edge of the top shaft was slightly crumbled, just like the one on the real cross. It was kind of Chase to tell me.

—You kind of look like Urlacher, I told him.

—I look like a mean penis?

I laughed, and Chase allowed himself to grin. He was resting his cold beer bottle on top of his swollen knuckles.

—Are you and Sadie still talking? I asked.

—Not since November.

—Why are the photos still on the fridge?

He shrugged.

—Might as well be something up there. It's not like I'm gonna have any other girl's photos anytime soon.

—There are, like, three thousand girls at King, Chase.

—You find one that wants to be with an ugly retard, you let me know.

—You're not—

—*He's* a fucking gargoyle, Chase said, gesturing at the TV screen. You know the only reason a girl would wanna be with a guy who looks like Urlacher? Because he's an NFL player. I bet he gets a marriage proposal every time he steps out of his house. What would they get from me? An ugly retard who played at a losing program and never even *started*? *Sadie* didn't want to be with me—she moved to fucking Boston so she didn't have to be anywhere near me. I call and call and this robot says the number's no longer in service, "Cannot be completed as dialed."

I watched him, waiting to see if he'd realize the slip he'd made about Boston; but he was too upset to understand what he was saying.

Chase stood suddenly and bumped the coffee table, spilling my beer.

—I'll get a—, I began, but he brusquely brushed past me into the kitchen and returned with a roll of paper towels and a bottle of cleaning fluid. He knelt to mop up the mess, and I stood behind him, watching how carefully he cleaned. I had stayed too long already, and knew I shouldn't have come here in the first place. And wasn't this what Chase deserved? Hadn't he practically imprisoned Henry while they'd been together?

But "imprisoned," that was Thao's word, one that seemed off when he'd used it that summer, and which seemed even more wrong to me now. Because, for how interwoven their lives were, Thao and Chase had met just the one time, during that disastrous night at Stefan Knows. Otherwise, Thao's sole knowledge of Chase had come from whatever Henry told him. Thao didn't know, like I did, the Chase that Henry had fallen in love with, the Chase you could only get in moments like this, the vulnerable, sweet, self-despising child who kept up sham photographs of an ex-girlfriend so he could have a reminder of the boyfriend he'd lost.

And was that fair? Didn't he deserve something better, something more?

And didn't I have some responsibility to help him? Wouldn't it be wonderful if *I* had someone I could talk to about what it was like to be a gay kid on the team? Someone who could understand my life in a way that Thao, no matter how much I told him, never could?

—Hey, I said, tapping his shoulder. Chase—

# SEVEN

My first chance to tell Thao I had come out to Chase was in Carsonville, around midnight. Like I said, the honesty Thao inspired in me was what made our adventure so exhilarating, and as I used the key he'd left in the mailbox to let myself into his house, I readied myself to honor that transparency, explain why I thought Chase deserved to have someone like me in his life, why I needed someone like him in mine. My resolve lasted the fifteen seconds it took to walk upstairs. When I entered Thao's room and saw how unconflictedly happy he was to see me, when I felt his innocent lips press into mine and heard his ingenuous questions about my last day of camp, I lost the nerve to tell him I had just confessed everything to the boy he loathed most in this world.

My second chance came the next morning, when we were both awoken by the sound of a recycling truck gobbling glass bottles. The lie had sat in my stomach all night long like an iffy piece of seafood, and I knew that forcing myself to puke it up now was preferable to letting it stay where it was and slowly absorb itself into my system. But then Thao flipped onto his back to stretch his arms, showing he was at full morning attention. Addressing that erection was infinitely preferable to eliminating it with words about Chase.

My third chance was during breakfast downstairs, though I'm not sure that even counts as a chance, since all eight of Thao's roommates ate with us. These boys were becoming nearly as important to me as Thao was, comprising as they did a community into which I was automatically, unquestioningly accepted, making as they had this house into a haven where the whole of me could be present and accounted for, a place where I could sit and talk without the usual desperate self-pruning. But they were also eight boys who loved Henry, and whenever Chase came up in conversation, they didn't pronounce his name so much as spit it. Why ruin breakfast?

I kissed Thao goodbye and drove to West Campus. I was enrolled in two real classes and two joke classes—a Melville seminar Professor Grayson was teaching and a survey of the New York School poets for the former, and The Golden Age of American Film and an introduction to cultural anthropology for the latter.

American Film was held first thing Monday morning, in a large auditorium that, intentionally or not, resembled a crummy old movie house—faded black walls, creaky chairs upholstered with ugly orange cloth, and little dotted stair lights that illuminated your steps while the film was in progress. My teammates had already claimed the last, highest rows when I arrived, and my pulse spiked when I spotted Chase. After getting fictionally castrated by these players not twelve hours earlier, I expected him to do something now to prove he still possessed his balls, maybe ask me where I had slept last night and listen to me stammer, maybe call me a faggot to watch me squirm. But I was pleasantly surprised. Chase only gave me a subtle chin lift before ignoring me.

The house lights dropped and a clip from *The Godfather* began. We open with Sonny Corleone, the family's loose-cannon scion, visiting the apartment of his pregnant sister Connie, who opens the door with her face turned away, trying to hide her blackened eyes and scabbed lips. When Sonny sees what his sister's new husband, Carlo Rizzi, has done to her, he bites his knuckle and prepares to rush out and murder his brother-in-law. But a teary, slightly slurry Connie tells Sonny *she's* to blame for her bruised face, she

hit Carlo first, was asking for it, and she makes Sonny promise he
won't touch Carlo. With frightening ease, Sonny's features relax.
He nods and kisses his kid sister reassuringly on top of her head,
telling her he wouldn't dream of making her child an orphan before he was born. In the very next scene, we cut to Carlo's New
York neighborhood on a hot summer day. Carlo and his goons
lounge on a short concrete stoop while kids play in the gushing
water of an open hydrant. Carlo is king of the stoop, dressed nat-
tily in a silk suit the colors of an orange Creamsicle and murmur-
ing lordly orders to his underlings about stopping taking action on
Yankees games. Then Sonny and Company screech up in a black
Lincoln. Carlo knows instantly what this is about and flees across
the street, but Sonny catches him by the scruff of his silk shirt and
hurls him into a garbage area in front of an apartment building, a
small rectangular space fenced in by a low wrought-iron gate. The
space becomes a cage for Carlo, and he can do little more than
desperately clutch a rail while Sonny jumps in to maul him—
punching him, kneeing him in the ribs, even throwing his own
shoe at Carlo's head. Sonny tries to loosen Carlo's grip on the rail
by biting his knuckles, taking us back to when he bit his own
knuckle in Connie's apartment, a harbinger of the violence to
come. When that doesn't work, he lifts a metal garbage can and
pounds Carlo over the head with it, then takes the can's lid and
smashes Carlo's face. By this point Carlo is half alive and crawls
out of the cage on his belly, kicked in the ribs again and again.
Carlo has just reached the curb when Sonny finishes him off with
a punt to the jaw. Carlo flops into the gutter, blood mingling with
the hydrant's runoff.

—You see Sonny's shoes? O'Connor said as we filed down the
auditorium steps. Those joints were tight as hell.

—They're called wingtips.

—What, like *wing* wings?

—Like a bird, young.

—Wingtips, O'Connor said, savoring the new term. I'm going to Nordstrom *tonight*.

We entered the hot, bright West Campus quad, the lawns and flagstone paths busy with freshly returned students. I had my Melville class coming up and broke away from the group, toward the English building. I noticed Chase walking in my peripheral vision, but we didn't acknowledge each other until we were out of our teammates' sight.

—Ordered my Urlacher jersey, he told me. They size them the same way they do condoms.

I smiled.

—What do you have now? he continued.

—Melville in the English building. You?

—Not Melville in the English building.

This exchange might seem mundane, and I guess it was, but mundanity was also what made it so extraordinary. I could sense a new evenness to Chase, a comfort in his own skin. Public Chase and Private Chase seemed to have collapsed into someone I hadn't met before, someone sustainable, someone who might be lastingly likeable. Was this the only Chase I'd know from now on? If it was, maybe I wouldn't even need to tell Thao what happened.

In twelve days' time the team would be in South Bend to play the University of Notre Dame for our first game of the season. Notre Dame was one of the most prestigious opponents in Division One, a nationally ranked squad, not to mention a program whose every game was broadcast to millions of people weekly on NBC. It was the biggest debut imaginable for King Football, and a public relations campaign was in full swing to generate excitement among our steadily growing fan base.

The latest step in that campaign took place the next evening, following practice. We dressed in our purple game jerseys and jeans in the locker room and migrated upstairs to the third floor, whose old, fusty trappings had been renovated into the futuristic football aesthetic you find at the country's great programs. A latticed steel-and-glass veneer had been overlaid on the drab white walls, the coffee machines with their singed hotplates were traded out for automated K-cup machines, while the entire back wall was now a bank of floor-to-ceiling windows that looked onto our stadium. The floor was split into four main areas: a King Football Hall of Fame tricked out with interactive displays; a chic restaurant called The Scepter that was to serve as a kind of on-campus extension of the King Club; a series of luxuriously appointed offices for members of the Crown Committee; and a ballroom complete with a custom-made chandelier fashioned out of curlicued iron.

Long folding tables had been arranged into a U in the ballroom, and we took our seats in the order of our game jerseys. Soon after we sat, the doors cracked open to let in a surprisingly heavy stream of fans, from infant boys in King Football onesies, to perma-bachelors in head-to-toe King gear, to a trio of walkered octogenarians who informed each and every player that they were the last surviving members of King's 1948 Rose Bowl team. With gold permanent markers we autographed complimentary posters with this season's schedule printed on them, footballs, baseball caps, old game programs, the backs of T-shirts, the thighs of jeans. Many fans were asking me to sign copies of the *USA Today* profile by Arnold Duffy, and I saw that, in addition to the free posters, Mary Sue Kim and other Athletic Department flacks were giving out copies of the paper.

Most of the fans had already read the article, judging from how often people stopped in front of Reshawn to ask after his mother's health, tell him they had someone in their own family suffering from MS. One sun-poisoned man in overalls was a preacher, and without warning he laid his right hand on top of Reshawn's head, removed a miniature Bible from his back pocket, and held the book aloft as he silenced the room with a resounding

—LOOOOOOOOOOORD!

People bowed their heads and closed their eyes, mothers shushing children.

—Lord GOD we ask that you *massage* your mercy into the legs of Reshawn's mother!

—Yes Lord!

—Take *away* her illness!

—Praise!

—ERASE her pain!

—*Please please!*

—We ask you to *FILL FILL FILL* her with the light of your truth, Almighty God, which guides us through this dark world every day! And we ask all this in the name of your only begotten son, Jesus Christ.

Reshawn kept his eyes open the whole prayer, looking up at the preacher with the intensity of someone trying to use only his neck muscles to prevent his head from being shoved underwater.

What a difference a year made. Last season I was so inconsequential nobody on the team cared whether I wore pads on the sidelines during games, while this year I was to be on the field against Notre Dame more than any other player—in addition to starting at Will linebacker, I was also a starter on the kickoff and kickoff return squads.

I was perfectly ecstatic about that, and when kickoff was called onto the field at practice the next afternoon, day turned to night and our practice field morphed into the glittering, bulb-bathed Notre Dame Stadium, complete with an 80,000-strong crowd emitting expectant surf-murmur as they waited for the kick. I locked hands with my fellow starters and ducked my head to listen to the huddle call.

—Break!

We fanned out to our positions. I sank my hips, swaying right-to-left in time with the crouching players ahead of me. The kicker raised his arm, the whistle sounded, and as the kicker lowered his arm and advanced toward the ball, I did too, slowly, slowly, until the ball was up and I was off, the crowd screaming as I sprinted downfield and keyed in on the Notre Dame snarler assigned to block me. My left arm crooked into a right-angled weapon I used to tear through that blocker's arms. Dip, rip, I was past him, now running so fast I felt I was in a kind of horizontal free fall, bearing down on the Notre Dame returner, on the verge of making my first tackle of my college career. But just when I was about to wrap him up, the back of my right shoulder pad was jolted and I was knocked off balance, redirecting me away from the returner and costing me the tackle. With that, the stadium reverted to the practice fields, night turned back to day, and I was staring at Barron Filmore, the freshman tight end who'd just blocked me illegally.

Our freshman class was more than living up to the hype. Of its fifteen members, thirteen had won either the starting or the backup spot at their respective positions, one had had his season ended with a torn Achilles tendon, and one had been knocked down to the bottom feeders. You guessed it—the disappointment was Barron, who'd struggled mightily to learn the offensive packages and was embarrassed badly in his freshman Oklahoma drill. To be the only freshman who wouldn't be traveling to Notre Dame was a humiliation Barron wasn't bearing well at all, and ever since his red practice jersey appeared in his cubby, he'd been picking fights in practice and the locker room, spouting conspiracy theories about how his black position coach had a vendetta against his white self, flailing desperately for some way, any way, to distinguish himself, change the coaches' minds, earn a seat on the plane to South Bend.

But as a bottom feeder he had no real avenue for doing so; the only thing he could do was run full-speed when he was under explicit instructions not to and perpetrate dirty hits on starters like me. Barron always ended up getting scolded for his stunts, as he was now:

—Don't be a fucking hero! Coach Hightower screamed. I see you pull that shit with one of my guys again and I'll shove my cock down your throat!

—Yeah, sure.

Hightower tilted his head.

—Say again, Filmore?!

—I said, yes sir!

The other kickoff starters were as angry as Coach Hightower, knowing they were just as susceptible to getting hit by Barron. So on the next kickoff rep, several of the starters diverged from their assignments to converge on Barron, crunching him between their bodies and leaving him to rise, wobbly, from the grass, blood dribbling down his chin.

*One of my guys*, I kept thinking.

CG: Welcome welcome welcome to this week's edition of "Talk to the Throne"! I'm your host, Carvell Gleason, and with me as always is the man himself, Head Coach George Zeller.

GZ: Hey there, Carvell.

CG: Hey, Coach! I think everyone'll agree *every* week is a special one on "Talk to the Throne" but, folks, this might be the specialest. In the studio tonight we got starting quarterback Errol Machen and the one, the only, Mr. Reshawn McCoy. First time we've had the triumpherate of King Football on the show. Reshawn, am I saying that right?

RM: Trium*vir*ate. With a *v*.

CG: Ha! Boy spells, runs, leaps buildings in a single bound. Can probably fix your carburetor, too.

GZ: Well, hold on now, Carvell—come Saturday night, we're gonna be able to spell that word both ways, ain't we?

EM: Yeah, Coach. That's for sure.

CG: Fair e-nough! Now, before we get to some of our callers, I wanna take advantage of the unique perspective here tonight. Coach is on the show every week giving us that 30,000-foot angle, but I wanna ask Errol and Reshawn about life in the trenches. What's the *feeling* of the team these days, fellas? First time King's played Notre Dame. Gotta be some butterflies there.

EM: Well yeah, there are, Carvell. But, like, you've got the good kind of butterflies and the bad kind. We only got the good. I wish we were in South Bend already.

CG: Reshawn, how about you? Gettin' nervous?

RM: About what.

CG: About what! Wish our listeners could see his face right now—Notre Dame players might take one look at him and just give up! All right, Randall from Greenville. You think you'd have the cojones to swap stares with Reshawn McCoy?

CALLER: Well, I don't know about that, Carvell. Twenty years ago, maybe.

CG: Smart answer there, Randall. What's the question?

CALLER: Customer at my garage had him one of those little fisty leprechauns on the back of his 4-Runner. I told him I'm a King man, through and through, and we got to talking about the game. I told him, Reshawn *and* Errol? We're gonna be tough to beat next Saturday. But this guy holds talent is only one aspect, and we just don't have the big-game experience. Like I said, I'm a King man, Carvell, been to every home game the last twenty-one years—

GZ: And we sure do appreciate that, Randall.

CALLER: Yes sir, Coach. But the man's point has been getting me a little worried. How we preparing for that kind of environment?

CG: Great question. Errol?

EM: Football is football. Coach Zeller keeps telling us we're gonna be playing the same game we always do. Hundred-yard field. Two goalposts, six points a touchdown, three for a field goal. It's all about this concept I've learned about in my classes, "interiority"—

*The Redshirt*

CG: Reshawn? You gonna add something?

RM: No. Sorry.

EM: [inaudible]. We'll be ready.

CG: Well—all right! Hey there, Graham from Morganton.

CALLER: Hey there, Carvell. More a comment, really. I am just fed *up* with this softness I'm seeing from a game that's supposed to be played by gladiators. I'm just putting it forward that we got a chance, a *real* opportunity, to show the country that *men* still can take the field. I thank you.

GZ: Love it, Graham! Gonna let you know the next time we got an openin' on staff.

CG: That strike a chord with you, Coach? Toughness?

GZ: You know it does. I tell my men every day—kill the softness, carve off the fat and feed it to the damn dogs. In Oklahoma drills we make the *punters* line up and tackle. I tell you, that disgust in Graham's voice? I know where that's comin' from. I feel that every day I go to the supermarket. The bank. The damn barber shop. Only place I *don't* feel it is with my men on the field.

CG: Reshawn, I think that's what makes you so blamed special. You're not afraid of confrontation. Other backs'll pussyfoot away from contact. But you got a hunger, don't you?

RM: Sure.

GZ: Errol's the same way. No sliding for him.

EM: Nope!

CG: Ha! Anita from Hope Mills. Always grateful for our female listeners.

CALLER: It's two parts, if that's all right, Carvell. A comment and a question.

CG: Yes ma'am.

CALLER: First I wanted to say I made all three of my boys read that article, in *USA Today*? It's just so precious whenever we get an example of true works.

253

CG: Yes ma'am. I find myself rereading it just about every day.

CALLER: And the question I have is, I was hoping for advice you might have for my sons, to go out and help their community.

CG: That's a hell of a—oops, I can probably be a little cleaner after Ms. Anita reminded us of works, can't I? Let me say that that gives us a *fine* segue to bring up something you wanted to mention tonight, Coach.

GZ: Sure does, Carvell. Friday evenin', the team's gonna be headin' over to the pediatrics wing of King Hospital to visit some very special kids. It tells you what kind of young man we got in Reshawn that he came up to my office last week and said he was so overwhelmed by people's response to what his mama's goin' through that he wanted to give somethin' back, to the community. So, like I said, we'll be at Pediatrics this Friday. If you'd like to donate, you can go to their website.

CG: Amazing. Just—amazing. All right, Octavio from Siler City.

With twice as many challenging classes as I'd ever taken and a hundredfold more football responsibilities than last year, I enjoyed only a few waking hours with Thao, late at night and early in the morning—times I had no desire whatsoever to ruin with the fights and misunderstandings and rushed explanations my confession would inevitably occasion. I would tell him. I *would*. Just later today. Just tomorrow. Just the day after that.

Meanwhile, Chase and I were finding excuses to be alone. We left class together and ended up walking the length of West; we intended to drive to Training Table and found ourselves crossing the county line as we traded stories about our lives as ambitious high school athletes who'd had desperate crushes on teammates, discussed the special exhaustion born of endless vigilance, and how that exhaustion gets stacked with all your other tiredness and puts you at a distinct disadvantage with your straight competitors. I talked about Coach Johannsen obsessively, while Chase talked about his father. There was one anecdote in particular he circled back to again and again. He was eleven, and his father took him on a day trip to Fernandina Beach, outside Jacksonville. This was the busiest, most ambitious period of Mr. McGerrin's career, when his mania to build his fortune kept him at the office from long before Chase woke until long after Chase went to sleep, and outings like this were rare for father and son. They got to Fernandina Beach early and spent the day swimming in the warm ocean, eating the fried chicken and potato salad Chase's mother had packed, and, best of all, standing in the sand and throwing a football, with Chase paying close attention to his father's instructions on how to grip the ball's laces, how to pretend to brush the ball against the top of his head just before he released. They were throwing the ball one last round that afternoon when Mr. McGerrin noticed something down the beach. He beckoned his son to come over, and Chase ran as fast as his young legs could carry him (he still dreamt about running, the sand sliding beneath his bare feet, preventing him from getting to his father). When Chase reached him, Mr. McGerrin took a knee, draped his arm around Chase's shoulders, and used the football to point to where the sand was being darkened by the rising tide. Two young men strolled there, wearing nothing but a matching pair of Speedos. Mr. McGerrin said, "You see those two, son? Those are queers." Said it matter-of-factly, as if showing his child a seagull.

Mr. McGerrin flew up to Blenheim the week before the Notre Dame game, and after practice Chase invited me to have a beer with the two of them. We drove to a hole in the wall in downtown Blenheim that Mr. McGerrin was fond of, a place called Dombey's with thick iron grates over the windows and a balding, portly white man behind the bar who spoke in a Cockney accent.

—Have a gooooood feeling about next Saturday, Mr. McGerrin said.

We carried our pints to a booth in the corner. We sat—Mr.

McGerrin, then Chase, then me—and raised our beers to toast King Football.

—How long are you here, Dad? Chase asked.

—Tomorrow night. The Crown Committee's touring the third floor of the Hay in the morning, and then we have a meeting over at Town Hall.

Mr. McGerrin's alcohol tolerance was undiminished; we had been sitting there all of a minute and his pint was already half gone.

—Meeting the mayor about a redevelopment project, he continued. We've put together a consortium. Real estate, architecture, design.

Mr. McGerrin took a pen from his computer bag and used the underside of his coaster to diagram the consortium's plan: The red brick warehouses downtown once used to store tobacco would be transformed into high-end condominiums; here you'd have a row of the kind of upscale shops that had once been the rule at the Blenheim Mall; there you'd get fancy restaurants for King parents who were visiting. A convention center, a multiplex, a greenway that would repurpose a mile-long stretch of abandoned railroad tracks.

—I love this place, he said, meaning the bar we were sitting in, though he lowered his voice so the bartender couldn't hear. We used to come here after games, and that *same guy* used to serve us, if you can believe it. But you can't lure tourists to a place with your old college drinking memories. I need to move on—*Blenheim* needs to move on. Forget Charleston, Atlanta, Nashville. Blenheim can become the cultural hub of the South. And don't think that's not relevant to the program. The more attractive you make this city, the better recruits we get.

Mr. McGerrin stopped, smiling at himself.

—Can't turn it off, can I? What were we talking about?

—Notre Dame, I said.

Mr. McGerrin reached his arm across Chase so he could squeeze my right biceps.

—Hardly recognized you at practice today, Miles. You've gotten *big.*

—Thank you, sir.

—Nervous?

—A little, sir.

—That's natural for your first start. I used to puke before every game.

I wasn't sure what to say. Chase looked to be in exquisite pain, watching us talk across him about the starting spot I'd stolen. Mr. McGerrin noticed, too, and put his arm around Chase, though he kept talking to me.

—Many of my old teammates coached their sons' teams to make sure their kids got in the game. But that's a disservice to the child, gives him misconceptions about how the world works. If Chase was ever going to play, it was going to be on his own merits. Same thing applies at King. I know a lot of fathers who'd be doing the wink-and-nod to Coach Zeller about the depth chart but my God, if someone had done that to *me* while I was playing?

He shook his head at the thought. He released Chase and stood, knees cracking loudly as he rose, to get us another round. Before walking off, he looked down at his son.

—I *told* you you were in trouble after that spring game last year. But you didn't listen, did you, Chasey?

The king was a lion cub who strutted on his hind legs, a gold crown flattening out his soft, pointy ears. The queen at his side was a baby hippopotamus, also upright, also crowned, with long eyelashes to make it clear she was female and a big smile that showed off two stubby, unthreatening tusks. Their dukes and duchesses followed in a jaunty train—a baby elephant, a baby giraffe, a baby flamingo—and looked around delightedly at the fantastical jungle they paraded through, pink palm fronds and orange bougainvillea blossoms, red banana trunks and yellow bamboo stands, high teal grass that swirled around their feet and fuchsia vines dripping from chunky branches.

Past the nurses' desk, the cub king and his court continued to appear on the walls of the pediatrics floor, except now the animals had changed into the same purple hospital gowns the patients here wore. In each area the walls featured the story line of a different animal's quest, so that in Radiology you could see the flamingo learning to fly, in Neurology watch the hippo practicing reading, and in Audiology and Speech look at the elephant lifting a floppy ear to listen to the musical notes that floated from another elephant's trumpeting trunk. The tableaux seemed to have their intended effect on my teammates, the players laughing and joking as we broke into groups and followed our assigned nurses to our assigned rooms.

Reshawn was in my group, which meant we were accompanied not only by a young Filipino nurse named Rhonda but also by Coach Zeller and a photographer from the Athletic Department. We entered the first room, where an eight-year-old South Asian boy with a white bandage wrapped around his scalp was sitting up in bed, his mother and grandmother standing next to him in bright saris. The boy was talkative and lively, and despite the fact that he had been flown in from New Delhi and didn't know the first thing about American football, he was overjoyed to receive the official team baseball cap and autographed poster Coach Zeller presented. But while the rest of us smiled at the boy's rapid-fire questions about our sport, Reshawn stood miserably in back, leaning against the door and giving skeptical glances to the photographer maneuvering around to take pictures. I knew Reshawn despised hospitals from all the time he'd spent in them with his mother, but I thought he could be trying a little harder to at least pretend he was happy to be here.

In the next room, the patient's father watched Reshawn in the held-breath way people do when they find themselves in the presence of a celebrity. The father was almost as young as me, white and redheaded, and wore a purple King College security uniform. His wife was black, young as well, and had a King College Cafeteria Services ID card clipped to one of her belt loops. Lying in bed was their light-skinned three-year-old son, whose nose and cheeks were splashed with freckles and whose arms were dappled with deep purple and green bruises. The boy was shy, the wife seemed tired, but the father talked enough for all three of them in a thick North Carolina accent.

—I'm tryin' to transfer over to the Hay facility, he was saying to Coach Zeller. Maybe you're the man to talk to?

—Well sure, Zeller said. Lemme see what I can do.

—Appreciate that, the father said, and then smiled generally at our group. Y'all dropped in during our little family sweet spot. Ellie works days. I got the night shift over at the King power plant, the one way out past East. We only got this hour between shifts where we overlap. But if I land somethin' on West Campus, that'll give us, what, honey, half an hour more?

—At least.

—Are y'all from Blenheim? Coach Zeller interjected, his accent even heavier than usual.

—Born and bred, the father replied. Played tailback over at Robert E. Lee.

—That right?

—Yes sir. Two-year starter. And it woulda been three if me and Ellie hadn't had our little surprise. King was recruitin' me. Wanted me, *bad*. Maybe I woulda made you wait a couple years before you got on the field!

He said this last part to Reshawn, who was again in the corner.

—Maybe, Reshawn said.

—I was *fast*, the father continued. Teammates told me it should be illegal for a white boy to run like I did. Nicknamed me Whitey Mouse. My 4.39 was *machine tested*. None of that hand-timed stuff. You can't get inducted into Lee's Hall of Fame till you been outta school five years, but I'll be gettin' the call. Read you was a 4.41.

Again, to Reshawn.

—I can't remember.

—Can't remember. I tell you what, if coach here puts in a

259

word for me and I get over to the Hay, maybe the two of us can line up and, *boom*, I'll show you what I still got.

The father was enjoying himself immensely.

—Maybe I shouldn't wait! he continued. Maybe we should figure out a race this week! What do you say, Reshawn?

—Maybe we should wait until your son's out of the hospital.

The father went quiet, and before things could get worse, our nurse Rhonda said we'd already taken up enough of their time.

We continued down the hall. Coach Zeller made Reshawn walk slowly with him at the back of the group, and though our coach kept his voice low, you only had to see his meaty finger poke Reshawn in the arm to understand what was being said. Once the scold ended, Zeller and Reshawn rejoined us and we all entered the next room.

I wanted to turn right back around. The patient was a preteen white girl, and standing next to her bed were her mother and the girl's identical twin. The sisters made for a kind of living, breathing before-and-after photograph: Before was plump with baby fat, her skin a rich brown from the summer sun, her heavy auburn hair pulled into a ponytail, and her mouth full of braces with rainbow-colored rubber bands. After, meanwhile, was so emaciated her neck seemed unequal to the task of holding up her head, and her pale skin was lined with layers of surprisingly long, downy brown hair. She was wearing both IV and breathing tube.

Thanks to Zeller's warning, Reshawn stood right next to the bed. He started out stone-faced, but his features loosened as the sick girl's mother told us how her daughter was Reshawn's biggest fan. The girl had gone to every home game last season before she'd fallen ill, and in her bedroom back home she had a whole wall decorated with nothing but magazine and newspaper cutouts of Reshawn.

The girl shyly asked if Reshawn would sign the baseball cap we'd come here to give her. The nurse loaned Reshawn her pen, and as he signed the underside of the hat's bill, I saw his chin begin to tremble. He handed the hat to the girl, and when she wished him luck at Notre Dame he finally lost it, sobbing so hard he had to bend down and hold on to the bed's plastic side rail with both hands.

The photographer had been snapping photos, but now he lowered the camera to his side. The sick girl didn't know what to do and just stared at the gold crown in the middle of the baseball cap she was clutching. Zeller and the rest of us were at a loss, too. It was left to the girl's mother to pat Reshawn on the back.

—Bless your heart, she said. We're gonna pull through. You'll see. She's gonna be just fine.

Saturday afternoon was graced with my favorite kind of football weather, late August weather, when the day is clear and hot and yet, if you know how to pay attention, you can sense that some of the summer's intensity has been scooped out of the light. There's an empty, secret space behind the glare waiting to be filled in by autumn, and if you're careful, if you attune yourself just right, you can momentarily slip into that space, let the emptiness envelop you. A week from today, we would be in South Bend. *I* would be in South Bend.

Following the team dinner we were instructed to return to the football building for what was being called a special meeting, though what was special about it no player knew. Back at the Hay, I joined the crowd of milling teammates in the second-floor hallway. Entry to the Team Room was barred by Coach Hightower, who stood before the door with his arms crossed and only smirked when players asked what the hell was going on.

Finally a knock came from inside the door and Hightower allowed us in. The graduate assistants had been busy draping a T-shirt on the back of every chair, and what I noticed first about the shirts was their strange shade of purple, somehow both lighter and deeper than the color I was accustomed to. But the odd color was nothing compared to the astonishment on the shirts' right breasts: a new logo for King Football. The gold of the King crown glittered, while the once-rounded points had been sharpened into spikes so that it looked less like a piece of regalia than a wearable weapon.

Manly squeals. Claps, daps, hugs. Many of us stripped off the shirts we were wearing on the spot and slid our new ones on, delighting in the feel of the virgin shirt cloth against our skin, running our thumbs over the new logo. The assistant coaches entered the room, with Coach Zeller sauntering in last, looking jolly as Father Christmas in a white polo shirt also emblazoned with our new crown.

—See y'all got y'all's surprise.

—YES SIR!

We sat. Zeller assumed a ship captain's stance up front, feet spread, chest thrust.

—Time was, you didn't have countries. The world was smaller and nastier'n that. Life was lived closer to the ground. Who could you depend on? Your family. Your *kin*. People called you son-of. And there was pride in that, men. Pride in what family you belonged to. Pride so great you created special symbols for it. You needed help in battle? You raised your eyes—

He did, scanning the air above our heads.

—and found what you trusted.

He thumbed the crown on his chest.

—*This* is your crest. *This* represents your real family. *This place* is our castle, and everyone out *there* is our sworn fuckin' enemy.

Players' legs pumped in place, hands clutching armrests.

—Forget the bullshit. The naysayers. Your professor made a crack about the team? Fuck her. A royal said, "King *Football*?" Get ready to spit in his fuckin' face. 'Cause *this*—

He slammed his closed fist against the crown.

—this is your shield! When you stand behind *this*—

He lowered his voice, breathing hard.

—nothin'll wound you.

It was cause for celebration, and after the meeting ended Jimbo instructed everybody to grab one article of clothing with our old logo on it. That done, we walked to the players' lot and, forming a long caravan led by Devonté's Grand Marquis, drove out of West Campus, out of Blenheim, and into the countryside, past nouveau riche subdivisions with their McMansions and three-car garages, past cypress swamps where the trees were flooded to their navels. We entered spreading farmland, acre upon acre of soft red earth turned a burning blue by the night. With a right, we rumbled down a long gravel road that cut through a tobacco field. We parked next to an old farmhouse and walked to an uncultivated patch of earth bordered on the far end by forest. The farm, I learned, belonged to one of Devonté's uncles.

As Jimbo unloaded the cases of Natty Light he'd grudgingly purchased as payment for his lost bet about Reshawn, Devonté led a group of players to fetch firewood from a half-cord stacked against the side of the farmhouse. There wasn't a cloud in the sky, only thickly clustered stars and a moon so near to full you had to stare to figure out where the missing slice was. The wood-gathering group returned and Devonté oversaw construction of the bonfire, proudly explaining how this field had been the site of Sanders family activities for three generations—graduation parties, pig pickings, haunted hayrides, footraces between boy cousins. The fire was lit, and as we waited for it to gain strength, we chugged beer and collapsed the empty cardboard Natty Light cases, feeding them to the flames.

I stood with Chase, sweating and laughing about my first day of camp last year, when he and Fade had told me I would be taken out to a field much like this and branded with an omega symbol. Chase needled me about my gullibility, while I relished just how far I'd traveled since last August, how much bigger, better—in every possible sense—I had become. The fire started to roar, and Jimbo told everyone to grab their article with the old King crown.

On his word, we threw the shirts, hats, shorts, and socks into the fire, chanting:

*One one two three*
*Who the fuck you came to see?!*
*King King motherfucker!*

Three hours later we finished the last of the beer, doused the fire, and got back into our cars to return to the Football House for a party. The drunkest of us drove down the wrong side of the country highway, racing the others home. I was bringing up the rear of the caravan, concentrating on steering between the lane lines, when Chase pulled alongside me in his truck. He rolled down his window and yelled over his engine that he stank of wood smoke—he was heading to his apartment to change into fresh clothes. This was code. He wanted me to come back to his apartment so we could have another of our secret talks.

We dropped our passengers off at the Football House and continued to Central. I parked in the lot next to Chase's building and texted Thao, telling him I'd be in Carsonville soon. He wrote back:

Gwen: I can't keep hard all night, you know.

I followed Chase upstairs. He went to his bedroom to change, and I went to the fridge for a beer. The Sadie photographs were gone. I was happy to see this.

—Get me one?

I turned to find he'd changed into a clean pair of cargo shorts and was bare-chested, a T-shirt slung over his right shoulder. Like all light-skinned football players', Chase's torso had a hallucinatory farmer's tan. The contrast between his sun-darkened neck and arms and his milky chest was so severe you'd have thought two different people had been stitched together.

I got him a beer, but when I tried handing it to him he slid between my arms and kissed me, gripping the back of my T-shirt.

Each of my hands held a bottle, his lips were much softer than they looked, and I could smell the Old Spice deodorant he'd just reapplied. He opened his mouth and tried to pry mine open with his tongue, which is when I finally made myself step back.

He was breathing heavily, and I could see the swollen head of his cock outlined in his shorts. He saw I had an erection too, but when he stepped up and laid his hand on it, I pushed him away with my elbow. He smiled and took the bottles from my hands, setting them on the kitchen counter.

—I'm supposed to be at Thao's, I said, trying to move past.

—Just sit with me.

—I need to go, Chase.

—Please?

I sat on one end of his couch, he on the other. My heart was still pounding, my cock confoundingly hard.

—Where are you meeting Thao? he asked.

—His house.

—And then what? You guys going to Stefan Knows? Or the Football House?

—No.

—Have you been on a date anywhere that's *not* at his place?

—Not yet.

He nodded.

—"Not yet." That was like me and Henry's *motto.*

—It's not the same.

—Why not? he said. 'Cause his house is bigger than a dorm room? You're still stuck inside. How many times have you guys seen each other on campus this week?

Not once. I didn't want to concede this, but I didn't need to; Chase already knew.

—You and me, he said, we could go anywhere we wanted. Nobody would think shit of it. You could come over here every night, no questions. And next year we could get a place together on Central. You two haven't fucked yet, right?

—That isn't your business.

He smiled.

—You're waiting? Until when? When we have a day off? But what happens if you get called in for a meeting or we have a special lift? Then you have to wait another week. Then another.

He slid over on the couch.

—There'd be no waiting with me. We could fuck right now. You could fuck me here. Or in the kitchen. Wherever you wanted.

His hand was sliding onto my lap, rubbing me through the fabric of my shorts, my pre-come darkening the khaki fabric. I tried to nudge him away—a nudge, not a push—and my halfheartedness only encouraged him to rub me faster. Then he climbed on top of me, straddling me, opening my zipper and pulling out my cock. His other hand pressed into my right shoulder, though whether to balance himself or keep me pinned in place I couldn't tell. He was stroking me too hard, and my erection was dwindling in his fist. I started to experience a kind of paralyzed hysteria. Given what Chase knew about me, I wasn't sure I had any choice but to sit here and let him do what he wanted, then do to him whatever he told me to do.

I punched him in the ribs with the heel of my right hand, a short jab that knocked the wind out of him. He fell against the coffee table, striking the top of his cheekbone on a corner. I stood and zipped my shorts. He was on all fours on the ground, pressing his palm against his face, and I left before he had the chance to say anything.

I was dumb with adrenaline as I sped to Carsonville, my shoulder bearing a phantom tightness from having been pinned to the couch. Turning into Carsonville, the adrenaline started giving way to fear, and that fear almost instantaneously boiled into anger. Reviewing Chase's every vulnerable word and gesture, I saw how he had been laying the groundwork for tonight. I thought about driving back to Central and throwing a brick through his truck's windshield, identifying a hundred opportunities I'd had to leave before things turned. *Why* did I keep coming back to him?

And had I just cheated on Thao?

I softly entered the house's living room. The lights were off. Thao and his roommates were on the green couch, watching a movie. Thao made room for me, sniffing.

—Where were you?

I tensed, thinking Chase's deodorant was detectable.

—You smell like a fireplace, he continued.

—The team had a bonfire.

—Shhhhhh!

Thao quieted, wrapping his arm around mine and leaning his head on my shoulder. I can't remember what movie we watched.

Each Sunday a different roommate was responsible for making breakfast, and the next day was Thao's turn. I woke to find him gone, off to buy groceries, and when I walked downstairs he was already busy cooking French toast while instructing his roommates on how to finish making the Vietnamese iced coffee. No one could find the can opener to open the condensed milk, and his roommates were helpless with laughter as they took turns puncturing holes into the tops of the cans with the claw end of a hammer. I checked my phone again, hoping for a text from Chase. I wanted an apology. An apology would allow me to forgive him, move on.

When breakfast was almost ready, I helped set the table with Abby Scone, a senior who was president of the campus LGBT association and an honorary roommate. Abby was one of my favorites of Thao's friends. She was from Iowa and had a midwestern way about her that reminded me of my family—deliberate without being abrupt, transparent but far from simple. She was also the only girl I'd ever met who knew more about football than I did. Her father was a high school coach in Cedar Rapids, and she had served as the team's water girl her entire childhood. She'd wanted badly to play football herself, but her father had forbidden it.

Abby surprised me by saying she'd bought her plane tickets to South Bend.

—You're going to the game? I asked.

—So are half the seniors I know. King's offering discounted hotel rooms near campus.

—People are that excited?

—Yeah! I mean, it seems like we might not lose by a hundred points.

She stopped, remembering who she was talking to.

—No offense.

Chase still hadn't texted by the time we finished eating, but that was fine. I could talk to him at the Hay, where meetings started at eleven. I drove over and entered the peaceful locker room. White paper McDonald's bags were rustling, hungover players lying on their backs on the carpet and speaking in soft hungover tones.

I carried my purple laundry net to my cube. Cornelius and a couple other players were already sitting in their lockers, and they quieted when they saw me.

## GWEN

The name was written in permanent marker on a torn piece of card-board that had been glued to my locker's nameplate. I was being watched. I needed to act like I didn't know what was happening.

—Who did this? I asked Cornelius.

—Chase came to the Football House last night with a big ol' gash under his eye and said he caught you texting gay shit to a dude named Gwen. Said he called you out and you clocked him.

—And people *believed* him? I said, forcing out a laugh.

—Shit ain't funny, Furling. You need to quash it, quick. Damn near the whole team was at the house last night.

The sign was glued to my nameplate with an epoxy, and I couldn't tear it off with my hands. I went to the equipment room to fetch Cyrus Pyle, who was in the middle of adjusting the air in Scan's helmet with a hand pump while Scan stood there. I pretend-ed to wait patiently for Pyle to finish, not wanting to seem too eager in front of Scan but knowing that all the while more players were filtering into the locker room, passing my locker.

Pyle finally followed me in. He was annoyed as he inspected the sign.

—That glue's going to damage the wood, he said.

He returned to the equipment room to see what he could find to remove it, and in the meantime I took a pen I kept in my locker and tried effacing the effacement, doing my best to ignore the players who shouted "Gwen!" as they passed our cube.

Chase walked in, setting his laundry net on his locker seat.

—The fuck? I said, walking up to him while pointing the pen back at my locker. What the fuck is that, McGerrin?

He looked at the sign, unconcerned.

—Your boyfriend's name.

—That's a *girl's* name, you moron. I knew you were stupid, but this—

—That's code for your faggot boyfriend.

Cornelius sucked his teeth.

—McGerrin, why you always trying to stir up shit?

—Why would Furling punch me in the fucking *face* if he wasn't hiding something?

Chase turned to me.

—If that's a girl's name, show them your phone. Show them the texts you get from "Gwen."

People in the cube looked at me, thinking I would show them my phone and clear everything up.

—This is some desperate shit, I said, throwing my pen at my locker.

Chase walked over to my cube to try and take my phone. I shoved him away.

—See! he said, regaining his footing. Faggot doesn't want me anywhere *near* it.

—Enough, Cornelius said, stepping up to me. Just give it.

He saw me hesitate—as did everyone in the cube, as did Jimbo and the other people from other cubes who'd come over to watch us.

—Furling, Jimbo said. Are you *serious*?

Cornelius was still waiting, and I could see he was clinging to his sympathy for me. He despised Chase for having been a nightmare roommate their freshman year; he wanted to believe me. Finally he just snatched my phone from my hand.

The amount of time it's taken for mountains to form and crumble. The eras in which whole empires have been built and razed. Those spans must have seemed much, much shorter than it was to watch Cornelius stare at my screen. And when he reached the text Thao sent me last night, he looked up from the phone with—it wasn't disgust. Not yet.

Gwen. Players knew this technically referred to the boy I'd been dating, but because they didn't have an actual human being to attach that name to, it existed as an abstraction that had an abstraction's flexibility—it could easily be used as a name for me, could serve as a handy way to differentiate between the boy they had in front of them and the boy they had known. Miles was the starting Will linebacker, the redshirt freshman from Colorado, the teammate, the friend. Gwen was the faggot, the infection the body of the team needed to reject.

Most players first heard the name in meetings, and when I walked into a room, I would see teammates lift their eyes to track me; and because it was so hard at first for them to believe I was what I'd been accused of being, many would lean over to me during film to whisper reassurances, to say that *they* thought it was bullshit, stay strong until the truth comes out. But this grace period was short-lived, since these doubters and defenders would be referred to one of two people—Chase, who was spreading his accusations as fast as his ugly mouth could spew them, or Cornelius, who stood as sober witness. By the time I got to the practice fields that afternoon, only a couple players walked up to pat me on the shoulder and halfheartedly say everything would be all right.

The whistle for stretch was blown, and I partnered with Reshawn. I hadn't seen him yet today, and my heart thudded painfully as I lay on the grass and raised my right leg, waiting to see him hesitate. But, as always, he took a knee next to me, his crotch only inches from mine as he cradled my upraised leg, rested my calf against his shoulder pad, and leaned forward to stretch my hamstring.

—Gwen! Errol yelled. Do semen really taste different if the dude you suckin' off eats pineapple?

Reshawn looked down at me.

—The fuck is he talking about?

I realized Reshawn was so far removed from the team's mainstream, so loath to linger in the locker room or any other place where teammates gathered, that he hadn't heard what happened yet.

—Who knows, I said.

From stretch we jogged to Special Teams period, where I joined the one huddle for kickoff. Like any other huddle, players held hands; but when I reached over to take the hand of Donald Hans, a junior fullback, he shook me off. We broke the huddle, and when the kick was up and we sprinted downfield, I felt like there was an invisible bungee cord tied around my waist that was preventing me from running full speed, a cord that only got tenser, tauter, the farther I ran, a cord that, were I to stop, would fling me backward into the woods bordering the field.

—Gwen, you got a dress I can borrow?

Chase asked me this when the linebackers gathered for Individual period. I wanted to unbuckle my helmet and beat him to death with it; but getting into a fight would anger the coaches, and that was the last thing I needed. The best I could do was trade places with others in the drill line so I faced Chase, collided with him, tried to inflict pain on him, maybe even injure him. But I was too distracted, and my form was sloppy. He overmatched me every time.

A text message from the real Gwen—or maybe I should say the less fake one—was waiting in my phone when I returned to the locker room. I didn't reply. I skipped showering and whatever special hell that would have entailed and drove to Training Table, which I did merely so I could get my name checked off the roll list the graduate assistants maintained for team meals. I bought food back on West Campus, not remembering I still had the stink of practice on me until the café employee crinkled her nose as I raised my arm to give her my cash. I returned to the dorm where Reshawn and I now lived—Mennee Hall, a Collegiate Gothic masterpiece in the center of West that had verdigris downspouts running up the sides of the façade and gargoyles grimacing on its eaves—and headed for the showers.

Reshawn was at his desk, exchanging the textbooks in his book bag, when I came back. I was wearing a towel, flip-flops, and nothing else, and from how hard Reshawn concentrated on handling his collection of Melville stories I could tell he'd finally learned what happened. I wanted to go back to the bathroom and take another shower, turn the water hotter than I could bear and stand beneath it for hours. Instead, facing away from Reshawn, I got a pair of boxers from my dresser, spread them on the floor, and stepped into the leg holes, shimmying the boxers up over my crotch so I wouldn't be naked when I took off the towel.

—Hey, I said, turning to him.

He looked up from his bag, doing his best to keep his face neutral.

—Hey, he said.

—I don't have to sleep in here.

—It's your room, too.

—That's—do you *want* me to sleep in here?

—I mean. You're not gonna crawl into bed with me, are you?

He was trying to give the situation some levity, but this only made me angrier.

—Fuck you, Reshawn. It's like—it's like I'm this fucking lockbox for all *your* secrets.

—Miles—

—Bribes? Running away from camp? I don't tell anyone *anything*, and now my life's getting ripped apart and you—you make a fucking *joke*?

—Sorry. Jesus.

—How was dinner, Reshawn? People in a good mood? You say anything to defend me there?

He shook his head, like I was too irrational to be taken seriously. He zipped his book bag and made to go.

—*No?* I said, taking a step toward him. No. Because you're too fucking self-pitying to think about anybody but yourself. You act like you're soooooo fucking different. You're no different. You're not better than any of them. You're the fucking *same*.

He threw down his bag.

—You don't know shit about me! I'm not the one who—

He stopped himself. I smiled sarcastically.

—Not the one who what? Fucked some boy?

The phrase made him even more uncomfortable.

—Fuck you, he said.

He grabbed his bag, and I threw up my hands and yelled as he walked out:

—*Nobody* can feel anything like *Reshawn McCoy* feels! Nobody thinks *his* thoughts!

He slammed the door. I slumped onto my desk chair, staring at textbooks I had no intention of touching tonight. I was ashamed of myself, knowing I had yelled at Reshawn because he was the only person I *could* yell at. And now what, Miles? Alienating the one teammate who wouldn't have been completely disgusted by you?

My phone buzzed with another message from Gwen. I didn't answer, but I did change his name in my phone to "Whitman."

Defense had lift at 7:15 the next morning, before classes started, but I couldn't think of a single player who'd be willing to be my partner, nor a scenario in which players between reps wouldn't yell out "Gwen!" or make some crack about me spotting them. I knew I would get punished for skipping the lift, but that was fine, I just needed some time, needed to extend my break from the ridicule a little longer. I turned off my alarm and slept through the morning.

I woke a few minutes before two and started for the Hay. Mennee Hall abutted West Campus's main quad, and when I stepped into the irritatingly lovely day I passed a group of kids who lived down the hall from me. They were busy building a large wooden bench that would stand in front of our dorm—a King tradition. Past them, royals were throwing Frisbees on the quad, or sitting in beach chairs and sunbathing as they studied, while a man with a trim blond beard—a postdoc, maybe—took a nap on the lush August grass with his forearm draped across his eyes. I felt an ache in my stomach that at first I thought was merely nervousness about seeing my teammates; but as I walked the ache kept yawning wider and wider, and when I passed a café I realized I'd forgotten to eat. It was too late to do anything about that. I needed to make sure I wasn't late to afternoon meetings.

I retrieved my playbook from my locker and walked to the Team Room. Coach Hightower was standing in the hallway outside the room, reading something in his binder.

—Coach, I began.

—Where were you for lift? he said, clapping the binder shut. A photographer from the *Blenheim Star* was here to take photos of the one defense.

—Fuck. Was that planned?

His expression soured.

—The fuck's that matter, was it planned? You were supposed to *be* here, son.

—Coach—

—You got a stadium tomorrow morning. Six o'clock.

We walked into the Team Room.

—Gwen! Why'd you miss lift—you run outta lube?

—Shut the fuck up! Hightower said, starting the projector.

After meetings I dressed quickly and went down to the practice fields, the first player to get there. It was an experiment: I wanted to see who among my teammates would stand with me, show solidarity. I watched the trainers set up folding tables, arranging hundreds of green cups they poured water or Gatorade into. Meanwhile equipment managers laid out cones, tackling dummies, purple nets filled with footballs. Players started arriving—punters to warm up their legs, quarterbacks to loosen their arms, linemen to practice footwork—but nobody stood with me. Nobody. The whistle blew for stretch, and Reshawn and I paired up. We hadn't talked since our fight, and when he stretched me he held my body gingerly.

The first period was Special Teams, and I joined the one huddle for kickoff. Donald Hans left his hand flaccid this time, forcing me to grab and hold it. Hunger scrounged around my insides.

—Break!

We fanned out to our positions. Coach Zeller usually floated around during this period, conferring with other coaches, leaving the special teams coach to manage his units. But maybe because Special Teams was the first period today, Monday, the first practice of Week One, and most definitely because he was nervous about Notre Dame, our head coach was standing right behind the kickoff team, watching us closely.

—Hold on, hold on. Furling!

I rose from my stance.

—Yes sir!

—Where were you for lift this mornin'?

—Coach—

—Where?!

—I missed it, Coach!

—No shit! Missed the photo session afterward too, didn't you?

—Yes sir!

He let out a roar.

—You think I got time for people who skip fuckin' *lifts*?!
—No sir!
—So what you gonna do about it?
—Run a stadium tomorrow, sir!
He shook his head.
—Not *nearly* good enough. Who's your backup?
No.
—I'm sorry, Coach!
Zeller laughed, incredulous.
—The fuck's "sorry" gonna do for me?
—Please!
—"*Please*"?! No one starts on my team with a fuckin' "please"!
He looked around.
—Who. Is. His. Backup?!
—Me, Coach! said Farrell, a freshman strong safety.
—Fine. Time to get ready for the big leagues, son. And Chase—
—Yes sir!
—You're back at starting Will.

Zeller wasn't the linebackers coach; Hightower was. I looked over at my position coach, beseeching him with my eyes to tell Zeller he'd overstepped his authority. But Hightower's arms were crossed. I had no choice but to yield my spot to Farrell while everybody—the ones, the twos standing behind them, the bottom feeders simulating Notre Dame's kick return, the other players on the sidelines—watched me do it.

One week. That's how long I'd been given to enjoy my promotion. *One week.* For no mistake on the field, no forgotten assignment, no missed tackles or blown coverage. *One week.* I caught Chase watching me during linebacker drills, trying to communicate something with his eyes. *One week.* Reshawn finally deigned to find me during a water break, but it was far too late for such a gesture; I walked off. *One week.* I've heard people claim that when they're in extremis they feel like they're at a great distance from their own bodies; but while I did feel a kind of separation, instead of being distant from my alienated self it seemed like I had to drag it around with me, and in the reps I got that afternoon it didn't feel like I collided with people so much as threw that self against them, like a measly bucket of water thrown at a burning skyscraper. *One week.*

Practice ended and the team started for the tunnel. I stood at the edge of the practice fields, in the shadow of the Jumbotron, and waited for Coach Zeller to finish a conversation with Cyrus Pyle. I would beg forgiveness, prove somehow that I would never, ever, make a mistake like missing a weightlifting session again.

I hoped to walk with Zeller into the Hay, but then I saw he was about to climb into the Gator with Pyle to hitch a ride. I ran over to stop him.

—Coach, I said. Can we talk?

It looked like that was the last thing he wanted to do. But he signaled for Pyle to wait a moment and stepped away from the Gator.

—What? he said.

—I know I let you down, Coach.

—You let your *team* down.

—Yes sir. I—

—How long you played football, son?

—Eleven years.

—Eleven years. And in that time, you ever had a coach who let you break team rules without consequences?

—No, no sir.

—I thought not.

He turned back.

—But didn't Reshawn break team rules?

Zeller turned and stalked up to me, eyes narrowing.

—What'd you say, boy?

—I—

—You *threatenin'* me?

—No sir.

—Uh huh, he said, nodding. Bet your ass you ain't.

I found my locker decked out with new gear featuring our new logo. Running shorts and T-shirts, knee socks and ankle socks, wristbands, headbands, durags, and gloves. My mouthpiece had a little crown fronting the front teeth.

The greatest gear, our new uniforms and helmets, were supposed to be revealed later on in the week, but as players finished showering, Jimbo went to the equipment room and sweet-talked Pyle into letting him briefly borrow them. He came strutting into the locker room dressed in our new purple game jersey, game pants, and helmet. The purple jersey and pants were glorious, made of a huggy material that gave Jimbo a seamless superhero's physique, with a white scimitar-shaped pattern that ran from armpit to knee. Our new helmet was even better, an aerodynamic model I'd only ever seen on NFL players that was painted in our new purple and had our new, jagged gold crown stamped on both sides. Jimbo walked in circles around the perimeter of the locker room like it was a catwalk, sashaying. He paused, jutted out his hip, fluttered his eyelashes.

—That's how Gwen walks!

I left without showering. Once again I was the first in and out of Training Table, this time packing a Styrofoam container with food to take away. I drove to West Campus and parked my Saturn in one of the lots used by royalty so no teammate would see me eating in my car. Just a few bites in, I set down the food and punched my steering wheel, punched it so hard my car started rocking.

I walked across West Campus, hating how much light remained in the sky. It wasn't even eight o'clock yet, and though I was falling behind in my classwork, though I was still expected to be studying my linebacking assignments for Notre Dame, I had no idea how I was expected to fill all the hours that separated now from tomorrow morning. And tomorrow? Tomorrow would be full in the wrong way: I had both of my joke classes, two fifty-minute sessions in which I would either wait for teammates to make cracks about me or squirm through their witticisms. Then meetings, then another practice, more of the living death of watching other people carry out reps that belonged to me.

The wooden bench in front of Mennee Hall had been finished, and when I saw Thao sitting on it I wanted to collapse into his arms. But like I said, it was still light out, and at any moment some of my teammates might return from dinner, on their way to their own rooms in Mennee. We needed to talk somewhere else.

I led him away from Mennee, taking a flagstone path that curved around the right side of the chapel. Behind the nave was a copse that was home to some of the tallest, oldest trees at King. A network of dirt footpaths wound through the copse, and lining the paths were finely crafted wooden benches alumni had donated to the school. Each bench had a gold-plated plaque screwed onto the backrest with a little dedication. The bench that Thao and I sat on read:

For Joaquim dos Santos, Class of 1987, from his loving father, Antônio dos Santos, Class of 1960. "The soul comes afterward."

I told Thao everything, spared myself nothing. Not the kiss with Chase that had preceded the assault, not the lies by omission and the lies by evasion and the bald-face lies I had been telling him the past week. The last of the sunlight extinguished, the lamp above us was only gradually brightening, and Thao's expression was hard to read. I assumed he was getting angry, waiting for me to finish before he raged. But when I reached the part of my story about Gwen and the last days' catastrophes, he didn't scream or huff away. He took my hand and held it with both of his. My teammates had mocked and prodded, heckled and ostracized me with no cause—and meanwhile here was a boy I had betrayed, lied to, maybe even endangered, who was taking my hand and bringing it to his lips to kiss whenever I reached another humiliating node in my story.

I finished talking, and only now remembered I hadn't showered after practice.

—I must stink, I said.

He lowered his face to my chest and sucked in a big breath. When he raised his face, I said:

—I love you.

It was the first time I'd ever said this to someone who wasn't my mother or father. I had always thought that when you told someone you loved them, it was simply a statement, a declaration. I realized now it could also be a plea.

—I love you, too, he said.

—I don't know when I can see you again.

—I know.

—Not until things calm down.

He nodded and took my hand again.

—Okay.

The dorm windows were dark, save for the occasional all-nighter. Birdsong dribbled from the oaks, and a few straggling insects bumped against the lights of the tall curling iron lamps spaced along the quad's edges. A security guard walked in the opposite direction on the flagstones and nodded absently as we passed.

The Hay was deserted, and I had to turn on the locker room's lights to dress for my stadium. Coach Hightower was waiting at the top of the tunnel when I got there, a gob of Skoal deforming his cheek. He wordlessly started down the tunnel, leaving me to follow. Our footfalls made dry squeaks on the rubber floor.

Dew coated the whitewashed concrete of the stadium steps, which made running up and down them tricky. I needed to sprint hard enough to satisfy Hightower, while not so hard I'd slip and tumble down the equivalent of a medium-height office building. I got into a steady rhythm, shoes pat-pat-patting, the sky beginning to blush while the stadium and game field remained blue. If I had just sat on Chase's couch and let him have me, I would be in Thao's bed this very moment. If I had just walked past Chase's apartment after the talent show, I would still be the starting Will. I wondered if Reshawn continued to dream about throwing himself off the top of the chapel.

Usually a stadium involved running up and down every staircase, but I was only halfway through my punishment when Hightower yelled:

—That's enough!

It was an unexpected kindness, and when we ascended the tunnel we walked side by side. I opened my mouth several times to speak but didn't manage to get words out until halfway up.

—I'm sorry, Coach.

Hightower spat chew juice onto the floor.

—You know how bad it looks for one of my guys to skip a lift? he said. *This* week?

—Yes sir.

—You ain't the only one with a boss.

—I know, Coach. I have to go to South Bend. My parents already bought plane tickets.

We stopped at the top of the tunnel. I needed to turn right to get to the locker room, while Hightower was headed left to the elevator bay. He contemplated something.

—Don't you breathe a *word* of this to anybody, he said.

I nodded, and waited.

—Yesterday morning, Coach Zeller told the coaches he wanted to make an example outta somebody. Get people on their toes. You drew the short straw. So let him cool off another day and I'll get you reinstated. Meantime, cut out that sloppy shit I saw from you yesterday. That ain't like you at all.

—Yes sir.

I practically skipped back to Mennee Hall. I slept through the

morning again, missing all my classes the second day in a row—
but this time it was because I wanted to rest so I could shine in
practice. I walked to the Hay at two, ignoring calls for "Gwen!" in
the locker room, then preempted anybody from denying me a seat
in the team meeting by sitting in the last row with the assistant
coaches. Another piece of cardboard with "Gwen" written on it
was glued to my locker when I returned downstairs to dress, but I
bottled the anger, would use it down on the practice fields.

Special Teams was the first period that day. I stood on the sideline, watching Farrell take my reps with the one kickoff. He was
twenty pounds lighter than I was, nowhere near my speed or power.

The twos were called in, and when I stood next to Devonté in
the huddle I left my hand at my side, expecting him to be as disgusted as Donald. But Devonté not only grabbed my hand, he squeezed
it. I realized then that he hadn't called me Gwen, not once, and to
this day I still don't quite know what he meant by that squeeze.

We were practicing an onside kick, and when the huddle
broke I bunched on the kicker's right side with six other players.
The kicker raised his hand and stutter-stepped forward, and when
he lofted the ball into the air I sprinted after it, desperate to recover it, show the coaches what they'd be missing if I wasn't starting
on this team. And can't you see that ball? Arching high, spinning
furiously, a brown blur against the blue sky? I would leap and grab
it, would fall to the field and curl around it like a mother shielding
its threatened child—

I was sitting on the bed of a trainer's Gator.

I looked around, blinking.

My shoulder pads were off. Helmet, too.

I saw that the one defense was on the field, lined up against
the bottom feeders. Offense-Defense period, which was held a full
hour after Special Teams.

Only now did I look down and notice that my right foot
was kicked out in front of me, an ice bag secured to it by an ACE
bandage.

—Hey, I said to a trainer walking by.

—Need anything? he asked, stopping.

I tried to rotate my right foot. Pain ribboned through my body. I didn't know what to say, and the trainer shrugged and continued walking. The whistle was blown for a water break, and players jogged to the sideline.

—Reshawn! I called out.

—How you feeling? he asked, catching his breath.

—What happened?

—To what?

—To my fucking ankle!

A group of players standing near us laughed.

—I don't understand, Reshawn said.

I closed my eyes and took a breath, trying to remember, trying to will away the injury. I opened my eyes again. My mind was blank, ankle still swaddled.

—The last thing I know, I said, was we were doing onside. I was going for the kick.

Reshawn nodded.

—Right. That freshman Barron hit you. J1 stepped on your ankle while you were down.

—I've been out since then?

Reshawn shook his head, distressed.

—No. You, you stood. The trainers helped you to the sideline. I came over here and we had a whole—you really can't remember?

—*What?* Remember *what?*

—We had a whole conversation. You've been sitting here for an hour.

The whistle was blown, break ending. Reshawn had to run back onto the field.

I sat on the Gator for the remainder of practice, trying to recover my memory, rotating my ankle, standing and trying to put weight on it, wincing and having to sit back down. I stopped another trainer, who said I'd be out for a week.

After Zeller gave his end-of-practice speech, I got a ride back to the Hay. But I didn't flee the building, as I had the rest of the week; I hobbled to the metal bench at the top of the tunnel, the bench players used to tie on their cleats, and ignored the smirks and snark of passing teammates. I was waiting for Gerry Veblen.

Veblen was the A/V man in charge of taping our practices. I followed him up to his office on the second floor and sat in the swivel chair next to his as he cued up film of the play that had injured me. The film started, the kick popping up into the air. There I was, number 42, sprinting to recover the ball. All the bottom feeders on the kick return were angling toward where the ball was going to land—save for Barron, who cut across the grain of his teammates and headed straight for me. I was looking up at the ball while Barron's head was lowered, aiming for my helmet, smashing it against mine. He upended me so that my feet were momentarily above the level of my head before I crashed to the ground.

When Reshawn said J1 had stepped on me, I'd assumed that had been as purposeful as Barron's hit. But now I saw I was just on the ground at the wrong moment. J1 tried to sidestep me, but he couldn't avoid cleating my ankle. After the play was whistled dead, J1 was the one who gestured wildly to the sideline for trainers to come.

Hightower ran up to me, too, taking a concerned knee next to me, then he stood and rushed over to Barron and got in his face, pointing toward the far end of the field, clearly telling Barron to run punishment laps around the practice fields. I took some comfort in seeing how angry Hightower was, but then I saw Barron, as he started running to the far end of the field, get slapped on the ass by several bottom feeders. They were congratulating him on what he'd done.

# EIGHT

—Can't you wrap it twice?

—"Tape," Mom.

—Wrapping tape! I don't know. Can't you do it extra?

—I can barely walk.

—Are they kicking this kid off the team?

—It's football, Dad. People get hurt.

—Our plane tickets are nonrefundable.

—You told me.

—We're going to lose—

—Five hundred—

—Five *hundred* dollars.

—So go anyway. You have the hotel room booked.

—And do what? Watch the game while you're sitting at home!

—Just go. You'll sit with the parents you've been wanting to meet.

—What's the prognosis again?

—One. Week. Mom, will you write it down for him?

—Don't talk like I'm—

—I'll be back in time for the Virginia game. I'll—I'll be playing the rest of the season.

—Maybe I should give Coach Zeller a call.

—Don't bother him, Dad. He can't sprinkle magic dust onto my foot and make it better.

—Will the McCoys be there?

—Senior, probably. I don't know how Ali's feeling.

—That poor woman. Do you remember Reneé from church? She had MS. She was in those mass petitions for *years*. She must have died.

—She moved to Greeley, Linda.

—Still. That poor woman.

—See? Go to South Bend. Annoy the McCoys.

—I don't annoy *anybody*.

—You can go to a service in the chapel. Light a candle at the grotto.

—They should let you come to Indiana. What if your ankle's feeling better by Saturday?

—That's not how it works, Dad.

—I *told* you not to get the nonrefundable ones, Carey.

—They were three hundred dollars cheaper!

—Good. Settled. Enjoy South Bend.

—Oh, let's not pity ourselves, sweetheart. This is a blip. Think of all the other games you'll play.

—I know. Look, I need to start this homework.

I hung up before they could say anything else. I was alone in the dorm room, sitting in bed, staring at the ankle that had been sprained three hours earlier. The bones were already swaddled in swelled flesh, the skin tinting blue. But maybe Dad was right. Maybe I could push through the pain, go to Notre Dame.

I lowered myself off the bed and tried walking to the door normally. Wincing, clenching my fists, sucking air through my teeth, I took ten careful, excruciating steps. By the time I reached the door I had to lean against it while I recovered my breath.

I tested my ankle obsessively the rest of that night, and in between bouts read a few more pages of "Bartleby," which we were to discuss in tomorrow's Melville class. I didn't finish the story until I was midway through icing my foot in the training room's cold pool the next morning, and when I hobbled across West Campus afterward I realized I'd retained virtually nothing of what I'd read.

Reshawn, though, must have read the story five times, and he was rereading it yet again when I entered the seminar room. Professor Grayson arrived a few minutes after me, and while Reshawn hadn't bothered to acknowledge my arrival, he now lowered his book to nod to Grayson, with Grayson warmly nodding back. I resented their relationship, resented that Reshawn was allowed to have a secret sharer while I had nobody, nothing.

I only tuned in to the lecture about halfway through class. Quoting the line "Every copyist is bound to help examine his copy," Grayson was saying:

—In "Bartleby," and indeed in much of Melville, there's an overpowering professional determinism. If you are known as a cobbler, then the world expects your whole existence to center on cobbling. If you are a woodworker, you work wood and only wood. But the battle is lose-lose. If you commit yourself whole-heartedly to your profession and *do* as the world demands? Like Captain Ahab, you'll be destroyed. And if you dare assert that you possess meaning *outside* your named function, like Bartleby? Let's look at the text again.

Grayson read:

"Turkey," said I, "what do you think of this? Am I not right?"

"With submission, sir," said Turkey, in his blandest tone, "I think that you are."

"Nippers," said I, "what do *you* think of it?'

"I think I should kick him out of the office."

"Ginger Nut," said I, willing to enlist the smallest suffrage in my behalf, "what do *you* think of it?"

"I think, sir, he's a little *luny*," replied Ginger Nut, with a grin.

"You hear what they say," said I, turning towards the screen, "come forth and do your duty."

Grayson looked up from the text.

—Bartleby steps out of the stream and is called insane. Yes, Silas?

Silas was a black sophomore. Pudgy with cornrowed hair capped by puka shells, he wore thick-rimmed glasses and, for so big a body, had an unexpectedly adenoidal way of speaking. Reshawn and I had become friendly with him last year when he lived in Stager Hall, and he lived even closer to us this year in Mennee, two doors down.

—I feel like Bartleby's getting romanticized, he said now. Nobody's forcing him to take this job. He gets paid to render a service, and he should render it. How else is the world going to function if people don't do what they're paid to?

—So you agree he should he be called a "luny," Grayson said.

—I mean, insanity's when you keep doing the same thing and expect a different result, right?

—But who says he's expecting a different result? Reshawn interjected.

Silas turned in his seat to look at him.

—Fine, Silas said. But maybe the opposite's true. Maybe if you keep doing the same thing and expect the *same* result, that's also crazy.

—He's protesting, Reshawn said.

Silas was skeptical.

—Protests want some kind of change to happen. And the way to accomplish that is for people to *understand* why you're doing what you're doing. Not just saying "I would prefer not to" and staring at a brick wall.

—But what about who Bartleby was before this job? Reshawn said. Who's to say he hadn't been protesting like that for *years*? Maybe this story just catches him when he's realized there's no point anymore.

For how despairing his argument was, Reshawn looked happy and vigorous, as he always did in class. I resented this, too.

Demoted and wounded, humiliated and scorned, I was supposed to submit, to acquiesce, to accept the ostracism and retreat like a leper to his cave. To agree, like I said, that Gwen and Miles were irreconcilable. But there was no Gwen, I told myself as I limped to the Hay that afternoon, there wasn't even really a Miles. There was just me, and if I showed these people that that me wasn't going anywhere, then slowly, surely, I could get past this crisis and heal in every possible way.

I changed into mesh shorts and a sweat-absorbing T-shirt in the locker room, ignoring players who said my ass cheeks looked a little chapped. I went to the cold pool, and when the other walking woundeds who'd been soaking their feet finished their rehab prematurely so they didn't have to share my water, I just sat at the edge, dipping my foot into the pool and feeling thousands of salubrious pinpricks. In meetings I was deaf to the provocations, the snickers, the snubs. On the walk down to the practice fields I hobbled alone to stay out of earshot.

Walking woundeds were expected to contribute to practice, and today I served as Coach Hightower's gimpy secretary while the linebackers moved through their periods—holding Hightower's binder, feeding him footballs, righting tackling dummies, arranging cones. I continued to take solace in Coach Hightower's fury at Barron's dirty hit, and today my coach made sure to thank me for my help, telling me to "stay close" during Team period. He clearly still didn't know what the players were calling me. The same coach-player delay that had led him to learn belatedly about me throwing Chase to the floor at Stefan Knows was now applying to Gwen. He would hear it eventually, but if I climbed out of this hole before then, if I made myself irreplaceable, he would be much less inclined to believe the name.

I screamed encouragements to my fellow linebackers. I wasn't so stupid as to pat anybody on the ass, or even tap the tops of their helmets, but my voice *was* my hands, and with it I clapped and hugged the boys who were, who would have to be, my brothers. Cornelius and most of the other linebackers received this coolly, which was better at least than Chase's mocking laughter. By now he sensed I was too weak to out him about Sadie. He must have realized, as I had, that the team wouldn't believe me even if I did try to accuse him of being gay.

But my ankle would heal by next week. Then we'd see just how well words protected him.

Throughout the 1970s and 1980s it had been an annual tradition for King College's president to speak to the team the first week of the season, a quick go-get-'em from the academic brass. But ten years before I matriculated, when King Football was in the doldrums of the nadir of one of the great losing streaks in college football history, "scheduling conflicts" began cropping up. The president was "traveling," he was "unavailable," he asked to reschedule at the last minute and never bothered to set another time. The subtext was clear: visiting the team considered most likely to get kicked out of Division One didn't jibe with our college's mission to hoard prestige, and to make time for an unimpressive enterprise such as ours must have seemed at best a waste of valuable energy and at worst to risk being infected by our virulent losing bug. Nor was this just King Football paranoia. During that same decade the president had been happy to address the college's other, *winning* sports teams, from field hockey to basketball to squash.

So it was a coup to have the college's brand-new president, Heinrich Aaronson, standing on the practice sidelines the day before the team departed for South Bend. A willowy Caucasian with a salt-and-pepper mustache, Aaronson was dressed in khakis and a tweed jacket that any person who exercised regularly would have soaked through in the 85-degree weather, but which didn't elicit a single drop of sweat from him. He watched us with genuine, though slightly bemused, interest, surveying our rituals and routines with the same keen focus he'd honed as an anthropologist studying remote Amazonian tribes before taking his career in an administrative direction.

The coaches were on their best behavior. No "anusface" or "clit-sucker," no grabbing a player by his face mask and screaming. Today they were our tough-but-fair leaders, our gruff-but-loving father figures, and from the eager, almost giddy way they ran around and laughed, they seemed to enjoy this chance to play the role of college football coaches.

Following conditioning sprints, the team took a knee around Coach Zeller and President Aaronson. Walking woundeds like me stood at the back.

—Let's give the president a big hand!

We applauded as Aaronson stepped forward. He proceeded to speak with the slow, patient, almost painfully clear tone he'd developed while sounding out English for Brazilian tribes who'd never laid eyes on Westerners.

—Thank you, gentlemen, and thank you, Coach Zeller. Some of you may know I was at Caltech before this, and I have to say, I always felt that that school was lacking a key . . . cohort. At so many elite schools, the focus is on excellence of the mind. But here at King we have students who cultivate body *and* mind—*you* all are what makes our college so special. That isn't to say we don't have our challenges. I know there can be something of a . . . border between the academic side of King and athletics. But Coach Zeller and I are intent on erasing that division. So I'll be shouting my lungs out for you all this weekend in South Bend, and Coach Zeller—

Aaronson looked to Zeller to see if it was okay to share the news. Zeller nodded.

—Coach Zeller has graciously agreed to be a guest lecturer in a certificate course on leadership next semester.

Vets chuckled.

—You're gonna be a professor? Devonté asked Zeller. Like, in a *classroom*?

—That so hard to believe? Y'all *know* I wear a mean suit and tie.

291

He turned to President Aaronson.

—Thank you, Mr. President. It's damn excitin' to strengthen our relationship. I tell these boys every day, they are scholars and athletes. In that order.

Coach Zeller placed his hand on President Aaronson's back and left it there.

—We got a tradition that ends practice with a special cheer. I should warn you, it's got a bit of profanity.

—I've heard a word or two in my day, Aaronson said.

Coach Zeller turned to the team, chuckling.

—All right, then. Reshawn, break us down.

Players shared apprehensive glances. In the abstract it made perfect sense why Coach Zeller would want Reshawn, our consummate scholar-athlete, to lead us in the cheer. But there was good reason why Zeller had never asked Reshawn to lead us in screaming "King King motherfucker!" before.

—I would prefer not to, Reshawn answered flatly.

Jimbo hung his head. Other players watched Coach Zeller, waiting to see how he'd respond. But while Zeller in any other circumstance would have lost his cool and told Reshawn he didn't give one *fuck* what he preferred, he could do no such thing now, not with Aaronson standing right next to him. Instead Zeller blurted out a hearty laugh and turned to Aaronson, who for his part seemed more fascinated by us than ever.

—This close to game time, Zeller said, Reshawn gets a little superstitious.

—Of course.

Zeller looked out at the team again, and though his mouth was still smiling, his eyes were pure ice.

—All right, Machen, he said to Errol. You do it.

At Training Table that evening, word spread that all players on the travel list were to voluntarily return to the Hay after eating to watch an extra round of film. I wasn't expected to attend—these meetings were about Notre Dame, involving assignments and strategies that would be obsolete by the time I got back on the field—but I decided to go anyway, wanting to show Coach Hightower the extent of my commitment.

Hightower was already in the linebackers room when we filed in, a case of Natty Light at his feet.

—Thought y'all deserved a treat for putting in the time, he said, extracting a can and popping it open.

The linebackers were delighted, since alcohol was usually forbidden in the Hay. As Cornelius handed out the beers, I hung back, thinking I would have to get my own can; but once everyone else was served, Cornelius tossed a can my way. I felt so grateful when I caught it, so *relieved*. I had been unfair to Cornelius. I just needed to give him time to adjust to the idea of me.

We sat while Coach Hightower remained up front, leaning his shoulder against the whiteboard as he sipped his Natty Light.

—We had, what, one televised game when I played here? he asked himself.

—Was TV invented back then, Coach?

—Fuckin' funny guy right there. We played SMU in—must have been '83 or '84. Best team in the country. Fuckin' *monsters*, man. Two national championships in the '80s. One of the greatest programs ever, you ask me.

—Y'all lose?

—We did, we did. But we kept it damn close till the fourth quarter. That was the first season I started Will. My grandma didn't have a TV, so my uncle picked her up and drove her two towns over so she could sit in a bar to watch me.

He smiled at the memory.

—First time that woman *ever* stepped foot in a bar, I can tell you that. She went to church every day of her life. Used to beat my ass *raw* if I said "darn" in front of her. But she went to a bar to see her Radon—drank a club soda with lime and told every lush in there that was *her* grandbaby playing on the TV.

I was surprised to find Hightower looking directly at me.

—Who you gonna be watching the game with, Furling?

—I'm—I don't know yet, Coach.

He nodded.

—Ain't you gonna be watching it with . . . help me out, McGerrin.

—Gwen.

—Right. Ain't you watching it with Gwen?

I kept my face neutral, my breathing even. Meanwhile, out of sight, I pressed my palms up against the underside of the table and tucked my feet beneath my chair. I rotated my right foot so that only the pinkie toe touched the floor, then rested my good foot atop my wounded one and pressed down, pressed until it felt like an electrical wire was severed in my ankle, twisting wildly, spitting sparks.

—You hear me, Furling?

—No sir. Sorry.

—I said is that shit *true*?

—No. McGerrin's a fucking liar.

The pace of Hightower's words quickened.

—Yeah? Is *Cornelius* lying, too?

He took a final swig of beer and dropped the can in the wastebasket on his way toward the computer in back. He killed the lights and started the projector.

And who *could* I watch the game with? Not the bottom feeders and walking woundeds who'd be watching at Stefan Knows, people who'd either called me Gwen or done nothing to stop others from doing so. They'd probably have tolerated my presence if I showed—a teammate was a teammate—but they would also have made it clear that was the best I deserved. So what about Dombey's, or another bar? I couldn't bear the idea of sitting in ugly anonymity. I knew I might explode if I had to listen to drunk men bludgeon each other with their expertise on *my* teammates, *our* strategies.

So where? Maybe I should just remain in our TV-less dorm room and sink into the self-pity Mom warned me against, listening to the happy voices of students out on the quad.

That seemed to be my fate until, just after sundown Saturday, there was a knock on our door. It was Silas, the boy from Melville class. He'd seen me limping into the seminar room and put it together that I wouldn't be traveling to South Bend this weekend, and he asked if I wanted to watch the game with him and some friends. A compromise, then, between Stefan Knows and a strange bar—a room full of boys who'd know who I was, but not what.

Silas's room was full already, with boys sitting on the two beds and on beanbags of various sizes and squishiness. As the injured/honored guest, I was given both desk chairs: one to sit on, one to keep my ankle elevated.

Silas handed me a Solo cup filled with a screwdriver.

—You must be so pissed, he said.

—You're Reshawn's roommate? another asked.

I nodded.

—He knows calculus better than I do.

—That's not saying much, Gary!

A pillow flew.

The television channel was changed, and I had the shock of seeing my teammates stretching on prime time. They were dressed in our new away uniforms, which were the inverse of the one Jimbo modeled in the locker room, the jerseys and pants white with a purple scimitar slicing down both sides. They were luminous. Players have preferences for home or away jerseys the way whiskey drinkers do for rye versus scotch, and I had always been an away man.

Meanwhile, our coaches wore white polo shirts, pressed khakis, black leather belts, and purple tennis shoes. Some of them buried hands in pockets and strolled stiffly between rows of stretching players, too tense to speak. Others knelt next to a wide receiver or defensive end to neurotically review audibles and assignments for the thousandth time. The shot switched to Coach Zeller, who was meeting Notre Dame's head coach at the 50-yard line. Both men's arms were crossed, conferring like prebattle generals.

The main commentator, an oaken-voiced white man of indeterminate age, promised to return with the kickoff after this commercial break. I'd already chugged my screwdriver, and after Silas made me another he went around the room distributing cans of Natty Light.

—Okay, he said. So that Ichiro doesn't go to the hospital again, we'll go slower than last Saturday.

Ichiro was a bite-sized international student sitting on one of the beanbags. He blushed.

—We'll do a swig of beer every time King gets a first down, Silas continued. Then three-second chugs whenever they score. Miles, does that work?

What Silas was asking was, did I mind the assumption that King's first downs and scores would be so paltry that Ichiro wouldn't have to be taken to the student clinic for symptoms of alcohol poisoning the second time in a week.

—Sure.

The broadcast returned. Notre Dame's cheerleaders were shown in profile, shaking pom-poms and wearing glazed smiles as they pretended not to notice the camera. Then a close-up of Notre Dame's leprechaun mascot, a boy in an Irish country hat and green cutaway suit, a gold vest, gold shirt and tie, and white tube socks meant to put you in the mind of tights. He didn't ignore the camera, he screamed into it, face blistering red as he held up an index finger. Next we were shown a long pan of cheering fans, including King's tiny section behind our bench. I sighed at the sight of my parents, proudly wearing the King Football gear I'd given them for Christmas. Mom sat next to Ali McCoy, talking the woman's ear off, while Dad leaned forward in his seat to talk across the wives to Senior.

We lost the coin toss and would be receiving. Notre Dame's

kickoff team fanned into position, the kicker raising his hand. The whistle was blown, and the crowd sound crested to a mighty "Ooohhhhh!" as the ball was blasted off the tee—a beautiful, soaring kick that Devonté caught on the goal line.

He was off, a tiny burst of person. Two Notre Dame players evaded their blockers and closed in on him, pincerlike—but Devonté exploded through their outstretched arms, then stepped left of Slo-Mo and the player he was blocking. He sped toward the sideline with only the Notre Dame kicker, the player of last resort, squeezing down, the kicker seemingly about to force him out of bounds at the 50. But here Devonté did a lovely lateral leap back inside, tangling the kicker's feet, and he was gone: 40, 30, 20, head swiveling to look over his shoulders, 10, seeing no one close, 5. When he reached the goal line he did a front flip into the end zone, landing on his back, throwing the ball into the air while ecstatically kicking out his hands and feet. Flags flew for Excessive Celebration as the teammates who'd been trailing Devonté ran into the end zone to pile onto him, slap his face mask, scream.

Silas's room was a madhouse, the Notre Dame stadium a mass grave. I obligingly lifted my beer and, with the others, chugged for one, two, three.

At least Farrell, my replacement on kickoff, didn't make the tackle when we kicked. Notre Dame's own return was your standard down-at-the-29 affair, and the game settled into a lull for the remainder of the first quarter. Notre Dame field goal, 7–3. King drives but has to punt. So on. Although we were noticeably smaller than Notre Dame, we were dominating, and the first round of beers, then the second, were quickly downed.

The ribbing of Ichiro was constant. He spoke far better English than anyone in here spoke Japanese, but there was still a slight delay between a joke being made at his expense and his response to it, a gap all the boys exploited, and none more so than an alpha geek named Raymond. Raymond cut off Ichiro, contradicted him, taunted him with idioms he didn't know. At first I was baffled why Raymond was acting so cruelly, but over the course of the first half I gleaned that he and Ichiro were roommates and understood Ichiro was disliked for tagging along to whatever social gatherings Raymond couldn't sneak off to—including the drinking session last Saturday that led to the emergency room visit and spoiled the other boys' fun.

Raymond was growing more blatantly mean-spirited as he drank, and by the middle of the second quarter Ichiro dragged his beanbag as far from him as he could, next to my chairs.

—Is this your first football game? I asked, looking down at him.

—No no, he said quickly, as if to reassure me. We have the X League in Japan. My team is Kanagawa.

—There's American football in Japan?

Ichiro explained the history of the sport in his country, how missionaries introduced it in the 1930s, the concept of *power hara*. I did my best to feign interest, but my real attention was on the broadcast, in particular the irritating inanities of the color commentator. A former backup quarterback from the University of Michigan, he had once been one of my favorite television personalities, but his aggressively knowing tone grated on me tonight. Before kickoff, Color Man had gruffed, "They better have ambulances waiting outside the stadium for these King kids, Jim." But by the third-quarter kickoff, when King was leading 17–10, Color Man acted like he wasn't recorded for a living and said, "I'm telling you, Jim, King's a team that's going to surprise a lot of people this year." George Zeller was "a player's coach, Jim. I don't think I've ever met a head coach so adored by his guys." There was the obligatory adulation of Reshawn, the talk of a son's love for his mother. But the player Color Man truly adored was our new starting quarterback. After Errol made a laser-precision twenty-five-yard throw to a receiver on the sideline, the camera lingered on him for a moment and Color Man gushed, "I had a chance to talk with this young man yesterday, Jim. He represents everything

George Zeller's doing right with King Football. Fantastic student. Natural leader. He knows he's been given a second chance, and by golly he doesn't want to waste it. I asked what he wanted this season, and you know, a lot of players will say 'All-American' or 'National Championship.' But Errol? He told me, 'I just want to make my teammates proud.' How about *that*?"

That's when I set down my beer and started playing the drinking game with my screwdriver. A long King touchdown drive of six first downs (six swigs) ended with a touchdown (chug one, two, three). Silas looked wary as he poured vodka and orange juice into my cup for the third time.

I didn't appreciate how drunk I was until the commercial break before the fourth quarter. My ankle had stiffened while I'd been sitting, and as I limp-wavered down the hallway I had to keep my right hand on the brick wall to steady myself. I'll spare you what happened in the bathroom—let's just say it involved an argument with a mirror. I was gone long enough that, when I returned to the room, I saw Notre Dame had scored a touchdown, stopped a King drive, and was now on King's 7-yard line, on the verge of tying the game.

Our goal-line defense was on the field, which meant Chase was in the game, lining up as I was supposed to be lining up, preparing to plug the gaps in the defensive line or brutalize anybody who crossed his path in the secondary. The ball was snapped. Notre Dame faked a dive and Chase was fooled into stepping up to the line of scrimmage, which freed a space behind him in the end zone. A moment later the releasing tight end was crossing behind him, was catching the pass, touchdown Notre Dame. As Chase hung his head in shame, my arms shot up to cheer.

Silas and the other guys laughed uncomfortably, as if I possessed an offbeat sense of humor. Ichiro, meanwhile, squinted at the screen, trying to understand what could have possibly led me to cheer against my own team.

I shuddered every time I took another sip of my warming

screwdriver. Two minutes remained in what was now a tie game. Notre Dame, rather than risk another Devonté return, squibbed the kick, the ball tumbling down the center of the field until Slo-Mo caught it and advanced with the grace of a yak. One Notre Dame player clung to Slo-Mo's waist, unable to drag him down. Another leapt on top of him. J2 was behind Slo-Mo, pushing him forward, until everyone finally crashed at King's 43.

The room's air was heating up with the agitated drunk bodies, and Silas propped the door open. Initially, royalty passing in the hall only glanced inside the room, but in time people began poking their heads in to see what the fuss was about.

King was driving. Reshawn gained eight yards but was tackled before he reached the sideline. Our offense entered no-huddle mode, Errol screaming the count over Notre Dame's howling fans. A pass for eleven.

Ichiro offered a portion of his beanbag to a small girl with tortoiseshell glasses named Suneeta.

Devonté jogged onto the field as a wingback, lining up in a trick play formation that had been concocted during camp. If I could have, I would have telepathically transmitted my team's secret to Notre Dame's coaches. Instead I had to watch, helpless, as the play was executed to perfection: Devonté went in motion, the quarterback stepped aside at the same moment the center shotgunned the snap, and Devonté caught the ball in the backfield and then beat the defender at the edge, sprinting free to the 30, 25, 20, 15, until he was finally brought down at the 11. Coach Zeller called the team's last timeout. Five seconds left.

At the commercial break, Suneeta looked up at me, laughing.

—What is *happening*?! she exclaimed. Isn't our team supposed to suck?

The broadcast returned, showing Coach Zeller consulting with the field goal team on the sideline. The whistle blew and the team jogged on.

And for a moment, for the length of time it took the field goal team to travel from sideline to right hash mark, I found myself hoping once more that King would win.

My ankle would heal, wouldn't it?

I could work my way back to starting Will, couldn't I?

Gwen was just a name, wasn't it?

—We got this, I said, under my breath.

But then the camera, waiting for the ref to blow the whistle, gave us a close-up of the King sideline, specifically of Jimbo and Cornelius holding hands. Their hands weren't joined in that perfunctory manly way in which one turns his fingers into a defensive flipper that he hooks onto the flipper of the other, nor was one of them leaving his hand limp while the other clutched it. No. Jimbo and Cornelius stood with fingers interlocked, joined in a solid hopeful loving grasp.

The camera returned to the game. I was talking to myself again, but now I was saying:

—Miss it. *Please.*

A bad snap sailing over the kicker's head. A rogue wind blowing the attempt no good. A freak Indiana sinkhole that swallowed both teams. But the snap was perfect, the hold golden, the kick an arrow shot through the heart of the uprights.

—GOOOOOOOOOOOOOOOOOD!

I gripped the underside of my chair as everyone else jumped, cheered, hugged, high-fived, the TV alternating between pans of the stunned Notre Dame student section and my euphoric teammates, who were sprinting onto the field, index fingers raised.

Coach Zeller was pushing through backslaps, hugs, and camera flashes, heading to the middle of the field to shake hands with Notre Dame's head coach. On the way there, Errol and Devonté, holding the handles of a Gatorade tub with the top removed, snuck up behind Zeller and doused him with a chunky yellow shower. Zeller bent over, laughing. Zeller was upright, running his hands through his hair, hugging Errol.

After commiserating with the other head coach, Zeller was

interviewed by NBC's sideline reporter, a statuesque woman with margarine-colored hair. In a happy hoarse voice, Coach Zeller answered:

—Well, it's all about family, Simone. These boys are brothers.

Somebody in the hallway stopped in our doorway to shout that there was to be a celebration out on the main quad. The room emptied. Ichiro extended his hand gallantly toward the door, insisting Suneeta go before him.

Silas and I were the last to leave the room. I leaned against the painted brick hallway wall as he hurried to lock the door.

—Coming? he asked me.

—No.

He ran to catch up. More royalty flashed past me, their shouts caroming off the walls. I started toward the bathroom to puke, steadying myself with the bricks again, and just as I was reaching the bathroom door I saw another group of my classmates spill out of a dorm room. The girls wore purple ribbons in their hair, playful little streaks of eye black on their cheeks. Several of the boys wore replica jerseys that featured Reshawn's number. They were chanting:

*One, one, two, three!*
*Who the fuck you came to see?!*
*King King motherfucker!*

When I limped into the Team Room the next afternoon, only a handful of players were there, starters mostly, so spent from the victory and drowsy from the late flight that several had improvised sleep masks out of hand towels.

—You think Zeller's gonna get Coach of the Week?

—What else you give somebody who took a team that didn't win a fucking game and two years later is beating *Notre Dame*?

—Not even two years, young.

—Better be careful what y'all wish for, Jimbo said. Zeller only signed a two-year contract.

—So? King's gonna give him whatever he wants.

—Yeah, unless he decides he wants a bigger program. I can name ten teams that'll offer him a job end of this year.

—Zeller wouldn't leave.

—Yo, y'all see that Simone chick talking to Zeller at the end of the game? She looked ready to bend over.

—Ah! Jimbo said.

He leapt from his chair and started the desktop computer that sat on a little counter recessed into the front wall. He used the computer to lower the projector screen. Once the screen was down, we could see what he was doing on the desktop: opening an Internet browser, searching for a video of last night's game.

—What, Jimbo?

—Hold on. The bottom feeders were telling me about this.

He found the video and pressed Play. It started with the post-game interview that people had just been talking about, which was also the last thing I'd seen on TV before Silas and I left his room: Simone, the sideline reporter, interviewing Coach Zeller. But the coverage hadn't ended there. After she finished speaking to Zeller, Simone had managed to lasso Reshawn.

—Great game tonight! she said to him.

Reshawn nodded, lowering his head to hear over the on-field jubilation.

—Tell me, she continued. How does it feel to have one of the biggest upsets in King history?!

—I would prefer not to!

Simone clasped her hand around her earpiece, the smile on her face indicating she thought she simply hadn't heard right.

—All right! Tell me then, 206 yards and three touchdowns. What is it about *this* offense that was able to outplay a bigger Notre Dame defense?

Reshawn nodded encouragingly, like he was hanging on every word, and when he answered, he sounded even more upbeat.

—You know, Simone, I'd prefer not to answer that!

Simone heard him this time, and flashed a panicked look at the camera. But, professional that she was, she recovered and tried once again, making what she must have thought was a master counterstroke by asking Reshawn a question no decent human being would answer facetiously on national television.

—This victory must be a special one for you and your family. Is there anything you'd like to say to them tonight?

Reshawn did something I never expected to see him do—he crossed himself and pointed up at the sky. Then he dipped his head and said the phrase once again, using yet another intonation, this one solemn though appreciative, graciously devout.

—I would prefer not to.

My ankle skin was a slush of sickening colors, soft-banana yellow, Popsicle green, Windex blue. And yet the hideousness was a good sign, and on Monday a trainer informed me I could try to practice half-speed tomorrow.

I was finishing the last exercise of my rehab regimen when a call came down from the fifth floor—Coach Zeller wanted me to stop by his office. My head coach hadn't deigned to speak to me since our post-demotion exchange on the practice field last week, not even to give condolences for my sprained ankle, and I had no idea what he wanted now.

I took the elevator upstairs. The secretaries seemed to be awaiting my arrival and immediately waved me back to the corner office.

—Close that door, Zeller told me.

I sat in a chair across the desk from him. Zeller was leaning back, fingers interlocked over his belly.

—How's the ankle? he asked.

I relaxed, forgiving him for not asking about my injury before. He was busy, it must have just slipped his mind. I felt guilty, again, for having drunkenly cheered against my own team on Saturday.

—Better, Coach. I'm allowed to go fifty percent tomorrow.

Zeller nodded.

—You've had a rough couple weeks, haven't you, son?

He knew. He knew about Gwen. He'd brought me here to comfort me. I wanted to lunge across the desk and hug him.

—Yes sir, I said.

—We get raised thinkin' women are the ones who can't stop gossipin', but you ask me, a sewin' circle of bra-burnin' feminists ain't *half* as bad as a college football team. These rumors, they're just mean-spirited. I don't believe a word, by the way.

—That means a lot, Coach.

He tilted his head, as if to say it was the least he could do.

—Names stick in football, don't they? he asked.

—Yes sir.

—They do. They do. And that's what's got me worried 'bout you, Miles. You still got four years of eligibility. Four years of gettin' called *that*? Just don't seem fair.

—I can ignore it, I quickly said. I'm gonna get back out there and shut people up with how I play.

He reached down to open a desk drawer and took out a can of Skoal, stuffing a plug of tobacco in his cheek. When he resumed speaking, he seemed not to have heard me.

—You know, he said. For all the guarantees us coaches make when we recruit players, it really comes down to a crapshoot. A boy's gotta choose a school and *then* see whether the place suits him. Suits his abilities, his personality. And I've been wonderin'— Coach Hightower, too—we been wonderin' if there ain't a program out there that's a better fit for you.

I crossed my feet beneath my chair.

—You *need* your teammates, Zeller continued. Coaches can support you all we want, but what it comes down to is foxholes.

—Foxholes.

—*Exactly*. I have no doubt you, uh, care for the men around you. But you need those men to care about you to the same degree. Otherwise the whole thing falls apart.

—I—

—You're a special player, Miles. Seldom have I seen some-body blossom like you have over the last year. And it just kills me to be sayin' this. But I got a responsibility to look out for the whole you, not just the player.

He paused, blowing air out of his nose resignedly.

—What I'm sayin' is, I think you'd be better off at another program.

I tried to say something again, but he held up his hand.

—That talent of yours, that'll make you *real* attractive to a lotta schools. Way more'n what were interested in high school. And when they find out you're only eighteen? Phew. I can think of a couple dozen programs that would just fall over themselves. Penn State. Florida. Alabama.

Zeller knew precisely what he was doing, dropping the names of those programs, places I'd spent my childhood fantasizing about. For a moment the bait-and-switch worked, as I relished the fact that a coach of Zeller's caliber was telling me I could play with the very best. But this was a sugar high that wore off fast, and re-maining beneath was my knowledge that, if I was indeed such a valuable prospect, Zeller would be offering to stand up for me, tell the team to cut out the Gwenning. What he was proposing amount-ed to off-loading me onto another, unsuspecting program. Like a lemon a used-car dealer buffs to a high shine. Like an iffy stock whose value you know is going to plummet soon after it leaves your hands.

—But I love it here, I finally answered.

And that was the truth. Hellish as my life on the team had become, I still loved King. Zeller was unperturbed.

—I'm sure you do. But think how much *more* you'll love a place where you're not dealin' with these kinds of rumors.

He lifted a wastebasket and spat.

—It's the right choice, son. Rest assured we'll keep you on scholarship while you're lookin' around. We got a whole year to find another place—though I suspect somebody'll snatch you up real quick. It's not every day a surefire All-American comes on the market.

He kept up the flattery a few more minutes, and when I stood to leave, he shook my hand and told me to put together a list of schools for him to contact. We would reconvene in a few days to get things started.

If there was anything resembling an upside to being forced off the team, it was that I gave up on secrecy, and after dinner that night at Training Table—where the players had already heard about my expulsion—I texted Thao to tell him to meet me in my dorm room. I did this because I felt liberated to, yes, but there was also aggression in my invitation, since I knew Reshawn would be in the room. I wanted to make Reshawn uncomfortable by having Thao over, wanted to force him—by which I mean force *somebody*—to accommodate me after a lifetime of making my own accommodations.

To my surprise, when Thao arrived, Reshawn not only made the effort to say hello but continued studying at his desk while we talked. Reshawn was offering an olive branch. But fuck him—too little, too late.

—Can't you stay on the team? Thao asked, sitting next to me on the bed. Like, dare Zeller to force you to leave?

—Scholarships are renewed annually. He just wouldn't renew it at the end of the spring. Anyway, even if I stayed here, I'd be a bottom feeder the rest of the time.

—A what?

"Bottom feeder" had become so engrained in my vocabulary that it took Thao's question to remind me how strange a term it was.

—A loser who doesn't play.

—What about—

Thao looked over at Reshawn uncertainly. I knew what he was getting at.

—Maybe I'll actually follow Coach Johannsen's advice at the next school, I said. Or maybe I'll just find a better way to hide.

—I'll move wherever you transfer, Thao said.

I squeezed his hand. After graduation he was planning on following a long-held dream to move to New York City and become a choreographer. Meanwhile, any D1 program worth its salt would be, at minimum, hundreds of miles away from New York. No, we would stay together only for as long as we both attended King.

The night was unseasonably cool, and Thao and I took a walk around West Campus. We held hands for the first time in public, moving slowly for the sake of my ankle—which, thanks to pressing down on it virtually the whole time I met with Zeller, had fresh circuits of pain sizzling through it. I felt a heavy, almost sweet sadness overtake me. I loved this part of West. Loved the tall, regularly spaced iron lamps, loved how the dark quad grass resembled deep water. I loved the archways that connected the residence halls, loved how the crenellations crowning the tops of dorms made this place look like the setting of a fairytale. I could have told you the name of every building I passed, which cafés were still open, where the best part of the library was to study after 8 p.m. King, I realized, had come to feel more like home than home ever had.

Going without seeing Thao for a week had been torture, and I simply couldn't conceive of living hundreds, maybe thousands of miles apart. Next year we would call each other often, maybe I would visit him in New York. But we would fall out of touch eventually, and I'd be left to spend the rest of my time on earth carrying around an amputated love.

—You hear someone spewed in the locker room last night?

—For real?

—Demetrius had a stadium this morning and stepped right in that shit as he was looking for the light switch.

—Getting drunk on a Tuesday night is ambitious.

—I bet you it was one of the Bobs.

—Nah. They were playing Madden at my place.

—Then maybe the coaches had a late celebration for Notre Dame.

—Maybe. Furling, what do you think?

"Gwen" was already starting to fall out of use with the players, but hearing my real name was almost as painful, since I knew it was being said out of pity.

I didn't answer J1's question and continued rehab. I was holding one end of a giant purple rubber band whose other end passed around the ball of my injured foot; the band created resistance as I moved my ankle back and forth, strengthening the tendons.

—Furling! Coach Hightower said as he ambled into the room. How's the ankle?

—Fine, Coach.

—Good good. Look, we're switching Farrell to linebacker from safety. Can't afford to be shallow at Will. I need you to help him adjust. Packages, stance, everything.

My ankle clicked each time it rotated, a wet, thick, horrid sound.

—You hear me, son?

—Yes sir.

I dressed in full pads, wearing a red practice jersey for the first time this season, and walked down to the fields with Farrell. He was a sweet-natured white kid from rural Ohio who'd never called me Gwen, and as we walked he talked incessantly about how nervous the position switch made him. I understood his anxiety: the transition from safety to linebacker required him to make a hundred little recalibrations that would add up to an existential shift. His stance and footwork and how he used his hands would all have to change, as would how he visualized the field, how he related to other players, how he moved through football's space. More daunting still, he was being asked to flush all the safety assignments he'd been stuffing into his brain over the last month and start absorbing a new, radically different set of tasks.

And how did I feel as I helped him start his adjustment? Did I seethe with envy and competitiveness as I watched this kid stumble through things I had mastered? Not really. I didn't feel much of anything. I was a grayness, I was mobile meat, I was someone who—I smiled mildly when I thought this—gave new meaning to the term "lame duck." Before today, I would have seen Farrell and thought he was taking "my" spot; but now I realized how foolish that was, how the spot had existed long before me, had continued to exist while I'd been injured, and would go on existing long after I moved on to whatever program I transferred to.

And when I transferred—couldn't I recover my color, my zeal? Within the football encyclopedia that was my brain, wasn't there entry upon entry of players who'd flamed out of their first programs only to then become phoenixes at the schools they'd transferred to, players who had gone on to become some of the game's greats?

Of course there were. But I was tired—so fucking tired—and the idea of starting over at another program, matriculating at a new school, was tantamount to telling someone who's just crossed the finish line of a marathon that, congratulations, you only have another twenty-six miles to go.

Nevertheless, I was still the good little soldier and dutifully drafted a list of programs for Coach Zeller. I brought the list with me when he called me up to his office an hour before Thursday's practice.

He was once again at his desk when I knocked, and once more he told me to close the door. But gone was the sweet-sad bonhomie he'd laid on so thick the last time. He didn't even look at me when I sat, too busy reading a sheet of paper. I waited, and waited, and once he was finally done reading, he tossed the sheet in my direction. The sheet had been folded into thirds, and its creased corners lightly scudded across the polished wood.

—You wanna explain this? he said.

On Thursday, September 2nd, Radon Hightower, line-backers coach at King, mocked me about a homosexual relationship I've allegedly been having with a fellow student. Coach Hightower called me "Gwen," a reference to a nickname for the student I've allegedly been sleeping with.

The letter went on like that, in the first person, single-spaced. It summarized the torments to which my teammates had subjected me, and the failure of the rest of the coaching staff to defend me, and ended with Coach Zeller forcing me to transfer from King. I read the letter twice, though not because I missed anything on the first read, just so I had a little more time before I had to look at my head coach.

—This some kinda threat? he said.

—No sir, I managed.

—Oh no?

He took an envelope from his desk drawer and tossed it my way. It was addressed to Arnold Duffy, USA Today c/o George Zeller.

—Give me your phone, he said.

—Coach—

—Now!

I handed it over. My heart thrashed as he paged through the call lists, which I knew were comprised entirely of calls either with my parents or with Thao.

—Who's this? he said, not showing me the phone.

—Who?

—"Whitman."

—A classmate from my Melville class.

—Melville *who*?

—He's—Whitman's just a classmate, Coach.

Zeller looked at me. He was squeezing my phone so hard the plastic started to complain.

—Let me ask you somethin', he finally said. You ever heard me call someone a motherfucker?

—Sir?

—Mother. Fucker. You ever heard me say that to one of your teammates?

—Yes sir.

—How'd you take it?

—Sir?

—You think I was saying that player has intercourse with his mother?

—No sir.

He nodded.

—You ever heard me tell a player he was a bitch?

—Yes sir.

—You think I was sayin' he was a female dog?

—No.

—All right. So what about "faggot"?

He let the word resonate like a struck tuning fork. A cramp was forming in my lower abdomen.

—What about "faggot"? he said again. You ever hear me call somebody that?

—Yes sir.

—You have. So tell me, why haven't any of those *other* players written an anonymous letter to goddamned *USA Today*?

—I—

—I'll tell you why, Miles. 'Cause it ain't personal. 'Cause these're *words* we use to . . . to motivate. We call you somethin' you ain't so you can prove what you are.

He was losing me. The cramp was worsening.

—So, he continued, the only thing that'd make you any *different* from those other players, the only thing that would make any of this legitimate, is if Coach Hightower used a word for somethin' you are.

—Coach—

He held up his hand.

—That's a question, Furling. The only thing I want comin' outta your mouth is an answer.

I pressed down on my ankle—not in increments but suddenly, causing breathtaking pain. Speak, Miles.

—Yes sir.

—Yes what?

—I'm . . .

I cleared my throat.

—I've slept with a boy.

He stared a long moment, and then did something that still robs me of breath whenever I remember it. He made that pinching motion people will make when they don't want to outright pick their noses—his thumb and forefinger clamping his nostrils shut—and began to twist his nose. He wasn't twisting lightly, though, but with such intense torqueing force that I, for a second, was convinced he was going to tear that nose right off his face, tear his whole face right off his skull, revealing—

But he released. He carefully set my phone on the table and nudged it toward me.

—So what do you want? he asked.

The sudden shift in power was nauseating, and I mean that literally. I had to stare at the edge of his desk, a fixed point to focus on while I waited for my stomach to settle.

And what *did* I want? To remain on the team? I had that leverage now, and knew I could tell Zeller to protect me from this day forward, to punish any player who dared utter the name Gwen. I could make him reinstate me at starting Will linebacker, could probably even have him fire Coach Hightower. I could stay. I could play at King. I could be the team's Will linebacker the next four years and, after that, maybe reach the NFL.

—I want to leave the team and keep my scholarship.

The words just appeared, like they'd been hiding behind me all this time. And once they were out, I had to keep talking in a rush, knowing that if I stopped I might not ever be able to start back up again.

—Everything still applies, I continued. Textbooks. My—my housing. I won't be coming to Training Table anymore, so I want extra stipend money to make up for that. All four years—scholarship. Summer funding, too.

There was a knock.

—Yeah? Zeller said darkly, still staring at me.

Miss Gemma, the head secretary, stuck her head in.

—Henry Purdy's on the line, Coach.

—Tell him to hold on.

The door closed. I knew who Henry Purdy was. He owned Purdy Motors, the most successful set of car dealerships in the state. Outside, in the parking spaces reserved for the coaches, sat a row of conspicuously new vehicles. Compact, minivan, SUV, or pickup truck, all of them sported a shiny silver decal that read PURDY MOTORS. In exchange for the cars, Coach Zeller appeared in commercials for the dealerships, presided over ribbon-cutting ceremonies for new stores, and always made sure to mention that Purdy Motors was a proud sponsor of this week's episode of "Talk to the Throne."

Zeller bit his lower lip, thinking.

—All right, he said. We'll say your injury's a lot worse'n we thought. Your ankle's not sprained. It's broken. Given—given the amount of time it would take you to recover, we decided to let you leave the team instead.

—Okay, I said. I can say that.

—Oh, you can? he asked sarcastically. Well then, I guess that's what you'll say.

There was a long, awful pause. He arched his eyebrows impatiently.

—Anything else? he asked.

—No sir.

—Then get outta my fuckin' office.

The Redshirt

. . .

That was the last thing Coach Zeller would ever say to me and the last time I'd ever step foot in the Hay, both of which I sensed then but wouldn't fully grasp until later. Nothing, really, was registering as I limped across West Campus, and when I reached Mennee Hall I sat on the wooden bench in front of the dorm, stunned and numb. Classes were letting out, and I watched students spill onto the sidewalks—economics majors, class presidents, a capella captains, sorority sisters, pre-laws, post-baccs. There was a tank-topped girl whose bare right arm bore a papery burn scar from elbow to shoulder. A boy on a unicycle making silly, expert navigations around the flagstones' pocks and ridges. All these bodies shouldering the sun, all these voices ringing, just as the chapel bells would ring later that afternoon. It was two o'clock, and when I realized the team would be gathering for meetings in fifteen minutes, I began to cry.

Once I collected myself, I texted Thao and asked him to come to West around nine. I wanted to see him, but not immediately. I went to my room and spent the rest of the afternoon in bed. I tried to sleep, but mostly I stared at the tree shadows playing on the ceiling.

When I heard our lock turn a little after eight, I hurriedly swung myself off the mattress, not wanting Reshawn to find me sitting in bed, thinking this would seem presumptuous, somehow. He walked in with a Styrofoam box of food from Training Table— dinner he'd put together for me. I had the urge to hug him but stopped myself, afraid something like that might make him uncomfortable. I wanted, *needed* to hold on to my new idea of him, and I understood that this new idea—that he was my friend, the best one I had at King—would be permanently sullied if he did something like recoil at my touch. So I made do with gratefully accepting the box of food he handed me.

—When did you write the letter? I asked.

—While you and Thao went on that walk.

I opened the box. I hadn't eaten since noon, but found I didn't have an appetite.

—What did the players say? I asked, setting the box on my desk.

He explained that they first learned I was gone when they walked into the locker room after meetings. My locker had been cleaned out by Cyrus Pyle; even my nameplate was gone. Zeller's broken-ankle explanation spread quickly, but this was a lie designed for the wider world, not the team, and nobody bought it. Instead they replaced this lie with their own lies, such as that I'd run away from King with my faggot boyfriend; that I'd killed myself by drowning in the cold pool; that I'd extorted Coach Zeller for not only my scholarship but also an exorbitant amount of hush money. Down at practice, the coaches were all in strange, sour moods. Coach Hightower one moment would be watching the leaves on the trees surrounding the fields, and the next slamming his binder against Chase's helmet. Reshawn's favorite reaction was Coach Zeller's: you wouldn't have believed the euphoric man from the Notre Dame game was the same one who'd screamed himself pink today.

Reshawn said all of this in what I can only call a vicarious tone of voice. When he finished, I said, apologetically:

—You've got what I want, and I got what you want.

He nodded, having clearly already thought this. He went to his desk and began switching the textbooks in his book bag for a different set.

—For now, he said. But if you can get off this fucking team, I can too. I just have to figure out how.

He left for the library, and I climbed back into bed. I thought about how my helmet and shoulder pads, wristbands and gloves, belt, hip pads, knee pads, thigh pads, and tail pad, my four pairs of shoes, my ankle and knee socks, my T-shirts and lifting shorts and girdle—how they all must have been returned to the equipment room to be washed before being sent back into general circulation.

I peered out of the iron-framed window that stood next to my bed, looking at the quad below. I spotted Reshawn. He exited Mennee Hall and turned left, toward the library. His eyes were down, his heavy backpack slung over his shoulder, and he paid no mind to the two students walking in the opposite direction who watched him pass. He climbed a short flight of stone steps into a dark archway, disappearing.

I looked right, toward the spotlighted chapel and the horse-shoe-shaped campus shuttle stop in front of it. Thao would be coming from that direction.

# Acknowledgments

Lisa Williams, the New Poetry & Prose Series editor, never balked at the idea that a novel about football could be a serious work of fiction, and for this I will be forever in her debt. Ann Marlowe's stress tests of every sentence made her title of copy editor seem inadequate indeed. And Patrick O'Dowd, David Cobb, Ashley Runyon, Jackie Wilson, and the rest of the folks at the University Press of Kentucky pooled their considerable talents to get my book to readers.

Kathy Daneman's keen intelligence and genuine enthusiasm made the publicity process a joy.

I find I have a healthy list of people to thank for favors done. Kyle Knight assured me I wasn't making too much of an ass of myself; Katie Freeman provided support during a particularly lonesome stretch; Adam Eaglin, who despite not being my agent generously gave important agently direction; Deni Ellis Béchard's comments significantly improved the prologue. And the Sewanee Writers' Conference allowed me to meet authors whose companionship will be a balm (and their talents a spur) for years to come.

Then there are the people who convinced a fanatical jock he was more than the sum of his body parts: Daniel McMahon, who introduced me to Ellison, Eliot, and Cervantes; Sherryl Broverman, whose urgent social consciousness I will always strive, and fail, to match; Hap Zarzour, who understood that something was wrong; Donna Hall, who made it clear *I* wasn't that wrong thing; the Duke teammates I let down and didn't punish me for it.

I am rich in family, blood relations and otherwise, and these acknowledgments would be endless if I described each person's importance to me. So a simple, strong thank you to Cindi Flahive-Sobel, Scott Sobel, Colin Runge, Sara Haas-Runge, Conor Runge, Holly Runge, Kylie Sobel-Kline, Marc Kline, Killian Sobel, Katie Flahive, Catherine Darby, Leonard Darby, Andy Stager, Josh Rickman.

Again, this book is dedicated to Seyward Darby, who at parties would never allow me to call myself anything other than a writer.

## A Note on the Text

Carmichael Stewart King is based on George Moses Horton (1797?–1883?). Horton was born a slave in Northampton County, North Carolina. As a boy he taught himself to read, and so prodigious was his facility with language that he soon could compose original hymn stanzas in his head. In his twenties, he earned both money and renown on the University of North Carolina's Chapel Hill campus for his ability to extemporize acrostic love poems for college students. With the help of various benefactors, he learned to write and started publishing his work, and by 1865 he had authored three books of verse that contain many poems of devastating beauty. He stopped publishing poetry after moving north at the end of the Civil War, a silence that would continue for the remainder of his life.

While the details and shape of Horton's journey differ in crucial ways from my character's, I should note that the research documents I used for my fictional purposes were found on the website of UNC's Documenting the American South initiative, available at https://docsouth.unc.edu/.

THE UNIVERSITY PRESS OF KENTUCKY
## NEW POETRY AND PROSE SERIES

This series features books of contemporary poetry and fiction that exhibit a profound attention to language, strong imagination, formal inventiveness, and awareness of one's literary roots.

SERIES EDITOR: Lisa Williams

ADVISORY BOARD: Camille Dungy, Rebecca Morgan Frank, Silas House, Davis McCombs, and Roger Reeves

Sponsored by Centre College

 CENTRE
COLLEGE